Acclaim for
EMBERHAWK

Finalist for **The Independent Audiobook Awards 2021**: Young Adult
Semi-finalist for **The Realm Award 2021**: Reader's Choice

"A heartfelt fantasy whose tinges of darkness don't threaten the endearing relationship at its core."

— FOREWORD REVIEWS MAGAZINE

"Brilliant fantasy with a unique and complex world of elemental entities, political machinations, and unlikely love."

— LOREHAVEN MAGAZINE

"*Emberhawk's* danger grips, the humor lands, and the romance smolders. Foley examines the beauties and hardships of pluralistic societies, and themes of faith, duty, and cultural expectations are skillfully woven into the narrative. Whether you're looking for an entertaining YA fantasy romp or something a little deeper, *Emberhawk* delivers."

— LINDSAY A. FRANKLIN, Carol Award–winning author of *The Story Peddler*

"Jamie Foley's ability to worldbuild opens an easy door for you to step into her creative world. With descriptions so vivid and beautifully written, combined with a fast-paced and exciting plot, you won't want to miss this new offering from Foley."

— BETH WISEMAN, bestselling and award-winning author for HarperCollins Christian Publishing

"An enthralling story about love in a world on the brink of war. Though I suppose I should warn you that her captivating world building, vivid prose, and compelling plot are certain to lead to sleepless nights and antisocial tendencies."

— ELIZABETH NEWSOM, author of *Captive and Crowned*

"*Emberhawk* has all the ingredients of a great book, tied together beautifully: heart-pounding danger, delicious romance, wonderfully complex characters, a fascinating magic system, and an explosive ending. I cannot wait to read the sequel."

— CATHERINE JONES PAYNE, author of *Breakwater*

"Fantasy at its finest! The rich world-building and gorgeous prose pulled me deep into the story, and the fascinating characters and brilliant story kept me turning pages well into the night. *Emberhawk* has it all: tension-filled adventure, a slow-burn romance, and witty characters who will steal your heart and tug your emotions."

— S.D. GRIMM, author of *Scarlet Moon*

"*Emberhawk* weaves intrigue, romance, and vivid worldbuilding into a tapestry of a story that readers will marvel at. The unique magic system, dynamic characters, and slow-burn romance create a riveting read that can't be missed!"

— R.J. METCALF, author of *Renegade Skyfarer*

"Vibrant worldbuilding and rich cultures make *Emberhawk* sing! Add to that a spunky heroine and snarky hero (not to mention that explosive ending) . . . and when can I read Book Two?"

— GILLIAN BRONTE ADAMS, author of The Songkeeper Chronicles

Silver Blood

Books by Jamie Foley

<u>The Sentinel Trilogy</u>
Book 1: Sentinel
Book 2: Arbiter
Book 3: Sage
Prequel: Vanguard

<u>The Busy Mom Guides</u>
The Busy Mom's Guide to Writing
The Busy Mom's Guide to Indie Publishing
The Busy Mom's Guide to Novel Marketing

Steampunk Fairy Tales Volume III

<u>The Katrosi Revolution</u>
Book 1: Emberhawk
Book 2: Silverblood
Book 3: Lotusfall

SILVER BLOOD

THE KATROSI REVOLUTION BOOK 2

JAMIE FOLEY

FAYETTE
PRESS

ROYAL PROVINCE
OF
VALINOR
REDFISH ISLAND
KOOA RIVER
VERIDIAN PLAINS
WAELYN'S PYRAMID
ODA'E'S RANCH
ROANOKE
THE GNARLED WOOD
SILVERMEAD RIVER
RIVER MOSSU
KATROSI FORESTS
to Darkwood
Jadenvive
Navarro
Tribal Alliance Territories
TRADE ROUTE
CORIANDER'S CAMP
LAKE MOSSU
Sekoiako
Rainosek
GRANNY ZELLE'S RETREAT
EMBERHAWK SOVEREIGNTY
PHOENIX BAY
Quin Zamar
RIFT OCEAN

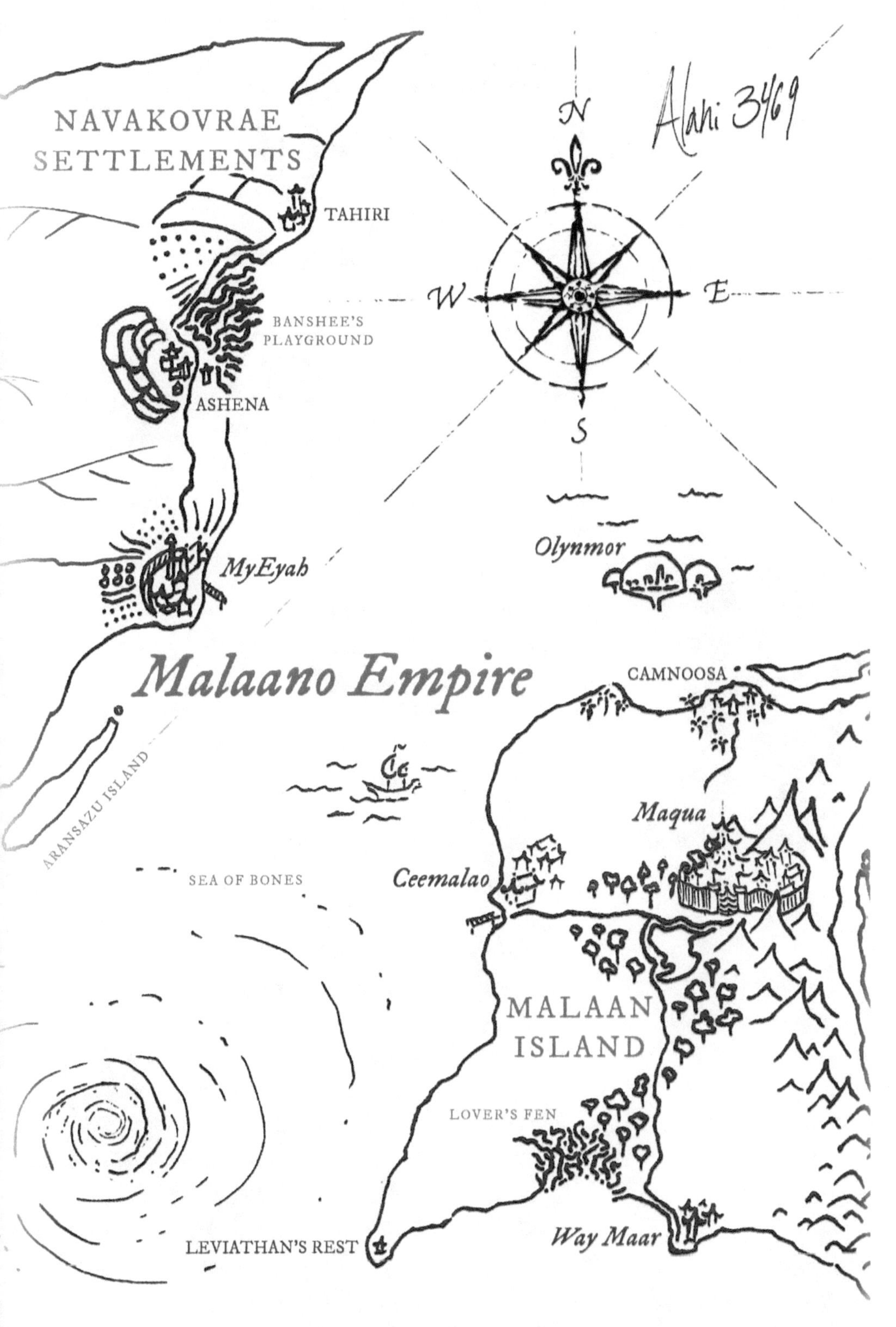

NAVAKOVRAE SETTLEMENTS
TAHIRI
BANSHEE'S PLAYGROUND
ASHENA
MyEyah
N
W
E
S
Alahi 3469
Olynmor
Malaano Empire
CAMNOOSA
Maqua
Ceemalao
ARANSAZU ISLAND
SEA OF BONES
MALAAN ISLAND
LOVER'S FEN
LEVIATHAN'S REST
Way Maar

Emberhawk Monarchy Family Tree

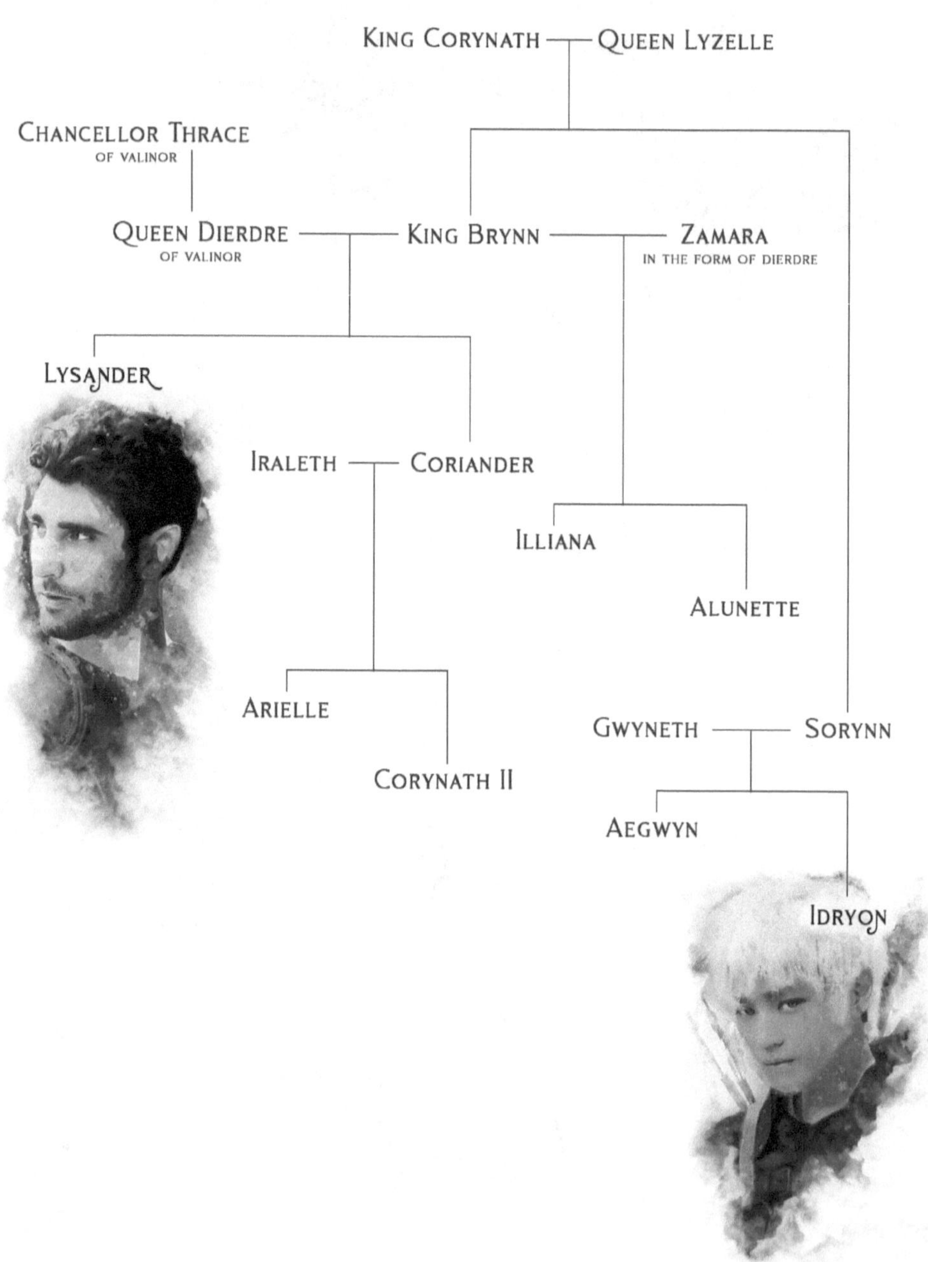

GLOSSARY

AEO — The creator god who formed the physical and spiritual realms and all races therein.

AEO LEYWA AI SHEA — A farewell wish in the Ancient language meaning, 'Aeo be with you and protect you.'

AETHER — A spiritual energy generated by one's soul.

ALANI — The name of the planet on which the story takes place.

AMOS — A semi-mortal shapeshifter who serves as the primary source of power for their element. There is one *amos* for each element.

BALEMBA — A Phoeran word meaning 'butterfly.'

D'HAKKA — A giant tree-scorpion with an appetite for large prey.

ELEMENTALS — Shape-shifting spirits created after angels but before humans, thus their nickname 'second born.' There are one *amos* elemental and seven *trai'yeth* elementals for each of the four elements: Malo (liquid), Terruth (solid), Aris (gas), and Phoera (energy).

RUPERO — Syn-forged coin currency used by the Phoeran tribes.

SYN — The silvery metal in a human's blood that allows them to control their element. Elementals control syn itself as well as their element.

TRACE CAT — An apex predator the size of a lion. They wield the Phoera element to manipulate light, disappearing without a trace.

TRAI'YETH — Shape-shifting lesser elementals who can remove syn from humans and redistribute it. Means 'sealing vessel' in Ancient.

TRIBES — The five tribes that immigrated from Illyria across the Rift Ocean hundreds of years ago: the Katrosi, Emberhawk, Roanoke, Darkwood, and Sekoiako.

XAVI — Like feathered velociraptors with the faces of dragons, xavi are native to the tribal lands and used as mounts by the Malaano Empire.

ZOTH — A frigid region of the spiritual realm occupied by exiled rebel angels, said to be devoid of the creator's light and warmth.

1

LYSANDER

ysander drifted from sleep and wondered why Zoth felt so familiar. Surely that creator-forsaken region of the spiritual realm was where an assassin like him should end up after a fiery battle in the skies over Jadenvive. A battle he'd lost.

He couldn't be in heaven—the pain radiating from his gut blended with nausea in a dizzying whirl, and the air smelled of smoke and rot from a forgotten butcher's cellar.

But he couldn't be alive, either, because his mother had killed him.

He grimaced through the mental fog. No, Zamara wasn't truly his mother—she was only an elemental shape-shifter, who fancied herself a goddess. A false goddess he'd failed to defeat.

So why was he still breathing?

Lysander winced at the pain and spat the taste of rust from his tongue. He blinked at letters burned into the charred wood of the ceiling, somehow written as elegantly as if with a quill forged from embers.

You're welcome, Oathbreaker.

Surprise mingled with dread and sludged through his tired veins. The only one who called him "Oathbreaker" was Felix, the elemental who'd given his power to Lysander in exchange for an oath of loyalty. So Felix had saved him and placed him . . . where?

Lysander hissed under his breath as he pushed himself to standing from a fire-scarred sofa. The charred husk of a room bore unnatural burn marks—dead coals and heat stains abruptly stopped halfway through the former living room. Ash flitted through the remains of a window frame on the left with a bright view of the treetop city and forested horizon beyond.

Clearly the work of the Phoera element. Felix must have stopped the blaze, then surrounded the sofa with the same flame-retardant goo that stuck to Lysander's boots.

He unbuttoned his leather jerkin and peered down at his chest. The palette of colors smeared colors across his skin were a sure sign of internal bleeding—the result of Zamara violently ripping the elemental power from his veins. *Did Felix cauterize my internal wounds?*

No wonder it felt like he'd been mauled by a gryphon.

A curse tumbled from his chapped lips. What had become of his gryphon, Sorrel? Had she been captured? Killed? Was she still waiting in the forest for his return?

What about Ryon? Had Felix saved him too?

How long had he been asleep?

Lysander ignored growling hunger as he maneuvered to the window. Far below, the wooden layers of platforms bustled with activity. Soldiers bearing the painted masks of the Katrosi tribe hauled boxes, stretchers, and unidentifiable remains.

So Felix had placed Lysander on one of the top levels. How in the stars was he supposed to get all the way down without the Katrosi catching him? His mother's Valinorian heritage made him stick out from tribesmen like a wild saber-tooth in a pride of royal striped trace cats.

He wants me to get caught. Lysander took a deep breath, and his diaphragm pinched in protest. *He should have let me die.* Zamara would flay him for trying to assassinate her.

Wait—if Lysander were still alive, and so was Felix, and Jadenvive hadn't burned to the ground, did that mean the false goddess was . . . dead? Zamara wasn't the type to surrender or retreat.

Lysander couldn't afford to entertain the notion. He had to get out of Katrosi territory before they executed him.

He covered his mouth as he coughed, hopefully not making much noise—his deaf ears couldn't tell. He reached out to the Phoera element and found it humming in his blood like a nest of ice hornets. Felix had stuffed him to the brim with elemental power.

Lysander made a fist and rubbed soot from his thumb. If Felix was giving syn to *him*, and in such generous amounts, Zamara must have been slain. She would have left behind a mountain of silver dust fraught with fiery potential.

The thought of freedom was too tempting to savor, so Lysander shoved it from his mind and summoned the Phoera element. The flows of sound energy appeared around him, flickering in different directions in his mind's eye—not discernable in nature, but in strength, like the feel of vibrations against his skin. Those sharp, quick bursts of energy were probably someone yelling beyond the wall behind him. And the deep, distant resonance could have been carts rumbling along the ground far below.

Lysander buttoned up his jerkin and made his way to the room's door, grimacing as the wooden planks beneath his boots reverberated with the sound energy—either creaking boards or maybe the squishing of goo on his boots.

His hand moved to the sheath on his right hip, then his left. Then his boot, and the hidden fold of leather underneath his cloak. All of his knives were gone.

Bleed you, Felix!

The door stuck in its frame and wouldn't budge. Lysander released a steadying breath and pulled his cloak's hood over his black hair. He wasn't about to climb down the crumbling firewood on the other side of the room, but opening this door would probably make enough noise to attract attention.

He kicked it open.

Jadenvive's main upper road stretched out before him, snaking between restaurants, shops, and taverns. Scavengers held cloths to their mouths against fading plumes of smoke that sifted through rope bridges, lower levels, and nets below.

If anyone noticed Lysander, they didn't approach him. He released a breath of relief, then shut the door behind him and joined the flow of the crowd as if he had a purpose of the utmost importance.

If Ryon's alive, he'll be at the orphanage. Lysander kept his head down, letting his hood drape as far as it could fall over his face. The wooden street below him glistened with frost—probably kept at an icy temperature by elementalists as a preventive measure against any remaining embers. *If there are any true gods out there listening, please let those kids be OK.*

He recalled the complex route to the orphanage in root-tunnels beneath the treetop city. He'd memorized the city's layout before for an assassination or two. But how much had become damaged and impassible in the recent events?

Sound energy vibrated before Lysander, directed at him. A hand appeared in front of his chest, forcing him to a sudden stop.

Lysander's pulse jump-started. He looked up into the dirty face of a middle-aged man. The man smiled and said something else, but his lips were partially covered by a bushy beard, and Lysander couldn't determine his words.

Great. At least the man's eyes didn't immediately brighten in recognition.

Lysander pulled his hood back just enough to reveal a pointed ear—they'd been cut to identify him as one of the deaf. "I can't hear you," Lysander said. "Can you sign?" He repeated his question in hand-language, making a gesture for each letter in the Phoeran language with his soot-smeared fingers.

Understanding dawned on the man's face. He pointed back to a tent behind him, where women in healer's garments tended to blanket-covered forms atop cots and palettes.

Oh, he thinks I'm hurt. I must look like I've crawled out of a volcano. Lysander rubbed his chin and found it coated with flaking dried blood. He scratched at it and pulled his hood back over his eyes. "I'm fine, thank—"

His words died in his throat. Beside the healer's tent, a troop of Katrosi amber masks guarded the bridge that sloped down to a lower level. They stopped every passerby and peeked in every bag before waving people through.

One of them was watching him. As they made eye contact, the man pointed at Lysander, and sound energy from his direction burst over all other vocal signatures.

Lysander cursed and turned on his heel. He ducked and ran through the crowd, angling for its most dense pockets.

At least they were only amber masks—the second-to-lowest rank. And he'd only spotted three of them at the checkpoint.

Lysander ducked into an alley and scoured his memory for the nearest secret path. Behind the Malaano-style inn called Het'saya, but wasn't that on a lower level?

He dashed to the edge of the platform and leaped over the railing. Something in his gut stretched in an unpleasant manner as he swung down between the crossbeams.

The thick wooden supports beneath the platform were suitable for climbing, just as Lysander remembered. He reached for one and ducked onto it as unidentified sounds rattled above him. He reached for the Phoera element and rejected the waves of sound energy around himself, making his footfalls and movements silent as death.

Lysander clung to a wooden strut and craned his neck to look toward the underside of the bridge. Pain in his stomach warned against acrobatics. He ignored it.

A man swung down on a braided rope ahead, hanging by a hook on the bridge's cross-beams. Red eyes focused on Lysander through a mask painted like a scowling yellow demon.

Lysander cursed and rushed back in the opposite direction. The amber masks might be the second-to-lowest Katrosi rank—above foot soldiers but below specialists and the chieftess' bodyguards—but they excelled in the defense of tribal villages. He should have known they'd be equipped with climbing gear in a treetop city.

He abandoned the Phoera element and instead focused on landing a risky jump to a metal-plated support. He glanced over his shoulder and made sure not to look down. The amber masks swung through the maze of beams with disturbing speed.

Lysander reached the edge and pulled himself up. Darkness danced around the corners of his vision. The railing raked across his back as he ducked beneath it. Where to hide: inside a building or within the crowd?

If only he were as skilled at Phoera invisibility as Ryon. The ability to become invisible and silent simultaneously would be great, too.

Lysander dashed toward a tavern and rounded its corner. Maybe if he could—

Something cracked against the back of his head, sending him down to one knee. He whipped around and planted an uppercut in his attacker's gut.

The man who fell wasn't even masked. *The guards got civilians involved?*

He looked up into faces of terror among the crowd, all focused on him, like he was a monster from the depths of Lake Mossu. His dulled ears picked up faint deep-pitched cries, like underwater screams.

Someone tackled him from behind. He threw them off and ran—right into a masked soldier.

Too many. His nerves rioted with pain as he recoiled from blow after blow, unable to anticipate them in the frenzy of the crowd. When he downed one attacker, they were replaced by three.

Lysander hit the ice-cold street and wrestled against the grips pinning his arms behind his back. He bit down against the agony in his gut and relented before the strain of resisting could re-open internal wounds.

I knew it was impossible. Lysander forced himself to relax as they bound his wrists. Perhaps their justice system could offer him some kind of penance for a life of self-indulgence and service to an evil queen. Where could he go now that Zamara was dead, anyway? He was a slave who'd forgotten how to live free.

What kind of game is Felix playing?

Lysander thought he saw a fox in the branches above as they hauled him up onto unwilling feet. Vibrant green eyes with no pupils narrowed at him, then disappeared into the leaves.

2

BROOKE

Rage swirled in Brooke's mind like a midnight typhoon, its lightning flashing with murderous intent. She gasped and pulled back from the aether, dampening her senses before they could consume her.

She opened her eyes. Dozens of patriarchs and matriarchs from the houses of Jadenvive crowded at the bottom of the stairs before her throne, packing the Great Hall more full than her bodyguards recommended. If this mob decided to grab Brooke and throw her from the crow's nest, they'd be unstoppable.

Regardless, she remained determined to hear the shattered voices of all her people. They mourned for lost loved ones, homes, and livelihoods. And they shared her thirst for revenge.

Brooke glanced at her new advisor, Ryon, who looked as disturbed as she felt. His loyalty was unquestionable, and yet the blood of their enemies flowed through his veins. Brooke made a mental note to assign a guard to him before nightfall.

"Bring him out!" the people shouted. "Give him over to us!" Their voices tangled and merged into a chant: "Execute! Execute! Execute!"

Creator, help me.

Brooke stood up from her throne in one swift motion, tossing her braids and headdress feathers across her leather armor. Silence blanketed the room.

"Lysander is being interrogated." She spoke with the booming voice that her father, the late chief, had taught her. "He could be of value because of his royal Emberhawk blood. I will not have him executed until he is of no use to us."

Protests resounded, and the head of the Blackthorne family, a burly merchant with flame-singed hair, stepped forward and yelled over the cacophony. "Blood for blood, Chieftess! Who will pay for the death of our city?"

"Jadenvive is not dead." Brooke lifted her jaw. "The Emberhawk will regret ever setting foot on our lands. We slew their god-queen. Now I will select their new monarch, and they will submit to us under the Tribal Alliance."

Shouts erupted throughout the room until Ryon held out his hand.

The Blackthorne representative called out, "So they attack us and you ally with them? Are you so terrified of the Malaano Empire?"

"I will never fight beside the blood-hawk!" someone yelled.

"They'd sooner stab us in the back and feed us to the Malaano!"

"The line of Stillwind chiefs ends here!"

Brooke closed her eyes and reached out to the aether. The room's tension nearly boiled over into an all-out riot.

She breathed deep and held out her hand, focusing on the last shred of peace in her soul and willing it outward. Stillness settled over the room like the first autumn snow. Subdued with her aether but not snuffed out— she could still feel their anger simmering below like a cinder beneath the ashes.

"I will meet with the elders and seek their wisdom," Brooke said, more softly now that the Great Hall had fallen into an uneasy quiet. "Use your energy to aid your neighbors, and I will give you justice." She opened her eyes and touched the quartz gem atop her headdress. "I swear it on my chiefdom."

Then she turned and strode through the ornate wooden door behind her throne. Mumbles and murmurs sounded as Ryon's footsteps followed and shut the door behind them.

The high curved ceiling and brilliant tapestries of the Chamber of

Elders did little to soothe Brooke's anxiety. If she couldn't somehow deliver the people's retribution to the Emberhawk, she'd lose much more than the remaining four years of her seven as Chieftess. She'd end the Stillwind legacy in shame and ensure that she would be the first and last female to lead the Katrosi tribe. And she'd certainly not be re-elected. That would make her a High Chief, as her grandfather had been—her childhood dream.

A foolish dream best left rejected and forgotten.

Brooke moved to the line of mannequins that displayed the armor of the previous chiefs. Her battle leathers looked so small beside the rest. Insignificant. Inept. Incapable.

She stared at the wooden head above her grandfather's d'hakka chitin armor and wondered for the hundredth time where his headdress had been lost to the ages. How could she possibly satisfy her people as he had as High Chief?

Declaring war on the Emberhawk only a decade after the Sacrificial War would drain both tribes and leave them vulnerable. Just like the Malaano Empire wanted. But how else could she exact true justice after so many innocent people had died in Emberhawk fires—behind the walls of their own capital city?

"I'm sorry," Ryon said as Brooke lifted her headdress. "I didn't realize how appointing me as advisor right after the attack would look. I'll step down."

Brooke glanced over her shoulder to face him. Ryon looked even more like an Emberhawk than his cousin Lysander, with short silver hair and a slender-yet-masculine build. His new lenses didn't hinder the sun-fire glow of his eyes—eerily similar to the flames that had ravaged her city less than a week ago.

"I won't accept your resignation." Brooke tugged a xavi feather that had snagged on a braid, and her handmaiden, Shaya, rushed to help. "You're not Emberhawk any more, and everyone knows it."

Ryon rubbed his forehead and crossed to a wooden table, where they'd spent sleepless nights pouring over intelligence gathered by Brooke's pale-masked soldiers. Dread blanched Ryon's olive skin as he leaned over the table. "Regarding Lysander, I won't hold it against you . . . if you have to . . ."

His words twisted in the aether, indicating a lie. Brooke frowned. Of course Ryon didn't want his cousin to be executed.

"Summon the Elder of Aether for me, please," Brooke said as her handmaiden wrestled with her headdress. "Invite him to dinner with me tonight."

Ryon turned to her and bowed. "Yes, Chieftess."

"Hey." She narrowed her eyes at him. "I told you not to call me that."

Ryon's smile looked forced, but his stature seemed to lighten. "Brookie?"

She cringed. *"Brooke."*

Ryon grinned like a fox. "Rookie?"

Brooke rolled her eyes. "I've been the chief for three years."

"You're horrible at Phoera, though," Ryon said. "Can you even light a candle?"

Brooke pursed her lips and grimaced as a braid was yanked. "Just because I don't study the element doesn't mean I'm a rookie."

He disappeared out the back door and called back, "Get some rest, Rookie!"

She grunted. Perhaps promoting him hadn't been such a fabulous idea after all.

Brooke thanked her handmaiden as the headdress finally came free. She collapsed onto the sofa with a sigh. Emotions from the next room threatened to overwhelm her—no, they resonated with her own energy. Sorrow, fear, hopelessness, and anger, crippling her ability to think. If she kept everything bottled much longer, she'd explode. Maybe she just needed to find a place to hide and cry.

She'd never seen her grandfather cry. Maybe they were right about the position of chief being a man's job.

"You did well, my lady," her handmaiden whispered. "They respect you."

Brooke swallowed hard and blinked back the wet blur in her eyes.

"Please don't, Shaya." She rested her elbows on her knees and slouched forward, draping her braids over her shoulders. "I know you mean well, but I just can't right now."

Shaya bowed and folded her hands over her tunic. "You're under so much pressure. Shall I prepare a hot salt bath for you?"

Maybe that's what Brooke needed, along with a full wineskin and some chocolates stuffed with jomoco jam. But she refused to give in to such luxuries while her people nursed their burns.

A knock rapped on the side door, and Brooke called in the messenger. He rushed in and bowed as he presented her with a scroll. "From Princess Illiana of Quin'Zamar."

Brooke inspected the wax seal of the Emberhawk royal family: a flaming bird with outstretched wings and a curved beak open in mid-cry. Illiana's first letter hadn't been sealed like this. Did it mean they'd passed on the crown after the death of the queen?

Brooke folded the letter's seal, cracking it in half. The rolled letter crackled as she unfurled it and read:

Chieftess Brooke,

> *I extend my deepest condolences, but we will not be able to provide aid to Jadenvive during this troubling time. Our resources are required to fight Coriander's rebellion. You have my word that I will put an end to them for the damage they have caused to our two noble peoples. My men will identify those involved in the attack, and I will give them over to you for execution.*

> *Even as I grieve the loss of my mother, Dierdre, my people need a ruler. I have been crowned as Queen. I look forward to many years of prosperity and peace with the Katrosi tribe, forsaking the wars of our fathers.*

> *However, I must decline the invitation to join your Tribal*

*Alliance. We have no border with the Malaano Empire,
and our navy is strong. We have no reason to believe they
are a threat to us.*

May Zamara's fire warm your spirit in this difficult time.

Queen Illiana

Brooke's blood curdled. The traditional Emberhawk farewell stung like thinly veiled gloating.

Surely Illiana knew her late mother was the shape-shifter Zamara instead of the true Queen, Deirdre. Or was she really stupid enough not to know everything that had happened? Did this teenage princess really expect Brooke to believe that Coriander's small band of rebels had razed Jadenvive?

No, this teenage *queen*. The crown shouldn't fall to her. Lysander was the oldest—he would have been king if he hadn't abdicated. So the new monarch should be Coriander, just as he'd been fighting his false mother for. Their younger sister, Illiana, must have had a better relationship with their mother if the crown had fallen so far down the family line.

Brooke's nails dug into her palm as she clenched a fist and re-read the letter. So, Illiana wouldn't join the Alliance either. Like mother, like daughter.

No reason to believe the Malaano Empire is a threat, huh? What an idiot. If the Malaano declared war at the eastern Katrosi border, the Emberhawk beaches would be next. Even the Emberhawk navy was no match for Imperial ships if they had no allies.

"Ill news?" Shaya whispered.

Brooke made an effort to appear relaxed. "It could have been worse." At least Illiana had been cordial about her lies.

"You look exhausted. I know you haven't been sleeping," Shaya said. "I'll make you some fadeleaf tea."

Brooke rolled the letter back up. "No, thank you. I'm—"

The back door swung open, and her best friend Nariellyn popped her head in, flopping her lopsided hairdo.

"You sure 'bout that?" Nariellyn sauntered to the table and clacked a clay mug down hard enough to spill brown liquid down its side. "Made some almost as bitter as your soul." That smile made her look half her age.

Brooke leaned back into the sofa but couldn't prevent a grin from escaping. "Not a good time, Nari." The young healer was the last person Brooke wanted to see right now, and she never knocked. She watched the drip of tea slide down the mug's glaze and hoped Nariellyn would leave on her own.

She didn't.

Brooke sighed. "Were you in the Great Hall?" she asked as the messenger took the scroll with a bow and retreated.

"Unfortunately." Nariellyn flopped down on a sofa covered with a trace cat pelt, opposite where Brooke sat, and stretched out her legs as if she owned the place. "Looks like the Stillwind reign's comin' to an end."

Brooke snorted. "Thanks for the vote of confidence." She took the tea and let the floral aroma fill her lungs. After taking a sip, she grimaced. Nariellyn wasn't kidding about it being bitter—she'd probably swapped the honey for some medicinal concoction to keep Brooke on her feet.

She took a deep swig and forced herself to swallow despite the stinging heat. "Since you know so much, if you could take over as chieftess, that'd be great."

"Ha!" Nariellyn slung a leg over the couch's armrest. "Even if I could kill all those beasties for trophies in my own headdress, the elders would choose a mudhoof over me."

Well, why did they choose me? Brooke stared down into the swirling steam. "What do I do? The people are angry enough to skin anything that looks like an Emberhawk, but another war would only amount to pointless bloodshed. I can't get them to focus on helping the wounded and rebuilding before winter."

"Mmm. Hard to say." Nariellyn scratched her wild hair. "They need to blow off steam somehow. I'm gonna need a bigger pipe."

Brooke glared at her. The only thing she *didn't* need was a bigger pipe. "Thanks for the reminder that you'd be a terrible chief."

Nariellyn's snaggletooth smile melted Brooke's anxiety. "Someone's gotta set the bar low enough for you to look good."

Brooke dipped her fingers in the tea and flicked them at her.

"Hey, now! We're running low on yaupon thanks to your addiction." Nariellyn wiped her face. "What've they got outta that prisoner so far?"

"Nothing," Brooke grumbled. "Lysander's an assassin. Apparently he's been trained to keep his mouth shut."

"Well, he can't keep his *mind* shut." Nariellyn tapped her temple. "You paid him a visit yet?"

Brooke stood and straightened the leather strips that hung like a split skirt below her belt. Lysander might just be the solution she needed. Maybe he knew the secrets of the dead goddess, or the weaknesses of his volatile tribe. He'd abdicated their blood-drenched throne, but perhaps she could convince him to reclaim it, then control him like the dog he was.

If not, a public execution would sate her people's bloodlust . . . for now.

3

KIRALAU

Jadenvive was a burned-out husk compared to the thriving treetop village Kira remembered from her first visit. She pushed her bandana further up her nose and grimaced at the scents when the wind stilled. Smoke. The sharp tang of spilled smother-coal slime. The dead.

Kira ducked behind her brother's back as a cart rumbled beside them. "Are you sure this is the right way?" she asked.

Tekkyn glanced over his shoulder at her, then lifted a thick arm so the crowd parted and she could reclaim her place at his side. "I remember the path to the Great Hall quite well from when I was dragged there."

Kira frowned and pulled her hood further over her face. The glares bore down on her like a stranglehold. If Ryon hadn't given her the scroll of invitation from the chieftess, they probably wouldn't have made it through the front gate. Many citizens of Jadenvive didn't hide their curiosity, their assumptions, their barely contained anger.

"Why did you people help the blood-hawk? How could you?"

"I heard they supplied the explosives. Every one of them should be in jail until this gets settled."

"Go home, umberhide, before I send you back to your precious Island in a body bag."

The drunk who'd said that last one had been silenced with a glare from Tekkyn, who looked like a badger-bear daring anyone to threaten its cubs. They didn't have time to explain to every passerby that Kira had slain the giant fiery hawk with shards from a shattered lift and a well-placed harpoon. That Tekkyn had protected orphans beneath the city's roots as the explosions rained earth and ash down on them. That their little brother, Lee, had lost his life protecting an escape route for civilians.

"Ryon will make sure we're safe as soon as we make it to the Great Hall," Kira murmured. "We're under the chieftess' protection."

"Assuming they let us in," Tekkyn growled.

Kira pushed up on her tiptoes to see above the heads of the crowd. The massive sequoia-wood pillars of the Great Hall stood unsinged, its banners with the five-pointed star of the Tribal Alliance waving in the wind. Men in carved masks guarded the front door, holding back a roiling crowd with the blunt ends of long spears. Protestors chanted and raised signs with Phoeran script and simple drawings of swords, skulls, and bleeding birds.

Tekkyn reached for her hand and held it tight. "Stay close."

Kira gripped her pack with her free hand as her brother stormed through the crowd, pushing people aside when they didn't move for him. Kira bit her lip and avoided angry gazes as Tekkyn marched right up to the closed double doors.

He shouted over the chanting, "We've come at the request of the chieftess!"

One of the guards faced them. His golden eyes flicked over both of them through the holes in his wooden mask. "Your summons?"

Kira slung her pack from her shoulder and pulled the scroll out. It'd been smashed between her jar of cherry preserves and spare tunic, but the broken wax seal still clung to the parchment.

The guard furrowed his brow at the seal, then unfurled the letter and glanced at the signature. Then he gestured upward and yelled something in Phoeran that Kira didn't catch.

Heavy doors creaked open just wide enough for Tekkyn to shoulder through and Kira to follow. The crowd erupted, and the doors shut behind her with a deep thud.

Kira clung to her pack and looked up at the empty throne. The last time she'd been in this expansive room—complete with thick pillars, a long table, and unnerving taxidermy—she'd met the decorated Katrosi chieftess and feared for Tekkyn's life. It was difficult to believe that Brooke now wanted them for some grand political purpose. Tekkyn might be a skilled swordsman, soldier, and Navakovrae Resistance spy, but she was just a farm girl whose hands seemed permanently stained from pitting countless cherries.

"Can I help you?" asked a heavy-set woman who strode toward them with a welcoming yet cautious expression.

"Tekkyn'ashi and Kiralau of Navarro," Tekkyn said. "We were summoned."

The woman's rigid posture smoothed, and her smile melted into a more genuine rendition. "Ah, yes. Welcome!" She turned and waved for them to follow. "You must be weary after your journey. Please, relax; you are personal guests of the chieftess. Your quarters are this way."

Kira's tension began to slough from her back as she scurried in Tekkyn's shadow. Maybe this wouldn't be so bad after all.

But where was Ryon?

She searched for him as they entered a hallway behind the throne, peeking into a library, an armory, and a quiet kitchen as they passed. The peaceful wealth stood in stark contrast to the angry chaos outside. Kira felt like there should have been more staff, as she seemed to remember from her last visit—perhaps they were out helping. The chieftess didn't seem the type to be pampered on a lofty throne while her people suffered.

"Here we are." The woman gestured to an open door at the end of the hall. Kira peeked in.

A bed of leathers and quilts was crowned with a night sky and treetops carved into the headboard. Tall, thin windows of clouded glass looked down on the city's levels and greenery below. The horns of a great stag overshadowed a hammock hung from glazed metal hooks in the corner.

Kira balked as the woman huffed and straightened a beeswax candle on the dresser, muttering something about a clumsy girl named Bekk.

"Can I fetch you some water?" she asked.

"Yes, please," Tekkyn said before Kira could decline.

"Um . . ." Kira fidgeted as the woman passed, and she paused to regard Kira with a patient curiosity.

"Is Ryon here?" Kira whispered.

"Idryon? Ah, yes." The woman squinted a playful eye. "I think he's in the map room. If you come with me, I'll show you."

Kira's spirit leapt as she turned to follow, but her escort eyed Kira's luggage. "Would you like to set your pack down first?"

Kira felt her face flush with heat. She awkwardly dashed past Tekkyn and slung her pack on the hammock, avoiding her brother's gaze. She didn't need to see it to know what it looked like—he'd been teasing her relentlessly the entire trip here.

"Behave!" Tekkyn called after her, and Kira scrambled for an escape.

The woman chuckled down the hall. "Brothers."

Kira's appreciative laugh came out high-pitched and tense. She wanted to smack herself on the forehead. *Stop acting like a little girl!*

"He's just as excited to see you, too, you know."

Kira choked on her own breath. "Really?" Did all of Jadenvive know they were an item, then?

The woman looked over her shoulder with an amused glance. "Unusual for a Navakovrae to go on *evadír,* but I'm pretty sure there's an exception for the goddess-killer." Her smile filled with pride and appreciation. "Ignore all of the naysayers. You're a hero and very welcome here. Just give the people time to recognize you." She stopped in front of a door marked with Phoeran script in white paint and dropped her voice to a whisper. "Besides, you two are adorable together." She winked as she slowly pushed the door open.

Kira swallowed a concoction of embarrassing emotions and forced an awkward smile as she peeked inside.

". . . need more orange masks to clear debris," a man's voice muttered from a table in the center of a square room. The walls Kira could see were crammed full of flags, trophies, and weapon displays.

"It would be better to keep the eastern flank on guard." Kira recognized Ryon's voice as he continued from somewhere beyond her sight. "Let's request more aid from Roanoke and Sekoiako."

"A little late for them to be on guard," the first voice grumbled. Kira identified it as an older man in leather armor with a line of skulls branded into one of his pauldrons. He stood at the table, which Kira noted was full of maps and figurines as she continued to creep inside.

"We need more space to set up tents for the homeless immediately," the decorated elder continued. "If anything else arises to defend against, they'll still be available to fight."

"But they wouldn't be alert or have a defensive line," Ryon said.

The other man snorted. "Why're you so scared of the Malaano, boy?"

"I'm not scared of the Malaano. I'm wary of the empire."

Kira caught sight of wild silver hair on a familiar figure, who faced away from her. Ryon leaned over the table, his half-cloak with the five-pointed Tribal Alliance star draping across one shoulder. The same shoulder she'd shot only weeks ago . . . Weeks that felt like months.

She allowed herself to admire the differences in his appearance and missed a few of his words. The rough scouting leathers and equipment had been replaced with sleek black cloth and strategic accents of xavi-scale armor, whose colors flitted from gold to orange to scarlet in the sconce-light.

Apprehension resurfaced, threatening to smother Kira's hesitant joy. Ryon seemed so different than when she'd first met him. The sarcastic enemy soldier in the d'hakka-infested woods was now a government official with royal lineage.

Or maybe he'd always been like this, and it just hadn't dawned on her until now.

". . . seen them first-hand. I listened in on their barracks in Navarro and Ashena and MyEyah. Their soldiers are weary but their officers are aggressive, and their emperor is looking for any excuse to invade." Ryon pointed to something on the map Kira couldn't see. "This is their perfect opportunity to strike, and they very well may have orchestrated it."

The older man pursed his lips. "We're well aware of the threat, Emberhawk. But we have limited resources and far more pressing needs." He crossed his arms. "It's clear that you're eager to prove yourself, but you're not an elder. You're an advisor. You speak, but we vote. The sooner you learn that, the sooner we'll get along."

Kira grimaced as Ryon's irritation grew tangible, even from her view of his back.

A long moment passed, and when Ryon spoke again, his voice was smoother. "I understand that, elder. And if you understood my hatred for the people who murdered my father and burned our city, you would not call me 'Emberhawk' again."

The corner of the man's lip twitched up in a barely perceptible smirk. "Very well." His arms unfurled, and he moved a small painted figurine from one point on the map to another. "We will leave half the guard in place for now and send the rest to aid with the tents. And perhaps when the Darkwood prince arrives, he will promise more aid as a wedding gift." He turned on his heel and disappeared from Kira's sight. "Adjourned."

Ryon's stature sagged as rustling sounded from other parts of the room and another door creaked open on the opposite side. Kira backed away but froze as Ryon turned and spotted her. His steely posture evaporated in an instant, and his fiery eyes ignited. "Kira!"

She grinned sheepishly and shrank in the slight opening. "Hi—"

His sudden embrace forced the breath from her lungs. She closed her eyes and hugged him back, drinking in the scents of mesquite and leather oil. Her apprehension fled, chased away by a sudden sense of security and acceptance.

"You made it," Ryon said as he released her and beamed down at her. "I'm sorry; I really should have escorted you in. Did you have any trouble? Did they let you in all right? I'm sorry the smoke's still bad. I hope being here doesn't bring bad memories, and I—"

"I'm fine," Kira interrupted. She looked down his height, admiring the new armor that complimented his form in a manner she felt guilty for enjoying. "Look at you, Mister Big Bad Advisor."

Ryon deflated with something between a grunt and a sigh. "Yeah, don't remind me." He adjusted his new lenses, pushing at their seat on his nose. "Oh, hey, I got you something!" He unwound a thread pouch on his belt and handed it to her with big, hopeful eyes.

Kira bounced on her heels with a surge of delight. She carefully worked to loosen the thread and opened the pouch. Nestled inside was a glass butterfly perched on a metal hairpin. Its smooth curves caught the light in a ballet of pastel colors, fading and reappearing as she turned it over in her palm.

Kira's breath snagged, then spilled out in awe. It reminded her of the way the oil-water danced with light at the Moon Festival, urged to life by masterful wavesingers.

"A *balemba* for the *balemba*." Ryon laughed awkwardly at his own pun. "Do you like it? The glass melter's pretty skilled, huh? I thought you might like it for your . . ." His attention flicked up to her hair, which had undoubtedly wrestled free of its bandana restraint, thanks to the last leg of the journey.

"If you say frizzy, I'm going to hit you."

"I was going to say gorgeous, obviously. Can't I spare a moment to admire my girl?" Ryon sported that playful smirk that made her insides melt. "I thought it would match Dad's—I mean, *your* bracelet."

Kira gathered a handful of curls and subdued them with the crystalline pin. "I love it. Thank you so much!"

"My pleasure." He shone with pride. "Have you seen Brooke yet?"

"No, we just got h—"

He stopped her with a sudden kiss, pulling her close in another warm embrace. Kira tensed, then relaxed as tingling energy trickled through her. Her daydreams didn't compare.

"Sorry." Ryon released her and grew an impish smile. "Am I allowed to do that?"

"Uh . . ." Kira blinked, regretting that he'd ended it so soon. "Of c—"

"No," Tekkyn said, and Kira nearly jumped out of her skin. Her brother watched them from further down the hallway with an unreadable expression.

"Uh, I—"

"Pardon me," someone said behind Ryon.

Kira backed up, mortified, as the elder pushed past Ryon. He raised a gray eyebrow at her as he passed.

She wanted to fly back to the cattle ranch and turn back time to last year's harvest, when she knew nothing about *evadír* or talking foxes or Zamara and everything made sense.

"Hey," Ryon chuckled as he stepped forward and grasped her hand. "I'm sorry. You'd think I'd have learned to control myself by now."

She cleared her throat and adjusted the butterfly pin, but she couldn't contain a grin. "You'd think, but I know better."

4

LYSANDER

"How many attackers were there?"

"Are there any other Emberhawk hideouts in Katrosi territory?"

"What's the name of your Malaano contact who supplied explosives for the attack?"

Lysander ignored the sign language interpreter as her questions repeated. He controlled his breathing and focused on the pain, lessening its sway over him. As long as they didn't use the porcupine quills or stingray barbs again, he'd be fine.

He wouldn't mind telling them what they wanted, really. The temptation burned as hot as the glowing iron they threatened him with. He didn't care about loyalty any more, now that Zamara's threats had vanished.

But if he gave them what they wanted, his usefulness would expire, and they'd execute him.

And just because he didn't want to live didn't mean he wanted to die.

The interpreter placed a slip of parchment in Lysander's lap with her questions written in hasty script. He closed his eyes and breathed in the sharp scent of the gooey leaf gel that slicked the walls of his cell that prevented him from burning the prison to the forest floor. They'd give up their interrogation eventually.

Something cracked against Lysander's jaw, sending sparks through his vision. He glared up at the guard, who pointed at the parchment with a baton.

Lysander moved his jaw around and found his teeth still in their places.

"You still haven't told me if Idryon survived. If he did, bring him here, and I'll answer his questions."

The interpreter exchanged a glance with the guard. She took the parchment from Lysander's lap, and the two abruptly left his full-metal cell, leaving him alone with only the bars and chains and the chamber pot in the corner that smelled like it hadn't been properly cleaned.

Relief trickled through Lysander as the pain faded from pulsing sharp to resounding dull. Ryon was a Phoeran elementalist—surely he wouldn't have been killed by any energy such as fire. But he could have run into one of the Emberhawk arsonists. Or pulled some fool-headed rescue in a collapsing building. Yeah, that sounded like something his younger cousin would do.

Lysander slouched on the cool metal bench. He was grateful for the generous length of chain that bound his wrists, leaving him some slack from the wall behind him. The Emberhawk weren't so hospitable to their prisoners.

A small white object near the cell door caught his eye. That hadn't been there before. Was it folded parchment?

Lysander looked around quickly. No guards. He reached out to the Phoera element and waited to feel the rhythmic vibrations of footsteps or the low hum of talking nearby. Every source of sound energy he could detect seemed distant.

He stood up from the bench and stretched his foot toward the parchment. His height was advantageous for once. His boot stomped on the small slip and dragged it toward him. The chain on his wrists was just long enough for him to grab it from the floor in front of the bench.

A lockpick fell out of the folded parchment as Lysander opened it. Black ink read:

> *Flames dine on the city in the sky*
> *Twin slaves the only to survive*
> *The chieftess sleeps, the slaves meet*
> *And return with freedom and pride*

He'd never been so happy to see one of Xavier's stupid poems. It must be him—the two of them had been Zamara's favorite pets, with Xavier being the firstborn of a noble house that opposed her tyranny and Lysander being the rightful heir to the throne. She'd kept a tight leash on the two of them for good reason—she'd had them trained as assassins to do her dirty work, and they'd tried to assassinate *her* more than once.

So "twin slaves" seemed accurate. "The only to survive" though . . . so Zamara really was dead, somehow? And Sylendrin and the rest of them.

Lysander released a ragged breath. He'd never thought he'd taste freedom again, but it tasted bland. Zamara had already ripped away everything wonderful from his former life. What good was freedom when he had nothing left to live for?

Well, maybe he should get out of prison before he celebrated.

He inspected the lockpick, hoping the thin metal would work on both of his cuffs and the cell door. The third line of the poem must mean that Xavier wanted to meet him tonight in the basement of the Jolly Satyr: the only place in Jadenvive where Emberhawk spies and assassins exchanged communiques. He couldn't miss that appointment—Xavier was much more skilled at light-bending, which Lysander would need if he wanted any chance of escaping Jadenvive.

Lysander braced himself and stuffed the parchment into his mouth. Whatever ink Xavier had used tasted like old horseradish.

He grimaced as he swallowed and reached out to the Phoera element again. He'd have to use the lockpick when he was certain no one would catch him in the act.

Rhythmic vibrations signaled footsteps nearby—probably down the hallway. Lysander growled as he recalled the naggings of his mentor to be patient. He stuffed the lockpick into his waistband.

Lysander almost didn't recognize Ryon as he appeared beyond the bars. A pair of lenses rested on his nose, and his xavi-scale jerkin shone with a polished gleam—a far cry from the wilderness-scarred equipment of a scout. His cousin's eyes glowed orange like twin summer suns, regarding Lysander with grave caution instead of their usual mirth.

"Brother," Lysander said, invoking the depth of their former relationship. Lysander and Coriander had grown up with Ryon in the glass palace of Quin'Zamar, never dreaming they'd end up on three different sides of the conflict wrought by their late fathers.

Ryon didn't respond as he stepped up to the cell door. He didn't open it.

A sick feeling slipped into Lysander's hope, withering it away. "Did you get the orphans out?" he asked.

Ryon raised his hands and signed: *"You didn't give me enough time."*

Lysander's heart clenched as Ryon continued, *"Everyone is fine. Except my fiancée's brother."*

Lysander blinked. "You're engaged?"

"Evadír," Ryon signed, and Lysander recalled the Katrosi three-month courting tradition that ended in a proposal.

A smirk grew across Lysander's lips. "That Navakovrae girl, huh?" Wouldn't she just be his girlfriend until *evadír* was done? So why was he already calling her his fiancée? Was Ryon that confident she'd accept his proposal after the three months? "I thought you were just 'escorting her to Jadenvive.'"

Ryon glanced over his shoulder at something out of sight down the prison's hallway. *"Listen, you're in deep trouble. I'm Brooke's advisor now, but I don't think my word is louder than the people's."* His forehead creased as his brows furrowed. *"You need to answer everything the chieftess asks and do whatever she says."*

Lysander harrumphed. "Why? So she can end my misery sooner?"

Ryon pursed his lips. *"Zamara is dead—she can't control you any more. You finally have freedom and so much to live for. Don't be a hard-headed idiot and throw it all away."*

"So much to live for? Name one thing."

Ryon's signing hand paused and wavered in midair.

Lysander spoke before Ryon could make anything up. "Zamara took my throne. She took my hearing. My family. Selene. Our own people call me the Slain Prince."

"Live for Granny Zelle, for Sorrel, for me and Aegwyn and Mom, and for your future family," Ryon signed.

Lysander huffed a laugh. "Future family? I don't exactly have as many girls throwing themselves at me as before the—"

He cut himself off as the chieftess strode into view, catching Ryon's arm and saying something Lysander couldn't hear. Behind her chalk-and-charcoal warpaint was an enchanting face despite her serious expression. Deep eyes matched the rich brown of her braids that trailed over wyvern-scale armor.

Lysander checked his expression, making sure he didn't gawk. She'd blossomed into a woman since he'd seen her last—no, it looked more like she'd been forged from the bloodthirst of war. An angel of death: the perfect union of beauty and violence.

How could she not be married yet? She must be twenty-seven now. Any red-blooded man would kill for her, and she was the leader of the Tribal Alliance and chieftess of the largest tribe—oh. Lysander remembered with a start. The people called her the Jade Witch . . . supposedly cursed to never wed or continue her family's line of Katrosi chiefs. They said she'd been engaged twice, and both young men had met terrible fates.

It was true for one of them, at least, because Lysander had been the first.

Brooke's mouth moved, and Lysander recognized his own name on her lips as Ryon interpreted beside her. *"Lysander. Terrorism isn't befitting of a former prince. I never thought you would stoop so low."*

Lysander sat up straighter on the cold metal and rested his chained wrists on his knees. "Stoop so low as to warn your people of the attack?" He nodded at Ryon. "Or trying to kill Zamara as soon as the attack began?"

"Your information was not specific enough, nor given early enough." Brooke glanced at Ryon as he signed. *"You should have come to me directly."*

Lysander snorted. "You'd have thrown me in this cell and not listened to a word I said."

"You're wrong. I can discern truth from falsehood." Brooke motioned to

her right, and the guard reappeared and opened the cell door. *"So you would be wise to answer my questions swiftly and honestly."*

Lysander steeled himself without surrendering his relaxed posture. Did the people call her the Jade Witch because of her curse, or because of the rumors that she could read people's minds?

Brooke strode into his cell and stood over him. She considered him silently, as if he were a board game with a hundred pieces.

Lysander didn't look away even as his pulse strengthened. Dark streaks of her face paint bled down into her pale cheeks like oily tears. Perhaps a design indicating that the Katrosi tribe was in mourning.

Not the paint of war. Interesting.

Brooke's lips moved and Ryon signed, *"I regret to inform you that your mother has passed away."*

Lysander frowned. "My mother was murdered years ago."

Brooke's brown eyes darkened while Ryon's flared like stoked embers. *"Zamara is dead."*

"Good," Lysander said.

Brooke tilted her head, shifting her braids across her armor. *"Then the crown should fall to you."*

"It should have passed to me when my father died."

Brooke turned and said something to Ryon that wasn't translated. Ryon left and returned a moment later with a chair. Brooke flipped it around and sat in it backward, resting her forearms across the chair's back.

She was eye-level with Lysander now. The paint didn't quite hide the freckles on her nose, and the powder graced her eyelashes like frost. Alluring, but not as beautiful as Selene had been. No one was.

"You had a problem with the queen taking the crown?" Ryon signed as Brooke spoke.

Lysander didn't miss the warning look in Ryon's eye, but he ignored it. "Zamara was the first queen of my people to play king."

Ryon's eyes bulged as he signed Brooke's response: *"You don't believe women should rule, then?"*

"I don't believe elementals should play god, murder the monarchy, and shape-shift to take their place," Lysander said. "Zamara was no woman. She was a fire-spirit with no true body, and I hope she's rotting in Zoth."

Something flickered in Brooke's eye, but Lysander couldn't discern what it was. *"You didn't answer my question."*

Lysander sighed. Why should she care what he thought? "You were elected by a council of elders, yes? You had to prove your worth alongside the men?"

"I proved my eligibility by killing two xavi, two trace cats, and two d'hakka." Brooke held up three fingers as Ryon translated. *"Agility, strength, and courage. The elders chose me over the others who completed the trials. Does this make me equal to a man?"*

"Regardless of how many beasts they slay, women are equal to men in value," Lysander said, "but not in role. But there are exceptions to every rule." A smirk tugged on his lips. "You've got quite a complex about this, eh?"

Behind her, Ryon looked like he was about to explode.

Brooke smirked. *"Just curious as to how you felt as the pet of an illegitimate queen."*

Lysander considered her for a long moment. What game was she playing?

Ryon's thumb made a slice across his throat—a gesture Lysander didn't have to know sign language to understand. Maybe it wouldn't hurt to explain a bit.

"The elders are the true rulers of your people. They elected you, and your people fear you. It's no concern of mine how the Katrosi rule themselves," Lysander said. "But in Emberhawk culture, the king and queen are sun and moon. The moon cannot govern the day any more than the sun can rule the night. The king must always have a queen to fulfill her diplomatic responsibilities; he cannot do both jobs at once. And if the queen tries to rule as king, she takes both powers for herself. The balance is broken, neither role is properly fulfilled, and the noble houses are slighted with their heirs becoming unable to marry into royalty."

Lysander tapped on his chains and wondered what kind of clinking sound they made. "This is why Coriander's rebellion is so strong: the people hate Zamara for ignoring the customs of our ancestors and breaking our rules of succession."

Brooke's face was as unreadable as Terruthian block-letters. Lysander couldn't tell if she was considering his words or listening at all.

The fear of acquiring a distortion in his voice rose again. He'd been deaf for two years now, unable to hear his own voice—did he sound like a kid trying to talk through a mouthful of honey drops?

Brooke finally spoke, and Ryon signed: *"Whom do you love more: your brother or your sister?"*

Lysander blinked. "I love them equally. Is that a threat? I've answered all of your questions, no matter how random they are."

Brooke tickled her chin with the tuft of brown hair at the end of a braid. *"Who should inherit the Emberhawk throne, then?"*

"If you'd been listening, you'd know that since I abdicated, it goes to Coriander. Not our younger sister, Illiana. And Cori's wife should be queen."

Brooke nodded and watched Ryon sidelong as he signed. *"Do you think that, as king, Coriander would have the Emberhawk join the Tribal Alliance?"*

"Probably," Lysander said after a moment of consideration. "His positions on peace and trade are popular."

Brooke watched him, unmoving, until an uneasy chill slipped down his spine. Maybe she was reading his mind.

Finally, she spoke. *"Illiana has crowned herself queen."*

Lysander's discomfort froze into shock, then shattered into anger. Brooke was trying to manipulate him, just like Zamara. "You're lying."

Brooke shook her head. She displayed no indication that she was deceiving him. Mild curiosity raised her brows.

It couldn't be true regardless. Zamara had wanted the crown to fall to

Illiana, but now that Zamara was dead, surely Illiana would want to set things right. The people would never stand for Illiana to rule as queen, especially because she was young and unwed.

Lysander looked at Ryon. The solemn look on Ryon's normally bright face told Lysander everything he needed to know.

He bit down on a curse. Why would his little sister do something so stupid? Did she think Coriander's rebellion made him a traitor to the throne, and therefore ineligible?

"Has there been infighting?" Lysander asked.

"Not that I know of," Ryon signed for Brooke.

That wouldn't last long. If Coriander hadn't already tried to storm the palace, he would.

Lysander stared down at his hands. He had to convince Illiana to give Coriander the throne. But how?

"I've given you information. Now tell me everything you know about the attack on Jadenvive."

Lysander sighed, commanding his unease to leave with his breath. "You already know everything."

Brooke shrugged and shifted in the chair. *"Tell me anyway so we can compare notes."*

"As soon as I do, you'll have me executed."

"That is not for me to decide, but the elders at your trial." Brooke's chair scooted forward until she was within arm's reach. A scent like jasmine wafted his way as her braids tossed with the movement.

Heat rose into Lysander's neck. He leaned back against the cold wall and looked away.

Ryon waved to draw Lysander's gaze. *"Look at her."*

Lysander stared at the ribbon-like design in the wall, as if the metal had been poured into a mold while molten and cooled in place. "I'm not interested in your magic, witch."

Ryon leaned into his line of sight. *"It's all right."*

Lysander glared. "So says the son of the traitor."

Hurt flashed across Ryon's face until he looked at Brooke, then back to Lysander. *"Just look at her. It'll be much more pleasant than an inquisitor."*

Lysander clenched his fists. He couldn't deny his curiosity.

He reluctantly met her gaze.

Brooke's irises seemed to warp and bleed out with streaks of brown and amber. He jerked back as the room faded into darkness, leaving only her eyes visible in a void bereft of time.

Panic shot through Lysander. He tried to look away, but he had no body. He was a lost soul drowning in an ocean of ink.

What are you hiding?

Brooke's voice rang through his head, clear and beautiful as a song after an eternity of deathly silence. He missed the meaning of her words and savored the sound like chocolate mousse prepared by the chef at the palace of Quin'Zamar.

I can hear, he thought, and his own voice rang strong and deep through his mind. Smothering emotion blossomed and choked him.

Somehow, he could sense Brooke's surprise. *Oh . . . I—*

What magic is this? Lysander demanded.

Brooke's surreal eyes flickered. *It's the aether of the mind.*

Teach me, he thought to her. *Teach me to hear again, and I will do anything for you.*

5

BROOKE

Brooke felt as if she'd been struck by lightning from an unseen storm. Lysander's sudden elation came from nowhere and everywhere at once, smothering her shock.

Had her voice in his mind been the first thing he'd heard since he'd lost his hearing? He hadn't been deaf when she'd known him as a teenager. How long had he been deprived of hearing the voices of others?

Teach me. Lysander's thought was loud yet tentative, joyful yet desperate. *Teach me to do this, and I will tell you anything you want to know. I will swear my life to you. I will put my brother on the throne for you. I will—*

Brooke retreated from his mind and sucked in a steadying breath. One moment she was inside the most damaged, hopeless, guilt-addled mind she'd ever encountered, and the next his exhilaration was enrapturing.

Her vision returned. The chained man before her looked as broken as the emotions she'd sensed. His black hair unkempt. His pointed ears streaked with soot. His maroon eyes pleading.

A husk of the arrogant prince she'd once known.

Lysander bowed as low as his restraints would allow. "Please."

Brooke took a step back, bumping into the chair she'd forgotten about. Ryon furrowed his brow at her, and she ignored him.

"I . . ." Her voice shriveled in her dry throat. She cleared it and composed herself, grasping for a response that would allow her enough distance to consider the abrupt change in negotiations. "I will consider it, depending on your sentence. Your trial is tomorrow."

Realization and depression crashed down on Brooke, and she struggled not to sway under their power. Those weren't her emotions. She cursed herself and struggled to pull all of her aether from Lysander's mind.

But most of it was already gone. A faint bond remained—one she hadn't realized was there. One she'd begun establishing without his knowledge while they were teens so she could spy on his thoughts. So she could determine that no matter how attractive he was, he was rotten to the core. So she could prepare herself for a life of a repeatedly, relentlessly shattered spirit—a certain consequence of an arranged marriage with such an entitled, self-centered person.

Brooke turned on her heel and fled from the cell.

She dodged Ryon and nearly ran headfirst into her lead bodyguard, Dimbae. He caught her with gentle hands as wide as a bear's. "All right?" he murmured.

Brooke squirmed out of Dimbae's grip, avoiding his gaze. She couldn't talk to him now or she'd lose it. Those deep brown eyes knew her too well. They'd discern her in two blinks, and she'd break.

The attack. The loss of life. The people's anger. The fracturing of the Alliance. The threat of the Empire. The Darkwood prince. And now this.

It was too much. Even if her mind could handle it, her heart couldn't. She needed a stiff drink and a cry somewhere no one could hear her.

"Brooke!" Ryon's voice followed her, and she quickened her pace. Exited the prison and veered for the nearby Great Hall. Ignored the salutes of guards and stares of civilians.

"Hey." Ryon jogged to come alongside her. "What did he do? Did he hurt you? I'll—"

"No." Brooke swallowed hard to remove the quiver from her speech. "You said Kiralau and Tekkyn'ashi arrived. Are they ready for me?"

A moment of silence passed as they marched along the element-frozen platform. "Yes. Shall I summon them for you?"

"Please."

Ryon ran ahead without further question. It was one reason she'd chosen him as her new advisor. Not many men understood when to talk and when to shut up and leave her alone. For all the social games she had to play as chieftess, her soul was restored in quiet places where no other thoughts or emotions could infect her. Retreats where she could read a scroll-story or craft with the soft white clay from the Sekoiako lands. Where she could pray and breathe and sip her favorite ginger tea.

But they'd said the Grove of Tomorrow beneath Jadenvive had burned. All of her late mother's weeding and pruning and seed selection gone in a single night. Where could she retreat to now?

I can't train Lysander, even if he somehow survives his trial. I don't have time. And he's too desperate. Too dangerous. And . . .

She couldn't admit that she still had a bond with him, somehow. She hated herself too much for it. Normally that would be considered a boon to speed his training, but she just couldn't. It was toxic. *He* was toxic.

And yet another side of her mind—the portion her father had honed and sharpened for leadership—insisted that Lysander could be the answer to her biggest problem right now: the Emberhawk problem. That was why she'd visited him in the first place.

Well, that, and to gloat a bit. Now regret swam in her gut and made her nauseous. Ginger tea would be heavenly right now.

Maybe the Elder of Aether could train Lysander if he didn't receive a death sentence. But surely the people would vote to have Lysander executed before the next day of rest, and the Elder of Justice would acquiesce.

Would she feel a sudden emptiness on the other side of their aether bond?

Brooke shoved the thoughts from her mind as she veered for the Great Hall's secret entrance. Dimbae wordlessly covered her with his invisibility, and Brooke tolerated the blindness and held his forearm for guidance until the flows of light met her eyes once again.

Emotions lost their grip on her throat as she marched for the map room. She swallowed the last of them to deal with later. She was the chieftess. She couldn't allow anyone to compromise her clarity of mind—least of all the tattered remains of a hollow prince.

Dimbae opened the door and scanned the room, and Brooke followed. Kira and Tekkyn sat attentively at the square table strewn with maps—details they probably shouldn't be seeing. But if she was going to entrust them with this next request, she'd have to trust them with far more than what felt comfortable.

"Chieftess," Tekkyn said with a nod as Kira stood, making her chair skitter as awkwardly as her bow.

"Kiralau, Tekkyn'ashi. Please, sit." Brooke displayed a smile she didn't feel. "Thank you for making the journey. I hope it treated you well."

Kira obliged as Ryon entered with a jingling satchel in each hand. Brooke felt his eyes on her as he waited.

"It did," Tekkyn said. "What can we do for you?"

Brooke noted his cool demeanor. Exactly as she remembered, and exactly what she needed.

She slipped into an opposite chair and allowed herself to relax more than her mother would have approved of. "I have jobs for both of you regarding the imperial princess, if you are willing." She nodded to Ryon, who set a jingling, bulging bag before each of them. Kira gawked at him with eyes the size of the third moon, and he waggled his brows.

Brooke continued. "I know few Malaano people personally, but you have both proven yourselves trustworthy."

"Princess Vylia?" Kira glanced at her brother. "Is she still . . . I mean . . . after the attack . . . ?"

"Yes, she survived. But she is in a coma, along with one of her bodyguards named Sousuke." Brooke adjusted her headdress, moving that annoying pin above her right ear. "Most of her entourage were not as fortunate. Two guards, her advisor, handmaiden, and translator were lost."

Kira cringed and Brooke continued, "I would like to hire you to replace her translator and handmaiden if you have the skill for such things, and to hopefully become her confidant." She turned to Tekkyn. "And for you to replace her lost guards."

"I . . . I don't have *any* of the skills—" Kira began, but her brother interrupted. "Was there a fourth guard?" he asked. "Normally Malaano nobles and diplomats travel with four."

Brooke relaxed a fraction, pleased that he seemed as knowledgeable as she'd hoped. "Indeed. The fourth, Hiro, was injured but recovered his health quickly. He returned to Malaan to inform the emperor that his daughter is alive and recovering."

Kira looked down at her hands in her lap. "What happened to them? Do the healers think they will make it?"

A twinge of stress pinched inside Brooke's chest. If the princess died here . . . she didn't want to think about the repercussions.

"They breathed too much smoke," she said. "The upper levels of Jadenvive are a bit more luxurious than the lower. I'd given Vylia a home in which to stay or establish a Malaano embassy. But the higher levels received the most smoke, and the flames below gave them no method of escape." Brooke leaned back in her chair. "My personal healer is seeing to them, but it is not known whether or not they will awaken. If they do, their injuries should be minimal unless their minds are damaged."

All was quiet for a long moment. Brooke felt Tekkyn's calculating gaze on her and met it.

"The rest of the entourage died from the smoke, then?" he asked.

How was he so perceptive? *I should hire him for my own guard,* Brooke thought. "No. The rest of them were assassinated."

Kira's mouth fell open. "Assassinated?"

Brooke glanced at Dimbae, whose disapproving look was nearly imperceptible. Ryon's approval, however, was far too obvious. She'd have to work with him on that. And his bias as well—normally he shouldn't be so keen on sharing highly sensitive information with foreigners.

But she knew Tekkyn's heart from the time she'd arrested him and invaded his mind after his unit had been involved in the assault on Jadenvive. That search had revealed two things: Tekkyn kept secrets so well that he'd successfully spied on the empire from within their own ranks for years, and that he was loyal to his family and his cause unto death. He'd be the perfect soldier if he didn't have such a hard head of his own.

And Kira was a hero of the city whose residents didn't know her yet. Perhaps Brooke could adopt her into the tribe when the time was right. But now that the people knew that a Malaano unit had aided the Emberhawk with arson, Brooke would have better luck adopting a d'hakka into the tribe.

Brooke took a breath to release her reluctance. "One of Vylia's guards turned on them, but Hiro and Sousuke ended him before he could get to Vylia. Hiro had an . . . interesting theory as to the assassin's motives."

"We were worried about that too." Tekkyn's thick frame leaned over the maps, his blue eyes flicking between markings and miniatures. "The Emperor is drowning in bloodlust. But to sacrifice his own daughter as an excuse to invade . . ."

Brooke restrained her surprise. "Who is 'we'?" Kira asked, horror plainly showing on her face.

"The effectiveness of the Navakovrae Resistance lies in its spies, as I told you last time we spoke." Tekkyn's smirk shone with pride. "We have contacts on the Island. They said the emperor replaced one of Vylia's veteran bodyguards at the last minute. That was out of the ordinary."

"You can't be serious," Kira whispered. "Of course we aren't the emperor's biggest fans, but do you really think he'd kill his own daughter?"

"I think he'd use her for political gain like every other ruler uses their children," Tekkyn said. "And because he didn't marry her off for an alliance, he used her for war instead."

Brooke's heart ached like an old bruise. She was no princess, but the predicament felt familiar nevertheless.

"Regardless of your decision, I can guarantee you safety inside Jadenvive. We are using every available resource for security, and more allies arrive with aid every day." Brooke fixed Tekkyn with a firm gaze. "You may have lost your cover as a Malaano soldier, but I will pay you double whatever they did to protect Vylia, befriend Sousuke, and relay any information you uncover to my spymaster. As long as Vylia lives, the emperor has no excuse to justify invasion to his war-weary citizens."

Tekkyn nodded. "I accept." He shrugged at Kira's bewildered expression with an energetic glint in his grin. "I was getting bored."

Brooke turned her attention to Kira, who shrank like a nervous puppy. "I . . . would love to help, but I don't know anything about dresses or makeup or etiquette. And I'm fluent in Phoeran, but there are still some words and phrases that I don't understand. And I'm horrible at reading it." She tucked her hands under her knees and glanced at Ryon. "And I'm on *evadír.*"

"Don't worry; you speak the language well enough. Just be Vylia's translator and friend if you don't have the skills of a handmaiden. Vylia's appearance probably won't be her foremost concern after what she's just gone through, anyway." Brooke gestured at Ryon. "I won't separate you from him. His family lives here, so you can get to know them and fulfill that half of *evadír* as we wait for the princess to wake." She offered a soft smile. "If you accept, and you decide to marry this idiot, I will fund your wedding."

Kira made an odd noise as she choked on a gasp. "Oh, no, I couldn't possibly expect you to—"

Brooke flicked a wrist to cut her off. "It would be the perfect way to honor your victory over Zamara and to celebrate a sort of marriage alliance to promote peace between our peoples. If that's what you want."

Kira bit her lip and looked at Ryon, whose grin lit the room. "She'll need a nice salary, too, yeah?" he said.

Brooke froze her smile in place before it could flatten. Did everyone think her treasury was a never-ending pit? It wasn't like she was an Emberhawk queen with a pyramid palace forged from translucent gold. And she didn't have a half-destroyed city to repair or anything.

"Of course," Brooke forced out. Hopefully she was preventing war on another front by caring for Vylia—if so, it was worth any cost. "In addition, your food and lodging will be provided for you here in the Great Hall. You are my personal guests—do not hesitate to ask if there is anything you require."

"Well, then . . ." Kira's skepticism melted into a hesitant smile as she glanced between the encouraging nods of her brother and her betrothed. "I accept."

6

KIRALAU

Kira knocked lightly on the door to the infirmary and stood up straight. Her nerves jittered and buzzed like a beehive.

"Calm down," Tekkyn murmured behind her. "If you pull on that bracelet any harder it'll shatter."

Kira hadn't realized she was nervously toying with the arm band Ryon had given her. The smooth circle around her wrist glinted softly in the light from a window down the hall that looked more like an arrow slit.

"Gold doesn't shatter," Ryon said from her other side.

"Gold?" Tekkyn snorted.

"It's translucent gold, forged by the master elementalist of Quin'Zamar," Ryon said.

Kira glanced back to catch Tekkyn rolling his eyes. She shushed them and knocked on the door a little louder. The last thing she needed was for these two not to get along, but she couldn't think about anything other than meeting the imperial princess right now.

Although the reminder that she was wearing gold—real, priceless, magically forged gold—warmed her with pride and affection.

"Hold your gryphons," came a hushed voice from the other side of the door. It opened slowly, and a pair of feminine, narrowed eyes glared out at them. "Who're you?"

"Kiralau and Tekkyn'ashi," Kira whispered. "We've been assigned to aid the princess."

"Oh, hi!" The door opened just far enough to reveal a spritely face.

Wild hair bobbed as the girl tilted her head. "The princess is still asleep, though." She pushed forward to glance down the hall, and Kira stumbled out of her way. "Where are the guards?"

"I let them take a bathroom break," Ryon said.

The girl shrugged and moved aside, opening the door. "Come in, come in! Just be *quiet.*" She elongated the word with wide, playful eyes, as if inviting them to a game of hide-and-seek.

Kira hesitantly stepped into the room. Four beds lined one wall, and two hammocks on the other. The ceiling was half-formed of thick, cloudy glass, allowing sunlight to grace two dark-skinned figures lying on the beds: a young man and a young woman.

"Where's the doctor?" Kira whispered.

"I'm the chieftess' personal healer," the girl said, crossing to a small table and closing a cabinet behind it. "If we could skip all the 'you're too young' stuff, that'd be great. You're pretty young, too."

Kira blinked at her. The healer couldn't be much older than twenty. "I didn't mean—"

"Yeah, you did, but it's fine." The healer hopped up on the table and crossed her legs, straightening her back to sit tall. "I'm an aether healer— the only one in the tribe. We have a traditional healer and a Roanoke herbalist check on 'em every night, too. They're both ancient, so you can trust 'em."

The girl's face was blank, so Kira gave a smile to hopefully mask her awkward feeling. "If the chieftess trusts you, that's good enough for—"

"What's your name?" Tekkyn interrupted.

"Nariellyn. Call me Nari if you feel like it." She picked at a fleck of dirt on her bare foot.

Kira stared. Hopefully the aether gift could somehow make up for the lack of dignity. Or maybe this was some kind of prank.

"I'll keep watch out here until the guards get back," Ryon said as he closed the door. Kira's heart sank as he disappeared from sight.

Tekkyn stepped closer to the beds and looked down on the sleeping figures. "How long have they been asleep?"

"A few days. Too long," Nariellyn said from the table. "Every day that passes means they're less likely to ever wake up." She sighed. "Sadness."

Kira quietly approached until the sun warmed her from the giant window above. A bowl filled with water sat on a nightstand, steaming with an earthy scent. Below a colorful quilt, a girl with a round face and flawless skin breathed softly in her sleep.

Is she my age? Kira wondered. Surely this couldn't be Vylia, daughter of the Emperor of Malaan. Without a crown or dress or colored powders around her eyes, she could have been mistaken for any other girl from the island beyond the Sea of Bones.

The sleeping soldier beside her was just as still. But bandages covered his shoulder, his side, and his hands. Bloody armor sat piled beside his bed.

I don't care where they're from . . . What they must have gone through was awful. Even more so if they were betrayed. Kira's nervousness melted into empathy. *Creator, please let them wake up.* She cautiously touched Vylia's hand, glad to find it warmer than her clammy face looked.

Kiralau.

The sudden voice in Kira's head made her jump. It was feminine, watery, distant—surely she hadn't heard it with her ears, because Tekkyn didn't react as he studied the soldier's equipment and complained that it hadn't been cleaned.

Kira looked around, trying to find the source of the unearthly voice. The painting on the wall? The vining plant in the corner? The orange salt-rock beneath the cabinets? It hadn't come from any particular direction, but from everywhere at once, like Brooke's thought-speak after she'd questioned Tekkyn in the Great Hall. But unlike Brooke's deep, rough voice, this had been sultry. Smooth. Surreal.

Gentle laughter flitted through Kira's mind. *Don't be afraid, little minnow. Do you not recognize my voice from your answered prayers?*

Fear lanced from Kira's heart to the pit of her stomach. Her gaze whipped to Nariellyn, but the healer was eyeing Tekkyn with an admiring interest.

Kira slowly turned back to Vylia's still face. "Who are you?" she whispered.

"Definitely the princess," Tekkyn answered. "Hard to tell without the makeup, but the portraits capture her pretty well regardless." He tipped his head toward the sleeping soldier. "And this is Sousuke?"

"Yep. Another of her bodyguards named Hiro went back to Malaan Island to tell the emperor his daughter is alive so this won't, you know, cause international upheaval or anything." Nariellyn's nervous grin shone with a flash of white teeth. "Are you okay, Kiralau? You look . . ."

"I'm fine." Kira swallowed the tension in her throat and took a step back from Vylia's bed. "I thought I heard something."

Nariellyn tilted her head like a curious cat. "Wish I could hear something else. I've been sittin' here for days listening to nothing but snores."

Kira forced a smile. "Right."

You know who I am. I am the seven-tailed fox.

Blood drained from Kira's veins, leaving her with hollow dread.

It couldn't be. The water goddess had been silent her entire life. Cold. Nonchalant. Nonexistent.

And if she did exist, Felix had said she was locked away in a stone, unconscious and powerless. And even if that weren't true, she was just an elemental—just like Zamara had been before Kira launched a harpoon through her crystalline heart.

Say my name.

Kira's lips felt dry. "Lillian?" she whispered.

An ethereal smile pressed into her mind. *Come back when we can speak in private, my child. I have need of you.*

7

LYSANDER

Lysander adjusted his bruised wrists in their restraints as the guards dragged him up another flight of stairs to the Hall of Judgement. The floor curved in an enormous crescent shape with rows of stacked seating full of onlookers and windows that looked down on Jadenvive from the city's upper levels. Like a gaping maw eager to swallow him.

He didn't have to hear the people's voices to know what they were saying. They glared at him as if they could ignite him with their stares alone. Only the elderly men, assembling on the far side of the room in seven elevated chairs, seemed oblivious to his entrance.

The guards shoved Lysander down in the center of the room. His knees were knocked out from under him and slammed into the floor. They tugged on his bindings and affixed them to a pole that rose to the ceiling.

Lysander closed his eyes and willed his jittery pulse to calm. He'd known the Katrosi would end him from the moment they'd caught him. It wasn't like an official death sentence would be a surprise. At least their strange trial system offered the possibility of a civilized execution.

Two strong vibrations rippled through the sound waves, and Lysander glanced toward their source. A middle-aged man lowered his robed arms as if he'd clapped, and now he bellowed something above the white noise of the crowd. Dozens upon dozens of people moved for their seats and settled.

Lysander looked toward the seven Elders, but Brooke wasn't there. Nor was there any sort of throne. He frowned and finally found the horns and claws of her headdress poking above the crowd on the far side of the room. The chieftess sat in a simple chair as if she were any other citizen. The paint of mourning appeared to drip down her cheeks like black tears.

She didn't return his gaze.

Does she have power here? Dread curdled in Lysander's stomach. What kind of ruler had no say in the trials of their people? The Katrosi system of governance was foreign to him. Powers separated like a finely balanced scale with three pans. He'd always thought it interesting until now.

Because yesterday he'd ruined an already awful relationship with the only person who might have kept him alive.

An elder with blue robes rose and gestured, his lips moving in soundless speech. Lysander took a deep breath as his hand-language interpreter slid into his view and sat cross-legged on the floor. Her eyelids drooped and her posture slumped. He wasn't sure which she hated more: him or her job.

"Thus begins the trial of Lysander of Quin'Zamar, firstborn of the late Emberhawk King Brynn." she signed. *"He is accused today of aiding the elemental Zamara, recently discovered to be Queen Dierdre, in her siege of Jadenvive. Thus he faces dozens of counts of assault, murder, and arson. As well as prior counts of espionage and assassination."*

Lysander gritted his teeth. *Zamara was* not *Queen Dierdre,* he thought. *Zamara murdered my mother and impersonated her to rule the kingdom for years. Get it right.*

Someone spat at him from the crowd on his right side. Lysander caught the movement and dodged, and the guards swiftly obstructed his view. The announcer, or whatever he was, said something the interpreter didn't seem to translate.

Lysander shifted on his knees, pretending to ignore the waves of hatred roiling among the people. Another burst of sound energy from one of the elders seemed to restrain them. He took a steadying breath and considered dulling his connection to the Phoera element to quiet the static that undulated all around him. But even though it was just commotion, it was better than deafening silence.

If only the guards hadn't found and taken the lockpick Xavier had given him. Not that it would have helped him escape the city, anyway.

When he looked back up, one of the elders was gone. The Elder of Aether, if he remembered correctly. These Katrosi had a crazy old man to represent every aspect of their crazy way of life. How the five tribes had originated from the same Phoeran people only a few hundred years ago and formed such different cultures, Lysander would never know.

The Elder of Aether appeared beyond the guards, shuffling in amber robes. Lysander couldn't decipher his expression beyond a tumbling white beard, so he focused on a knot in the wooden floor instead.

Look at me, Slain Prince.

Lysander's throat constricted as a masculine voice echoed through his mind, clear as a morning-bird's call. Not nearly as lyrical as Brooke's thought-voice, but welcome nevertheless. Any true sound—even a mockery of it—was welcome.

Lysander looked up at the elder and met his cloudy hazel gaze.

You know they call you that, yes? The elder sat in front of Lysander, his hunched back bringing his wrinkled face uncomfortably close. *Why are you called this?*

Lysander stared back, wondering at the futility of a conversation with this man. Had he come to mock him?

It is customary for me to determine the motives of the accused at the beginning of every trial of this magnitude, the elder said. *Intentions play a role in the dealings of justice. Now, why are you called the Slain Prince?*

Lysander determined not to back away or avert his gaze, though he had no idea what the man's question had to do with this trial. *Zamara took everything from me,* he thought, assuming the elder could hear his internal musings as Brooke had. *I was raised as the crown prince. Then she murdered my mother and impersonated her through shapeshifting. My father killed himself from sorrow and shame. Zamara took my lover, my hearing, and my throne. I am unrecognizable from the child I was. Thus they call me "slain."*

The elder listened, quiet and cool as winter in the deep forest. *How could she take your throne? It is known that you abdicated of your own will.*

It was not my will. When my father died, Zamara brought my love, Selene, and my brother, Coriander, into her inner room and ordered me to abdicate. When I refused, she—Lysander paused as a bloody memory flashed through his mind's eye—*killed Selene. Then she threatened Cori and I . . .* Lysander closed his eyes and took a deep breath, coming back to his senses in the courtroom for a brief moment. *What else could I do? Cori finally believed me about Zamara after that, and he escaped to form his rebellion.*

A somber darkness seeped from the elder's presence in his mind. Lysander wondered if the old man could discern whether or not the claims were true.

And she took your hearing?

Two years after my abdication, I couldn't stand it any more. She used me like a dog, sending me to commit the murders and spying you accuse me of. I tried to kill her and failed. She . . . He couldn't finish the thought. *She punished me. The few sounds I've heard since then have only been what would be absurdly loud to most, and even then, they are difficult to discern.*

The elder watched him with an unreadable expression. *Were you under Zamara's control for the attack on Jadenvive?*

I've been under her control since she took Selene. But I have been supporting my brother's rebellion against her however I can. I warned my cousin, Ryon, and I turned on her during the attack. I failed to kill her again, and I'm surprised I survived that encounter. Lysander huffed a breath. *Not that it mattered, since I won't survive this trial.* He leaned back and shifted in his restraints, holding his chin high. *I don't care if you kill me. She's dead. That's all that matters.*

The elder remained still for a long moment. *Creator have mercy on you, child. Ask him for forgiveness, and he will satisfy you with his justice and heal you with his love.*

Lysander rolled his eyes as the old man got to his feet with the help of a guard. At least he'd heard another person's voice before the end, however unwelcome a religious rant was. What had the creator ever done for him?

Sound energy reverberated from the announcer's direction. The translator grew lax with lazy movements as the conversation bounced around the courtroom and the minutes dragged on.

Lysander closed his eyes. If Zamara hadn't infiltrated his family, he'd probably be at the palace of Quin'Zamar right now—rather, at Quin'Alor, the grand pyramid's former name. He'd be dressed in d'hakka silk dyed in the rarest shades of violet and blue. His Valinorian mother, Dierdre, would still be alive to dote upon him, and his father to angrily disapprove of his every action. He'd be married to the daughter of the Katrosi chief, who would not have grown up to become chieftess herself.

Brooke.

Lysander stared through the crowd until he caught a glance of her. Those big brown eyes had sharpened as she'd grown. Her playful, styled hair tightened into braids. Her curvy features toned into the firm-yet-feminine stature of a spearmaiden.

It wouldn't have worked between them, anyway. She was too strong-minded—they'd clash against each other like swords. And he had no idea how to treat a woman, at least in an appropriate way. Selene hadn't finished teaching him.

Brooke met his gaze, and he couldn't tell if the tear was genuine or from her dripping warpaint. She looked away.

Lysander frowned and turned back to the interpreter.

Her hand signs were stiff and cold. *"The people have voted, and the Elder of Justice has sentenced you to death. Your soul will be delivered to the creator in three days."*

8

KIRALAU

Kira squinted at smudged writing at the top of the Phoeran schematics. "Crossbow," she murmured as she read. "Designed so a bolt shot at high speed can penetrate heavy armor." At least, that's what she thought the flowing script said.

"Wonder what kinda fish they got in that lake." Tekkyn lifted a fish hook above his head, examining it in the light from the ceiling windows of the infirmary. "I heard they got whisker fish as long as a man's leg."

Kira reined in her frustration as she tried to calculate how much force the collection of pulleys could exact upon the bowstring. "I'm sure the river Mossu has the same trout that the Silvermead does. They're only separated by the Gnarled Wood."

"Yeah, but the Silvermead empties into the Rift Ocean, while the Mossu feeds Lake Mossu. So we might get more salt-fish swimmin' upstream from the ocean while the lake might have fish that don't like the salt."

"We're a long way from the ocean, though," Kira muttered, tilting the schematic sideways as she counted strings.

"Well yeah, but you should see how far them redfish will travel at the right time of year."

Kira blew out a breath as she set the scroll down in a crackling protest. "Why don't you just go fishing and find out?"

Tekkyn tore his eyes from the gleaming fishhook to glance at her. "Gotta watch these Islanders."

"I'm watching them."

He frowned. "I'm bein' paid well to—"

"It doesn't take two people to watch them sleep," Kira said.

Tekkyn smirked. "My job's to guard them, whether they're awake or not."

A frustrated growl rumbled in Kira's throat. "We're in the Great Hall—the safest place in the entire city—and they aren't going anywhere. I'll send for you if they wake up, okay?"

Tekkyn pursed his lips. "As tempting as that sounds, I'm a soldier, and I never leave my post."

Kira gave him a blank look. "Then be quiet so I can study. If I have to listen to you talk about fish for five more breaths, I'm going to turn into a shark, okay?"

Tekkyn chuckled and crossed to her. He tousled her hair before she could lean away. "All right, fine, Frizz. I'll just check out the docks and come right back." He strode to the door and slipped the hook into a pouch on his belt. "I'll call for an extra guard outside in case you need to use the restroom or something."

"And they could call us if we're actually needed! What a novel idea!" Kira shooed him away and retrieved her scroll as Tekkyn shut the door behind him.

Yeah, the shark comment had been dumb, but she was more flustered than she cared to admit. Lee had loved fishing, too, and no matter how much Kira treasured her remaining brother, she couldn't become his new fishing buddy. The memories hurt too much. The wound was too raw.

And with Tekkyn gone, Kira was finally alone with the two sleepers . . . and that mysterious other presence.

Kira carefully rolled up the schematics and placed it next to the other scrolls from the Jadenvive library. She glanced at the door as she stood and moved to stand where she'd last heard the disembodied voice.

"Lillian?" she whispered.

Kiralau. The voice echoed in her head, undulating with warmth and peace. *It seems we may speak freely now.*

Kira's blood chilled, half excited and half horrified that the being had answered so quickly. It must have been listening.

"What are you? How are you doing this?" She looked down at Vylia's still face. What sorcery had the royals conjured on the Island?

Did you not just acknowledge my name? Laughter passed through Kira's mind like a summer breeze. *You truly speak to the goddess of water, little minnow. The seven-tailed fox. The deity of fertility and generosity. Lady of the Endless Isles. True ruler of the Malaano Empire.*

Kira blinked in surprise. Lillian thought herself the ruler of Malaan? Then what of the emperor?

She tightened her fists. "You can't be Lillian. I called out to her my entire life, and she never answered my prayers. My people suffered through years of drought, and she either abandoned us or she wasn't powerful enough to help. Now why would I suddenly hear her voice here, in a foreign land?" Blood thudded through Kira's veins. "I know you're just a mind-reader like the chieftess. Show yourself."

A moment of silence passed, and a feeling like crawling spiders skittered across Kira's skin.

What a remarkable fire you have. I see now why you have bound yourself to a Phoeran. The voice remained smooth and calm. *Tell me, faithless girl: does your land still thirst for water?*

Kira froze. They'd had gentle, consistent, intermittent rain for over a week now. Not so much to have caused a flood—just the right amount for the land to absorb and heal. The right amount to help the Katrosi put out the fires. The right amount to restore a vibrant green to their fields and feed their starving cattle.

A sliver of fear trickled down Kira's spine. She said nothing.

I speak to you now through my mirror, a powerful artifact within Princess Vylia's belongings. You may know it as the Malo Stone—the source of the Malo element.

The trickle of anxiety turned into a gush and flooded Kira's belly with dread. Her eyes flicked to the folded dress and other delicate accessories on a thin table behind her. She slowly turned and spotted an opal the size of her fist. It glittered and gleamed every color even in the stillness, swirling like a magical storm trapped behind glass.

Kira's breath faltered. *Is this the stone that Felix said Lillian was imprisoned within?*

"Are . . . you . . . trapped inside?" she whispered, staring into the depths of the stone.

The voice made a noise akin to a snarl. *How does one trap a god? Within a rock, no less? Blasphemy.*

Kira clenched her fists until her nails dug into her palms. "They say the creator bound the four greater *amos* elementals for disobeying his laws and abusing humans."

The creator is dead. I killed him myself along with the other amos, *and we absorbed the power from his dying breath. His laws were tyrannical and his judgements harsh. No one misses him except the blind pagans.* The voice changed abruptly from vitriolic to nonchalant. *Now, my child, if you will put aside these baseless beliefs and return to me, I have chosen you to perform a simple task. Do this for me, and you will be rewarded beyond your mortal imaginings.*

Kira remembered to breathe. She glanced back at Vylia and Sousuke, then at the door. Nothing had changed.

Well, Lillian's claims aside, it couldn't hurt to know what she was after. "What is it you want?" Kira whispered.

The voice's candor turned sweet. *I'm fond of relics, as you can see. The children of Phoera have stolen one from me. Tell me: what do your pagan leaders say of the keystone?*

Kira blinked in surprise. "The big quartz gem in the chieftess's headdress?"

One and the same. Retrieve it for me, and I will add its power to my own. With it, I can easily aid my people, such as yourself, at the edges of our ever-expanding empire. Droughts needn't last so long, even so far from Maqua, hmm?

Kira's jaw fell. "You want me to steal Brooke's—"

The door opened and Kira jumped. Ryon's smiling face popped in through the breach. "Hey, *balemba!*" His grin faded as he caught her expression. "Everything okay?"

"Yes, uh . . ." Kira straightened and hurried to him, far too aware of the surreal presence at her back that made her skin raise into bumps. Something in her hair flopped with the sudden movement, and she fumbled with the butterfly pin Ryon had given her. Tekkyn's teasing must have knocked it loose.

Thankfully, the voice said nothing more as she left the room. She had to tell Ryon about this strange development, but not here. Perhaps Lillian couldn't hear her elsewhere in the city, away from the "mirror."

Kira landed in Ryon's arms. "I'm fine. How are you? I heard Lysander . . ."

"I'm trying really hard not to think about that right now." Ryon held her tight. "I'm still on duty but thought I'd check in and say hi. Do you have any plans for tonight?"

"No." Kira dared not look back. "What did you have in mind?"

"Mom's making venison empanadas for dinner." Something in Ryon's eye implied that empanadas were something special, whatever they were. "Since we're on *evadír,* you know, I thought actually spending time with family might be a good idea."

Oh, right. The purpose of *evadír* was to meet each other's families, wasn't it?

Kira's tension began to hesitantly melt. "That sounds great, but . . ." She looked back at Vylia's sleeping form, waiting for the quilt over the princess's chest to rise and fall. The opal burned in her peripheral vision.

"Spend just a few minutes on break with me. I really need a distraction right now," Ryon said. "I passed Nariellyn on the way here. She said she's coming for a routine checkup. And she'll be back tonight as well, so I'm sure it wouldn't be a problem if you left for a little date."

Kira turned back to him with a sly smirk. "Date, huh?"

"I've got plans." Ryon's eyebrows bounced. "Oh, and Tekkyn is invited to dinner too. But not the afterparty."

Kira rolled her eyes and leaned forward, hoping to provide the support Ryon needed after his cousin's death sentence. And she wanted out of this room as soon as possible.

"I'll leave Tekkyn a note, but he'd only be interested in *fish* empana . . . nadas. We won't need a chaperone for this 'afterparty,' do we?"

Ryon's grin widened. "Nope."

9

BROOKE

"I answer your summons, Chieftess."

Brooke watched the middle-aged man kneel before her throne, his dark cloak whispering around fine clothes and clean boots. Good thing he averted his gaze, because if she looked half as tired as she felt, even her war paint couldn't mask the dark circles under her eyes.

Sleep had evaded her during her brief midday nap. She'd lost count of the meetings she'd already had today. Two more to go.

She wanted nothing more than a few minutes of shut-eye, but she refused to rest until her people could.

Brooke tilted her head toward her handmaiden. "Another yaupon tea, please."

Shaya raised an eyebrow, silently voicing her disapproval.

Brooke waved her off. So what if it was her fourth cup of the energizing brew?

Shaya bowed and shuffled down the steps toward the Great Hall's kitchens.

"It's good to see you, Ulysses," Brooke said to the man. "I hope the fire didn't cause your family any suffering."

"It didn't. Our house is in the upper levels, but the smoke drifted to the other side of the city." Ulysses looked up at her with a dark, hollow gaze. "If I may speak frankly, Chieftess, I'm surprised you would care about the wellbeing of my family after what my mother did to you."

Brooke frowned. It was true that she hated his mother more than any other creature on the planet. When Ulysses and Brooke had competed for the title of chief three years ago, his mother was the one who'd started the rumor that Brooke was a witch in an attempt to inflict political damage.

He must think it humiliating to kneel before me now.

"Rise," Brooke said. "You might have heard that I lost my vice in the attack. I'd like you to be his replacement."

Ulysses froze halfway to standing and stared at her with wide eyes. "You . . . what?" He looked back down at his feet. "Surely you can't be serious. The elders didn't choose me that day, so why do you think I would make a good chief if something happened to you? I was . . . arrogant and awful."

A smile tugged on the edge of Brooke's lips. "Your admission confirms you aren't like that any more. It's been three years." She stood up from the throne, hoping the movement would force some blood back into her exhausted limbs. "But one thing didn't change: you'd make a good vice for the same reason you were good competition on that day."

She omitted the other reason he could probably guess: making an alliance with her political rival would strengthen her own support from the people during a tumultuous time.

Ulysses's brow furrowed in thought. "Thank you for this honor. But I'll need time to think on it." He straightened his leather jerkin with an annoyed tug. "And I'd have to ensure my mother wouldn't cause trouble."

Brooke suddenly felt lighter. Maybe this wasn't such a bad idea after all. "The position is yours if you want it. You have three days to decide."

"Thank you." Ulysses bowed his head. "This is yet another reason the elders chose you. I don't think I could forgive my enemies like this."

"We are not enemies," Brooke said, "but if we were, haven't you already forgiven me?"

Ulysses's lips parted, but he didn't say anything. Then his shoulders seemed to relax a bit. "I can't forgive you for being chosen. That's not a crime."

"It's practically a crime for you to not see how you're the perfect candidate for my vice." She smirked. "I wouldn't have offered you the position if I didn't think you'd make a good chief if something happened to me."

His expression turned into an intimidating mix of dark and playful—that competitive gleam Brooke knew well. "Obviously you're wrong, so I'll just have to make sure nothing happens to you."

Not exactly comforting. Aeo, I hope I'm making the right decision.

Brooke nodded. "You are dismissed."

Ulysses turned and exited, leaving the Great Hall empty except for the unlit braziers, guards, and Shaya as she quietly returned. And the invisible Dimbae, who was probably leaning on his favorite pillar.

Brooke adjusted her headdress and groaned, wishing she could remove the heavy wyvern horns and aether stone. But the annoyance was probably helping her stay awake.

"I'm going to be late, aren't I?" Brooke asked Shaya as she stood and took her leave.

"Very," the handmaiden replied. "I'll have your tea sent as soon as it's ready."

"Thanks. Dimbae, are you going to follow me to the . . . uh . . ." She really must be tired if she couldn't remember the name of one of her favorite places in the city.

"The Grove of the Ancients?" A tall, thick figure shimmered into existence on her left. "You should know by now that I follow you everywhere."

"You don't have to. The Elder of Aether is one of the most powerful beings on the continent," Brooke said. She'd heard some interesting reports about how the Emberhawk attackers who'd crossed him had fared.

"The Elder of Aether is an elder," Dimbae said. "Yes, he held his own in the battle, but it left him exhausted. Does anyone know how old he really is?"

"Respect," Brooke warned as two guards opened the massive, intricately carved double doors for them to pass through. Outside, wooden steps led down to a wide platform that glistened with frost. Brooke made a mental note to let the elementalists focus their attention elsewhere now that the threat of fire had passed.

She smirked up at Dimbae, appreciating the head-and-a-half of height difference. "Although he's probably old enough to have tended to Vanya as a seedling." She gestured at the giant birch holding the platform aloft—one of three great trees that supported the city-in-the-sky.

Dimbae's grin stretched wide. "Don't let him hear you say that."

The headdress drew both smiles and glares as Brooke made her way to the elevator—another reason she wished she'd removed it. Only half as many Katrosi civilians could recognize her in plainclothes without warpaint.

Dimbae kept all but the children at bay. "We're gonna get the bad guys, right?" a young boy asked with fire in his eyes.

Brooke reassured the child with a heavy heart. Why did no one acknowledge that most of the Emberhawk attackers and Zamara herself had already been killed? Did they not realize what a miracle it was that a foreigner—a teenage girl, no less—had vanquished a false god with a harpoon and the shards of a broken elevator? Would her people not be satisfied until they crushed the entire Emberhawk tribe in another bloody war? Would they not rest until another generation of men was wiped out?

She tried to clear her mind as she strode under the vined archway that signified the grove's entrance. The elder might chastise her for projecting such troubled thoughts into a sacred place.

The path wound around ferns and fig trees, comfrey and chamomile. Each section of the garden had been planted with care, placing species that complimented each other together. Corn, beans, and squash flourished in the sunniest spot as if fire hadn't blazed overhead just days ago. Only flecks of ash on a few leaves betrayed the façade of peace.

"Well, look who decided to show up," Nariellyn said from her cross-legged position on a large sandrock beside the pond. She opened a mischievous eye and grinned.

"Sorry. It's not like I was busy leading the tribe or anything."

"*Aish,* you two." The elder shooed Nariellyn away with a leathery hand. "You're done for the day. Practice your mental shields." He stood with obvious effort and brushed at his long, white beard. "I'm sorry, Brooke, but aether training is over. The tribe may need you, but my lunch also needs me."

Brooke frowned. "I understand. Sorry, Master."

"It is all right." The old man placed a hand on her shoulder and squinted at her under unruly eyebrows. "You are troubled by many things today. Sit by the water and clear your mind."

"Actually, Master, I . . ." Brooke swallowed as she watched Nariellyn go. "I was hoping I could at least speak with you for a moment."

He sighed, and clacked his cane on the gravel until he arrived at the sitting stone by the falls. "What is it?"

Apprehension tightened Brooke's throat. "We've both seen inside Lysander's mind."

The Elder of Aether watched her, still and silent.

Brooke swallowed. "He's not innocent, but he was used. Manipulated. Forced to obey Zamara's commands. Didn't you share that with the other elders before the vote?"

The old man's gaze wandered to Dimbae, then back to her. "I did. It is not accurate to say he was forced. He was not bound—he chose to obey her."

"Zamara was threatening his sister. She'd murdered an innocent to control him before."

"And he allowed himself to be controlled out of despair and shame. He did her bidding for years and spilled blood in her name." The elder leaned on the cane beneath his beard. "Why do you argue this now? His fate has already been decided."

Brooke clenched her fists. "Because this is more mob rule than it is justice." She took a step closer and lowered her voice. "He could be the key to peace with the Emberhawk. You felt his heart just as I did. He is broken, but he could help us. He *wants* to help us."

"And what do you want, young one? I can see your soul more clearly than I can see your crooked headdress."

Brooke froze. The weight on her head did feel a bit off. She adjusted it and straightened her spine. "I want healing for my people. I want to honor my father's and grandfather's legacy. To avoid more bloodshed. And for us to all sleep without worry for tomorrow."

The elder stared at her, motionless, until she had to fight the urge to look away.

"This is called lying by omission," he said in that slow, crackly voice. A snicker-bird chittered from the nearby fig tree as if to laugh at her.

Brooke bit the inside of her cheek. "Okay, I also want a family, just like everyone else. Why is this suddenly about me? Perhaps you could appeal to the council for Lysander. He is the rightful king of the Emberhawk; he could be a great asset—"

"Perhaps you are more attached to him than you should be, since you were promised to each other at a young age." The elder tilted his head. "Do you share an aether bond with him?"

Brooke recoiled. "Not in the truest sense. I . . ."

He just stared at her, those hazy eyes piercing her to the core. Like a butcher removing her heart with swift precision and displaying it on a plate for the world to see.

Brooke remembered her training—*his* training—and took a deep breath, then released her unease with it. Most of it, at least.

"I formed a bond with him as a youngling," she admitted. "I thought it would have deteriorated by now."

"Spirit bonds do not diminish with time or distance," the elder said. His gaze softened. "The death of someone you are bonded to is always difficult. I am sorry for that. But it is your responsibility as chief to enforce the will of the people."

Brooke nodded. "Always." She crouched before him, her boots sinking into the rich soil. "Please, then, tell me what to do. Our people thirst for

Emberhawk blood, and I don't think Lysander's will quench them. Illiana has stolen the throne from her brother Coriander and refuses to join the Alliance. She'll be every bit the tyrant her mother was while the Malaano grow more threatening by the day—who knows how they will react to the loss of Vylia? It looks like this was all a manipulation to push us closer to war. And our city is in ruins. How can I possibly resolve all of this? Or *any* of it? I've agreed to marry the Darkwood prince but even that sacrifice may accomplish nothing in the end."

The elder listened quietly, then spent another minute stroking his beard in thought. "Our situation is dire indeed. I will beseech the creator for wisdom on your behalf." He placed an aged hand on her arm. "For now, go to the prison and tell Lysander goodbye. Acknowledge whatever he is to you, or whatever he was. Then you must let him go. Clear your mind. For the sake of our people."

Brooke nodded slowly as a grim determination settled over her heart. "Yes, Master."

By the time sugary citrus tarts had been served for dessert, Kira had almost forgotten about Lillian. Almost.

Her future mother- and sister-in-law were too good to be true. Wasn't she supposed to not get along with in-laws? Gwyneth's heart seemed as kind as her cooking was divine, and Aegwyn must have inherited a dash of the same light-hearted humor that Ryon had. Kira wondered what their father had been like and wished she could have met him.

"All right, off to bed with you." Aegwyn shooed the orphans from the table to a chorus of disapproval. "Tell Miss Gwyn 'thank you' for dinner."

"Thank you," the children echoed.

Kira grinned as they left, little Mayla lagging behind with her floppy ragdoll. They functioned like a family . . . Kira wondered how they'd feel if any of the kids were actually adopted out. Ryon said a year had passed since the last adoption, and the older the orphans got, the lesser their chances became.

Mayla looked back and waved at Kira, who grinned and returned the gesture. Maybe it wouldn't be so bad to grow up in the root tunnels, beneath the treetop city and all its toils. With a loving matron, half a dozen playmates, and the best cooking this side of the Silvermead River. And Ryon bringing them stolen delicacies from afar.

"Thanks, Mom," Ryon said as he pushed an empty plate away. "You could open a restaurant, you know."

"Oh no, I'd be much too rushed. And having to stop every five minutes to settle a dispute adds to the flavor." She winked and gathered the dishes. "Thanks for the venison. The rest is drying in the oven. If you can gather some berries, I'll buy some fat tomorrow, and we'll have plenty of pemmican for the winter."

Ryon's expression hitched, but Kira couldn't determine why. She stood to help Gwyneth with the dishes but was waved away.

"Did you . . . shoot this deer?" Kira asked Ryon.

He smirked and tapped the edge of the lenses Felix had given him. "It's easy to forget Zamara messed up my sight thanks to these. Just have to get used to holding my bow differently." His chair scooted across the smooth stone floor as he stood and held a hand out to her. "How about a tour?"

Kira felt her cheeks warm as she took his hand. He never mentioned the blemish Kira had received from that same battle: the scar she bore in the shape of Zamara's handprint around her neck. She hated the bumpy feel of it and felt certain people noticed. She'd planned to hide it by wearing her bandana around her neck, but this season was too hot for a neck-scarf.

Well, if her betrothed didn't mind, she didn't care what anyone else thought.

"Haven't you given me a tour already?" Kira asked.

"You haven't seen the half of it, my dear," Gwyneth called from the kitchen. "Thank you for joining us for dinner. It has been a pleasure getting to know you." Her proud smile shone under hanging garlic braids and drying herbs. "My Idryon chose well."

The warmth in Kira's face spread to her ears. "Thank you. It has been wonderful getting to know you as well." She was certain she'd butchered the Phoeran word for "wonderful."

"Visit us as often as you like," Gwyneth said. "You two have fun."

Kira's fingers tingled in Ryon's hand—he hadn't let go. He moved toward an opening behind the children's playroom, pushed it aside, and beckoned her forward with an excited light in his gaze.

Her own excitement mingled with a timid flutter in her chest. "Where are we going?"

"You'll see." Ryon chuckled as he watched her from the corner of his eye. "Your nervousness is adorable."

Kira pursed her lips. "Is there any emotion I can have that you *don't* think is adorable?"

"Nope."

Kira sighed. She'd walked right into that one. Of course, her fiancé thinking she was cute wasn't a bad thing. She'd just like to be respected every once in a while, but most people only saw the short, harmless girl she appeared to be.

Except Brooke, who seemed to appreciate the intellect that Kira sharpened beneath. Tall, muscular, intimidating-as-a-wyvern Brooke.

"Everything okay?" Ryon asked.

Kira cleared her throat. "Yes. You?" She ducked under a twisting root as she followed him. "You seemed a little off when your mom was talking about pemmican." She dared not mention Lysander and hoped that wasn't what his strange reaction had been about.

"Ah. You're a perceptive one." Ryon forged onward, not turning his face back to her as he spoke. "No big deal. It's just not as easy to find the time to hunt and forage now that I'm Brooke's advisor. But with the pay increase, I can just buy the berries she needs. Assuming anyone is willing to sell food right now . . . Everyone is hoarding whatever they can."

Kira searched for the source of emotion behind his tone. "But you were able to bring that venison home."

"Yeah, and I still feel guilty about how long that took, even if most of the time I spent hunting was before dawn." Ryon turned down a path that broadened beside a shriveled root. As they roamed farther from the light of the orphanage, he withdrew a candle from his belt. He snapped, and the wick burst into flame.

"Sounds like you've got the new job jitters," Kira said.

"Well yeah, and Brooke is dealing with a lot of problems right now," Ryon said. "As if a third of the city being damaged or destroyed wasn't bad enough, the Malaano princess is a huge problem. And Brooke agreed to marry that d'hakka-of-a-prince from Darkwood. He'll arrive soon."

Kira had heard a surprisingly small amount of gossip about the royal wedding. Perhaps people had too much else to worry about at the moment. "So you're concerned for her mental state?"

"Overall health is more like it," Ryon muttered. "I'm shocked that the Emberhawk didn't try to assassinate her during the attack."

"They probably did," Kira mused. "I heard they killed the former vice. But isn't Brooke always surrounded by a bunch of invisible guards—the most skilled warriors in the tribe?"

"Not always." Ryon tapped his foot, and little ripples in a puddle underfoot reflected the candle's light. "Watch your step."

Kira noted the slick spots on the tunnel floor and avoided them. "It's good of you to think of her safety, but you're not her bodyguard."

"Yeah, my job is more important than that. I guard her mind . . . and her heart, if I can."

Kira tugged at Ryon's hand, and he stopped to look back at her. His brow knitted like storm clouds overshadowing the happiness he'd shown with family only minutes before.

"Is that in your job description?" Kira asked, trying to keep any jealousy off her face.

Ryon's expression softened. "No," he admitted, his rigid stance relaxing. "I just . . . she's been more than my boss for a couple of years now. She's one of my closest friends. That's why I think . . ." He clenched his jaw for a long moment. "I think she made a huge mistake making me her advisor."

Kira frowned. "Is that what's been bothering you? You think you're not good enough?"

"I *know* I'm not good enough. Advisors are supposed to be old—you know, wise. They're supposed to have a flicker of a clue what they're doing."

Kira's heart ached for him. "I thought only the elders were supposed to be old. How old was the last advisor?"

"Older than me." Ryon looked down at her hand in his. "I just . . .

There are probably hundreds of people in the tribe who'd have been a better choice than me. She just picked me because I'm her friend. And she was wrong."

Kira took a step toward him and placed a hesitant hand on his jaw. His short stubble was scratchy, but she loved the way it felt regardless. "Maybe she wanted someone who knows the land and its people better than anyone else. A scout who knows the hearts of the tribes because he's travelled to each of them. A spy who knows the enemy more intimately than any city dweller."

Ryon's eyes widened a bit, then hardened. "She doesn't need someone who 'knows hearts.' We're on the brink of war—she needs someone with strength and experience."

"Doesn't she want peace?" Kira asked. "She has an entire city full of enraged people. Maybe she needs someone to remind her that her enemies are human. And as an Emberhawk yourself, you are a constant reminder to the Katrosi people that not all Emberhawk are violent. An Emberhawk *royal,* at that. You represent a hope for peace that otherwise seems impossible right now."

Ryon stood still for a long moment. He said nothing.

"Doesn't the creator say to love your enemies?" Kira whispered.

"Yes, but . . . it's complicated. There is forgiveness, but there is justice, too."

"You are the perfect person to find the balance." Kira pushed up on her tip-toes and kissed his cheek. "I believe in you."

Ryon turned his head and found her lips with his. He kissed her gently, then deeper as he pulled her close. Kira's skin alighted, pulsing a yearning energy through her veins.

He pulled away far too quickly, still holding her tight as he grinned down at her. "Thanks, *balemba.* What would I do without you?"

She didn't want to catch her breath. "You'd have died from infection."

Ryon smirked. "Or I wouldn't have been shot in the first place."

"Would you shut up and kiss me?"

He chuckled and released her, leading her with a gentle touch. "This way."

Kira grumbled after him through a winding maze of caverns bored by massive roots. An intersection of an ancient taproot and branching rhizome had been washed clean by an underground river, creating a spacious room. Mushrooms clung to the cave walls, glowing with faint teal, aqua, and green light. The water reflected the glow and harmonized with its own luminescence from the small fish darting beneath the surface.

Kira's breath faltered as Ryon's candle snuffed out with a whisper of elemental frost. He watched her awed reaction with a hopeful expression. In the absence of the firelight, the mushrooms seemed to glow brighter.

"Worth the trip?" he asked.

Kira couldn't find the words to do it justice, and she didn't want to mispronounce the word for "wonderful" again. "It's . . . breathtaking."

Ryon strode to a pile of furs beside the water, where the ethereal light coalesced brightest. "It's a secret. You'd better not tell anyone." He stretched out on the hides and sighed in satisfaction.

Kira couldn't tear her gaze from the swath of intermingling colors strewn across the ceiling like a painting. "You found this place?"

"You just reminded me that I'm a scout, yeah?" He winked. "This is kind of a safe spot in case something goes bad upstairs. You know, like the whole city being on fire. I make sure everyone at home knows their way down here in case of an emergency." He scratched the faint stubble along his jaw. "Come to think of it, Tekkyn might know about this place if they evacuated during the attack."

"It's incredible," Kira said. "It makes me wonder how many more gorgeous places the creator buried beneath the earth that no one has ever found."

Ryon shrugged. "Good question." He patted a spot on the furs beside him.

She snuggled up next to him and relished the joy that blossomed in her chest. "How am I so lucky?"

Ryon wriggled his arm under her neck and stared up at the luminous ceiling. "Felix is the deity of luck, you know."

Kira cringed. "I think he hates me."

"He makes everyone think that," Ryon said with a laugh. "If he talks to you at all, he likes you."

Kira took a deep breath. The humid air had an interesting musty scent, almost like a greenhouse on a cool day. "Do you really think Felix has some kind of luck magic?"

"No," Ryon said. "Every elemental has some sort of domain in the elemental religion, but it doesn't mean anything. I just say that to tease him because he hates everything about the idea of humans worshiping elementals."

"Why? Just because he's not really a god?"

"Because it's disrespectful to the creator. One of Aeo's laws is to not worship anything except for him. He created everything, including the elementals, so worshipping something that Aeo made—something mortal—doesn't make sense, yeah?" Ryon said. "Felix is smart enough not to disobey the creator."

Kira studied a vein of speckled stone in the cavern wall as she considered his words. "I don't understand how the creator can be loving when his own followers are afraid of him like that. And aren't some of his laws kind of strict?"

Ryon's shoulder moved beneath her head, and she shifted to rest against his chest, not caring about the rough feel of his tunic on her cheek.

"He's like a father," Ryon said in a low tone. "He loves you more than anything and would die to save you. But he has rules to protect you and will punish you if you break them so you don't grow up to be a brat."

"Too late for that," Kira muttered. "I never realized how spoiled I was until I left the ranch. Yes, we had our troubles, but so many people have it so much worse." She folded a smooth deerskin over her belly and stroked the fur. "If the creator is good, and he is all-powerful, why does he let bad things happen to good people?"

Ryon grumbled something akin to a growl. "Does everything always have to be a deep philosophical discussion with you? Will I ever be able to just take you on a date and relax?" He tickled her, and she squirmed away, but he pulled her back with a firm grip. "Theologians have been trying to answer that one forever. The histories say that in the beginning everything was flawless, but human wrongdoing fractured the perfection. We lost our immortality and brought a curse upon Alani. The curse is where things like death and disease and agony come from."

Kira vacillated between listening and defending herself against another tickle strike. But Ryon's hand on her side was light and still as he continued.

"I think it's because the creator wanted to give us free will," he said. "That means we have the choice to do genuine good, but unfortunately we also have the freedom to hurt others. But there will be true justice in the afterlife. And Aeo does intervene to give peace and help to anyone who asks him."

"Hmm," Kira mused. That would be a thought to chew on later. Ryon was right that she needed to enjoy this moment. This place was uniquely beautiful beyond anything she'd ever seen.

But she couldn't relax until she told him about Lillian.

"I have to tell you something," she confessed.

Ryon toyed with her hair, tickling with a feather light touch. "Yeah?"

Kira tried to prepare herself for how strange this would sound. "Lillian has been speaking to me."

His hand hesitated. "What? You mean you . . . want to worship her again?"

"No, I mean she has literally been speaking to me. Audibly. Well, not through my ears, exactly . . ."

Ryon turned on his side and shifted until he could see her face. Concern etched his features.

Great, now I've ruined the moment, Kira thought. "Well, it's only happened a couple of times when I was in Vylia's room. The voice said it was Lillian speaking through the Malo stone. She called it her mirror."

Ryon's fiery eyes widened. "Is this a joke? The Malo stone is here, in Jadenvive?"

Kira nodded. "I wish it were a joke. The stone is in Vylia's belongings. It looks like a big water opal."

"I noticed the opal, but I had no idea it was the Malo stone," Ryon said. "But it's not supposed to do any talking, regardless. Lillian is supposed to be asleep."

"I have no idea. But she wants me to steal that big quartz gem from Brooke's headdress."

Ryon balked. "She wants the keystone?"

Kira nodded. "She said she could use its power to help the empire. Which she thinks she rules."

Ryon's mouth hung open for an awkward moment. "You . . . We have to tell Felix. According to legend, the keystone is the artifact that the creator used to seal the *amos* elementals away. The chiefs have passed it down in their headdresses to protect it through the generations. If Lillian got her hands on it . . ." His thumb rubbed his other fingers nervously. "Just the fact that the keystone and the Malo stone are in the same city is beyond dangerous. If Lillian were released somehow . . . Aeo help us all."

The look on Ryon's face scared Kira more than his words. "What should I do?"

"Tell Felix and hope he knows what to do. If the Malo stone is one of the princess's belongings, we can't just take it, but since she's unconscious and might not ever wake up . . ." Ryon's musing trailed off. "I'll try to summon Felix as soon as our date is over."

"I'll come along and watch you do the cuckoo dance." Kira grinned sweetly.

Ryon narrowed his eyes at her. "I would have paid a thousand rupero to see you do it."

"Ha! You'd have to pay a thousand more for a chance at me ever doing that again."

Ryon leaned on his elbow and grew that lopsided grin. "What are my odds?"

Kira looked away before his charm could fully entrap her. "Ill advised."

He huffed a challenging laugh. "Well, I've got something else to show you, if we can forget that the world is falling apart for a second."

Kira raised an eyebrow, intrigued. "Do your best at helping me forget that I was chatting it up with a dead goddess who apparently wants to use me to get out of prison and rule the world."

"Eh, she's powerless inside that stone. She's not going anywhere unless someone manages to steal Brooke's headdress, then get past the guards to Vylia's room, then figure out how to let her out. Even then, I'm not sure it's possible since there's a prophecy about the *amos* awakening at the end of time. Regardless, we'll make sure she never gets out."

Kira nodded and tried not to think about the fact that he'd apparently been wrong about Lillian being asleep. What else could he be wrong about?

She forced a smile. "What do you have to show me, then? It had better not be something you stole."

Ryon chuffed in a display of innocence. "I don't need to steal any more, beautiful. I'll be swimming in rupero within a few months." He rolled onto his back, closed his eyes, and held his hands out toward the ceiling.

Kira watched in silence for a long moment. Then another. And another.

"Am I supposed to be seeing something?" she whispered.

"Give me a minute," Ryon said, moving his fingers ever so slightly.

A ray of light appeared above them, faint and blurred. It swayed, seeming to absorb the glow of the mushrooms until it stretched into a long, colorful swath. Green and blue and indigo light waved slowly like a banner on the breeze.

Kira stared, mesmerized. "How are you doing this?" she whispered, afraid of breaking his concentration.

Ryon inhaled sharply and the lights vanished. Sweat glistened on his forehead as he turned to look at her. "What'd you think?"

"That was . . . beyond words," Kira said. "What on Alani was that?"

"It's called sky paint. When the tribes left Illyria . . . to settle this land hundreds of years ago, some went much further north . . . even above Valinor." Ryon paused for a moment to recover his breath. "Then a few decades ago, one of their ships found us. There was a great celebration, and they told us that in their new lands, the whole sky can be painted with floating lights." He wiped his forehead. "Not the easiest or the most useful way to use Phoera, but it's pretty neat, huh?"

"'Neat' doesn't even begin to cover it," Kira said. "Thank you. This has been so amazing, and I'm sorry I kind of ruined it."

"I wouldn't say it was ruined, but . . ." Ryon smirked. "Guess we'll just have to try again."

11

LYSANDER

Lysander loathed fear. It made his joints rigid, his stomach sour, his focus blurred.

Why should he fear death? Every man died. Every animal and plant. Every living creature—even elementals. Such was the curse on this world.

He wished he would have died when Zamara ripped the Phoera from his blood, tearing through him like a storm of blades. Why had Felix saved him, knowing he'd die anyway by Katrosi hands? So he could suffer for a few more days as punishment for breaking his oath?

Better if death would have taken him on the battlefield, sudden and swift.

Lysander stared at the shackles around his wrists. After Zamara died, Felix had given him enough of her syn to melt the metal chains like water. But what was the point of being free if he had nothing? No home, no job, no friends, no family. No palace. No hearing. Nothing but his guilt and a smoldering pile of regret.

No point in trying to escape.

Curse Brooke for tempting him with hope. It made everything so much worse.

The door beyond his cell opened. Lysander squinted against the light, and the shuffling of his two fellow prisoners meant they'd noticed as well. His fellow murderers awaiting their date with the executioner.

Ryon entered and lit the wall sconce with a wave of his hand. He avoided stares from the prisoners and came to stand before Lysander's cell door.

Lysander watched his cousin warily as he stood in silence. Ryon's skin seemed a healthy color, and yet his eyes drooped as if from exhaustion. And he still wouldn't meet Lysander's gaze.

At least his presence was a decent distraction.

Ryon's hands finally moved, forming gestures for common terms and symbols for spelling. *"Brooke will be here in a few minutes."*

Lysander tried not to groan. Brooke was the last person he wanted to see right now. The way he'd begged her during their last encounter was the crowning glory on his pile of regrets.

"You'll have to take care of Granny Zelle," Lysander said. "If Cori took her in, the rebellion would only put her in danger."

Ryon's face contorted into a grimace. *"Think she'd be willing to move to Jadenvive?"*

"From King Corynath's pyramid to the root tunnels? Yeah, I don't think so."

Ryon rubbed the back of his neck, then signed, *"I tried everything. But even Brooke doesn't have any authority with—"*

"I know." Lysander leaned back on his metal bench, his chains skittering with the movement. "It's fine."

"It's not fine!" Ryon's gestures quickened and strengthened. *"I never dreamed I would be in a position of power, but it doesn't seem to matter a bleeding—"*

"Justice is blind," Lysander interrupted. "Be glad that the Katrosi system isn't corrupt enough for you to manipulate it."

Ryon finally looked at him, his face reddening. *"The elder was supposed to see your memories. He was supposed to see that you're innocent."*

"But I'm not truly innocent. I could have refused Zamara and died instead. It is what it is." Lysander took a deep breath, wishing he could accept the reality himself. "Thanks anyway, brother. You can sell my dried herbs and oils and poisons. They're labeled well, and the rare ones will fetch good prices. And Zamara paid me with a mithril bar once—it's hidden under a floorboard in my room . . ."

He trailed off at Ryon's flustered gesturing, then decided to ignore him. "And please make sure my gryphon gets back home."

Ryon's protests stopped. *"Where is Sorrel?"*

"She's probably still in the forest nearby, waiting for me. She'll be madder than a trace cat that I haven't returned."

Ryon frowned. *"How do I find her? If she doesn't remember me from when she was a chick, she'll eat me."*

"She knows you." Lysander's heart ached for his bird. If only he could snuggle into her golden feathers and soft white fur one last time. The gryphon would probably miss him more than any human would.

Ryon nodded slowly and signed, *"I'll find her."* He looked back up with stress lines between his brows. *"Did you get right with the creator? Have you asked for forgiveness?"*

Lysander snorted and leaned forward, resting his elbows on his knees. "I've asked for forgiveness from any deity that I could think of, but I doubt it'll matter."

The far door moved again, and Lysander squinted against the sunlight. The silhouette of a young woman entered, and the door remained open for long enough that at least one invisible guard could have entered. Lysander barely recognized Brooke without her war paint and headdress. Her simple tunic, leathers, and cloak included a hood, which she drew back to watch him with a wary gaze.

Ryon bowed and backed away to give Brooke his place in front of the cell door, but she motioned for him to stay. Her umber eyes met Lysander's without hesitation. Her lips moved with words he couldn't hear.

Ryon signed, *"The verdict was not what I'd hoped. I've come to tell you goodbye."*

Lysander wished Brooke would have thought-spoken to him, then reconsidered. The fact that she hadn't connected with him mentally spoke clearly enough.

He harrumphed. "You speak more bluntly than any woman I've ever met."

Brooke's stone-cold visage warmed a bit. *"Unfortunately I don't have the time or patience for formalities,"* Ryon signed for her.

The door opened again behind her, and a petite handmaiden offered a cup of steaming tea on a china saucer. It carried the smooth, sweet scent of yaupon. Brooke took it with a thankful nod and drank deeply. *"I truly am sorry. I did everything I could for you."*

Lysander felt his neck warm. He couldn't fathom why Brooke would have lifted a finger in an attempt to save him from her people's wrath. If their arranged marriage would have gone through, he'd probably have cheated on her a dozen times or more. Not because she wasn't attractive in her own right—it was just the selfish way he'd lived without consequence as the crown prince. And she must have known it. Everyone did.

His heart lurched at the thought, and he struggled for a response. Maybe he could be honest, just this once. What did he have to lose? But even in this circumstance, his pride would scarcely allow it.

He glanced at Ryon, who studied him with narrowed eyes. Perhaps his cousin understood somehow. Ryon nodded slowly, as if to encourage him to let it out.

Lysander looked down at his well-worn boots, whose fraying leather was in dire need of care. "I'm sorry for everything." He took and released a deep breath. "It's good that nothing happened between us. I would have had even more to regret right now."

He couldn't see her reaction, but the air thickened with tension. He forced himself to look up.

Brooke's tea cup froze in her hand. She said something to the side he couldn't discern, and the bars of his cell door swung open. He stiffened as a bull of a man shimmered into existence and freed him of his chains.

Energy surged through Lysander's veins as freedom tempted him, but he remained sitting on the bench until the man vanished, the cell door closed, and the lock dropped back into place. His chance of getting past that huge man, Brooke's most skilled guard—Dimbae, if memory served—was less than zero.

A disturbance in the sound waves indicated that the prisoner in the cell to his right protested, but Brooke appeared to silence him with a glare.

"Thank you," Lysander said, unsure if he was interrupting or not. He slowly rubbed his wrists, hoping that an invisible assassin hadn't slipped into his cell to gut him as soon as she left. "Though I don't understand why."

Ryon began signing again. *"She says it's the last mercy she can give. For what your fathers envisioned for the two of you, and for the peace that might have been."*

Lysander looked back up at her, stunned. Ryon had probably translated that wrong. And yet Brooke's eyes were like dark pools, concealing restrained emotion within their depths.

Surely she didn't actually wish that they'd been married? After he'd fallen into sins no one could forgive and she'd risen to the most powerful position among all the tribes?

It made absolutely no sense. She couldn't possibly be a little girl craving love under all of that prowess and acuity.

Lysander swallowed to moisten his dry throat, but it didn't help. "I would have been the worst possible husband, and our marriage would not have prevented the Sacrificial War."

He ignored Ryon and read Brooke's response from her lips. "I would have done my best to love you anyway," she said.

Brooke downed the rest of her tea, shoved the cup and saucer at her handmaiden, and turned on her heel.

Wait!

Lysander thrust the thought at her with all the will he could muster—with all the desperation and sorrow that threatened to drown him.

She paused. Glanced back at him over her shoulder. Blinked in surprise. Had she heard him?

You have natural talent for aether. Brooke's voice rang like a song through his mind. Her eyelids drooped. *Such a waste.*

Lysander struggled for composure. *Set me free in secret. I can become one of your guards—invisible. I can help you establish peace with the Emberhawk. No one would—*

I will not defy the will . . . of my people. Her voice was firm, yet accompanied by a maelstrom of emotion. *You will . . . meet the . . . creator. I'm . . . sorry.*

Confusion and fear branched out from her thoughts like twigs from a dying tree. But they weren't directed at him. Weariness overwhelmed her, bleeding out from her presence and infecting him with exhaustion.

Abruptly, the mental connection was severed, leaving Lysander alone and empty within his own mind once again.

Brooke swayed and Ryon caught her. She put a hand to her head as she slid to the floor.

Lysander rushed to the bars, ignoring the protest in his muscles. "What's wrong?"

Dimbae reappeared and cradled Brooke. He and Ryon spoke so quickly that Lysander couldn't read their lips.

"What's happened?" Lysander yelled.

"She's exhausted," Ryon signed as Dimbae held a hand to her forehead over peacefully closed eyes. *"Just needs sleep."*

"No, something's wrong. She didn't just pass out; I felt her fear." Lysander reached his hand through the bars. "Give me that cup."

Ryon looked doubtful. *"We've been trying to get her to rest—"*

"Give me the cup!"

The handmaiden's eyes were as wide as the shaking saucer in her hand. At Ryon's nod, she carefully held the cup out.

Lysander snatched it and dunked his finger into the last remaining drops. Tiny fragments of crushed leaves clung to his skin. He smelled it, tasted. Closed his eyes.

Beneath the strong flavor of yaupon, between the layers of citrus and ginger and faint sweetness, lay a mild taste undetectable by most: dreamthistle.

Perennial herb. Purple leaves. White buds. Roots infused with concentrated poison. His favorite for silent assassinations.

"She's been poisoned." Lysander glared at the horrified handmaiden and shoved the cup back at her. "The antidote is on my belt. Give it to me, and I'll save her."

Ryon looked from him to Brooke and back again, then at Lysander's equipment hanging from hooks in the wall below the sconce.

Dimbae lifted Brooke's limp form as if she were a child. He said something to Ryon, then turned to leave.

"Did you hear me?" Lysander yelled. "It's dreamthistle. She's going to die unless you let me treat her *now!*"

Dimbae opened the far door with one hand as he cradled Brooke to his chest, unhindered by the warning—as if he couldn't hear it.

Lysander closed his eyes and reached out to the Phoera element. Sound vibrations echoed all around him. He honed in on noises from Brooke's direction. The soft rasp of her breathing was too faint. The fluttering beats of her heart too far apart.

"Check her pulse!"

Dimbae paused. Ryon slid beside him and placed two fingers on Brooke's neck. His face drained of color.

Lysander hoped his voice sounded as deep and authoritative as his father had taught him for addressing a large crowd. "Set her down and open this door."

Ryon said something to Dimbae, and the response included something about another healer.

"There's no time!" Lysander gripped the bars and tried to rip them open to no avail. "She's already asleep which means we have only seconds. Open the bleeding door, and you can kill me after I save her!"

Ryon's signing was sloppy as Dimbae yelled something at the handmaiden. *"Tell me which vial—"*

"Open the door!" Lysander roared.

Ryon grabbed a key from the wall and rushed to the cell door. Dimbae moved to prevent him, but couldn't stop him while holding Brooke.

The lock clanged open.

Lysander burst through the door and ran right into an invisible blade.

Pain seared across his neck as a second guard flickered into vision, this one wearing the azure mask of Brooke's elite. He held the handmaiden by one hand and a sword at Lysander's throat with the other.

Icy terror shot down Lysander's spine. How deep was the cut in his neck?

He raised one hand above his head in a show of innocence and stretched the other out to the leather sash hanging from the wall. Glass vials clanked as he skimmed over them. Blissroot, aloe, fadeleaf, muddlewort . . . He pulled an oiled herb mix free with his mouth and slowly backed toward Brooke. The blade followed him.

Lysander eyed the azure-masked guard and uncorked the glass bottle with his teeth. "Tilt her head back."

Ryon gently opened Brooke's mouth, and Lysander poured the oil onto her tongue.

She didn't respond.

Warm blood trickled down Lysander's neck. *Creator, if you're there, and you're her god, then let me save her!*

Brooke's eyes fluttered open, unfocused. Her brow furrowed. She coughed and moaned.

Tangible relief engulfed the room. "Lay her down," Lysander said as he looked at the handmaiden. "Water. Quickly."

The second guard might have said something behind his mask, but Lysander couldn't see his lips to read them. He kept his grip on the girl's arm and his blade to Lysander's throat.

"Quickly," Lysander repeated as he fumbled for a pouch at the end of his leather sash. He doubted the horror-stricken handmaiden was the assassin. But even if she were, she couldn't escape the city any more than he could.

A moment passed, and the azure mask released the handmaiden. She ran.

Dimbae and Ryon gently laid Brooke on the floor as Lysander tore into the pouch and found a bulbous rhizome. "I need a thin slice of this." He held out the paper-skinned root to the azure mask, who moved only to press his cold steel deeper into Lysander's skin.

Ryon grabbed the rhizome and cut it with his dagger, producing a thin slice of orange flesh. Lysander grabbed it and slowly leaned over Brooke, wincing as the blade's edge drew more blood. Ryon yelled something, and the azure mask's sword hesitantly retreated.

"Brooke." Lysander held a finger over her pale face, but her eyes didn't focus on it. "Can you hear me?" He gently opened her mouth and slipped the rhizome slice under her tongue.

He dared to touch her neck, searching for her pulse. As he waited, it grew stronger. Faster.

Brooke's eyes closed tightly. She coughed and swallowed, her jaw fumbling with the rhizome under her tongue. Her eyes opened again, cleared of their former haze. She squinted at the faces hovering over her.

"We've got you," Lysander murmured, his battered muscles relaxing. "It's safe to rest now. You're okay."

A tentative presence reached out to his mind, bewildered and weak. *Did you . . . do this?*

No. A dart of pain pricked him—did she really think he'd try to murder her? Hopefully she could determine the truth in his claim. *But I think I know who did. We'll get him.*

Brooke's aether slipped from his thoughts as she fell back into unconsciousness. Dimbae cradled her as the handmaiden returned too late with water.

Lysander's relief smelted into something darker as he struggled to remember the phrasing of Xavier's note.

> *Flames dine on the city in the sky*
> *Twin slaves the only to survive*
> *The chieftess sleeps, the slaves meet*
> *And return with freedom and pride*

Anger flared inside him, incinerating every competing emotion. He'd interpreted it wrong. The chieftess sleeping hadn't meant they should meet after dark. It had meant dreamthistle and death.

Lysander cursed Xavier and his stupid riddles aloud.

Ryon glanced up at him. *"You know something."*

Bile rose in Lysander's throat, and he swallowed with disgust. Why would Xavier do such a thing after the attack was over? They weren't bound by Zamara's will any longer.

He must want true freedom. Killing the chieftess would mean Zamara's assault hadn't been a failure. Returning with victory to the Emberhawk monarch—whoever that might be—would be equivalent to returning from battle with their enemy's head on a platter.

But in exchange for Brooke's blood . . . it wasn't right. She wasn't some bloodthirsty enemy warlord—she was the Alliance leader who'd strived for peace at every opportunity. The Emberhawk had razed her city, and she still hadn't marched on Quin'Zamar, for the love of the sky.

"Xavier." Lysander muttered. "I know where he's hiding."

12

LYSANDER

Lysander adjusted the makeshift bandage on his neck. The cut hadn't stopped bleeding yet, but he wouldn't pause and risk letting Xavier escape. Neither would Ryon or the half dozen azure masks all invisible on the crowded street behind him.

He didn't want harm to befall his comrade, but what Xavier had done to Brooke felt somehow . . . personal. Conflict tore at his soul. But if helping the Katrosi capture Brooke's attempted killer would be one of the last things he'd ever do, it felt like a good choice. Why should his loyalty remain with the Emberhawk after his people's rejection and Zamara's abuse? At the very least, this last taste of freedom was better than spending his final hours in a cell.

Lysander took a steadying breath and opened the door to the Jolly Satyr.

Scents of pork, freshly baked bread, and spilled alcohol buffeted him. The wide room seemed as lively a tavern as any, with a collection of cheerful patrons, a polished bar, and a healthy fire in the hearth. Sound vibrations from dozens of different sources made Lysander wince and weaken his connection to the Phoera element.

At least the noise made the private booth in the corner the perfect inconspicuous meeting place. It was the go-to spot for Emberhawk assassins and spies who infiltrated Jadenvive, but it was empty at present.

Lysander slid onto the leather-clad bench and felt underneath the table's furthest side, near the metal support in the center. His fingers met a slip of folded parchment, held in place with sticky tar. He pulled it free.

It appeared to be blank. Lysander summoned warmth to his hand and held the paper over his palm. Faint ink bloomed across the parchment.

Have a way out. Waiting until you find me or they end you.
Vanya platform, storage barn beside tanner's workshop.
Hurry up. I'm craving pitas.

Lysander snapped, lighting the candle in the center of the table. He propped the note up beside it, wagering that the Katrosi were familiar with the invisible ink. No doubt the azure masks would retrieve the note and follow him.

He left the Jolly Satyr casually enough to prove he wasn't trying to escape. He couldn't see them, but he could feel their eyes on him like owls in the dark.

The rope bridges and streets on the way to the great tree, Vanya, were crowded and busy enough that no one seemed to notice Lysander under his hood. Or maybe one of the masks was extending invisibility to Lysander, since the risk of someone recognizing a man on death row entailed consequences they weren't willing to risk.

Lysander glanced down at himself and did a double-take. Yeah, someone was definitely making him invisible. He made a note to avoid bumping into anyone in the crowd who had no idea he was there. Or did he look like a floating pair of eyes to any onlooker? Well, maybe that wasn't such a rare sight in Jadenvive considering Brooke's invisible soldiers.

Had he been invisible in the Satyr too? The azure masks should tell him these things. Or maybe it was Ryon, who was so skilled at light-bending it was practically an art.

Lysander reached out to his element to silence his footsteps. He wove through the masses until Vanya towered before him with platforms and bridges and buildings clinging to her ancient white bark. The oldest part of the city: the trade district.

The tanner was on the south side of the main platform, if memory served. A constant thrumming buzzed over the rest of the sound energy as he approached—perhaps the neighboring blacksmith's hammer?

Lysander struggled to calm himself as he spotted a storage barn behind the storefronts. He released Phoera and fell into deafening quiet. If Xavier were here, he wouldn't make any noise anyway. And that rhythmic banging was rattling his bones.

He moved to the door and paused. It was unlocked.

For Brooke, he told himself. Obviously she didn't care for him, but she represented the most precious thing he could fathom: a second chance. Hope. Even if she couldn't prevent his execution, she'd told him of another way to communicate and connect with people. A magic he would have given anything to learn.

And she reminded him of a better time . . . before he'd lost his family. Before the war. When all he'd had to worry about was palace politics and not publicly shaming his father, the king. If only he hadn't squandered it all.

Lysander's feet felt glued to the frost-chilled platform. Regardless of how jumbled his feelings toward Brooke were, she was as close to his enemy as one could get. How could he betray his own tribesman for the sake of a Katrosi? Xavier was his fellow survivor of Zamara's cruelty and the one who'd had his back for years. The friend who'd managed to slip him a lockpick under the tightest security in Jadenvive. The comrade who'd risked his life by staying and waiting for him before escaping to safety.

Lysander swallowed hard. No backing out now. He could practically feel a dozen eyes of the most elite warriors in the city drilling into his back.

He glanced down at his hand. The invisibility was gone.

He slid the barn door open.

Scents of cedar wood and leather oil welcomed Lysander into the dark, dusty space. He stepped inside and recognized xavi saddles hanging from a loft as his eyes adjusted. Skins stretched like canvases across the wall on his right beside a tool-strewn workbench. Crates and barrels had been stacked in the area on his left.

Lysander pulled his hood down and hesitantly reached out to the flows of sound energy once again. He saw no one, but this must be the place Xavier had meant.

The fact that he'd left the door open behind him would be Xavier's first warning that something was wrong.

A flicker from the loft caught Lysander's eye. A young man's face smirked at him from the rafters.

"Took you long enough," Xavier signed.

Lysander's heart slammed against his ribs. He crossed his middle fingers—their wordless sign for danger. If the Katrosi knew it, he'd feel a blade through his back any second.

"Did you poison Brooke?" Lysander asked.

Faint light gleamed from the ajar back door, accenting Xavier's silver pony-tail as he tilted his head. He didn't respond.

Lysander glanced at the loft's ladder. A large crate blocked the top.

"She just wants peace. We can have it now that Zamara's dead," Lysander said.

Xavier frowned at him for a long moment, then signed, *"Why are you using present tense?"*

Sweat trickled down into the bandage on Lysander's neck. It cooled as something passed by him—either the breeze or a whisper of death.

"I saved her," Lysander said as he clenched his fists, erasing the subtle sign in his fingers. He'd given Xavier enough clues—his life was in his own hands now.

Xavier hopped up on the railing, revealing long stretches of fabric between his arms and sides. A Katrosi glide suit.

Lysander recognized the word "traitor" on Xavier's lips. Then the assassin jumped and flew out the back door.

Masks appeared all around the barn. One jumping to slash a sword at Xavier and missing as he passed. One halfway up the ladder. One with a bow whose arrow slammed into the barn door's edge.

Lysander bolted out the back door and watched as Xavier—with his arms and legs outstretched and glide suit billowing between each limb—slowly floated downward beyond the lower platforms and drifted toward the forest beyond the colorful fields below.

Bursts of sound energy exploded behind Lysander, followed by thumping vibrations of sprinting footsteps. Ryon appeared beside Lysander, leaning over the railing and squinting after the disappearing figure. The archer nocked a second arrow but didn't fire, probably not wanting to risk the lives of civilians below if he missed.

Pain sliced into Lysander's shoulder blade. He grimaced and raised his hands.

Now he would pay for Xavier's escape. But at least his friend and the chieftess were both alive. For now.

The pain subsided as Ryon stepped between Lysander and whoever had attacked him. Lysander slowly turned away from the railing to face whoever had cut him, his hands still raised.

A slender man had pulled his mask back to yell at Ryon. Lysander caught the meaning of some of his words, which were more difficult to lip-read through his anger. " . . . signaled him somehow! . . . your *cousin,* Emberhawk." He accentuated the word "cousin" with a slow dip of his head, like a predator who'd identified its prey.

Lysander couldn't see Ryon's face from his position, but his response was just as animated.

Whatever Ryon said stunned the man. He paused for a half-second before his snarl returned. "You do not command us, boy," Lysander read from the man's lips.

Ryon stood up straighter and began signing, though it was still difficult for Lysander to interpret from behind. *"You don't respect me—I understand that. But you will respect the title I hold if you claim to be a man of honor. The advisor may not command you, but the law does, and I speak the truth."*

Another azure soldier put a hand on the man's arm and leaned in. Lysander couldn't see his lips beneath his mask . . . the mask with the same design as the one from the prison. The one who'd sliced his neck.

The angry one's eyes widened. He looked up at Lysander. Tipped his head slightly and turned away.

Surely Lysander hadn't seen that right. He ducked as three orange masks leaped off the railing beside him and spread the wings of their glide suits. The remaining soldiers vanished in various ways, and the small area behind the barn was suddenly empty save for confused bystanders.

"What just happened?" Lysander whispered.

Ryon gripped the railing and stared after Xavier and the pursuing Katrosi as they slowly drifted into the distance. A weary smile spread across his face. *"Thank you."* He gave a sidelong glance full of gratitude, yet lined with suspicion. *"You're free."*

Lysander had no idea what he meant by that. "I didn't signal him. I led you to him as promised."

Ryon's brows dipped in doubt. *"I'm sure you tipped him off somehow, but I meant thank you for saving Brooke."* His hand clapped Lysander's shoulder, and the pain reminded him that it needed medical attention. *"And thank the creator for that timing. I couldn't bear to lose you, even if you are a lying, depressive idiot."*

Lysander just stared at him. "What are you talking about?"

"I've invoked asha'ai, *a Katrosi tradition. You saved the chief—your greatest wish will be granted."* Ryon's grin spread. *"I'm guessing you'd like to not die, yeah?"*

13

BROOKE

Brooke was dead. She must be.

Her eyelids felt heavy and her body detached as she drifted from dark dreams. This new scene was blurry, too, but familiar. Tall cedar pillars, carved with heroic scenes from the past, held an arched ceiling aloft. Ancient plaques and weapons wielded by chiefs past adorned the walls. And beyond the wide bed she lay in, she could see the roaring maw of the bearskin rug she'd pretended to ride as a child, when her grandfather had been chief and these quarters were his.

Brooke groaned and shifted under the violet d'hakka-silk quilt. Too hot. So hot.

Someone moved from a couch by a bookshelf in the corner. Nariellyn's face became clear as she drew nearer.

"I'm here." Nariellyn placed a hand on Brooke's forehead and frowned. "You're okay. How do you feel?"

Brooke doubted she was real. In one of her nightmares, Nariellyn had been Zamara in disguise.

She closed her eyes and felt some relief from the pounding of her pulse through her head. "Am I alive?"

"Mostly." Water trickled as Nariellyn wrung a white cloth out into a bucket on the nightstand. "You've been dead on the inside for a long time now."

Brooke couldn't stop a smile. That was the real Nari all right.

"Shut up. Smiling hurts."

Nariellyn smirked and placed the cool cloth on Brooke's forehead. "What hurts the most?"

Brooke furrowed her brow as she took account of every part of her body. Everything felt stiff, sweaty, and sore. "My head."

"That's a good sign, according to Lysander."

Brooke growled as a dozen different emotions flared inside her tattered heart. "What happened?"

"Well, the azure masks aren't sure yet, but here's what I know so far." Nariellyn stood and spoke as she strode to the door. "Shaya prepared your seven hundredth cup of tea and somewhere between the kitchen and the prison, an Emberhawk named Xavier poisoned it with dreamthistle. He must have been hiding in the city since Zamara's attack." She opened the door and whispered something to a guard outside, then closed it again and continued. "They say if you fall asleep from dreamthistle you never wake back up. But Lysander had the antidote in his equipment, and Idryon let him out to give it to you." She flopped back on the bed beside Brooke, her wild bun bouncing with the movement. "So I guess you're alive or whatever."

Brooke struggled to keep up through the migraine. "Did they find the assassin?"

Nariellyn poured ice water from a weeping pitcher and handed the glass to Brooke. "Yeah, Lysander led the azures to a barn where Xavier was hiding in the trade district. But as they closed in, he flew off with a glide suit. The orange masks pursued him into the woods, but they lost him." She wiped the nightstand of shed water droplets and set the pitcher back in its place. "The council set Lysander free under *asha'ai.*"

Brooke nearly spewed the water halfway across the room. "What?"

"Well, he saved your life," Nariellyn said. "Good thing he was there or we'd be organizing another election right about now."

Brooke's headache somehow hurt even worse. She stared into the element-chilled water and tried to make sense of it. Her memory bled together with the surreal dreams.

"So Lysander is just . . . running free around the city? Did they adopt him into the tribe? They'll kill him in the streets!"

"No, he's basically hiding in Idryon's room here in the Hall." Nariellyn pulled her legs up and crossed them on the bed. "The elders want to talk to you before making the public announcement tonight, so it's a good thing you finally woke up."

Brooke groaned and rubbed her eyes. "I wish I would have died."

"Hey, only I can joke like that." Nariellyn put a hand on the soft silk over Brooke's knee. "They'll give you time to rest and recover, of course. Or, at least . . . a day." She offered a terribly awkward smile. "Or is Lysander that bad?"

"He complicates everything." Brooke drank deeply and relished the cooling effect. "I wish he never existed."

Nariellyn snorted. "How can you say that about a man so *fine?*"

"You can have him." Brooke set her empty glass down on the nightstand with a loud clack.

Nariellyn's cheeks drooped in an exaggerated frown. "I don't think you mean that."

"Can we talk about anything except Lysander, please?" Brooke flipped her goose-feather pillow over and laid back down with a sigh. "What in the skies am I going to do?"

The spacious room was quiet for a still moment, save the chattering of a bird beyond the reinforced window above the headboard. Finally, Nariellyn spoke. "Something else happened while you were asleep."

Brooke refused to open her eyes again—her migraine seemed to prefer the dark. "What? The Malaano invaded, and we're all slaves of the glorious empire?"

She heard Nariellyn chuckle. "At least you wouldn't be in charge any more."

"It's not that I don't want to be in charge. It's that everything is exploding at the same time, and my people hate me for doing what's right," Brooke grumbled. "Grandpa Torvyn and Dad didn't have to deal with nonsense like this."

"No," Nariellyn said slowly. "But High Chief Torvyn had to deal with Navakovrae settling on tribal land, and your dad led us through the Sacrificial War. And let's not forget the famine and the plague and the wyvern attacks."

Brooke sighed. Maybe she was being a tad self-focused. "You're right. I'm sorry." She rested her forearm over her eyes. "What else happened?"

"Why don't you just get some rest? It's not important. The Hall Matron can deal with it for now, and we'll see how you feel tomorrow."

Something felt off. Brooke opened an eye to peer under her arm at Nariellyn as she realized what was wrong: Nari wasn't telling any jokes.

"Tell me now."

Nariellyn sighed and looked away. "The Darkwood prince has arrived."

Brooke's stomach clenched, and her throat closed up. Moisture welled in her eyes, and she squeezed them shut, willing the tears not to fall. She controlled her breathing as the Elder of Aether had taught her. In . . . and out. Control. Peace. Clarity.

Nariellyn whispered an apology, and Brooke lost it.

She wept for her people and their lost security. For the next generation and their lost prosperity. For herself and her lost dream of a marriage filled with love.

Her best friend held her without a word. Listened to her barely comprehensible explanations. Encouraged her to let it out. Scolded her for holding it in for so long.

A knock on the door jolted Brooke from her weeping. She sat up straight, wiped her tears, and donned her mask of steel.

"I don't have to answer it," Nariellyn whispered.

Brooke's head was already throbbing harder—the guaranteed headache after tears was another reason she hated crying. Her body felt like she'd been mauled by a wyvern. She probably looked the part, too.

She sniffed and blinked to clear her eyes. "It's fine."

Nariellyn watched her with a disappointed frown. "Are you sure you're okay?"

"I'm fine. The azures wouldn't let anyone disturb us unless it were important." Brooke straightened the covers around her, then offered her friend a weak smile. "Thank you. I'm all right. Let them in."

She hated lying, but she had a job to do. The Katrosi tribe needed their chief. And she wouldn't let the assassin have his way by taking her out of commission.

Nariellyn moved to the door with slothful reluctance. She opened it and the Elder of Aether shuffled in.

Brooke bowed her head and pushed a fallen braid from her face. "Master."

"How are you, my child?" The old man hobbled closer with concern etching his weathered face. "We feared the worst, but you are looking well."

Brooke doubted that, but the elders never lied. Well, maybe he was half-blind in his old age. "The fairypox were worse."

"Good," he said, "because you must leave Jadenvive tonight."

Shock filled a moment of silence. Brooke waited for him to break into a smile or wink or anything to indicate that he was jesting.

"I mustn't have heard you right," she said.

He leaned in close enough for her to smell his jojoba beard oil. "I beseeched the creator on your behalf, and he spoke to me." His wide, clouded hazel eyes didn't quite focus on her. "You are in danger. If you don't leave at nightfall, you will die."

Brooke cringed. "What will happen?"

"The creator did not say." He reached out for her hand, and she provided it to his wandering grasp. "But he was very clear. I am gravely worried for you, my dear."

Dread settled like a stone in Brooke's gut. "Master, I just survived an attempt on my life—"

"You will not survive the next if you don't listen." The elder waved in Nariellyn's direction just in time for her to push a chair up for him. He gripped the wooden arms and slowly lowered himself onto the seat. "The creator has provided a way to preserve our people. You must take

Lysander with you and remove Illiana from the Emberhawk throne. Her heart is hardened; she will not join the Alliance. We need the support of all five tribes to defend ourselves against the empire should they attack."

Brooke leaned to the side to brace herself on the bed as a wave of heat slammed into her. She took a steadying breath. "Lysander may be the rightful king, but he abdicated."

"No, his younger brother Coriander must be king. He is next in line; he is older than Illiana, and their custom is for only a king to rule beside his queen. And even better, Coriander and his wife already have heirs. The Emberhawk people will accept him as the new monarch." The elder paused to catch his breath. "But Illiana claimed the throne first, so the palace and its guards and nobles are loyal to Illiana. You must bring Lysander as a negotiator to remove her and place Coriander on the throne without violence."

Brooke looked down at her nightgown and pressed the fabric between her fingers as her mind spun. If she could accomplish such a thing, Coriander would be indebted to her and inclined to join the Alliance. She'd been hoping for an optimal solution, but how could *she* possibly make that happen? Couldn't Lysander do it himself? Why did she have to go with him?

"I can't abandon my people. They need me now more than ever."

"The elders will take over your duties as we do in your every absence. You'd leave your doppelgänger, of course, and your advisor, and Ulysses could accept your offer to become your vice at any moment. The people will never know you're gone until you return victorious."

Brooke glanced at Nariellyn, but her friend didn't wear an appalled look. She just shrugged. "I'll go with you."

They couldn't be serious! And yet, it was a rare occurrence when the Elder of Aether claimed to receive word directly from their god. He'd never been wrong.

"There's no way I'd leave in secret," Brooke murmured as she turned possibilities over in her head. "I'll tell the people I'm going to put a monarch I can control on the Emberhawk throne. Perhaps that will sate their thirst for vengeance, especially now that Lysander has been set free . . ."

The elder's white head shook firmly. "You must go in secret. Otherwise you'd need much more security, and our soldiers would be more than willing to follow you. It would result in a bloodbath, and the missing men from our defenses in Jadenvive would leave us vulnerable to attack from the Malaano."

"We are already vulnerable thanks to the fire." Brooke tossed the covers from her legs, not caring about impropriety against the heat searing outward from her core. "If the people found out that I left them in secret before all of our dead are buried, I'd be impeached."

"I will share the memories of my vision with the elder council. Everyone will agree and defend you if need be. I would take the blame in that worst case scenario. I will also share memories with the heads of family houses if I must. Which I will probably have to do for Lysander's *asha'ai* as well." He squeezed her hand. "This is not my will, child. This is the command of the creator."

Discomfort squirmed in Brooke's stomach. "The creator rarely commands things be done in secret."

"He's right, though," Nariellyn said. "The Emberhawk have spies and informants everywhere, just like we do. If you announce it publicly, Illiana will know your every move. She'll double down, and taking the palace will be that much harder. She'll send forces to kill you on the road. And if Lysander leads you to wherever Coriander is hiding, she'll have you followed to kill him and his heirs."

Brooke pursed her lips. There were too many moving parts, too many risks. Why should she sacrifice so much for a tribe that had just attacked hers and nearly murdered her? A people whose bloodthirst had resulted in her father's death. How could she abandon her own to help her enemy while Jadenvive suffered?

"The Darkwood prince just arrived. Am I supposed to subject my double to *that?* And what if he finds out she's not me?"

Nariellyn grimaced. "Yeah, that's bad. But it's her job, and she's very good at it. How much time have you spent around the prince, anyway? He won't know it's not you, and the wedding won't be scheduled very soon in light of recent circumstances." She tapped her fingers on the medical pouch fastened to her belt. "Dealing with him would be one less thing you'd have to worry about right now."

Brooke pulled her hand from the elder's, grasping for any reasoning to throw against this ridiculous idea. "Am I even well enough to travel? I feel like I'm being grilled in a fire salamander's nest."

"I'll go get Lysander," Nariellyn said as she suddenly bolted for the door.

"W-wait!"

"He knows more about the antidote and stuff," Nariellyn called as she slipped out.

Brooke squeezed her eyes shut and sighed. What kind of bundle of nonsense had her life become?

"I'm sorry, Master. This is all just very . . . sudden."

"The burden on you is great. This is why the creator has sent you help."

She smiled weakly. "He sends help in the strangest packages, doesn't he?"

The elder returned her smile with radiant joy. "I have already spoken with Lysander. He was born of evil, but he is repentant. His heart is pure for you. You can trust him."

Brooke recoiled and hoped it didn't show. The elder's half-blind eyes might not notice, but his mind's eye was sharp enough to pierce the soul.

"Is there anything else you can tell me?" she asked.

"I will go to pray and seek more guidance before you depart. Otherwise, I will see you again upon your return." He stood from the chair and laid a hand on her shoulder. "Be vigilant, my child. *Aeo leywa ai shea.*"

14

VYLIA

Vylia reeled from nightmares of fire and smoke. A bird like a giant phoenix soared by with a dragon's cry, its flaming breath blistering her skin. A black cloud billowed, inescapable and impenetrable, burning her lungs and smothering her mind.

Colors brightened as Vylia opened her eyes, squinting against the firelight. But now, somehow, it seemed more like daylight as the ethereal smoke cleared.

A thick glass ceiling bent over her, allowing the sun to softly warm her skin. A gentle mist, smelling of sweet herbs, drifted beside her and evaporated around the small room. A bed lay on either side of her, one empty and one holding a young man.

Sousuke.

Memories slammed into her.

Sousuke!

Vylia shot upright, and the room spun, smearing shades of brown and green across her vision. She leaned back on her elbows on the bed for support, closing her eyes against the sudden dizziness.

Someone exclaimed in a language she didn't know. A chair groaned against the floor. Footsteps hurried in front of her.

"Princess?" said a tentative voice in her own tongue.

Vylia opened her eyes, and the dizziness mercifully faded. A Malaano girl about her age crouched at her bedside with wide blue eyes. A bandana held her wild curls at bay. Her smooth, ebony skin was even darker than

Vylia's—she wasn't from Malaan Island. A settler to the harsh tribal lands?

"Don't worry. You're safe," the girl said. "I'm Kiralau of the Navakovrae, and I'm here to translate for you and help you. How do you feel?"

Vylia took a deep breath in an attempt to steady herself. "Where are we?"

"You're in the Great Hall in Jadenvive—the safest place in the Katrosi forests. You're well-guarded." Kiralau turned her ear to a spritely tribal woman beside her who said something quickly in the Phoeran language. She nodded and turned back to Vylia. "This is your healer, Nariellyn. Can she tend to you?"

Vylia's heart sank as her mind slowly churned over the information. She wasn't safe. She was in enemy territory. And all of her guards were dead. Except . . .

She slowly slid off the bed, but her legs barely held her. She flopped onto Sousuke's bed as Kiralau lunged forward to catch her.

"Careful, Princess! You must be weak after your long sleep."

Vylia gasped for breath, her lungs burning as if she'd just sprinted the length of a leviathan. "How . . . long . . . ?"

"About five days."

Five . . . ?

It was then that Vylia realized how hungry she was. And how her mouth felt like a desert. And how she really shouldn't have moved from bed.

"Princess, please, lie back down. I'll help you."

Vylia grimaced through the nausea and reached a hand out to Sousuke's face. His skin was warm. He breathed slowly. But he didn't stir at her touch.

She struggled to slow her breathing. "Sousuke!"

"He's asleep, just as you were." Arms slid under her shoulders and gently lifted. Vylia's limbs felt too weak to resist as another Navakovrae laid her back on her bed—this time, a young man who shared Kiralau's coloring. He placed her in a sitting position. "Forgive me." He bowed as he backed away.

The Katrosi healer handed Vylia a bowl of broth that felt too heavy to hold. She stared down into the steaming liquid, and something fell into it with small ripples. She hadn't realized she was crying.

"It's okay. We're doing everything we can for him." Kiralau knelt beside her bed and offered an awkward smile. "Please, eat and regain your strength. It hasn't been easy keeping you alive."

Vylia didn't need prompting to devour the savory broth. She caught her breath in between slurps and didn't care that any sense of propriety had long since flown out the oddly curved window. Slowly, her dizziness and hunger began to fade.

She couldn't tear her eyes from Sousuke as she ate. What had become of the others? Aoko had killed so many . . . but what about Hiro? Sousuke couldn't die and leave her alone in this foreign land. He couldn't.

"Thank you." Vylia held her bowl out, hoping for a refill. "Why am I here? Does my father know of the attack? Was I the target?" At least she wasn't in chains, and these people didn't give her the impression that she was a captive.

Kiralau glanced at Nariellyn, who pursed her lips. She took the bowl and handed it to the young man, who strode out the front door. Vylia spotted two guards outside before it closed.

The healer touched a listening device to Vylia's chest and uttered a word in Phoeran.

"Breathe normally," Kiralau said. "She's listening to your lungs."

Vylia obeyed the deliverer of delectable broth as the device moved to her back. "Answer me. Please."

Nariellyn nodded and hurried to the cabinets on the other side of the room as Kiralau spoke in a low tone. "The Emberhawk attacked the city, but failed to destroy it." Her blue eyes shone with concern as she paused. "Do you remember what happened to your people?"

Vylia wished she didn't. Pain throbbed through her chest like a deep, old bruise. "We were betrayed."

Kiralau frowned. "I'm so sorry."

Vylia lifted her hand and examined her palm. Her skin tone appeared healthy, and yet she barely had enough strength to hold her arm upright. "I need to speak with the Katrosi chieftess."

Kiralau's frown deepened. "She is recovering from poison."

Then . . . this must not be solely about me. Vylia leaned her head back against the headboard. "Please wake my bodyguard up."

The Navakovrae's brows knitted in confusion. "He's in a coma."

"In Malaan, we have priests gifted in the use of aether. Some can use thought-speak. Have you tried that?"

Kiralau's bright eyes widened. She turned and spoke Phoeran to Nariellyn, who in turn spoke to the guards beyond the door. Their conversation lasted a few minutes.

Vylia watched them, missing her translator desperately. "Do the Katrosi have any thought-speakers?"

"The chieftess herself." Kiralau stood and smoothed her tunic and split skirt. "She's on her way."

Five days. *I'm lucky to be alive.*

While Vylia waited for the chieftess, Nariellyn had tried to explain the techniques used to prolong her life as well as Sousuke's—from using Phoera to keep their muscles stimulated with energy to having a Navakovrae elementalist keep them hydrated and fed with broth—but the details were either lost in translation or simply above Vylia's understanding.

Vylia closed her eyes and recalled the meditation garden at the base of the Beresai Falls in Maqua. Water cascaded from such a height that it was said to be the grace of the goddess falling from heaven.

But Lillian had abandoned her at the most crucial time.

Vylia winced at memories of blood and wine. She glanced at the hot water vapor drifting upward into the air from the bowl beside her bed. She reached out for it, calling upon the power of the Malo element in her blood.

It didn't respond.

She felt nothing.

Tears welled in her eyes, and she closed them before the healer could see and think something else was wrong. Wasn't it enough that she'd almost died, lost her mentor, Uma, and the rest of her entourage? That they'd been betrayed by one of their own? Now she had to mourn the loss of her ability to command the element of water right after she'd graduated as a wavesinger.

Vylia took a deep breath, trying to stamp the emotions down. Her father had placed the treacherous Aoko on her team of four bodyguards. And Aoko had said something about doing the will of the emperor as he'd murdered her people.

Aoko didn't seem like the type to kill for fun, though Vylia supposed that could be the case. But something deep inside her leaned toward another explanation. Something darker.

Her father seemed like he actually loved her as she'd left the palace. She'd known then that his aura was different. Unrecognizable from the cold nonchalance he'd normally regarded her with. But she'd wanted so desperately to believe it were true. To go on this mission and finally make him proud. Finally earn his love.

She swallowed as a wave of nausea hit her. She'd never seen him love anyone aside from her late mother. It was like the empress had been his last vestige of humanity, and his heart had died with her.

And so he'd used his daughter in a game of politics like every other ruler did. Except instead of marrying her off for an alliance and peace, he'd traded her for war, like sacrificing a rook to maneuver for victory.

Suddenly marrying that lord from Ceemalao didn't seem so detestable. Maybe if she hadn't refused, the tribal peoples wouldn't be threatened by slaughter from an empire they were powerless against.

A tear slipped free as Vylia opened her eyes. She turned her head to Sousuke beside her, watched his chest rise and fall, and pondered his still, peaceful features, for once free of his usual stern expression.

Wake up, soldier. I need you.

A knock on the door stole Vylia's attention. She swiped the tear from her cheek as Nariellyn hopped down from her perch on the table and opened it.

Vylia nearly called out in disappointment at the clear breach in protocol. But Nariellyn didn't need to ask her permission before inviting others into these chambers. These weren't Vylia's chambers, she wasn't in Malaano territory any more, and Nariellyn wasn't her servant.

She didn't recognize the chieftess at first as she entered. Without her war paint and headdress, she could have been any other brown-haired woman on the streets of Jadenvive. Only her athletic physique, feathered braids, and commanding aura gave her away.

"Princess," Brooke acknowledged as she strode forward. "It's such a relief to see you alive and well." Her Malaano sounded clear and practiced with a staccato accent.

Vylia noted how long the door stayed open and wondered how many of Brooke's invisible guards filed into the room.

It was too much effort to assume a regal stature and formalities. "It seems this attack was not an attempt on my life alone," Vylia said. Her voice sounded too soft, as if it had lost its strength just as her arms had.

"No." Brooke grabbed a chair beside the dresser. "It was an attack by the Emberhawk tribe. I cannot express how sorry I am that you were caught up in this." She flipped the chair around to sit in it backwards, resting her arms on its back. "I sent a squad of my best men to retrieve you, but when they arrived, they found you and your people . . ." She trailed off, apparently in search of the right word.

"Slaughtered." Vylia's voice cracked. "Their deaths were no fault of yours. We were betrayed from within."

Brooke's expression darkened as she frowned. "I fear the attacks were coordinated," she said quietly. "We have evidence that the Malaano supplied the explosives the Emberhawk used in the assault."

Vylia blinked. "Evidence? I know nothing of this." Such an accusation could be interpreted as an act of war. And yet, it wasn't so difficult for Vylia to believe when it aligned with her own theory.

Her heart felt like it had begun to rot. "And yet it doesn't surprise me. I think . . ." Her voice twisted, but she forced the words out. "I think my father intended for me to die here so he'd have an excuse to declare war."

Brooke watched her for a long moment with the eyes of a lioness. "Your bodyguard, Hiro, survived with minimal injuries. He left for Malaan days ago with the message that you are alive."

Relief mingled with dread in Vylia's gut. "Then they could try to kill him, too," she murmured.

"I sent a pair of guards with him at his own request. Hopefully we'll receive word from him soon." Brooke reached out and touched the edge of Vylia's bed. "I signed an agreement of peace with you. The Katrosi will do everything in our power to protect you." Her brown eyes hardened. "What can I do for you?"

Vylia had no idea what to ask for, except . . . "They say you know the ways of aether." She gestured to Sousuke. "In Malaan, our thought-speakers connect with the minds of those in a coma and can sometimes bring them out of the long sleep."

Brooke studied Sousuke with furrowed brow. "I've never heard of that, but it could work, I suppose." She stood from her chair and moved to his bedside. "It's more difficult to enter one's mind without eye contact . . ."

"Please try. He's . . ." She didn't want to admit that he was all she had left. "He's important to me."

"I'll do my best." Brooke knelt, placed a hand on Sousuke's forehead, and closed her eyes.

Vylia's hope drained further with each passing moment. After several minutes, she almost reached out to Brooke to tell her she'd done enough.

The chieftess paused to adjust her position, to ask Nariellyn something in Phoeran, and to murmur something to herself, or perhaps to her god.

Sousuke took in a deep breath, and Vylia's anxiety shattered along with her composure. Tears poured from her like a broken dam as Nariellyn rushed over and guided Sousuke through awakening. Kiralau translated the healer's instructions: move slowly, sit up carefully, breathe deeply.

"Vy?" Sousuke blinked at her with concern. "You're okay?"

"Yes," she answered, savoring the familiar voice that always made her feel safe. "Mostly."

Sousuke flexed his hand and lifted it, frowning down at his body. "Not good." He managed to sit up and took a bowl of broth that Kiralau offered.

"We're alive. That's all that matters." Vylia turned to Brooke. "Thank you," she said, determined to stay in bed and not to make a mess of her floppy limbs on the floor again, though she wanted to hug Sousuke's neck regardless of propriety.

"Thank the creator and your own healers for the idea." Brooke stood and stretched. "You're lucky to have this one in your service."

"I know," Vylia said with a smile, wondering what Brooke had seen inside his mind. She wiped her tears with the sheets, enjoying the flush of Sousuke's ears as he slurped the broth down.

Nariellyn spoke in Phoeran as she examined Sousuke, and Brooke nodded. "You both appear to be in decent health, but you'll need time and exercise to regain your strength." She stood. "Unfortunately, I must go, but by the time I return you should be fully recovered."

Something about the way she said it pricked Vylia with worry. "You're leaving?"

"Tonight." Brooke didn't seem happy about it. "A sort of diplomatic mission to the Emberhawk lands."

Vylia cringed. Her first—and last—diplomatic mission had ended in unprecedented disaster.

She didn't know what to say. Brooke was the only local she knew, and only just. Was she supposed to lie here, helpless in a foreign city, waiting for the next assassin?

But what was the alternative? How could she possibly return to her father now?

Unless he truly did love her. He could welcome her back with open arms, never let her leave the palace again, and she'd live in luxury for the rest of her days.

Or she could trust Brooke, recover here under guard, and await word from Hiro. His loyalty was unquestionable, as was Sousuke's.

Suddenly she wished Hiro had never left.

"I can offer more luxurious or secretive accommodations if you wish, but you are safest here in the Great Hall." Brooke waved at the door, and a few heartbeats later, Kiralau entered with the young male Navakovrae who'd helped her before and a young tribesman she'd never met. "I presume you've already met Kiralau—she will be your translator. She may not be familiar with the customs of your handmaidens, but she is responsible for felling the giant ember hawk that attacked us."

Vylia raised her eyebrows at Kiralau. "Is that so?" The Navakovrae girl looked about as intimidating as a branch runner.

Kiralau tipped her head with a flash of pride. "I had some help."

"Tekkyn'ashi will guard you as your man recovers. He is a former Malaano soldier now under my employ." He bowed low as Brooke introduced him.

"And this is my advisor, Idryon. He's new to the job but he has the authority to procure nearly anything you need." Brooke gestured at the young tribesman with striking orange eyes. He seemed a different ethnicity somehow—distinctly from the Phoeran tribes, but the slant of his eyes appeared more cunning. Like a fox, perhaps.

Idryon bowed, swishing the half-cape over his left shoulder. "At your service, Princess," he said in near-perfect Malaano.

Vylia returned his bow with a tilted nod. This might have been the best Brooke could offer considering the circumstances, but she still . . . "Must you go?"

Brooke's weariness laid on her shoulders like a mantle too heavy to bear. "I wish I didn't have to. Truly. It's difficult to explain." She placed a hand on the end of Vylia's bed. "It is a miracle that you've returned to us from the long sleep. Stay here in safety and recover your strength. Let's not tempt fate again."

15

LYSANDER

The way the Katosi patriarchs looked at Lysander made him wish he were still in chains. He stood between two soldiers on the upper dias of the Great Hall, near the throne where the elders gathered, and the tribesmen glared at him as if they could ignite him with their stares.

Their scapegoat had escaped.

The Elder of Aether stood at the base of the steps with a line of impatient people stretching out before him, waiting to see the memories he offered. He gently touched chins and looked into seeking eyes, one after the other.

Lysander assumed transferring thoughts for a line that long must be tiring. And he sincerely hoped that the old man wasn't sharing the private memories he'd accessed from Lysander's mind after Ryon had appealed for Lysander's freedom.

But even if that were the case, it would be worth it. Lysander was no stranger to public shame.

Finally, the line diminished, and the expressions in the crowd turned from anger to grim acceptance. Some even looked at Lysander with an admiring gleam. That's when he realized that the elder must have only shared the bare minimum—the recent memories of apparent heroism and the genuine desire to save Brooke.

Most of them knew he wasn't a hero. But he'd take the package deal regardless.

"And thus the council has granted asha'ai," the Elder of Justice declared,

and the hand-language interpreter repeated. *"What the creator has decreed, let no man deny."*

The crowd responded as one, loud enough for Lysander to feel the vibration through the floorboards.

"So be it," the translator signed.

The Elder of Justice turned to Lysander and gestured at the soldiers who flanked him. *"You are free."*

Lysander bowed as the soldiers retreated. "Thank you."

The elder ignored him and turned back to the crowd. *"For the next order of business, turn your gaze to the brazier."*

The translator didn't have enough time to finish signing before the fire pit in the center of the room ignited into a bonfire. A fire dancer stood among the flames in flowing strips of traditional leather, gesturing with wide motions. Fire followed her movements in flashing images of trees and beasts as Lysander tried to keep up.

"From the towering pines comes the firstborn of King Raven Eye and Queen Hidden Xavi, dragon slayer and d'hakka master, Lord of the Black Forest and heir to the Darkwood throne: Prince Soaring Heron!"

The brazier's fire erupted in blue, and Lysander took an instinctive step back. Something passed on his right, and he barely avoided a shove from a man covered in tattoos and knife-sheaths. No doubt a bodyguard for the man on his other side who reeked of royalty: he bore a gleaming silken cape, a crown of silver spikes protruded from perfect hair, and he exuded enough arrogance to choke the room.

The people lit up, brightening the hall just as much as the dancing flames.

Lysander didn't care to keep the disgust from his face. It was like looking into a mirror from his own past, just a different culture where apparently shirtlessness was a thing.

"He comes to take the hand of our chieftess in marriage and add the might of the Darkwood warriors to our own!"

The crowd's response bellowed through the sound waves, but Lysander didn't need to feel it to understand their clueless joy-filled faces. Anyone with half a brain would know that a woman like Brooke wouldn't want to marry a boy like this. But of course, what she wanted didn't matter.

Lysander turned and headed for the door behind the throne. Someone caught his arm. He turned back and met the gaze behind an orange mask. The soldier shook his head and pointed toward the grand double doors on the far side of the hall, beyond the crowd.

Lysander frowned. So he was just an ordinary citizen now with no access to the Great Hall? No, just a foreigner.

He'd never been average before. From prince to Zamara's right hand to nothing.

No. He was still Emberhawk royalty, even if that didn't mean much any more.

"I need to speak with Brooke," Lysander said.

The soldier shook his head and pointed again to the far doors.

Thankfully, the translator jogged toward him. She didn't seem quite as cold as she'd been in the prison. She signed the soldier's words: *"Did she summon you?"*

"No, but she'll want to speak with me."

"That's for her to decide."

"I'm an herbalist—I've been aiding her recovery from dreamthistle."

"You've been doing that from a safe distance, by speaking only with her healers, correct?"

Lysander opened his mouth to retort but stopped when the translator began her own conversation with the soldier. Lysander couldn't see the man's lips behind his mask, nor could he see the woman's as her back was turned to him, so he waited and hoped.

A moment later, the translator turned back to him with a victorious grin. *"We'll escort you."*

He returned her smile. "Thanks."

Tapestries that told stories of generations past adorned the wooden hallway. Lysander tried to distract himself with them as they passed one of the elders' chambers. One he'd snuck into before. And if anyone ever found that out, his newfound freedom would surely meet its end at the edge of a Katrosi blade, *asha'ai* or not.

He clenched his fists as sweat slicked his palms. What if Brooke wouldn't meet with him? Or what if she refused to teach him the magic of thought-speak? Could he find someone to teach him in Quin'Zamar? Or should he dare to show his face in the palace ever again, since Xavier had called him a traitor and was surely halfway to the border by now?

Lysander nearly tripped when he noticed that the translator had stopped in front of him. She knocked on the door.

He clenched and unclenched his fists. Why was he so nervous? He wasn't used to feeling emotions so . . . intensely. How long had it been since he'd cared about anything?

The door opened, and the translator welcomed him inside the chief's chambers.

Lysander's blood surged faster than it should have as he entered. These people were idiots to trust someone like him in the most secure place in Jadenvive.

Brooke stuffed bundles of cloth and leather into a satchel. She didn't bear any face paint, and her braids were tied up in a long strand of ribbon. She wore common clothes, and a long hood trailed down the dark cloak on her back.

Lysander frowned. *Where is she sneaking off to?*

Brooke glanced up and waved the translator away. Her words were plain on her lips. "I don't need translation, thanks." She pointed at the soldier. "You, stay."

So not all of them were idiots.

Lysander cleared his throat as the translator left behind him. "I, uh . . . They granted me *asha'ai*."

Good. Brooke's voice rang like an angel's song through his head. *You deserve it.* She continued packing with haste.

Yearning billowed up inside him, smothering all fear. It wasn't like hearing again, but it was so close. So beautiful.

He needed it. He'd do anything.

Lysander swallowed. "Please teach me your thought-speak."

Brooke only paused for a half-second. *I can sense your feelings along with your thoughts, you know.*

Horror dawned on him. "Y-you can?"

Was that a smirk on her face?

First you'll need to learn to harness aether, then to craft a sort of shield around your mind to protect yourself.

Lysander straightened his back. "I learned those things as a boy to prevent spying and manipulation on the monarchy."

Oh, good. That'll save a lot of time. Brooke grabbed an etched knife from the wall and slipped it into a sheath. *Assuming you're not lying. You have no mental shields at all even though you know I'm a thought-reader.*

He felt his face flush and cursed his pale skin for showing it. "I didn't know you were an empath as well."

There's a lot you don't know.

Lysander clenched his jaw as she took a long spear from a mount on the wall. "Where are you going?"

To the Emberhawk Sovereignty, and you're coming with me. We're putting your brother on the throne.

She might as well have slapped him in the face. He mustn't have heard her right, and yet her voice in his head was as clear and apparent as a sunny day.

"Shouldn't you be recovering from dreamthistle?"

Illiana refuses to join the Alliance or take responsibility for Zamara's actions. She seized the throne, upending the proper line of succession. Brooke wrapped twine around a bundle of cloth, cinching it tight. *Since you abdicated, the crown should fall to Coriander. Isn't that right?*

Foreboding lodged in Lysander's chest. "Yes, but there's nothing we can do about it. Illiana was Zamara's chosen heir since she branded Cori a traitor."

Doesn't that fly in the face of your laws? Brooke said. *Didn't you say your people always need a king and queen to rule, and that one cannot rule without the other?*

"Yes, so I'm sure Illiana is seeking a husband and will marry quickly." He lowered his voice. "My people do not get a say in politics as yours do, unless they are a noble house bound to the monarchy through marriage."

Well, we're going to give them a voice. Brooke shoved the bundle into her bursting pack with excessive force.

Lysander watched her for a long moment. "It's a fool's errand."

Then you can ask the Elder of Aether to teach you.

"I didn't say I wouldn't go," Lysander blurted.

Brooke wrapped the leather strap around a bone hook, wrenching the pack closed. *Oh, you prefer me to teach you?* She smirked up at him. *The elder has half a century of experience and taught me everything I know. Why me?*

Lysander grasped for a response that wasn't a complete lie, as she would certainly discern it. "You don't have a beard."

Her laughter flitted through his mind, rich and deep. *See my requisition officer for any supplies you'll need.* She slung the pack over her shoulder. *We leave before nightfall.*

"What about the Darkwood prince?" Lysander regretted the words the instant they left his mouth. But he'd already stepped in it. "You must know he just arrived."

Brooke's expression soured. She grabbed the spear and inspected its metal tip. *Thank you for saving my life.*

Lysander blinked. She had a habit of evading topics she didn't like. Definitely a politician.

He shrugged. "I didn't have anything better to do."

Brooke fell quiet for a long moment as she ran a hand along the polished spear, paying special attention to the knots in the glazed wood. *I know I'm asking a lot of you.* She looked up at him and caught him in an enrapturing copper gaze. *Can I trust you?*

Lysander forced himself to look away, glancing at a shelf full of scrolls and books instead. "I think you already know the answer to that, or you wouldn't have asked me to come."

It was her turn to flush, though it didn't show as strongly on her tanned complexion. Perhaps his eyes deceived him.

That remains to be seen. Brooke stepped close and stared up at him, spear in hand. *Regardless, I do not fear you.*

Nothing about her composure gave him any reason to doubt her words—she stood strong and unwaveringly confident before him despite their vast difference in height. The lines of stress that faintly graced her face did little to hinder her beauty.

But perhaps because of their former relationship, or perhaps because of the bond lashing them together, or perhaps because of his former aether training, Lysander sensed she was lying.

16

BROOKE

Brooke opened the dark pantry and inhaled the scents of dried beef, scarlet long pepper, and mesquite smoke. Strips of jerky, too numerous to count, hung by hooks above racks of cranberry pemmican.

She allowed herself a moment to relish the fond memories the scents evoked. Hunting trips with her father. Camping with her mother. Her solo expeditions into the Gnarled Wood, hoping to slay two d'hakka and wear their tail spikes in her headdress if she could pass the trials and be selected as chief.

The size and complexity of that confounded headdress took up an entire pack on its own. Bringing it was a risk and a burden, but she'd decided it was necessary in case she needed to reveal herself or prove her identity to Coriander. Dimbae could carry more bags than an ox, anyway.

How many provisions to pack, though? Two women—herself and Nariellyn—but Nari had a taste for sweets, so she'd have to pack extra honey drops to keep her from griping along the trail. And three men— Dimbae, another azure mask, and Lysander. The trip to the Emberhawk border wasn't far, but where was Coriander's hideout? Surely not so far as Quin'Zamar on the southern coast, as he'd want to keep his family as far from the palace as possible.

Brooke rapped her fingers on the pantry's doorpost. Probably no more than a week's worth of food was needed. So she'd pack for two. She didn't want to spare the time for hunting or foraging.

"Here's all the journeycake we've got on hand," said the plump chef from the kitchen island. She folded cloth over yellow bread with dizzying speed and tied the corners. "If you've got a half hour to spare, I can make a dragon's weight in anything you'd like."

Brooke did a quick calculation and grabbed several pounds of jerky and pemmican. "That's all right. I'll just take some nuts and dried fruit."

A servant girl took Brooke's handfuls as another dashed for a stack of baskets near the ovens. The chef finished her wrapping and stacked the loaves. "Aye, and we'll send some fresh jomoco—they've got a good shelf life. First of the harvest came in just yesterday. The winds are with you, Stillwind." She winked, then put a hand on a voluptuous hip. "You could stop by Monty's if ya need more provisions in a hurry. I happen to know he's well-stocked at the moment." Her eyeroll delivered more meaning than her words.

Brooke couldn't help but grin. "He kept you up late cooking again? Luckiest man in the city."

The chef sighed as she moved to stir an iron cauldron over the wide hearth. "Why don't you tell him that on your way out? Of course demand is high right now as people stock up, and that's all right, but a woman's gotta rest when she gets home from a hard day's work. Don't you agree?"

Brooke prevented a selfish retort from tumbling out of her mouth. Instead she hoped her genuine smile was still intact. "Completely."

The chef's mirth dimmed as she stepped forward and laid a soft hand over Brooke's. "You're doing a great job, my lady. These tough times won't last forever."

Brooke relaxed a fraction. She'd never been able to hide anything from the master chef, whose cupboard she'd stolen biscuits from as a child. She'd normally been caught with a laugh instead of a reprimand.

She placed her other hand over the chef's. "Thank you."

The chef bowed her head. *"Aeo leywa ai shea."*

"There you are."

Brooke turned at the sound of Lysander's voice. He stood at the kitchen doorway, apparently wary of entering the fray. Brooke ensured that Dimbae gathered the provisions as they were prepared, silently adding them to a bag with care.

She crossed to Lysander and did her best to prepare for whatever bad news he was bound to deliver. First an attack on the city by *his* unit, then one of *his* friendly assassin comrades trying to kill her, and now *his* deformed family tree would have to be uprooted and replanted by her—the unluckiest woman in the cosmos. Now what other lovely circumstances would he deliver?

"It would be great if you could give me a mask or badge or a letter with a seal of authority or something," Lysander said as she approached. "Do you have any idea how hard it is to even get within speaking distance of you?"

Brooke summoned her aether to speak her thoughts directly to his mind. Her energy brightened within her soul and filled her body with gentle peace. *Strange,* she said to him. *It's almost like assassins are trying to kill me and the guards are on high alert or something.* She eyed a small satchel in his hand. *What is it? Are you ready to go?*

"Yeah. Ready when you are." Lysander held the satchel out toward her. "Here's an antidote blend for your tea."

Brooke shouldered past him without taking it, relieved that Lysander wasn't associated with pandemonium this time. "Thanks. Help Dimbae carry our provisions if he needs it, please." She said it both out loud and in her thoughts, creating a strange echo.

She suppressed a shudder. Hopefully Lysander could read lips instead of that becoming a regular dizzying sensation for her.

"I don't need help," Dimbae's deep voice sounded behind her, as expected.

Lysander's footsteps followed her into the hall. "I can read lips most of the time. I learned it for my . . . previous occupation before I lost my hearing."

Brooke stopped and looked back at him. *I didn't send that thought to you.*

He shrugged. "Well, I heard it."

Alarm unsteadied her. That wasn't normal. Either he had more previous aether training than he'd let on, or he was some sort of prodigy with thought-speak.

Perhaps she should work on her own mental shields.

Lysander held out the satchel again. "You should take this now if you want to feel well tonight," he said. "Without it you will probably start to feel the side effects again. It'll take a few days for your body to rid itself of the dreamthistle completely."

Brooke gave him a sidelong glance over her shoulder as she strode toward Nariellyn's quarters. *It doesn't look like tea.*

Lysander looked confused. "I said it's a blend for tea."

She turned a corner. *Do you expect me to chew dry herbs?*

"Have you forgotten how to brew tea, Your Majesty?"

Brooke stopped short and turned on her heel. *I've got a few more important things on my plate right now. If you'd like to help, perhaps you could pull your own weight.*

Lysander glared down at her with maroon eyes. "Sorry, I guess I wasn't pulling my weight when I saved your life."

I thanked you for that. Brooke clenched her teeth. *Look, I'm grateful for your remedies. Just have it brewed if you want me to drink it. I'm kind of busy. All the time. I thought that was obvious.*

Lysander leaned to one side. "I didn't sign up to be your servant. I just got away from Zamara, and I'm not doing that again."

Anger ignited within Brooke, smothering her inner peace. *Are you accusing me of treating my servants like Zamara did? My grandfather abolished slavery in the Katrosi tribe at great cost of life.*

"Skies, you're defensive. Do you not realize how lucky you are to have survived dreamthistle poisoning? You must not if you think the antidote isn't important enough to take two minutes to brew some tea."

Brooke snorted and wished she had her warpaint and headdress on. Perhaps then he'd show some respect. *I had a feeling you'd make this trip difficult, but I didn't anticipate you'd start before we even left.*

Lysander stared at her, motionless, for a long moment. "Why do you hate me?"

Responses swirled in Brooke's head, each fighting to be selected. Because he complicated everything. Because he was a dark stain on her childhood memories. Because he was the definition of untrustworthy. Because he made her feel uncomfortable in the strangest way. Because he had no responsibility on his shoulders while she carried the world on hers.

Because his thoughts were woven with fondness for her, but only because she could help him "hear" again. He was selfish even in his shallow version of love.

Too late. About fourteen years too late.

Brooke released a hot breath. *I don't hate you.*

Lysander's eyes widened. "You still . . . ?"

Panic lanced through her. Surely he couldn't sense her emotions, too?

No, there was nothing for him to sense!

His sharp features softened. "It's all right. We were just kids. I'm sure I hurt you, somehow . . . I'm sorry."

Brooke's throat squeezed shut. "No, it's not like that. I don't . . . It was a long time ago. And I never did. Really." She could feel herself sweating despite the element-enforced chill in the air. She realized after she'd blurted it out that she hadn't used thought-speak and he probably didn't understand her mashed jumble of denial.

Lysander shrugged. "Okay."

Humiliation crashed down on her. Clearly he didn't believe her. But wasn't it obvious she detested him? He'd said so himself! She'd severed any attraction to him years ago.

Muffled shouting down the hall provided a blessed distraction. "Sir, you can't go back there!"

"If you won't tell me where she is, I'll find her myself!"

Brooke felt her blood drain to her toes. That was the voice of Prince Soaring Heron.

He rounded the corner, coming into view too late for her to react.

Sharp, dark eyes latched onto her and traveled up and down her features.

"Chieftess." Soaring Heron stopped as a crowd, including her doppelgänger in full regalia, a handmaiden, and four guards came up behind him. "Would you please explain what sort of deceptive charade is going on?"

Brooke hoped she'd managed to contain her cringe. She glanced at her people, who bowed low behind him without a word. She dismissed them with a wave.

"Wait." Soaring Heron pointed at Brooke's double with his lip curled in disgust. "I understand that you maintain this façade for cowardly 'security purposes.' But this one actually tried to convince me that she was you. Multiple times. In Darkwood, we cut out the tongues of liars."

"Then you'd have to cut out my tongue, too. Good thing we aren't in Darkwood." Brooke nodded at her doppelgänger, whose face paint accentuated her expression of terror. She bowed again and disappeared behind the guards.

Brooke smirked. "I wondered if you'd recognize me without my paints."

Please let this work, she prayed as her pulse slammed through her skull.

A playful fire ignited in Soaring Heron's eyes. Light from a glow-shroom torch on the wall accentuated the flowing tattoos across his bare chest. "Her body isn't as . . . athletic as yours." He came close enough to look down on her. All the way down. "What game are you playing?"

Brooke's trepidation soured into nausea. His attractiveness couldn't be denied, but it held little pull on her for a reason she couldn't define.

She considered her words carefully. Unfortunately, the truth might be the best option . . . If he caught her being deceptive again, it could cause international problems.

"You must swear to secrecy."

Heron drew a knife and cut his third finger without hesitation. He held both out to her.

Brooke did the same, cursing herself for forgetting the Darkwood oath tradition. She shook his hand, mingling their blood as she lowered her voice. "One of our elders is a prophet. He foresaw my death if I do not leave the city before sundown."

Soaring Heron's brows knit together. "Who would dare? I'll kill them."

"He doesn't know, but I must obey. I was lucky to survive the last assassination attempt."

The prince's red-orange eyes shifted behind her to pierce Lysander. "Let me guess: an Emberhawk?"

Brooke glanced back at Lysander, who looked like a statue carved from marble.

She sidestepped to remain between them. "Lysander saved my life."

Soaring Heron tilted his head back, but he wasn't tall enough to look down on Lysander. "What's he doing here? I heard he's disabled."

Brooke frowned, hoping Lysander hadn't lip-read that. "He's going to accompany me on a diplomatic mission to the Emberhawk lands. Hopefully things will be safer when I return."

"You must be joking," Soaring Heron said. "Please tell me you're not going to interfere with the sibling squabbles of a foreign monarchy."

It sounded so much worse when he put it that way. Brooke looked down at her hand and squeezed the bleeding cut together. "Coriander is the rightful—"

Soaring Heron huffed a laugh. "That's none of your concern!"

"I agree." Brooke sighed as an azure mask appeared and offered her a bandage. She took it, and he vanished the next instant. "However, that was also part of the prophecy. I have no choice."

Soaring Heron ran a hand through his long hair, narrowly avoiding the spikes of his crown as he muttered something about religion. "It would be exceedingly ill-timed and dangerous."

"Agreed."

He put his hands on his hips and glared at Lysander. "Perhaps I could have a talk with your prophet."

"I'm sorry," Brooke said. "I don't want to go, truly. But I'll be back within a fortnight. In the meantime, I'll ensure you're given the finest accommodations."

Soaring Heron snorted. "Not during a time like this. Your people would loathe me straight from the start." He motioned to an iron-jawed guard behind him with more angular tattoos. He whispered something before turning back to Brooke. "We haven't unpacked yet. My guard and I will accompany you."

Brooke's stomach clenched. "Like you said, it's dangerous—"

"All the more reason you need me to protect you."

She bit down on a flash of panic. "Please, Soaring Heron. If anything happened to you, it would be a political nightmare."

"And the same can't be said for you? Meddling with the government of another nation can be considered an act of war, you know." He tilted his head as the dark, playful smirk returned. "Call me Heron."

Brooke stepped closer to him and lowered her voice. "Please. I couldn't bear it if you got hurt."

He pulled her into a warm embrace and kissed her before she realized what was happening. Her heart pounded, but her blood lacked the zing that had coursed through her when her second fiancé had kissed her. The one who'd died in a hunting accident. The one who'd strengthened rumors of her curse.

The curse that Heron, her third fiancé, was now subjected to.

Brooke forced herself not to pull away, aware that she must have felt stiff and cold in his arms. But she couldn't have enjoyed it if she'd tried.

Lysander's presence lingered behind her. The Emberhawk's aether simmered with negative emotions. Anger on the surface, but below, something . . . colder.

Heron finally released her. "I came here to be with you. You'll be mine soon, and I'll never leave you again."

Brooke plastered a smile on her face. "All right, if it's just the two of you. I'll leave one of my guards behind." She tied the bandage around her finger and cinched it tight. "We must leave within the hour. Discreetly."

17

RYON

Ryon never thought he'd have an office. Tapestries and taxidermies adorned the wooden walls. The metal crest of the Katrosi chieftain sat on his desk, beside the Tribal Alliance crest, waiting to stamp yet another decree. He kept the wax hot and the stamps cool with Phoera, grateful for the distraction from the papers his assistant kept piled high.

Apparently he had an assistant now.

But the glamor of becoming Brooke's advisor had faded far more quickly than he'd imagined. The people were outside, constructing a halfway house in the midday sun. Distributing relief supplies. Tending to burn victims. But he sat here, signing and stamping papers behind a desk as if he were someone of import.

Ryon rubbed his eyelids before he could finish reading the next request for treasury funds to restore a historic monument in the trade district. Before the end of Jadenvive's restoration, he'd have about as much life left as the treasury would have *rupero*.

He couldn't stop wondering about the man who'd sat in his chair only weeks before. How he'd coped with the stress of the job. How he'd decided which requests were important enough to send to Brooke. How he'd determined how many funds to allocate to each request.

How he'd died in Zamara's fire.

"Sir!"

The door opened before Ryon gave permission. His assistant rushed in with his head ducked as if the stuffed trace cat would return to life and gnaw on his head.

"Excuse me, sir. This is urgent." He held out a folded piece of parchment stained with ink blots. "It's meant for the Malaano princess, but the chieftess should see it first. But I can't find her."

Ryon raised an eyebrow at him as he took it. The lotus blossom seal was broken. "Who's it from?"

"One of the princess's bodyguards, or so the courier believes. He stressed secrecy."

"Who broke the seal, then?" Ryon asked as he opened it.

"The azure masks screen everything that goes to the chieftess during times of heightened security, sir."

Ryon grunted his acknowledgement and read the Malaano script:

To Her Highness Princess Vylia, or to her guardian Sousuke,

I hope with everything in my being that you both have awakened, healthy and safe, as you receive this. Unfortunately I bear grave news.

Word of your death spread faster than I could travel. Along the road, every tongue spoke of war. In Navarro, the troops seemed restless and on high alert. And in MyEyah, I heard that the emperor executed the families of his daughter's bodyguards.

I haven't confirmed it myself, but surely some escaped. We will find them, Sousuke. House Rhu could not have been fully eliminated. And that snake Aoko was surely working for the emperor—he couldn't have killed his family for doing his own bidding. But then, it seems he betrayed us all.

I was too late. I'm sorry.

Your Highness, forgive me, but it seems clear to me now that your father intended from the beginning of your mission to use you as a sacrificial pawn. Your death was to be his excuse for declaring war on the tribes. And now that I've committed treason for saying so, I urge you to hide yourself away. If you have survived (Lillian let it be so), and the emperor learns of it, there could be other assassins sent after you. Once it became clear to me that we were manipulated and outplayed, and when I learned they'd already murdered our families, I decided not to tell anyone you survived the fire, for your safety.

I've made contact with the Lotusfall. They have connections to more than one powerful house; they are the only ones who can keep you safe now. The people tire of bloodshed, and if you still draw breath, Your Highness, you could be the key to ending your father's reign, if that is what you wish.

Regardless, my vow to protect you remains unbroken. You will make an excellent empress one day. Lillian let it be soon.

Trust no one.

Burn this letter. I'll make contact as soon as I can.

Hiro

Ryon's mouth felt dry as he squinted at the handwriting. He'd never heard of the "Lotusfall"—that should be how the Malaano characters sounded.

He stood up from his desk, sending his chair screeching across the wood floor. "Why can't you find Brooke?"

"I . . . Her double is meeting with the public today. She's not in her chambers or the Grove of the Ancients. The azures won't tell me anything. I'm not sure where else to—"

A knock interrupted him. Once again, the door opened without Ryon's permission.

Brooke entered with a hood deep enough to cover her face entirely, but Ryon recognized her anyway. Lysander stood in the hallway behind her.

"I must speak with you in private." Brooke turned a dark gaze on the courier. "Quickly."

The courier bowed and left, and Lysander took his place in Ryon's office. The door shut behind him.

"Good timing." Ryon held out the letter for her to take. "What's with the getup?"

Brooke ignored it. "I'm leaving for the Emberhawk Sovereignty with Lysander, Dimbae, Nariellyn, and Prince Soaring Heron and his guard. Secretly."

Ryon blinked at her. "What?"

"The Elder of Aether had a vision. I must leave before nightfall." She glanced at the window behind his desk. "I trust you to handle things while I'm gone. Hopefully no more than a week."

Ryon felt like he'd gone to watch a drama-play but somehow missed the first half of the story. "What are you going to do? You don't really mean to leave me in ch—"

"We will put Cori on the throne," Lysander said.

A flare of hope sped Ryon's heart before his head caught up with it. "You'd need an army to remove Illiana." He signed as he spoke, even though Lysander apparently didn't need it.

"Coriander has loyal men, but hopefully it won't come to that," Brooke said. "You can do this. The elders handle matters of justice and disputes. You have the authority to handle everything else, but if you need me, just stall until I get back." She pulled an arm from her cloak and slipped a signet from her finger. "Here."

Ryon stared down at it, unmoving. "Brooke, seriously, you have a great face for dice, but this isn't funny."

"It's not a joke. You knew when you accepted the position of advisor that you'd be third in line of authority. Or tenth if you count the elders."

"I'm supposed to be third behind a vice! And I think you're forgetting that my experience in this job is approximately five seconds. And that I'm not qualified in the first pl—"

"We're about to have a vice," Brooke interrupted. "Ulysses will accept my offer within the next couple of days."

Ryon watched her serious expression in disbelief. She looked exhausted, as if a buffalo-sized leech were stealing her life away. And her brain.

"How are you going to receive his oath if you're not here?"

"My double can do it."

"Brooke!"

She couldn't be serious. This whole thing was beyond stupid. He'd served her for years, prizing her intellect above all.

The poison must have gone to her head.

Brooke sighed. "Don't look at me like that. I don't want to do this, trust me. I don't have a choice." She set her signet ring on his desk. "I'll be back as soon as I can."

Ryon remembered the letter in his hand. He held it out limply. "At least look at this before you run off. It's kind of important."

Brooke took it. Her eyes flicked over the ink. "Have the azure masks guard the princess in my absence." She handed the parchment back to him. "The healers have them on bedrest, so they won't be going anywhere until I return."

Ryon stared down at the paper and considered the consequences of resigning.

Brooke's hand weighed on his shoulder. "Things are crazy right now. It's hard—I understand that better than anyone else. But you can do this."

"I'm just a scout," Ryon whispered. "Choose someone else. Anyone else."

"I don't trust anyone else." Brooke straightened, but he refused to meet her gaze. "You swore an oath to me, Idryon of Quin'Zamar, and I hold you to it."

Anger sliced through Ryon, and he snapped a glare down at her. "I am Ryon of Jadenvive."

"Prove it."

He clenched his jaw. "You are a professional manipulator," he growled, then turned his glare on his cousin. *"Don't let anything happen to her,"* he signed.

Lysander nodded.

"I'll bring some chocolate back for the orphans." The corner of Brooke's lip curled into a smirk as her face disappeared into the shadow of her hood. "Just remember that my absence is a secret. Only the elders, azures, and the kitchen staff know." She took a step back toward the door. *"Aeo leywa ai shea."*

Ryon released a hot sigh as he bowed. *"Aeo leywa ai shea."*

Ryon pulled his lenses down and squinted at the messenger, but the new perspective didn't help the report make any more sense. "What kind of anomaly?"

"Definitely a Phoeran light distortion, sir." The young man paused to catch his breath. "It's just abnormally large. And it's slowly moving east to west."

Ryon tapped his fingers on his desk as he considered the news. Of course something weird like this would happen right after Brooke left.

He'd have a hard time forgiving her for leaving him with this mess.

"It's moving toward Jadenvive?" Ryon asked. "From the direction of the Malano border?"

"Yes, sir," the messenger said. "Sorry for not clarifying, sir. I ran here as fast as I could."

Ryon wished the guy wouldn't call him "sir." He'd been a scout, too, less than a month ago. The same rank.

"But you have no idea what it actually is?" Ryon asked.

"I have ideas, sir, but it's not my place to say." The messenger stood straight and avoided eye contact, as if Ryon were a king or something.

"Since the apparent danger is potentially beyond my ability to handle alone, sir, I thought it best to return and report in before investigating further."

"You made the right choice." Ryon stood and his back ached for a stretch. He removed the half-cape that identified him as the chief's advisor and tossed it on top of the mound of papers on his desk. "Would you like to go back there?"

The young man's brows knitted together as he watched Ryon move to the corner and strap his belt on, adjust his machete sheath, and grab his bow.

"Y-yes, sir."

"Good. I'll grab a few pale masks, and you can lead us to where you saw this . . . anomaly." Ryon pulled his mask on and tied the ribbon behind his head, savoring the familiar scent of pine and the linseed oil that sealed it.

"You're going, sir?"

A chance to get out of this cramped office? To escape the job he didn't want, at least temporarily? To return to the scents and sights and sounds of the forest? Of course he was going.

Ryon scribbled a note with charcoal, then remembered that Brooke always complained about his handwriting and that Phoeran was Kira's second language. He flipped the parchment over and started again.

Balemba,

> *Scout reported an anomaly of light-magic approaching*
> *from the east. Going to check it out. Back soon.*

He hesitated, knowing how worried she'd be if she happened to see this note before he returned.

> *Dinner at Het'saya? Just me and you this time.*
>> *Ryon*

Ryon's heart soared. He hadn't realized how much he hated cities until he'd made it past the gates. Well, he could never hate Jadenvive—maybe he just loved the wild that much more.

The fresh breeze that smelled of recent rain. The crooning of distant birds and clicking of insects. The tree lizard that titled its head at him from beside the path, jutting out its neck in a colorful display.

Being alone was the only improvement Ryon could imagine. Or swapping out the men who followed him with Kira. At least they didn't talk much.

The young scout stopped ahead. He whipped his head back over his shoulder to look at Ryon, his face painted with fear.

Then he disappeared.

Ryon gestured to the men behind him and followed suit, cloaking himself in darkness. He allowed light to touch his eyes only and quietly dashed to the tree line, where his floating eyes might be mistaken for those of a curious animal hiding in the brush.

The crickets stopped chirping. The birds stopped calling. The melody of the forest was overshadowed by a distant thumping. Like rhythmic footsteps. Hundreds of them.

Ryon squatted behind a birch, leaning on its bark for support as he stared down the trail. His eyes must be playing tricks on him. He pulled his lenses off and realized that he'd yet again forgotten to acquire a soft piece of silk for cleaning them.

The trees warped down the path like a heat distortion rising up from the earth. Trunks swayed as if they were as flexible as branches.

Ryon's throat closed until he could scarcely breathe. It would take a massive concerted effort to make an area that large invisible. He'd only seen such a feat accomplished once before—at Coriander's camp in the Emberhawk jungle. But whatever was being hidden here was mobile, making the feat that much more impressive.

How many elementalists were working together to make this possible? And how far did this distortion stretch beyond what he could currently sense?

Staying to find out was too dangerous. Because Ryon could imagine only one scenario in which this made sense: an invading army was approaching, and the Emberhawk were covering for them.

18

KIRALAU

If the chieftess has been poisoned, now is the perfect time to retrieve my keystone from her wretched crown.

Kira closed her eyes. She couldn't respond to Lillian, lest Vylia think she'd lost her mind.

All she could do to give a negative answer was to glare at the Malo stone where it sat on the dresser. Hopefully that would communicate to Lillian that Kira wasn't gullible or stupid enough to steal Brooke's headdress.

"Are you all right?" Vylia placed a hand on Kira's arm, jolting her from her brooding.

Kira tried to remember how to smile. Vylia's eyes were still puffy from tears, and Sousuke sat like a broken statue in the far corner. After that horrifying letter the courier had delivered, the last thing they needed was their new translator declaring that she'd heard a sultry voice from a rock encouraging grand larceny.

She couldn't believe Vylia had taken Hiro's news so well. Maybe she had some politician's ability to hide her feelings away until a better time. Maybe she was trying to be strong for Sousuke as he mourned the executions of his family. Maybe she was masterful at hiding her grief or confusion or anger. Or maybe she was just in shock.

"I'm fine," Kira said. "Are you sure there's nothing I can get you?"

"Time." Vylia's smile was faint. She looked from the Malo stone back to Kira. "Are you familiar with that?"

Kira tilted her head. "With what?"

"That stone on the dresser. You've glanced at it more than once," Vylia said. "It's called the Malo stone."

Kira swallowed. Lillian's so-called mirror would be a good distraction topic right now, so she'd jump into it even though she'd have to consider her words carefully. "I'm familiar with it, yes. It's a wonder to behold—I wasn't expecting to see such a treasure in my lifetime. Isn't it said to be the source of power for the Malo element?"

"Yes." Something in Vylia's acute blue gaze hung on Kira's every word. "Are you a wavesinger?"

"No," Kira said. "I've always wanted to be—ever since I saw the dancers at the Moon Festival as a girl. But I'm just a commoner; I don't have enough syn in my blood to practice the element."

"You don't need to be a silverblood to practice," Vylia mused. She glanced at Tekkyn'ashi as he sat near the door, then at Sousuke. Neither appeared to be listening.

She leaned closer to Kira and whispered, "Have you ever heard a voice when you're near the stone?"

Kira's heart kicked like a jackrabbit. "She speaks to you, too?"

Disgust turned Vylia's gentle expression. "Do not listen to a word she says. She is evil."

Kira looked over her shoulder at the opal, but her mind remained quiet aside from her own trepidation. Lillian either couldn't hear them or she'd decided to fall silent.

Something like a scream sounded in the far distance. Kira listened but heard nothing else.

Kira turned back to Vylia and whispered, "What does she say to you? She wants me to steal a gem from the chieftess' headdress."

"She demanded the same of me." Vylia pursed her lips. "If I were a pagan, I'd say she's trapped within the Malo stone and wants the keystone to free herself somehow."

Solace washed over Kira and rained around her with a gentle sense of peace. "I must be a pagan, then. At least if she's trapped inside, she can't hurt us."

Vylia frowned. "She nearly killed me by preventing me from using the Malo element at a dire moment. She meant for me to die for not doing her bidding. She hasn't spoken to me since, so I assume she chose you as her new pet."

Kira felt a sliver of nausea. Perhaps it was good that she wasn't an elementalist after all. "What should we do?" she whispered.

"I will return her to the temple in Maqua." Vylia's face fell. "As soon as circumstances allow . . ."

"Wouldn't it be safer to destroy the stone if she's that dangerous?" Kira said.

I am a goddess, fool. I cannot be harmed. If you will not obey, I will simply find another. You mortals have the lifespan of fleas. It is only a matter of time before one of you accepts my offer of power.

Kira turned and stared at the stone. "If you speak to either of us again, I will take a boat onto the Rift Ocean and cast you into its darkest depths. I wonder if any fleas could hear you there."

Tekkyn glanced over his shoulder and lifted an eyebrow. Kira gave him an innocent look, and he turned back to the door as someone knocked.

The silence in Kira's mind was tentative bliss.

Vylia's eyes were wide. "Did she respond?"

"No. You?"

"No."

"Good." Kira stood and took a sheet from the spare bed. She wrapped the Malo stone in thick layers, careful not to touch the glittering teal surface with her bare skin. She set it back down on the dresser, hoping the barrier would muffle Lillian's ability to see or hear them somehow.

She looked back to Vylia. "Think that'll help?"

Vylia seemed more relaxed as she sat on the bed. "I feel better regardless. We must prevent her from deceiving anyone else."

Kira nodded as the door creaked open behind her. She turned to see

Tekkyn holding it open for Ryon, who rushed to her.

Her joy at seeing him crashed back down as she studied his features. Forehead speckled with sweat. Tight jaw. Eyes darting to the curious imperials.

"What's wrong?" Kira whispered.

"An army is approaching," Ryon said in a low tone. "The empire."

19

LYSANDER

Lysander inhaled the scent of soft mulch from recent rain and enjoyed the gentle breeze that tousled his hair. The blackened treetop spires of Jadenvive had disappeared into the forest hours ago, but the elation of leaving still buoyed his spirits.

He'd never thought he'd leave that city alive.

The only thing that could possibly dampen his joy was that Darkwood prince. Leading Heron to Coriander's camp was a foolhardy security risk for the Emberhawk rebels. The Darkwood had better relations with the Emberhawk than any other tribe, and that could spell trouble for a perceived usurper like Coriander.

Regardless, Lysander didn't have a choice, so he led the group southeast as the sun fell behind the tree line in a burst of orange and pink.

It didn't really worry him—nothing worried him any longer. He was free, and alive, and Brooke would teach him to hear again. With a magic that surpassed his lost ability to hear in the first place.

He could hear Brooke's thoughts every once in a while, even with the little practice he'd managed so far. Not anyone else's, though—he assumed this was because of the aether bond he could sense between them, like a silken thread tying them together with magic of old.

Hopefully he could blame his spying on the bond if Brooke called him on it. He didn't want to accidentally push her any further away than she already was, but after hearing nothing for two years, the resonance of an ethereal voice was intoxicating. He couldn't just *not* listen to her whispers across the bond, whether she meant to send them or not.

The promise of power was invigorating. Better than just something to live for—it was the promise of a new life entirely. And he wouldn't let this one go to waste.

Fun, isn't it?

Lysander pulled on the reins of his xavi. That wasn't Brooke's voice.

He looked around. Brooke's young handmaiden was smirking at him.

Do I look like a handmaiden to you? She snorted as her xavi trotted past his, its scales flashing in the leaf-shadowed light. *Call me Nari.*

Lysander urged his mount forward. *You know thought-speak too?* he wondered.

It's kind of a basic aether skill. Nariellyn glanced back over her shoulder and looked him up and down. *Brooke asked me to assess where your skills with aether are. I think I've heard enough to determine that.*

Heat spread from Lysander's neck to his cheeks. *Your spying isn't welcome.*

Don't like the taste of your own herbs, eh? She raised a thin eyebrow and turned back around, stray tufts of wild hair dancing around her bun with the movement. *Brooke asked me to teach you some basics, too. Obviously your mental shields need some work.*

Lysander glared at the back of her head. *Brooke promised to teach me.*

She said you chose her because she doesn't have a beard. Nariellyn tilted her head, making a show of scratching her chin as her xavi pranced along the road, feathers bouncing on the top of its head. *I don't have a beard.*

Lysander looked over his shoulder at Brooke, whose lips were pressed thin under her hood. Was she aware of this? Maybe Nariellyn was making this up . . .

You're adorable, Nariellyn said. *A wolf on the outside, a pup on the inside.* He could feel her impish grin through the tenor of her thoughts. *I could just tell Brooke what I've heard and explain why you want to learn from her, specifically.*

Lysander gritted his teeth. The prince in him burned to teach her respect, but that wasn't the person he wanted to be. And apparently, this feisty girl could provide a path to his goals as well.

Swallowing his pride felt like swallowing lava. *I would be most appreciative to learn from you.*

Nariellyn twisted around in her saddle to inspect him with wide eyes. After a moment, her grin returned. *All right, handsome.* Her pink and violet xavi slowed to come alongside him, allowing him to regain the lead. *It seems you know how to sense your own aether, and Brooke's thanks to your bond with her. But do you know how to harness it?*

Once, he admitted. *A long time ago.*

No worries—you'll pick it up in no time. It's obvious you're a natural. Nariellyn's spritely gaze seemed admiring, drinking in the sight of him. Annoying, but something he'd grown used to years ago. Although having female attention again felt . . . nice.

The elements are like flares of the sun, and the aether abilities are dark craters of the third moon. Passion coursing through your blood versus whispers in the back of your mind.

Lysander felt like he was a kid again, back in magics class. *I know that; I can feel them both. But the difference between sensing aether and controlling it is like seeing a plume of smoke and trying to grasp it.*

Hmm. Nariellyn scratched her whiskerless chin. *That could be your problem: seeing is simply observing, but feeling is more of a connection. You need to focus on your aether more deeply, then use your will to command it.*

Lysander closed his eyes and breathed in the scent of recent rain. Felt the bouncing of the saddle. Discerned the coil of anxiety in his chest. They should make camp for nightfall soon. Then hit the border by lunch tomorrow.

Perhaps now was not the best opportunity to clear one's mind.

It's all right, Nariellyn said. *Just practice whenever you think about it. No one becomes an aethryn overnight.*

Lysander opened his eyes and corrected his xavi's wandering path. *Thanks.*

Something moved in the underbrush beside the road. Lysander hastily reached for his bow as a gold and white gryphon burst through the tree line.

"Sorrel?" Joy burst through Lysander as he leaped off the xavi and ran between the gryphon and the drawn weapons of Dimbae and Soaring Heron's guard. "It's okay—she's mine!"

The gryphon leaped and raced to Lysander, crouching in a playful stance. Lionlike claws dug into the road as a grin seemed to break across her beak. The tuft of her tail twitched in the air like a frisky cat's. If house cats were the size of horses.

Lysander tackled her in a furry hug. "Were you here the whole time, you rascal? You should have gone back to Granny Zelle's!"

Sorrel's mane bristled, her feathers standing on end. Golden eyes stared pointedly at his xavi.

"Aww, don't be jealous, girl. He was awful." Lysander rubbed behind her ears. "Worst mount ever. Bumpy and scaly and dumb as a slug."

The gryphon flopped onto her back in a flurry of feathers and tossed about happily.

I assume it's tame? Brooke's voice flitted through his mind as she hopped down from her saddle and stretched.

"Very," Lysander said as he petted Sorrel's belly. "For me, at least."

Soaring Heron said something as he rubbed his lower back, and Dimbae slid from his alpha xavi to lumber off into the woods.

We should make camp for the night, Brooke said. *Dimbae will find a spot for us far enough from the road. Bandits may have grown bold in light of recent events.*

Lysander nodded while Sorrel purred, sending familiar vibrations through the sound waves around him. He nuzzled into her fur and didn't care to hide his affection and contentment. He'd raised the gryphon since she was a clumsy, fluffy chick, and now she was a graceful and intimidating presence more than double his size. How many years had it been?

Her adoring faithfulness had helped him survive Zamara's abuse and the loss of his hearing. The great beast didn't understand or care that he couldn't hear any more. She was a constant source of joy and love, oblivious to the troubles of the world and utterly carefree.

With her at his side again, everything suddenly seemed better.

A flash of light from the forest caught Lysander's eye. He thought he saw a pair of glowing green eyes before they vanished behind a shadowed birch.

Felix?

20

VYLIA

Vylia opened her eyes, but it only invited her pounding heartbeat to join the cacophony.

Not again.

The screaming grew louder. Closer. Sounds of battle reverberated through the Great Hall's thick fortifications.

It was like she should have died in the fires, but had awoken to a living nightmare instead. Nothing seemed true—only real enough to be horrifying.

"Let me out," Ryon said to the guards, who'd moved inside the room for cover and barred the door.

"No," said a man whose blue mask bore more intricate markings than the other.

"I bear the chief's seal." Ryon showed a signet ring on his hand, but the guards didn't look. Didn't respond.

Sousuke paced from the guards to the window and back again, his hand on his sword hilt.

"Sit down," Vylia ordered for the third time in as many minutes. "You're wasting the little strength you have."

Again, he ignored her.

"The chieftess gave me her authority until she returns," Ryon said. "Stand aside! I need my bow."

"Brooke's gone?" Kira blurted.

The masked men glanced at each other. "Our authority surpasses the chief's in combat situations," one of them said. "Since you are now in leadership, you will not be permitted to engage the enemy."

Ryon chuffed. "What if the enemy *does* permit it? I need my weapon!" He switched to the Phoeran language but got no response.

Thick silence flooded the room as the sounds outside drew nearer. Cries of pain. Shouts of command. Thundering footsteps.

The guards exchanged another glance.

Vylia couldn't remain on her bed any longer. She stood with effort, and Sousuke jumped to her side to hold her arm. He looked barely able to support his own weight, yet his grip was steady and firm.

"Did Brooke make it out of the city?" Vylia asked, breathless.

The guards either didn't hear her or didn't respond, but they'd seemed to understand the Malaano she'd spoken before.

She took a deep breath and asked again, channeling her desperation into her voice. "Is Brooke safe?"

"We believe so," one of the guards murmured. "Don't worry, Your Highness. She assigned her own guard to you before she left. We are the most elite warriors among the tribes, and there are more of us than you can see. I swear by the creator, we will keep you safe."

"That's not my concern." Vylia closed her eyes and gripped Sousuke's arm tighter. "They're here for me. Give me over to them, and your city will be—"

"No," Sousuke snapped. "They think you're dead. They're here to take the city. Like vultures."

"They are our people," Vylia whispered. "If I reveal myself, they'll stop this madness."

"You know that's not true. You heard Aoko." Sousuke tapped the bandage on his wounded shoulder, where the traitor's blade had pierced. "I'm sorry, Vy, but your father wants you dead."

His words cut into her, and yet she felt numb. Her gut said he was right, but her heart said she should do everything in her power to stop the sounds of suffering.

They'd already lost too much.

"It's worth the risk," she said.

"Your sacrifice would accomplish nothing," Kira said before Sousuke could retort. She knelt to catch Vylia's downturned gaze. "We have all been assigned to protect and help you, and that's what we're going to do."

"This is my fault." Vylia squeezed her eyes shut against a sudden overflow of tears. "Can't you hear it? People are dying because of me."

"No," Sousuke said. He took her arm and drew her close as if to emphasize his words with the distance between them. "Because of the emperor."

His voice hadn't sounded like that before. Deep and ravenous.

Vylia shrank back but he held her gently. Wiped away her tears.

She'd just wanted to go on a simple diplomatic mission. To help end the hostilities. To make her father proud.

She should never have left the palace.

Sousuke shifted in front of her. His green eyes bored into hers. "I'm taking charge now."

Vylia blinked up at him. He'd always taken orders from her. "What?"

The door creaked open behind Sousuke, and a new voice spoke in hushed tones. Vylia looked to Kira for translation.

"The Hall has been breached," Kira translated, her eyes wide. "They're going to extract us to a safer place."

Fear knifed into Vylia's stomach. Hadn't Brooke said the Great Hall was the most secure location in Jadenvive?

Sousuke grabbed her hand as the group filed out of the room and down the hall. His other hand held his sword.

The world began to tilt, then slowly spin. She wasn't prepared for this. Even if her body felt stronger, she wasn't ready.

She wanted to ask where they were going but decided to save her breath and focus on her steps. Through a locked door. Along a dark passageway. Down a stairway with steep steps. Wooden stairs that seemed carved from the walls themselves—lines in the wood flowed down from one wall, through two or three stairs diagonally, then up the opposite wall.

It spiraled down in a barely perceptible arc. And seemed to never end.

Sweat permeated Vylia's gown and dripped into her eye. She gasped for breath. "I . . . I need—"

Sousuke sheathed his sword, picked her up, and carefully continued the descent.

She clung to his shoulders and rested her head on his breastplate. How could he have so much strength when they'd gone through the same ordeal? He'd also taken Aoko's sword to the shoulder. Nariellyn must have healed it with her magic somehow. Still, Vylia made note of his bandage and avoided it.

Fifty steps? Seventy-five? She lost count. It grew colder the further down they went.

Her breath wouldn't return. Sousuke began to pant. Vylia tried to put her feet on the ground, but he held her tight.

The azure masks ahead suddenly stopped as the stairway brightened. They muttered something in Phoeran that Vylia didn't understand, but she didn't need to comprehend their language to know it wasn't good.

"Let me down," Vylia said. "I can walk now."

Sousuke acquiesced after a moment's hesitation. He set her down and drew his sword carefully in the tight quarters. "Stay close."

Vylia found Kira behind her. A worried expression hung from her dark face, but her blue eyes sparked in the luminescence of mushrooms hanging from planters embedded into the walls. The air hung thick with humidity.

"What are they saying?" Vylia whispered.

"Ryon has a safe place for us," Kira translated. "The masks are going to make us invisible and silent while we run. You won't be able to see or hear anything—covering a group takes a lot of concentration, so they'll only be able to focus on allowing their own eyes and ears to be exempt from the magic. So we're going to have to hang on and trust them as we follow, okay?"

The proposition sounded terrifying to Vylia, but she nodded.

"Stay behind me." Sousuke took her hand as the world snapped into darkness.

Vylia gasped but couldn't hear it. She brought her hand up but couldn't see it. She touched her cracked lips just to ensure her fingers were still there.

Sousuke tugged at her, and she rushed forward while clinging to him with the little strength she had left. The earth was a void, but somehow it still existed beneath her feet. The floor gave way to something softer. Soil, perhaps?

The combination of terror and helplessness was beyond what she'd ever felt. She called for the Malo element in a plea for some form of security, but her senses didn't even tingle with recognition of the power in her blood.

Vylia cursed Lillian's stone in its embroidered pouch. She'd been in training to become a wavesinger from childhood, but not even water answered her call for aid any longer.

Sound suddenly burst back to her ears as someone jerked her aside— Sousuke? She stumbled into whoever it was as the sound of a grunt and the clash of metal split the air. A sword fight? She still couldn't see!

A strong grip on her wrist pulled faster than Vylia could run. She fell and bit down on a cry. Her knees sank into something cool and wet.

Strong arms lifted her, and she recognized Sousuke by the musky scent of his armor polish. She jostled in his grasp as he ran.

She gripped his armor until her fingers clenched up. A tear slipped down her cheek. *Gods spare us!*

Light blinded her as her vision blared back into focus. She squinted as the sounds of battle clashed behind her. She craned her neck to look past Sousuke's arm as he dashed to follow Tekkyn'ashi and Ryon. Kira followed behind, wielding a strange blue blade that looked more like some kind of animal's stinger than a knife.

Two azure masks fought a crowd of soldiers in gleaming armor. Flashing swords. Clashing shields. Cerulean tabards. The white lotus smeared with mud and splattered with scarlet.

Vylia's bones chilled at the sight, rendering her stiff and frigid from the inside out.

They were running away from them. Her own people. The symbol that had always represented security now pined for her blood.

Sousuke took a sharp left and slammed into the bark of the great tree. His panting sounded shallow, desperate. Vylia pushed away from him again, and this time he didn't resist as she took her own feet.

Tekkyn'ashi gave quick orders, and Ryon translated: "You're all Malo by blood. Sousuke will say he's escorting Malaano citizens to safety. I'll stay hidden. Follow my footsteps." He vanished from sight before he'd finished speaking.

Vylia tried to slow her breathing and maintain her balance as footsteps squished in the mud before them. Sousuke once again drew his sword and brandished it in his right hand while reaching back for Vylia with his left. They lurched forward, following Ryon's trail as Kira took the rear.

Platoons of soldiers swarmed Jadenvive's underbelly and choked the elevators. Vylia stole a glance at the main road leading to a massive gate that stood open. Twin catapults stood taller than the far walls. How had they managed to slip such machines and such a force through the forest undetected?

One soldier eyed them. Then another. She lost count. But they never spared more than a glance before continuing toward the elevators, or to a skirmish in the pepper field, or to a barn being stuffed with terrified civilians and crying children.

Vylia's tears swelled and blurred her vision as she staggered forward.

Sousuke released his grip. "I'm sorry, I—"

"It's okay," Vylia whispered.

"Here," Kira said.

Vylia wiped her eyes as Tekkyn'ashi and Sousuke stood on either side of a hole beneath a giant birch's root. Kira ducked inside, and Vylia followed.

Ryon reappeared in the root tunnel before them, knife bared. He quickly sheathed it as a silver-haired woman ran to him and hugged him tight. They exchanged hushed words in Phoeran, then the woman waved them hurriedly down the tunnel. Ryon rushed back to the entrance with a spyglass in-hand. He passed by them and vanished out the way they'd just come.

"Don't stop," Tekkyn'ashi said as he jogged forward to follow the woman, his sword still drawn. "This grows into an extensive cave network. We'll be safer further in."

Sousuke nodded at Vylia, then followed with his own weapon, daring anything else to enter.

"What's Ryon doing?" Vylia asked.

"He was a scout before he was the advisor. He'll be okay," Kira said, though her face was at least one shade lighter.

The path through the caverns never seemed to end. Vylia was certain she'd meet her death if she lost her way without a guide, both from exhaustion and delirium. Her body had never before felt so weak. Her knees threatened to give out at any moment, as did her frantic heart.

From a palace to a treetop suite to a dreary cave. From her own troop of bodyguards to foreign strangers she didn't know. From the darling of her people to a sacrificial pawn.

She stumbled and Kira caught her.

"Whoa, it's okay." Kira offered a faint smile. "I know it must be hard but you're doing great. You can rest soon."

Vylia did her best to return the smile as Sousuke thanked Kira. "This place is beautiful," she said, trying desperately to focus on anything else. The same glowing mushrooms from the spiral staircase lined the cave walls in droves, creating flowing lines of aquamarine light.

Sousuke stumbled and caught himself on one knee.

"Are you injured?" Vylia rushed to him but he waved her away.

"Fine. Just . . . tripped," he panted.

An obvious lie. The bandage on his shoulder was stained red, and the sweat that soaked the cloth between his armor plates was too profuse for the chilly underground air. But Vylia knew he'd say the same thing if his leg had been bitten off if it would make her feel safe.

"Let's rest here," Tekkyn'ashi said, but the silver-haired woman said something in Phoeran and beckoned him around a bend.

The cavern opened up into a large space with a clear stream whose waters reflected the phosphorescence of countless mushrooms. Several children splashed in the water with shrieks of delight, apparently oblivious to the horrors above.

Two of the little ones ran to Tekkyn'ashi and hugged him tight, drenching his clothes. He sheathed his sword with great care and hugged them back.

Vylia stared in disbelief as Kira spoke with another tribal woman, then turned back to her with relief lifting her features. "These are Ryon's mother and sister. They care for these orphans, and they all got here to safety with some supplies." She gestured to a bedroll that the older woman laid out on a smooth patch of stone opposite from the stream. "I told her you two are recovering from comas. You can rest here."

"Thank you." Vylia's voice came out like a squeak. She motioned for Sousuke to lay down first, but he just stared at her until she did so instead.

Her body ached as she lay down on the soft leathers, and Ryon's mother laid a soft quilt over her with a broad smile. "Gwyneth," she enunciated as she tapped her chest.

"Thank you, Gwyneth," Vylia said, hoping she'd understand. "I am Prin . . ." She trailed off. "Vylia."

Gwyneth nodded and retreated, shushing the children and speaking with Kira in hushed tones.

Sousuke stretched out beside Vylia on his own bedroll, and it wasn't long before his breathing evened out. Vylia willed her numbed mind to calm as her body relaxed. Her thoughts swirled but didn't go anywhere, like a stormcloud that threatened with thunder but never rained.

She felt herself slipping into sleep as Ryon returned with a grim expression. He spoke softly to Kira and hugged her tight.

Vylia waved Kira over and whispered, "What did he see?"

Kira appeared to be on the verge of tears. "The Great Hall is lost," she murmured. "The empire now controls Jadenvive."

21

BROOKE

Brooke spun and slashed her spear down, then pulled back before the bone tip could slam into the ground. She twisted and stabbed the cool morning air behind her, finishing the *kata* with a controlled exhale.

Her footprints in the dew marked her path through the lazy grass of the clearing she'd chosen for practice. The footwork wasn't bad, but not being able to make any noise threw off her regular pattern. And it wasn't nearly as fun without being able to hit anything.

She took a deep breath and closed her eyes, inhaling the pure scents of the forest. Being physically removed from so many of her problems gave her a relief that she felt guilty about. Just because she wasn't near the source of her issues didn't mean they didn't exist. But not being able to do anything about it was freeing, somehow. For now.

Brooke opened her eyes and decided to practice a different technique for another round. Her party should begin to wake soon, and she had no desire to end this moment of peace any faster than she needed to.

"Remind me not to get on your bad side."

Brooke spun and thrust her spear in the direction of the voice. Lysander leaned against a distant tree, raising his hands innocently.

She swallowed and lowered her weapon. *You're an early riser,* she thought to him. She glanced in the direction of the sun. It was just beginning to peek through the trees, tickling the bottoms of scattered clouds with swaths of orange and pink.

Lysander crossed his arms over his dark leather armor. "I thought everyone agreed that you weren't going to take a watch."

Brooke turned to begin her next *kata*, spreading her feet into a ready stance. *I let Nari sleep.*

"Does she know that?"

Brooke harrumphed and thrust her spear forward. She didn't answer.

Lysander didn't say anything, either.

She focused on the motions, trying to ignore his presence. Spin, sweep, slash. Left, forward, duck, right, backward, stab.

Brooke glanced at Lysander as she finished. He just stood there, watching.

You're kinda creepy, you know that? she thought to him.

His brow furrowed. "Sorry. I didn't sense that you felt nervous or uncomfortable."

Brooke cursed under her breath and called for aether to protect her mind. *Spying on my thoughts is even more creepy.*

"Isn't that your favorite pastime?" he said.

Brooke pursed her lips and thumped the end of her spear into the ground. *Can I help you with something?*

"You've already done that."

Her pulse thudded harder than it had from the *kata*. She grasped for something to say that wouldn't directly order him away. She was on a break from ordering people around.

Lysander pushed off from the tree and flexed his hands, testing the fingerless elementalist gloves he must have requisitioned from the quartermaster. "I can remove the sound if you want to practice properly. Pulling your strikes isn't healthy."

Brooke opened her mouth to decline but paused. That would be really nice, actually. And it was kind of him to offer—sound manipulation was a high-level Phoeran art far beyond her ability. Perhaps it wasn't so difficult for a royal silverblood like him. His maroon eyes seemed to glow softly in the fading darkness as dawn crept closer. He must have held a great amount of syn.

She cleared her throat and stood straighter. *All right.*

He nodded.

Brooke assumed her ready stance and began again, this time with her favorite drill. She glanced in the direction of their camp and hesitantly struck the earth with her spear.

It made no sound.

She stepped awkwardly as her footfalls were deathly silent. Her breathing muted, and the chirping of distant insects fell quiet. She spun and slammed her weapon on the ground again. The grass quivered, dew scattered in every direction, and the sensation of the impact travelled through her boots, but not so much as a whisper reached her ears.

So strange. And yet instead of feeling fear as she thought she should, overwhelming calm flooded her as she flowed through the movements. No hustle and bustle of the city. No voices demanding or accusing or whispering their own manipulations. No thoughts of her own anxiety plaguing her like a flock of birds constantly diving to peck at her flesh.

Just her and her weapon.

Brooke controlled her breathing as she whirled and struck. As blissful as the silence was, she couldn't imagine being trapped in it forever. Was this what Lysander experienced every day, never able to escape?

She finished the *kata* and couldn't stop a smile. *Thank you,* she thought to him.

He smirked. "Any time."

Brooke relished the chill of the morning breeze on her skin as she started toward their campsite. The recent rains must have broken the last of the summer heat. Harvest season was already here. She wondered how many of Jadenvive's burned fields would be salvageable, then tried to shove the thought away. Worrying about it wouldn't do any good.

"Why Darkwood?"

Brooke stopped and looked back over her shoulder. *What?*

Lysander stared down at the vials that slung from his shoulder to his waist in a bandoleer. "It appears that an alliance with Emberhawk would be more beneficial to the Katrosi than Darkwood."

She turned back and tilted her head. *Both are important if any of us are to survive a Malaano incursion. Why?*

"I don't have to use thought-magic to tell that you hate him."

Brooke balked at Lysander. Was he serious? Could he possibly be jealous?

What are you implying?

"Just that you could consider other options. You don't hate me any more, do you?" Lysander looked up at her with those dark eyes. "We both know how we feel, so it would be childish not to address it."

Brooke's throat clenched until she was out of breath again. She strove to remember her father's training. Show no emotion—give the opposition nothing to take advantage of.

We also both know that political alliances are not made based on feelings.

Lysander nodded. "But if you have the choice, why wouldn't you?"

The choice has already been made. The color of Brooke's knuckles lightened from her grip on her spear. She focused and willed her body to relax. *It seems you're not on friendly terms with Illiana, so your marriage might not have any political benefit, anyway.*

"Of course I'm friendly with my sister! And I'm still the firstborn son of King Brynn. You know that carries weight regardless of who's on the throne."

Brooke pursed her lips. *I asked the queen for your hand months ago, but you were too busy doing her dirty work.*

Lysander flinched. "I . . ." He seemed to notice something, or perhaps a new thought occurred to him. His voice wavered. "Zamara is dead. Things are different now."

Yes, they are. My city lies in ashes and my people would revolt if I married one of the arsonists. Brooke turned and stomped toward camp without waiting for his response.

So what if she'd rather marry Lysander than Heron? It was like having to choose between soggy bread or molded bread.

Lysander was disconnected from reality if he thought she could break a signed marriage alliance contract with no repercussions just because she felt like it. But then again, he'd grown up a spoiled prince, so he was probably used to getting whatever he wanted just by asking.

Brooke nearly walked face-first into Heron as he stepped out from behind a tree.

He didn't look at her—he was glaring at something behind her. "What were you doing out alone in the woods with *him?*"

She gaped up at Heron as her heart kicked like a trapped rabbit. "I was just practicing with my spear. I haven't been able to in weeks."

Heron sidestepped around her and marched toward Lysander.

"Aish, don't assume!" Brooke said as she followed Heron, but he ignored her.

Lysander didn't move as Heron moved in close. "I know you can't hear me, you point-eared disgrace," Heron growled, "so I'm going to have to make this clear enough for you to understand." His words grew slow and emphatic. *"Stay away from my fiancée."*

Lysander looked down on him with cool nonchalance. "How embarrassing to feel threatened by a point-eared disgrace."

Heron's nostrils flared, and Brooke thrust the butt of her spear between them. "Stop."

"It's dishonorable and inappropriate for you two to be alone out here, and you know it." Heron turned his fiery gaze on Brooke. "I'm beginning to think you're untrustworthy, Chieftess."

"I was only here to protect her as a bodyguard," Lysander said. "You're welcome."

Heron twitched. "He's a guard?"

It took all of Brooke's composure not to react. She'd never asked Lysander to be a bodyguard, had she? No. That might be the height of foolishness. Although he *had* saved her life.

"I asked him to help Dimbae just for this trip. Since we need to keep the headcount low, I left my other azure mask in Jadenvive to make room for you and your guard," she lied. Well, it was only a half-lie. Anything to prevent these two from fighting and further soiling relations between the tribes.

Heron snorted and backed away from Lysander, then stomped toward the camp.

Brooke released a silent breath. She avoided Lysander's gaze as she chased after Heron.

"I command you to stay away from him," Heron said.

"You're not my husband yet," Brooke said, "and I won't take kindly to unnecessary demands even when you are. I am not one of your servants."

Heron clenched his fists. "Where I come from, a man leads and his wife follows."

"Where I come from, a man leads with integrity and strength and love, and his wife follows out of respect and honor."

Heron stayed quiet for a long moment, and Brooke wished she could see his expression as she walked behind. The muscles of his shoulders seemed tense beneath his tattoos.

"I want all of those things for us—it is not my desire for you to obey me out of fear or demands. I recognize that you are a stalwart woman and a leader." He gave her a sidelong look and smiled. "I look forward to taming you."

Brooke admired Sorrel as the gryphon pranced along the road, leading the group with Lysander bare-back as if he weighed nothing. Her golden feathers and white fur reminded Brooke of the great eagles she'd seen as a little girl on a diplomatic mission to Valinor with her father.

Sorrel was as happy as a puppy. Brooke wondered what it must feel like to be so carefree. The beast probably didn't even worry about its next meal, whereas Brooke had temporarily escaped the pressures of leadership only to have two unworthy princes barking at each other over her.

She tugged the reins to the side, and her xavi trotted closer to Nariellyn's. *Hey,* she called through thought-speak to evade eavesdroppers.

Nariellyn glanced at her with a bored look. *My butt is so sore. I hate you.*

Brooke barely contained a laugh. *You must not have ridden in a while.*

Nariellyn faced forward and jutted her bottom lip out. *And I'm hungry.*

By the skies, you're a child. Brooke fished into her pack and withdrew a honey drop. *Here.*

Nariellyn enlivened as she snatched the candy and popped it in her mouth. *Maybe you're not so bad after all.*

Brooke rolled her eyes. *I have an aether question for you.*

Nari grew an impish smile, displaying sharp white teeth. *I offer consulting at five honey drops per question.*

Brooke glanced over her shoulder to see Dimbae, Soaring Heron, and his guard trailing behind. *Did Master ever teach you how to sever an aether bond?*

Nariellyn's brows knit together as she studied Brooke. *You know I just kid around—*

I don't want to cut our bond, goober. She looked away and sat up straighter as she bounced in the saddle. *Just wondering if such a thing is possible.*

Nariellyn glanced from her to Lysander and back again. *You should be asking how to sever a marriage alliance agreement.*

Brooke pursed her lips. *Obviously that's not possible unless I want to damage relations with Darkwood when we need them the most.*

Cool, so just sell out the rest of your life for more troops. Nariellyn held out a hand expectantly. *Idiot.*

You think I'm happy about this? Brooke handed over a second honey drop. *I don't have the luxury of marrying for love like you do—I've known that since I was five. So if it keeps everyone alive, yeah, I'll make that trade.*

So you love him? Nariellyn waggled her eyebrows. *I knew you'd grow a heart eventually.*

Brooke strengthened her mental shields before Lysander could sense her irritation or Nariellyn could sense too much. *Obviously not. Do you know how to sever an aether bond or not?*

He's like ten times hotter than Heron. Like an elemental in human form, but better!

You would marry a frog if you thought it were attractive enough.

I mean, sure, if it also had a dragon's stash of rupero *and a really nice house.* Nari grinned and held her hand out again.

Brooke ignored it. *Answer my question.*

Nariellyn shrugged. *You think I can sever an aether bond if even time can't? There's probably a way out there to do it, but I've never heard of it.* She wiggled her fingers.

Brooke bit the inside of her lip and absentmindedly handed over another candy as their mounts plodded along beside each other. She'd hoped that her confusion about Lysander—and whatever that irritating mass of feelings was—originated from that old bond. If she couldn't get rid of it, was she bound to feel . . . *something* for another man even after she was wed to Heron?

At least she could put distance between herself and Lysander after this monarchy drama was dealt with. He'd probably live in the palace of Quin'Zamar once his brother took the throne, and she'd be able to forget him over time.

Right?

For some reason, she wasn't confident. Emotions in general were foreign to her. They showed up every once in a while like a burglar and held her heart ransom. A ransom she never knew how to pay.

Seriously though, I think you'll be miserable with Heron. Nariellyn's thought-voice had lost its glimmer. *He strikes me as a really rotten person. If you find any way out, you should take it.*

Brooke gathered herself and set her jaw. *They're both rotten.*

Lysander was *rotten. Heron is presently rotten. There's a big difference.*

Brooke watched Nariellyn from the corner of her eye. *Wouldn't it be better to choose someone not rotten if I had the choice? Like my second fiancé?*

Everyone is rotten. It's just a matter of how much decay you can smell on them. Nariellyn leaned forward into the feathered crown of her xavi. *You can probably sense a lot more about Lysander than I can because of that bond. But you must trust him to some degree to ask him to come along.*

Brooke closed her eyes and released a deep breath. *Look, I know you're right, but I don't have the pleasure of choice. If only the timing . . .*

Nariellyn gave her a loaded look with a mischievous smile. *I was right about more than one thing, yeah?*

Brooke narrowed her eyes at her. *It doesn't matter.* She flicked another honey drop for her friend to catch.

She yanked the reins sideways, urging her reptilian mount to the side of the road. "Hold!" she called aloud.

Lysander glanced back, then patted Sorrel's neck and murmured soft noises to her. The gryphon swung around and trotted toward Brooke as the rest of the group gathered around.

"We should be nearing the border," Brooke said, glancing up and down the road. "I'd rather not deal with the guards on either side of the bridge, so let's cross the river. Downstream, in case the current steals something."

Sorrel stretched her wingspan wide with a yawn as Lysander nodded. The group followed Brooke as she veered from the road and forged a path through the trees.

Judging by the sound of rapids, the river wasn't far. Brooke dismounted as she approached the bank and gazed over the glistening water.

She couldn't see the bridge, so it couldn't see them. Perfect.

A sudden gust of wind flurried her braids as Sorrel took flight and landed on the opposite side of the river. She stared as Lysander sat up straight on his gryphon's elegant back and patted her feathered mane.

I know what I want for the next Festival of the Gifted King, Brooke thought. Gryphons were native to Valinor, but maybe she could pull some strings.

Brooke sighed and trudged down an embankment, slickened from recent rain. Her xavi snorted but followed as she tugged on the reins. She uttered soothing noises as she climbed back into the saddle and urged it into the waters. The beast splashed forward on two thick legs, then sank into a slither, waving its fan of tail feathers back and forth through the deep current.

One by one the mounts made it to the other side, and just like that, they'd crossed into the Emberhawk Sovereignty.

"Not another step!"

Brooke cringed and slowly turned toward the sound of the unfamiliar voice. It came from the direction of the bridge.

Two men clad in gold and ruby regalia bore the symbol of the monarchy: a phoenix with outstretched wings. Emberhawk royal guards. They approached slowly with bows drawn and aimed.

"You're under arrest," one of them called. "Put your hands above your heads."

"Sheath your weapons," Lysander said as he rounded Sorrel between the Emberhawk and Brooke's entourage. "Don't you recognize me?"

The guards' eyes went wide and their bows lowered. "Prince Lysander!" They each took a knee and bowed their heads. "Why didn't you approach at the border crossing, sir?"

Brooke gripped her reins so tight that her palms hurt. She translated through thought-speak for Lysander, since he probably couldn't read their lips with their faces downturned.

Lysander gestured to the group behind him, his travel cloak billowing with the movement. "I've brought new slaves. The Katrosi would not have allowed me passage, as slavery is illegal in their land."

Brooke followed the guard's gaze over each one of them and landed on Soaring Heron, who looked like anything but a slave with his proud countenance and disgusted expression.

What was the chance of them recognizing Heron? Or their chance of recognizing *her?*

She cursed herself for not having her hood up. Lifting it now would raise suspicion.

"Ah." The guards returned to their feet. "Welcome home, Your Majesty.

Shall we send word to the queen that you've returned?"

"Please," Lysander said. He squinted through the forest as if searching for something. "How secure is the road to Quin'Zamar? I've heard rumors of bandits."

"Allow me to send for an escort for you, sir."

"Very well." Lysander's voice sounded different somehow. Detached, perhaps . . . like it'd sounded when Brooke had first seen him in prison. He dismounted and stretched.

Brooke's stomach knotted. What was he doing?

The guards bowed and turned to march back in the direction of the bridge.

She didn't hear Lysander's movements as he reached into his belt with one hand and drew a dagger with the other. His footsteps were silent as he rushed the guards. Shot one with a blowgun and stabbed the other in the back.

Sound returned as the men crumpled to the ground.

A strangled gasp clawed from Brooke's throat. He'd moved faster than she could react. Horrifyingly fast.

"Why did you do that?" she cried, jumping from her xavi's saddle. She rushed to the fallen men to determine if they were dead, then wished she hadn't.

"They would have told Illiana about us," Lysander said as he pulled a dart from one guard's neck.

Brooke looked away from the Emberhawks' frozen agonized expressions before she lost her breakfast. "Couldn't you have told them not to? They were submissive to you!"

"I couldn't have trusted their word. And it would have raised suspicion." Lysander uncorked his waterskin and poured the clear liquid over his bloodied blade. "Not worth the risk."

Brooke balked at his nonchalance. "They were *your* people!"

Lysander wasn't watching her lips. "Hmm?"

Brooke gritted her teeth and sent him a thought: *They were your people!*

"They were Illiana's, and Zamara's before that."

They were Emberhawk—your own blood!

"The weight of a human life is always the same regardless."

She stormed up to Lysander and planted herself in front of him, glaring up into his maroon gaze. *This is my mission.* She sent her aether with enough force to stagger any mind.

His eyes narrowed. "You're in my land now. Risking the lives of my brother. My sister. My father's throne. I won't take any chances."

Brooke balled her hands into fists. *You will not kill anyone else without my permission. Understand?*

"Everybody dies, Chieftess. It's just a matter of when." Lysander's eyes sparked with a fire that reminded her of Ryon, but darker. Colder. "I'll do whatever I deem necessary to keep you safe."

His thought-voice brushed against her shields, amateurish and weak, yet strong in tone. *I'm one of your guards now, remember?*

"Well that was fun," Soaring Heron said as his xavi strode by. He looked down his nose at the bodies. "But if you ever refer to me as a slave again, your death won't be as swift."

Lysander appeared to ignore Heron, whether or not he could read his lips.

Brooke tried to swallow her bundle of frustration to no avail. Pride throbbed like a bruise in her chest. *It's true that we're in Emberhawk territory now. But we're working together on this, right?*

He studied her for a long moment as he wiped a cloth over his dagger. "Right."

She sighed and rubbed her eyes. *Please respect me in this, and I will try to respect you as well.*

Lysander's gaze deepened. Softened. Saddened. "As you say." He sheathed his blade and mounted Sorrel, who chirped happily.

Brooke tasted something foul. She'd forgotten his true nature.

He was a killer.

22

KIRALAU

Kira tipped the wooden bowl in her hand and watched water swirl around its edge. Access to clean water would quickly become a problem.

She glanced up at the cavern wall illuminated by flickering torchlight. Water trickled from ferns that clung to the rock, either sliding down the slick, rippling stone or bowing lacy fronds with each drip.

The amount that flowed in wasn't enough to create much of a current for the underground pool below, which was outlined with soft moss. Not nearly enough water to provide for the needs of the dozens of people who huddled in the large but crowded cave behind her.

Kira stacked the three bowls and moved to where Tekkyn attempted to cook without fire—smoke would have caused an even greater problem without ventilation. Instead, a teenage Phoeran elementalist kept the dented pot warm enough to simmer Tekkyn's culinary creation.

"You're getting compliments," Kira said as she held out the first bowl.

"That's a shock." Tekkyn poured steaming stew into the bowl with a silver ladle that didn't match the rest of his hodgepodge cooking equipment. "Whoever heard of chili without beef or pork?" he muttered.

"It's *so* good, Mister Chocolate!" The slate-haired orphan named Mayla beamed a smile from across the empty space.

Kira shushed her with a finger to her lips as she grinned. "People are trying to sleep," she whispered.

Mayla puckered her lips and mouthed, "Oops!" before returning to a game of rock organizing played by the younger kids.

Tekkyn sighed as he handed Kira the bowl. "Guess life ain't much different for them, at least."

Kira nodded as she watched the older children giggle and snicker softly amongst themselves as they searched for tiny aquatic salamanders in the pool. She wondered if Gwyneth had told them what had transpired above. That the city they knew was gone. Stolen by a greedy empire that had no claim to it.

How many people had been killed? Or were the Malaano wanting to keep the citizens alive? Perhaps to enslave them, or to take the product of their labor, or to subjugate them with high taxes?

She closed her eyes and took a deep breath, then regretted it. The smells of terrified, trapped people weren't pleasant.

Creator protect him, she prayed.

If Ryon didn't return soon to lead another group to escape through the root-tunnels' exit in the forest far from here, she didn't know what they'd do. The twisting series of caves were a labyrinth that would spell death for anyone who didn't know the way. Only an experienced scout with a dagger-sharp memory had a chance of navigating it without getting hopelessly lost in the black depths.

Ryon was the only candidate for the job. But with Brooke gone and no vice, he was third in line to rule the Katrosi tribe. Interim chief. At the worst possible time.

People had already begun asking Ryon questions that made his eyes as wide as eggs, so he would disappear—literally—and return with information the masks could use to outsmart, avoid, and resist the oppressors.

Except there was no resistance. The tribesmen were weak—first because of drought, then the Emberhawks' arson, and now this. Many had nothing left.

Kira bit the inside of her cheek and urged herself to stay strong. They would survive this, just like they'd survived everything else. Aeo had already provided a safe haven in this very same cave Ryon had planned their last date in. She could still vividly recall the sky paint he'd made in radiant lights above the crystalline waters.

Now the space was huddled with homeless people in shock and mourning. Some gazes full of horror, others dead and blank. They just wanted to get out of this cursed city, some said. The Jade Witch's curse had spread to Jadenvive itself.

She had to be strong for them. Joyful for the children. Reassuring for the traumatized. Trusting for Ryon. Hopeful for his return, because she refused to imagine any alternative.

A shout of joy sounded from the lookout at the cave's entrance, and Kira nearly dropped the second bowl as Tekkyn filled it. She craned her neck for a better view, stretching the scar from Zamara's hand she hadn't yet grown accustomed to.

An azure mask stepped through the breach—one of the few Katrosi combatants who'd survived. Behind him was a man of stature with an unfamiliar face, followed by a second azure. Kira's spirit leapt as Ryon emerged, looking dead on his feet.

He no longer wore the small gray cloak on one shoulder that bore the five-pointed star of the Tribal Alliance. The other man bore it instead.

Kira's gut knotted as the people cheered—loud enough to possibly compromise their location, even so far underground.

The man with Ryon's cloak bowed as Ryon stepped forward and raised his voice. "We still have not found Brooke, but she offered Ulysses the position of vice before the invasion. He accepts it now!"

"At your service." Ulysses's bow dipped lower as he fell to one knee. "Strength and humility. Justice and mercy. Discipline and joy. Between great sacrifice and great love shines the creator's glory."

The echoing cheer made Kira certain they'd all be caught. But considering the drastic change in the atmosphere, perhaps it was worth it. Life returned to the defeated as swiftly as a rising gasp from deep waters.

Kira glanced at the twin piles of furs where Vylia and Sousuke still slept soundly. The teen elementalist sitting nearby gave her a goofy grin and a thumbs-up.

Is he preventing them from hearing the noise? Kira wondered. Either the teen was really talented or he just wanted to impress her and got lucky—the princess and her guardian were so exhausted and weak they probably could have slept through a harpy attack. Regardless, Kira smiled back and nodded her thanks.

"I will only assume the chiefdom until Brooke can be found," Ulysses said as the people gathered around him. "There is another holdout in the merchant's quarter. I will be moving back and forth between these two locations, coordinating . . ."

Kira tuned him out as Ryon caught her gaze and headed in her direction. She set the forgotten bowls of chili down and hugged him tight as he crashed into her.

"Thank Aeo you're safe," she muffled into his leather armor.

"Thank Aeo that Ulysses is safe," Ryon whispered through her curls. "I was more likely to die from stress than from being caught by a Malaano patrol."

Kira pulled back and admired him. She removed his dirtied lenses and rubbed the glass with her tunic. "Good thing you're a professional scout."

"Spy." Ryon winked.

Kira narrowed her eyes at him. "You've lied to me about your job so many times I'm about to believe you're actually a circus monkey."

He shrugged with a lopsided grin. "That too." He took her hand, leading her beside him toward an empty spot by the water. "That's why I make a dragon's stash of *rupero, balemba.*"

Kira would have rolled her eyes if she wasn't so happy to see him. "Okay, so did you find anything besides Ulysses on your scouting spying monkey mission?"

"Lots of things. One you're going to need to sit down for." He squinted down at the water's edge and hesitantly sat on the rock. "But first, can I just . . . lie down for a bit?"

"Of course," Kira said as he stretched out on the stone and closed his eyes with a raspy exhale. "Are you hungry?"

"I'm a lot of things." Ryon rubbed his eyelids. "Mostly grateful for Ulysses right now. Thank the stars I don't have to play chief any more." He peeked an eye open under the crook of his arm. "And you. *Aish,* you're gorgeous. How'd I get so lucky?"

Kira felt heat rise in her cheeks and smirked. "Felix must have rubbed off on you." She noted how a clasp on his shoulder strap tightened as he stretched. She set his lenses down beside him and worked to loosen the leather. "When was the last time you slept? I can't keep track of what time of day it is down here."

Ryon grunted and closed his eyes again. "I can sleep when I'm dead. Which probably isn't too far off."

"Not without my permission, you won't." Kira pulled hard on the leather strap and was rewarded with a release of tension, both from the buckle and from Ryon. "Oh, I almost forgot!" she said. "I saved a couple of chicken eggs for you."

Ryon gasped and beamed up at her. "Really?"

Kira chuckled. "Yeah, I couldn't help but notice you love eggs. And you get me gifts all the time, so . . ."

"You love me!" Ryon grabbed her around the waist and pulled until she lost her balance, squeaked, and fell over him. He nuzzled into her shoulder and made a purring noise.

Kira grinned and enjoyed the awkward embrace. "Okay, okay. Let go so I can make them for you."

Ryon released her but took hold of her forearm. He pushed up into a sitting position. "I need to ask you something."

"Oh?" Kira remembered his lenses and handed them back. As Ryon slid them in front of his fiery eyes, she regretted not having done it herself.

"Our *evadír* isn't technically over yet, but . . . I'm not technically Katrosi, and neither are you." He grinned sheepishly. "Do you want to marry me?"

Kira's thoughts and breath eloped, leaving her to stare at him like an astonished statue. "I . . . Are . . . Are you proposing? Because *of eggs?*"

"No! I mean yes. Well, kind of." Ryon's olive skin flushed in the dim light. "If I were, what would you say?"

Kira swallowed in an attempt to fix her pitchy voice. "I would say yes."

Ryon's smile stretched wide. "Good, because we aren't promised tomorrow, and I don't really like waiting." He scratched his neck awkwardly. "Do you?"

A small "no" was all Kira could manage.

"But I mean, I want to actually ask you in a better place than this. Because anywhere is better than this, and I have plans. And I have to ask your father, too."

Kira's joy dimmed. "My father is in the barracks in Navarro. And I'm not sure what he'll say."

"He already gave permission for me to *evadír* with you. I'll do whatever it takes." Ryon's expression transformed in a way she couldn't discern. "But he's not in Navarro. He's much closer."

"What?"

"He led the invasion," Ryon whispered. "Commander Oda'e is now the imperial governor of Jadenvive."

23

LYSANDER

Lysander couldn't shake the feeling that he was being watched. Maybe Felix looked on from afar, or maybe Heron's presence was grinding a hole through his sanity.

They were close now—closer than anyone realized. The forest grew tangled with dangling vines, the humidity thickened, and branches burst with tropical flowers. Even this far north from the coast, and despite the recent drought to the east, the jungle flourished.

Lysander might have been able to see Coriander's camp through the vegetation if it weren't cloaked by Phoera light-benders. Maybe the elementalist guards were the source of his unease. Maybe they wouldn't reveal themselves to him since he led such a strange group.

What's wrong? Nariellyn's voice broke through his mind as she urged her xavi to trot alongside Sorrel.

Lysander scolded himself. *My mental shields obviously aren't working.*

No, you're improving quickly. Just keep practicing and you'll be out of the rookie phase in no time. He could feel Nariellyn's gaze on him, but he didn't meet her gaze. *Why are you so . . . anxious?*

Lysander considered brushing her off, then decided it probably wouldn't hurt to tell her. *We're very close to our destination. I'm reconsidering letting Soaring Heron in.*

Why? Nariellyn asked.

Because he's untrustworthy.

She inclined her head out of the corner of Lysander's vision. *That's probably true.*

Lysander appreciated that he wasn't the only one who disliked the arrogant Darkwood prince. *Is there a way with thought magic to prevent him from knowing the camp's location, or . . . ?*

Nariellyn's xavi tossed its head and bobbed its thick, pointed tail. *Advanced thought-readers can create false memories, but they can't erase real ones.* She leaned forward and patted her mount's neck. *You could just assassinate him.*

Lysander snorted, then realized it might give their secret conversation away. He yearned to glance back at Brooke, wondering if she were listening in. He barely resisted the temptation to pry into her thoughts.

I never take a life without good reason, he thought.

Uh-huh, Nariellyn's thought-voice was flat. *So, you should woo Brooke with intellectual stuff. Like philosophy or riddles or whatever. You know, boring stuff that smart people talk about.*

Lysander nearly fell off his gryphon. *What?*

Normal flirting won't work on her—she's heard it all because of politicians trying to suck up to her. So gifts and compliments and stuff don't really mean anything because it's almost always followed by someone wanting a favor.

Lysander didn't know how to interrupt her without tipping Brooke off to a conversation he really, really didn't want her involved in.

He gathered himself for a straightforward response. *Thanks, but I'm obviously not interested in pursuing her. She's engaged, in case you hadn't noticed.*

He's a pile of dung, in case you hadn't noticed.

Lysander grunted. *There's nothing I can do about it.*

You could talk to her.

I already did, and she doesn't want me, okay? Something between shame and defeat corkscrewed into his heart. *I appreciate your aether training, but I didn't ask you for advice. If you want to play matchmaker, she's the one you need to bother.*

He didn't hear a response from Nariellyn for so long that he assumed she'd fallen back in line with the others—he didn't want to look to check and risk burning her with his glare.

She does want you. You're just too dull to realize it.

Lysander sat up straight in the saddle and whipped his neck around to find Nariellyn, but she was already giggling at something she whispered to Brooke, who rolled her eyes and smirked.

A growl vibrated in his throat, and he didn't care if it was too loud. Nariellyn must have no idea he'd already been forward with Brooke and taken a brutal rejection. Starry-eyed girl.

Dimbae replaced Nariellyn at Lysander's flank as their mounts crashed side-by-side through the brush. The bodyguard said something Lysander couldn't discern, so he asked Dimbae to repeat it, and watched his lips carefully.

"I sense Phoera," Dimbae mouthed slowly.

Lysander pulled on Sorrel's reins and held up a hand to signal that the group should stop. The trees looked familiar, especially the giant one with the black scar down its middle where it had survived a lightning strike years ago. Wasn't that tree *inside* the camp the last time he'd visited?

He patted Sorrel's soft neck as he squinted into the jungle before them. The tree canopy above remained still—too still. Phoeran magic choked the air, surrounding them and clouding his senses.

"I am Lysander, firstborn of King Brynn!" he yelled. "We come in the name of peace. I have brought the Katrosi chieftess to aid your cause!"

The jungle shifted and shimmered. Vines seemed to move and light dimmed, then abruptly, the group was surrounded by men dressed in furs and painted with camouflage. A dozen arrows and spears targeted Lysander's chest.

He slowly raised his hands as a familiar face pressed through the line of warriors and barked something at them. Their weapons lowered as his little brother took a proud stance and grinned.

"I know who you are," Coriander signed, then bowed to Brooke. "Welcome to the rebellion."

24

BROOKE

Brooke gazed in fascination as the Phoera invisibility dissolved all around them, revealing a camp nestled into the jungle. Walls of rough-hewn spikes surrounded tipis camouflaged with giant leaves. Curious children watched from a fire pit in front of an expansive lodge as green-splotched soldiers awaited a command from their leader: a pale-skinned Lysander lookalike who could only be Coriander.

The brothers embraced and slapped each other on the back—hard. "Hey, has your voice finally dropped? I can't tell," Lysander quipped.

"Hey, you finally hobbled your way here. Did you make yourself a cane yet?" Coriander signed as he spoke. "You know, I hear the newest thing for people your age is called dentures—false teeth—so you can eat solid foods again! I have some old broken nails you could use."

Lysander huffed a laugh. "A cane would probably be a good idea to remind you who's stronger. And better-looking."

Humor relieved Brooke. She hadn't been convinced that the brothers would be on friendly terms. Although that still wasn't entirely clear.

A noise of awe slipped from Nariellyn. Brooke glanced over her shoulder to find her friend gaping as the spikes they'd nearly trotted into became visible.

Dimbae caught Brooke's gaze with a question in his eye. She motioned for him to stand down despite the dozens of nervous weapons that surrounded them.

"Yes, the healer's hut should have whatever you need," Coriander was saying. He turned his eyes to Brooke. "Chieftess." He approached her xavi and bowed with a flourish of his leaf-colored cape. "What a pleasant surprise. Welcome to my little home away from home."

Brooke nodded, impressed that he could recognize her without her headdress and war paint. Well, it was only a guess between her and Nariellyn, after all. "I apologize for the intrusion," Brooke said. "I have urgent business to discuss with you, Your Majesty."

Coriander's dark brows raised as he glanced at Lysander. "Well, I'm not sure that title is fully earned yet, but I have a feeling that's what you're here for."

Brooke tugged on the reins of her xavi as it pawed the ground, cracking fallen vegetation underfoot. Perhaps it would be best to state her intentions outright and answer the question in his expression. She got the feeling that he didn't mind discussing such matters in front of his men, and having weapons sheathed would be an improvement.

"I am here to support your claim to the throne in hopes that you will join the Tribal Alliance."

Coriander's face brightened with a roguish grin that reminded her of Ryon. "You are very welcome indeed," he said as his men whooped. "As soon as the rest of the Emberhawk recognize my leadership, it would be my honor to join the Alliance and finally bring lasting peace to our two peoples."

Brooke returned his smile as a flicker of hope lit in her heart. That was . . . way too easy. Maybe the Elder of Aether wasn't crazy after all.

"We can discuss details over a feast tonight," Coriander declared in a raised voice, and his men cheered again. "But first, I'm sure your journey was exhausting. Let me offer you a place to rest." He motioned to a soldier and whispered something, then turned on his heel and waved them into the belly of the camp, where Brooke felt like a bonfire was missing in the center of a collection of dozens of mats, crude benches, and chairs. Perhaps they only had this small fire pit because any more smoke would give away their location.

Soaring Heron pulled his mount alongside Brooke's as they slowly moved along a foot-path, now greeted by waves from tent flaps and squeals of delighted, dirty children.

"So primitive," Heron murmured. "Are you sure these people are worth allying with?"

The first good news in days and of course he had to squash it and insult their prospective allies before a deal was struck. "You know this is a rebellion, right? They should be in a translucent gold palace." Brooke said, not caring to hide her annoyance.

"I don't see any gold," Heron muttered. "How long do we need to stay here?"

"As long as it takes," Brooke said as she kicked her xavi forward.

Coriander led them to the stables, where the mounts were refreshed with water and feed. As Sorrel began to preen herself on a bed of straw, a young woman with a round belly appeared with two young children in tow. She approached Coriander with a kiss, then hurried to Brooke with a curtsy. "I am Iraleth, Coriander's wife—"

"Queen," Coriander corrected as the little girl and boy each clamped onto one of his legs. He bent over and tickled them with a playful growl.

Iraleth grinned. "Allow me to show you our accommodations. If the women would follow me, please."

Heron moved into Brooke's shadow. "I will sleep with my fiancée."

Brooke's heart leapt into her throat. "No," she blurted before her mind could catch up. "I will room with Nari."

Heron's lips pursed. He opened his mouth, but closed it again a moment later. Coriander led the men down a winding path through the encampment, and Heron followed.

Brooke didn't realize she'd been holding her breath until Heron fell out of sight. A touch on her arm jolted her back to reality. She found Nariellyn's angry gaze beside her.

"You look like you woke up in a d'hakka's nest and just realized what it's gonna do to you," Nariellyn whispered.

Brooke cleared her throat in an attempt to regain her composure. She forced a smile for a concerned Iraleth. "Shall we?"

Iraleth led them in the opposite direction down a thickly wooded trail. The sticks of a tall tipi stuck up through the underbrush, shrouding the stretched leather and furs with natural camouflage. A wooden platform elevated the tipi from the ground. Brooke examined the smoke flaps at the top and made a mental note to gather firewood before nightfall.

"Here we are. It's not fit for a chief, but I'm afraid it's the best we have to offer at the moment." Iraleth rested a hand on her pregnant belly with an apologetic smile. "Dinner will be served in about an hour. Please don't hesitate to let me know if there's anything I can fetch for you."

Brooke thanked her as she left. Modest accommodations would be a welcome change, and definitely safer than sleeping alongside the road.

Nariellyn crooned at how "cute" the tipi was as Brooke ducked through the tent flap and ensured her pack wouldn't catch on the folded entrance. Wooden supports extended upward to hang five empty hammocks. Beside each hammock sat a small table with shelves, topped with animal figurines a child might have made and painted with berry juices and charcoal. Ashes sat in a stone fire pit in the center.

She wondered how long Coriander's men had lived here. When she'd seen tipis on diplomatic missions, they normally didn't have permanent fixtures like platforms to hold them aloft from insects that skittered along the ground at night. Especially the guest accommodations.

". . . listening?" Nariellyn pouted as Brooke tuned back in. Her friend swung herself in a hammock, pushing against the supports with her toes as she stretched.

"Sorry." Brooke chose a hammock across the wide space and set her pack down. She tested the woven hammock before lying down. It felt . . . lovely. She closed her eyes and breathed in the scents of tropical flowers and leather tanning oil. The air was thicker this deep in the jungle. Packed full of moisture and life. Even the crude animal miniatures were a lively and amusing change from the ornate works of art in the chief's quarters.

Nariellyn was quiet for a long moment. "You seem . . . conflicted."

Brooke released a long breath and refused to open her eyes. "Just enjoying the moment."

"So we're going to pretend that didn't just happen, huh?"

Brooke's brow furrowed. She pulled an arm up to rest it over her eyes. "We're in a beautiful place. A safe place. Coriander has basically already agreed to everything I'd hoped. And there's nothing I can do about anything else right now, so I'm going to take a moment of rest."

"I'm so proud of you."

Brooke smirked and peeked an eye out. "Shut up. I rest sometimes."

"Yeah, like every other equinox." Nariellyn pulled a deerskin over herself and snuggled in. "Can you at least acknowledge how awful Heron is?"

Brooke dropped her arm back down over her eyes. "Darkwood culture is different than ours. He's honoring me by respecting our customs."

Nariellyn chuffed. "It's not just that. Lysander—"

"Emberhawk don't require marriage or engagement at all," Brooke interrupted.

"But Lysander wouldn't—"

"Enough, Nari! For the love of the stars." Brooke struggled to temper her frustration. "I refuse to have this conversation again. What's done is done, no matter what you think about it."

A long moment of silence followed. Then, "I just don't want my best friend to be miserable for the rest of her life."

"I understand that. And I appreciate it. But it's not your choice or your place. And you constantly complaining about it is driving me mad."

Though Brooke saw only darkness, she could feel her friend's hurt from across the space. Still, her words had been true. And if Nariellyn pestered her one more time, she might explode without as much control.

"Yes, *Chieftess*," Nariellyn muttered. Brooke heard her roll out of her hammock, stride to the entrance, and open the flap.

"Wait," Brooke called as she lifted her arm. "Do one thing for me, please."

Nariellyn glared back at her with thinly veiled anger.

"Go speak with Soaring Heron."

Disgust slid into Nariellyn's expression, followed by disbelief. "Is that an order?"

"It's a request." Brooke stared up at the trees through the tipi's smoke opening. "I need to talk to Lysander, and I don't want Heron to catch us together."

Nariellyn's eyes lit in surprise. "I thought . . . Okay." She glanced outside, then back to Brooke. "How much time do you need?"

"Maybe ten minutes. Please."

Nariellyn left without another word.

Brooke took a deep breath, savoring the clean jungle air as she recalled the elder's words: *". . . tell Lysander goodbye. Acknowledge whatever he is to you, or whatever he was. Then you must let him go. Clear your mind. For the sake of our people."*

Well, she'd botched every part of that order. She'd tried to tell him goodbye in the prison and then promptly been poisoned.

She had no idea what love truly was, so acknowledging it seemed impossible. Surely she hadn't actually loved Lysander as a teenager. She didn't have the *balembas* in her stomach as most girls did, which was an entirely stupid and unhelpful description. She'd never swooned over anything in her life except for a well-made spear or blade. And just because she could appreciate a handsome man didn't mean her brain would fly out her ears at the sight of one.

But she could acknowledge that she felt some sort of bond with Lysander. It was probably nothing more than the aether bond that she'd so foolishly forged years ago. When the Sacrificial War broke out and their marriage alliance was severed, she hadn't been able to break off whatever feelings had started for Lysander. She couldn't stop thinking about him, even though he'd suddenly become the son of her father's enemy. And a detestable spoiled prince at that.

So she'd decided to hate him instead.

It had seemed to work at first. She'd smothered any feelings of affection at the thought of him with loathing instead. Crushed any positive thoughts with the reality of the situation: the brutality of the Emberhawk monarchy and their evil goddess. They sacrificed anyone they deemed dangerous or worthless on their golden altar, draining their blood and siphoning the Phoera syn within to empower themselves. It was so vile that Brooke's father had gone to war to stop it after a band of Katrosi merchants had been accused of trespassing and sacrificed. Thus, the Sacrificial War.

But Lysander didn't represent that any more. He'd done what he could to stop Zamara and subvert her attack on Jadenvive. No one hated the former elemental queen more than he did. She'd wrecked the Emberhawk royal family and taken Lysander's hearing years before she'd set her sights on Jadenvive. Brooke couldn't fault him for any of that.

Now that Lysander had suddenly reappeared in Brooke's life, all of her former feelings tumbled back in a confusing mess. Her default reaction of hatred had won without her realizing it, and she'd treated him with more vitriol than he deserved.

She owed him an apology for that. Especially after he'd saved her life. And how he'd agreed to help her cause, even after her people had sentenced him to death.

The slate should be swept clean. Lysander deserved that much, and Brooke couldn't make sense of her situation without a return to neutral ground. If she could let go of whatever old feelings she had for him—positive, negative, or ambiguous—then she could finally clear her mind as the elder had instructed.

Brooke forced herself from the hammock, assuring her tired bones that its comfort would be hers tonight. Then she could take her boots off, too.

She peeked out of the tent flap. Only the thin trail, nearby spike wall, and distant tipis could be seen among the trees. She slipped out. Snuck to the foliage. Wished Ryon were here to share his expert invisibility.

Hadn't Coriander pointed out the healer's hut to Lysander when they'd arrived? Perhaps Lysander wanted to restock on his supply of herbs.

Maybe he was there now.

"Where are you going?"

Brooke nearly jumped out of her leather armor. She whirled toward the sound of Dimbae's voice.

He stood among the trees, not ten feet from her, waiting for her response.

Brooke straightened. "You're a little closer than usual."

His dark face remained flat. "I have reason to believe you require a tighter guard as of late."

"You don't trust Coriander's band?" she whispered.

"I don't trust anyone," Dimbae said. "But they are not to whom I was referring."

A sick feeling flopped like a dying fish in Brooke's stomach. He could only mean Heron.

"Thank you, but I will not require . . . overnight protection. I want you to get plenty of sleep."

Dimbae remained as still as the trunk he stood beside. "Then I will take shifts with Lysander, if you truly mean to make him one of your guard."

Brooke bit the inside of her cheek. She certainly didn't intend to offer Lysander such a position long-term, and she doubted he'd want to become an azure mask even if she offered. But she didn't want to tell Dimbae that right now and have him guard her alone night and day.

"That's not necessary," Brooke said. "I'm going to speak with Lysander now." She patted the dagger sheath on her belt. "I'll be fine, really. Please go and relax. We all need some rest, and yours is well-deserved."

He just stared at her for a long minute. Finally, he bowed. "As you wish."

"Hey," she called as he turned away. "Thank you. For everything. I'll get you back to your family soon."

Dimbae's rigid stance eased. "Thank you, but they are safe. I am here to serve as long as you need me." He vanished into the greenery.

Brooke removed her gloves and flexed her fingers, trying to shake her tension out with them. She stuffed her gloves in a pocket and moved in the direction she guessed the healer's hut might be. Nariellyn would hopefully be distracting Heron by now. She had ten minutes.

The encampment was so heavily wooded that sneaking between buildings didn't seem too difficult, even without the Phoera element. The land seemed waterlogged, but there were still leaves to crackle or soggy spots to squish, so she moved with caution. Soon she found a sort of wigwam surrounded by herb plots, raised garden beds, and hanging baskets with vines trailing down their edges. An herbalist, to be sure—most of these plants were more medicinal than they were edible.

Lysander was nowhere in sight.

Now what?

She felt like a child. What was she doing, sneaking around as if she were up to no good? Was she going to act like this every time Heron didn't approve of something?

Brooke mentally kicked herself. She would talk to Lysander because it was the right thing to do, and she wouldn't apologize for it. She had an aether bond with Lysander—whether she liked it or not—and she could use it to her advantage now.

Aether surged at her command, swirling through her like a mist. Gentle but eager to be used.

Lysander?

Hey.

Brooke turned in the direction she sensed his thought-voice originating from. *Can I speak with you for a moment?*

Do you have permission from your Darkwood?

Brooke gritted her teeth. *No, and I do not require it.*

Her mind fell quiet for a moment. Then she heard, *All right.*

Where are you? she asked.

I found a spring by the herbalist.

Brooke noticed the downward slope of the earth to her right. She ensured no one watched as she stepped onto the path and followed Lysander's aether signature. It felt faint and dark, somehow, yet with a warm hue, if aether could have color. Deep red, perhaps. Calm and steady. It had to be him.

Ferns sprang up to ankle-height as she walked, tickling her pants and split riding skirt with delicate fronds. She heard the spring before she saw it, trickling with a soft melody. Lysander sat at the edge of a small pond, surrounded by pouches and bowls with organized reagents. He worked with a mortar and pestle and acknowledged Brooke's arrival with a nod.

She focused on her balance as she approached over slick moss-covered stones. *Your thought-speak is much improved.*

"I have Nariellyn to thank for that," Lysander said aloud.

Brooke nodded, but he wasn't looking at her. *What are you doing?*

"Making a modified version of my antidote," Lysander said. "I ran out of a few herbs recently."

Brooke winced and hoped he didn't see it. He was probably referring to the dreamthistle remedy he'd been supplying her. The one she'd scorned back at the Great Hall.

I can pay you, Brooke offered.

"No need."

Brooke chewed on the inside of her cheek. *Thank you again for saving my life. I probably haven't seemed very appreciative.*

"It's fine."

Silence.

Brooke swallowed hard, but her trepidation remained. *Listen, I . . . I owe you an apology.*

Lysander glanced up at her with curious maroon eyes. His pestle didn't stop its rhythmic grinding.

Brooke looked away. She stepped closer and sat on a rock nearby, letting her boots dip into the pure water.

She took a deep breath. Told herself to just force it out and be done with it. She was used to stamping down on her pride while dealing with foreign dignitaries. So why was it so difficult now?

When we were younger, I didn't know how to break my bond with you when the war broke out. So I started . . . hating you instead. It felt idiotic to admit, especially considering her thoughts might be accompanied by a rising mess of emotions. She felt her cheeks heating. *I've been awful to you without really realizing that. An old bad habit. And I'm sorry.*

"You've been under a lot of stress," Lysander said as he added more leaves to his mortar. "Too much for one person."

No, that's not an excuse, Brooke insisted. *Leaders shouldn't take their stress out on anyone. Especially someone who's gone so far out of their way to help.*

Lysander paused his work for a moment. "I think we both know our history is too complicated to expect a normal relationship." He set to grinding once again. "It's all right. I've grown accustomed to much worse."

Brooke grimaced. *I won't treat you that way any more. I'm sorry. I really appreciate everything you've done.* She watched the water coax mud from her boots and carry it away in the lazy current. *I want a blank slate between us.*

Lysander tilted his head, the splotchy sunlight accentuating his short black beard as he examined her. "Okay, then. I'll forgive you if you forgive me."

Brooke almost asked what to forgive him for, since nothing recent sprang to mind. He must mean his past. All of it.

That shouldn't be too hard to release him from at this point. He'd been a teenager, after all. If she'd had the same pampering as a youth, she'd probably have acted the same.

I forgive you, Brooke thought, and as soon as the words left her, she sensed a new awkward peace between them. Fragile and hesitant.

Lysander's slow grin lit his features in a way she'd never seen before. "All right, then." He poured the crushed herbs from his pestle into a cup, then reached out to the pure spring water. The water tossed inside the vessel as it filled, then suddenly steamed in his grip.

He handed her the cup. "Your last dose. Then you should be fully recovered from the dreamthistle." His gaze flicked from her forehead to beneath her eyes to her fingernails like a wise matron checking her feverish granddaughter for symptoms.

Brooke took the tea and savored the warmth between her hands. The steam smelled of honey and mint as she breathed it in. *I thought I'd recovered days ago.*

"That's because you have an expert herbalist." Lysander winked as he rubbed his tools clean in the pond. "It normally isn't so pleasant."

Remembering how she'd felt upon being poisoned, Brooke imagined that was true. She took a drink and was taken aback by the delightful mix of sweet citrus and berries. It tasted more like a cup from the kitchen of the Great Hall than medicine.

"It's delicious," Brooke said, taking another sip before she remembered he couldn't hear her.

But he was watching her reaction with a slight grin. "Good." He lifted a small branch from his collection of dried herbs and began stripping it of leaves.

It's different than before, Brooke thought to him. *Did the herbalist have what you needed?*

"Not everything." Lysander carefully dropped the leaves into the mortar, then repeated the process with another twig. "What you're drinking is missing the most powerful reagent—I ran out. It's rare, but I've got more growing at my grandmother's pyramid."

Brooke wondered if he meant the grandmother on his royal side or his Valinorian side, then recalled that Valinorians lived in castles, not pyramids. So he must mean the former Queen Lyzelle, if Brooke remembered the Emberhawk monarchy family tree correctly.

Lysander continued. "So I added ginger rhizome for your stress and joyberries for taste instead."

Brooke nearly protested that she didn't need anything for stress, but stopped and scolded herself for nearly denying it. Why fight a fact that was apparently plain for all to see? She hadn't realized how tight the muscles in her back and neck were until she'd relaxed on that hammock.

The thought of a quiet moment with this tea and that hammock was worth fantasizing over. Her burdens were being relieved one by one, from arriving safely at Coriander's camp and his favor toward the Alliance to a fresh beginning with Lysander—something she never thought she'd have. Surely that deserved a celebratory respite until tonight's dinner. Maybe she could even take a nap.

She took and released a deep breath, relishing the warmth of the tea in her hands and the steam on her chin. *Thank you.* The spring bubbled quietly as she paused. *I need to apologize for one more thing.*

"Hmm." Lysander raised an eyebrow. "Unfortunately you've already met your quota for that today. Apologies don't suit you."

Brooke huffed a laugh. *All right, then. How can I buy another ticket?*

An awkward smirk grew across Lysander's face. "You can solve my riddles."

She couldn't determine whether or not he was serious. *Riddles?*

"Mmm. I wager a mind like yours shouldn't have trouble with them."

How odd. Yet she enjoyed riddles and puzzles. And if she got them wrong, she'd have an excuse not to admit to him that letting those border guards go probably would have endangered Coriander's people and compromised everything. She also didn't want to admit that it was her own fault for not going further up the river and using Phoera to ensure they were undetected.

Riddles were a much better alternative. She had the time, for once. Why not?

Let's hear them, then. How many?

"Just three." Lysander tossed the stripped twigs into the creek and set his pestle to their leaves.

> "What lives, breathes, moves, and eats
> But has no heart, lungs, feet, or teeth?"

Too easy, Brooke thought to him. *Fire.*

Lysander nodded. "We're just getting warmed up."

> "What shines without light
> Hides in plain sight
> Turning, yearning
> To match its siblings in flight?"

Brooke lowered her cup to sit on her knees and rapped her fingers on the glazed clay. Perhaps some form of water that reflected light? No . . .

A cloud? she guessed.

Lysander's expression grew devilish. "Nope."

Brooke pursed her lips. *Some kind of shiny winged insect? A firefly?*

He shook his head. "Think nighttime."

No, don't give hints—ah. Brooke snapped her fingers. *The third moon! The dark one.*

"Yes." Lysander carefully poured the crushed leaves into a vial of golden liquid. "Okay, last riddle. Give me a second." He looked up at the vines hanging from trees above, appearing to rehearse in his head. "And no thought-spying."

Brooke couldn't believe she hadn't thought of that herself. Though it would have ruined all the fun.

She took another luxurious drink of tea as she waited and shifted on her stone seat. It felt so nice to have nothing hanging between them. No more shadows of negative emotions weighing her down at the sight of him. Sure, she'd probably have to struggle with her old grudge again at some point in the future, but for now she actually found herself enjoying this time with him. His work was intriguing to watch, and so was he. She hadn't known many Valinorians in her life, and none recently. The contrast between his dark hair and light skin was . . . aesthetic. Even his pointed ears, though created with a cruel scar, were unique and somehow attractive.

Maroon eyes glanced up at Brooke, and she nearly swallowed her tongue.

"Okay. Are you ready?"

She cleared her throat and nodded.

> "Who defends the weak
> Rewards the meek
> Tames the wildest heart
> Dances the swiftest art
> With beauty fierce and bold
> And legacy forever told?"

The creator, Brooke answered instantly. *I thought the last one was supposed to be the hardest.*

"Wrong."

She frowned. *But every description fits Aeo. "The swiftest art" is creation.*

"Well . . ." Lysander tilted his head. "So is your spear *kata.*"

Brooke sat dumbstruck. *No, it's not.*

Lysander laughed. "I wrote it."

Then . . . does he mean . . . ?

Lysander wore an amused grin. "It's you."

It must be a joke. That riddle fit her like a tunic fit a mudhoof. But Lysander's expression was serious, yet lighthearted. Unwavering. Unapologetic.

Something bloomed inside her. Something tentative and awkward and delightful. Something intoxicating and terrifying and forbidden.

Suddenly she knew why it was described as having *balembas* in the stomach.

A lifetime of training in speechcraft failed her. She could negotiate trade deals, arbitrate for peace, and debate for justice. But now she had no idea how to respond.

She set the cup down, stood, and left without a word.

25

KIRALAU

It took all of Kira's self-control to walk with her back straight. Shoulders squared. Chin high. As if she wasn't terrified of the imperial soldiers who guarded every platform, ramp, and rope bridge. As though the haunted emptiness of Jadenvive didn't feel entirely surreal. As if she belonged there.

She was one of them, after all.

"Breathe, Frizz," Tekkyn said behind her. "I've already arranged for us to talk with Dad. No one'll stop you."

Mentally, she knew that. But her heart refused to believe that their father was the man to blame for all of this suffering. With every step she took toward the Great Hall, her blood pounded harder, coursing dread through her veins.

"Is it really him?" she whispered.

"Remember what I told you about him a few weeks ago?" Tekkyn murmured. "All's well."

How could he even utter such a phrase when they were surrounded by such devastation? The invasion hadn't caused that much more damage to Jadenvive, but the taverns and restaurants were still blackened and charred, the workshops empty or collapsed, and the homes felt like prisons for their own families with patrols everywhere. The people had focused more on healing the wounded and scavenging fire-scarred crops before reconstruction could begin. Now Kira wasn't sure the city would ever recover to its former glory.

But she knew what Tekkyn meant, and why he wouldn't repeat it out loud. He'd said their father was with the Navakovrae Resistance. An organization of Malaano settlers to the tribal lands who were no longer loyal to the empire. A rumored band of rebels who opposed the high taxation and being forced to fight the empire's wars.

If that were true, though, then why had Oda'e captured a tribal city in the emperor's name?

"This way."

Kira snapped out of her musing at a guard's beckoning. She looked up, and her apprehension drained to her feet, rooting her in place before the ornately carved double doors of the Great Hall.

Heavens help me.

Tekkyn took her arm and gently but firmly led her beside him.

The Hall was just as she'd remembered—thick wooden pillars supporting an impossibly high ceiling and wide stairs leading up to a throne flanked by long tables. But the braziers were unlit, the guards wore metal helms and tabards instead of masks and leathers, and the chief's throne was empty.

Kira closed her eyes for a moment and steadied herself. *I killed a goddess. I can face my father.*

Why did this feel so much harder?

The guard led them to the back rooms, which she remembered for the joyful reunion with Ryon just days ago. Now the halls were dark, empty, and silent.

Kira pulled her cloak tighter around herself as she followed Tekkyn. The Katrosi didn't deserve this. Hitting them before they'd had a chance to recover . . . It was brutal. Undignified. Unfair.

Their guide peeked his head inside the war room, hesitated, whispered something Kira couldn't hear, then opened the door for them to enter.

It wasn't one of the elders or the chieftess who leaned over the map table, but their father. Towering muscular frame, dark skin, silver plate armor, and ocean-blue eyes, which Kira and Tekkyn had inherited.

Oda'e's rigid stance melted as he saw them. He grew a weary smile and opened his arms.

Kira crashed into his breastplate and gripped him tight, though her hands couldn't meet behind his thick back.

"Dad." Tears came unabated. She couldn't stop them.

She didn't want to ask the question she didn't want the answer for. "Why?"

Kira was vaguely aware of Oda'e motioning for the guards to leave and the soft sound of the door closing. "Baby girl," he murmured, hugging her back gently. "I'm so sorry."

"Commander," Tekkyn said with a bow.

Kira could hear the disapproval in her father's voice even before he spoke. "We are alone."

"May I speak freely, then?" Tekkyn whispered.

Kira felt Oda'e nod as she refused to let him go. "The former rulers of the city used to discuss their plans in this room. It should be safe against eavesdropping as long as the door is fully closed."

"Can I confirm it?" Tekkyn asked.

"My guards have," Oda'e said. "They are trustworthy."

Kira shut her eyes, squeezing more tears free. *Former* rulers?" She pulled away and looked up at her father's stern face. "So you're the new chief, huh?"

Oda'e's azure gaze dimmed. "Only temporarily. I—"

"How could you?" Kira's voice broke. "We've been fearing war all this time, and now that it finally happens, it's *you?*"

"This was set into motion months ago," the commander said in a low tone. "I would have been court-martialed had I refused. But this places us in a good position. With—"

Kira slammed her palm into the colorful shell fragments that decorated his left breast, indicating rank. "Better you be court-martialed than for all these people to lose their lives!"

Tekkyn grabbed her from behind, but Oda'e said, "Let her go." He leaned down to look close into Kira's eyes. "That's exactly why I did it," he whispered. "With me in command, I could ensure the lowest loss of life and the least destruction."

A tear ran cold down Kira's hot cheek. "It shouldn't have happened at all."

"I agree, but that wasn't our choice." Oda'e gently touched her face with a gauntleted hand. She flinched but didn't move.

"I need you to keep a secret," he whispered. "One that could get us all killed."

Kira swallowed hard, but only a fraction of her anger and hurt were buried with it. She nodded.

"This is the first big play by the Navakovrae Resistance. I will protect the civilians and weed out the soldiers loyal to the empire as we settle in." Oda'e's eyes flashed with something akin to determination or excitement—she couldn't tell which. "Then we will reveal ourselves, declare our independence, and give control of the city back to the Katrosi in hopes of forging an alliance with the tribes. With luck, the chieftess will allow Jadenvive to become the home of the Resistance and serve as a safe haven for any Navakovrae who wish to cross the border to flee the imperial tyranny."

Kira blinked at him as his words sank in. Surely she hadn't heard him right. "You want to just . . . give the city back to the Katrosi?"

Oda'e nodded. "As soon as it's safe. Then my Resistance soldiers will expel anyone loyal to the empire and defend the city."

It sounded ridiculous. Kira swiped a tear and narrowed her eyes again. "I saw countless Malaano soldiers on the way here—"

"The majority of my men are Resistance."

She just stared at him. "How is that possible?"

"We've been planning this for over a year now," Tekkyn murmured as he stepped beside her, eyeing the door. "Dad's had plenty of time to organize troop transfers for those who were found to be loyal."

Kira shifted her disbelief to her brother. "You knew? Before the Empire did?"

"Taking Jadenvive was the only strategic move that made sense according to imperial tactics." Oda'e's expression smoothed into something peaceful—that expression he used to make before he grabbed her in a snuggle-hug or revealed a gift he'd brought home from town. "Don't worry; everything is under control. It's going to be all right. You're safe."

She wanted to believe him, but nothing made any sense. "But isn't the Resistance just a few farmers and ranchers? And how can you be sure your men are loyal to you instead of the empire?"

"You know how unpopular the draft has been." Oda'e tipped his head toward Tekkyn, who looked more like their father than ever before. "You know Tekkyn'ashi was named after a tribesman—my best friend growing up. The empire is forcing a generation of men to take up arms against their neighbors."

Kira frowned. "But the tribes aren't as friendly toward us."

"They were a generation ago, before the empire became more aggressive in their hostilities. Do you know what Navakovrae means in the Phoeran language?"

"Friends from the east," Kira muttered.

"Friends," Oda'e repeated. "The tribes have done nothing to us but share their land, trade, and help us when we ask. They share their healers and their techniques to help survive the heat and drought. At least, the Katrosi and Roanoke do, and the Sekoiako most of the time." He motioned toward chairs tucked beneath the table and took a seat. "The only one who wants this war is the emperor to expand his domain."

Kira slowly sat and tugged on the end of the bandana that held her curls at bay. "Okay, but how can the tribes and a few farmers hope to beat the Empire?"

Tekkyn snorted. "Farmers have more strength, endurance, and skill with tools than the more 'sophisticated' vocations on the island and larger cities. They also have more land—more to protect—and therefore have more motivation."

Kira glanced at him sidelong. It was almost eerie how much he sounded like their father.

Oda'e nodded. "Farmers and ranchers make fine soldiers. I would take a dozen of them over a hundred academics any day."

Kira twirled the cloth between her fingers, tickling her ear as she stared at the maps and flags on the wall in thought. "Okay, but are most of the Navakovrae Resistance actually willing to die to fight for the tribes? Because if the empire finds a traitor . . ."

"We are fighting for our own independence, Frizz," Tekkyn said, his aura growing fierce. "Against taxes and tyranny and bloodshed. We just want to live in peace, with representation from our own people. Leaders who could understand what it's like to live off the land during a drought. Locals who know what a trace cat is—not some faraway beaurocrat who only cares about their shipment of 'exotic' jomoco and chocolate and d'hakka silk."

Fear slithered up Kira's spine and coiled around her throat. She leaned forward and reached for Oda'e's glove. "Dad, listen to his voice—it's just like that time he ran after that trace cat that took one of our calves. He's going to get himself killed!"

"Hmm. But you've never set traps in the Gnarled Wood, fought trace cats, or chased an enemy soldier into the forest, have you?" Oda'e smirked.

Kira stopped toying with her bandana as her mind blanked. "I . . ."

"Some things are worth fighting for. But we have no intention of dying." Oda'e took her hand. "Can you trust me?"

Kira pressed her lips together. "I really want to," she whispered. "Do you have Brooke in custody?"

The commander shook his head. "We haven't been able to locate her, thank the tails."

The tightness in Kira's chest loosened a bit. "What about the elders?"

Oda'e frowned. "We have four of them—they're safe. Two are missing. And unfortunately, one didn't make it."

Kira's breath halted. "Who?"

"The Elder of Aether. He used magic to try and stop the siege at the gate, and it must have been too much . . . He was very old."

Tears welled up again, but Kira blinked them back. "You said you did this so people wouldn't die."

"So not as many people would die," Oda'e said quietly. "I'm sorry I couldn't protect everyone."

"This is war, Frizz," Tekkyn said softly. "There will be more, and the blood of every one of them is on the emperor's hands."

She clenched her teeth. She knew she sounded naïve, but she didn't care. One life was too many, and the loss of an elder was surely a crushing blow to the Katrosi.

Kira glanced at her brother. Had he already told their father about Vylia—that she was alive and under their protection? Was it safe to tell him?

Oda'e turned his attention to Tekkyn. "Is the new leader settling in well?"

Tekkyn nodded. "Everyone seems to know Ulysses and respect him already. Spirits are a lot better, and they're gettin' more organized."

"Good," Oda'e said as Kira's jaw fell open. How much did he know?

Oda'e pulled a jingling pouch from his belt and slid it across the table to Tekkyn. "If *rupero* isn't worth anything at the market any more, just let me know, and I'll have rations delivered. Get me another list of specific needs and we'll place them at a drop-off point."

Kira watched her brother pocket the bulging bag. "You're . . . supplying the refugees in the caves?"

"Just as I feed my own troops instead of draining local resources." Oda'e leaned back in his chair and rapped his fingertips on the charcoal map. "Even the emperor doesn't want to devastate the region. He wants to siphon their wealth, just as he does our own, so the situation must be handled delicately."

Kira frowned. "Then he wants to enslave the tribes? Or tax and control them?"

"Not sure yet. Both are probable." Oda'e eyed her quietly for a long moment. "You don't trust me."

His accusation knifed into Kira's heart. What was he implying? "I do," she said, but her voice constricted.

He pressed his lips into a thin line. "I did not know about the threat to the princess until it was too late. We knew Sa'alu was going to be instrumental in manipulating a war, but never dreamed the emperor would sacrifice his own daughter." Dark anger lit in his eyes. "Thank the tails she survived."

Kira's eyes widened. So he knew everything then?

"Her survival is more important than I can express. The Lotusfall are interested in collecting her." Oda'e leaned forward, capturing Kira in his gaze. "Does she trust you?"

Kira shrank. "I think so. But I've only known her a few days." She glanced at Tekkyn. "The Lotusfall?"

"A secret society from Malaan. They have been undermining the dynasty since before Pappy built the dairy. And they're joining us." Oda'e lowered his voice. "They believe Vylia is the key to overthrowing the emperor. She must be protected at all costs."

Kira's palms began to sweat. "She and her bodyguard are hardly protected. They're just sleeping on the floor of the cave. Not to mention they just woke from comas; they need medical attention."

"Do you trust me?"

Kira took a deep breath and released it. "I do," she said, but she wasn't certain she believed her own words.

"They're better protected than you think," a disembodied voice said.

Kira nearly jumped out of her boots as Ryon appeared next to her. She balked up at him. He winked.

"I thought I said coming along was too dangerous!" Tekkyn barked.

"You did," Ryon said, adjusting the soft rabbit-fur moccasins that had replaced his boots. "If you think I'm going to let Kira go somewhere dangerous and not be at her side, you don't know me at all."

"*I'm* at her side," Tekkyn said.

"Well done, Idryon." Oda'e said with a grin.

Ryon raised an eyebrow. "I believe I introduced myself as Ryon, sir."

"Indeed, you did." Oda'e chuckled. "Tell me, Ryon: could you use those skills to safely bring Vylia here to meet with me? Secrecy and her safety are of utmost import."

"Yes, sir." Ryon bowed his head. "And then I have another matter to discuss with you in private, if I may."

Ryon didn't look at Kira as he spoke, but his fidgeting made her guess at what he wanted to discuss with her father. Trepidation and excitement sprouted within her.

If the appreciative and intrigued way that Oda'e regarded Ryon was any indication, he was sure to give his blessing for his daughter's hand in marriage.

26

VYLIA

The platform streets and bridges of Jadenvive were eerily empty, as if a plague had swept through and no one dared leave their homes. The only vestige of life left in the market square was the occasional guard where two paths crossed.

Vylia supposed the empire was a plague of sorts, spreading at any opportunity.

"Going dark again," Ryon whispered as they neared the corner of a bakery that had smelled divine when she'd toured the city as the Malaano ambassador. The Great Hall shouldn't be too far from here, if Vylia remembered correctly from her brief tour of the treetop city before her world had been inverted.

She couldn't see her escort who stood only a few feet in front of her—based on the sound of Ryon's voice—but she'd grown accustomed to his strange disembodied directions and floating orange eyes when he glanced back to check on them.

Sousuke reached for Vylia's hand, and she took it. He was clearly on high alert—squared jaw, sharp eyes, low crouch. But for some reason, despite everything, Vylia felt no fear as she waited for Ryon's surreal darkness to fall once again.

Maybe it was the new plainclothes Kira had found for her. No one would recognize a foreign princess without her crown or dress or makeup. Assuming any of these soldiers had laid eyes upon her before, anyway.

Or maybe it was the fact that this Commander Oda'e already knew about her and she hadn't been killed in her sleep in the cave. Apparently the new leader of the city had even been supplying the hidden refugees with food and other necessities. And he was the father of two out of the three people in Jadenvive she could probably trust.

What a peculiar stroke of luck.

"I think I'd like to do something for the people of this city," Vylia whispered as the world evaporated into darkness once more, shrouding her in Ryon's invisibility.

"This isn't a time for jesting," Sousuke hissed.

"I'm not," Vylia said as they slowly started forward, one foot blindly in front of the other. "The children have found ways to have fun already, but the adults look like their souls have fled."

"These aren't your people, Vy. You don't have to be a princess right now."

"But I want to," she whispered back. Truthfully, as her body recovered from the coma and she spent more time awake, she found she needed something creative to do with her hands—anything to help, somehow. "Maybe I could make some decorations for the Moon Festival."

She heard Sousuke's frustration in his breath. "I don't think they'll be celebrating. And risking your life for some hanging tassels and ribbons is beyond foolish."

Vylia pursed her lips. He never used to speak to her with such a blunt lack of decorum. "I could at least make some corn husk dolls. Someone else could hand them out. It wouldn't be dangerous. Ryon, could you nab some ears of corn from the field?"

"Yes. Now *shhh*," Ryon hissed from somewhere in the blackness before her.

Vylia frowned. She'd never been shushed before.

Well, she'd spent much of her life wanting to just be treated as a normal person. So maybe she shouldn't complain.

She abruptly realized that the Moon Festival was a Malaano holiday, anyway. Even if the Katrosi celebrated it as well for the few Malo-heritage people who called Jadenvive home, putting decorations around the city would probably send the wrong message.

She could still make some dolls, though. The orphans would love them regardless. Especially the little girl named Mayla who'd asked Vylia approximately seventy-eight questions about what it was like to be a real princess.

Ryon's footsteps stopped, and so did Sousuke. He pulled her close with one arm, and she knew the other was ready on his sword hilt.

Something squeaked—Vylia guessed it was a door hinge. According to the plans Ryon had laid out beforehand, it should be the kitchen door to the Great Hall. They crept forward once again.

Vylia's vision returned with a flash of color, making her simultaneously squint and blink. Smells of garlic and roast beast filled her senses. She missed her regular diet of lobster and angel tuna and rice, but Katrosi cooking certainly had its own appeal.

"Oh, hello, Idryon! You look completely drained, sweetheart," said a plump woman whom Vylia assumed was the chef because of her sauce-smeared apron. She handed Ryon what looked like a wheat bun with crusted cheese on top as Sousuke closed the door quietly behind them. "Take a moment to rest."

"I'm fine," Ryon panted. "Do you know . . . the guards' schedules?"

The woman's smile grew wide. "No need. All of the soldiers in the Hall are on our side." She winked and pressed the roll into Ryon's hand. "If this had to happen, it was the best possible way, yeah? God is good." She took another roll from a stack on the kitchen's island and offered it to Vylia with a bow. "Pleasure to meet you, Your Highness."

Vylia took the food and curtsied, forgetting that her dress had been replaced with a flowing beige tunic and a simple drawstring skirt. "Were you the one who prepared the red soup for my first dinner with the chieftess?"

The chef's brown eyes brightened. "The long pepper, aye. I was hoping it wouldn't be too spicy for you."

"It was the perfect amount of spice! Absolutely delectab—"

"All right, let's go." Sousuke took Vylia's hand again and wove through the kitchen staff to a door on the opposite side between baskets of pumpkins and gourds.

"Hey!" Vylia tore her hand free. "If we're safe, I have a few seconds to have a chat." She stared up at Sousuke's sharp green eyes. "You've been awful bossy recently."

Sousuke sighed and rubbed his nose, his plate armor clanking with the movement. "Kitchens are not secure. You might have noticed we just strode right in from the street. I'm just trying to keep you safe."

"As usual, but you don't have to be a grump about it." Vylia took a defiant bite of the roll and was momentarily distracted by how soft and buttery it was. "I've been living in a cave for . . . for . . . I don't know how many days because there was no sunlight! Let me have a little human interaction, please."

Sousuke watched her for a long moment, and slowly the hard lines of his face smoothed. It wouldn't have passed for a smile on anyone else's face, but Vylia knew him. "You're ridiculous," he said. "I've never met anyone who could actually be positive in this kind of situation."

"Ridiculous?" Vylia wrinkled her nose in a disapproving look. "I have no more tears left to cry. Should I be more like you and always be miserable, even when we receive a ray of hope?"

Sousuke's lips flattened into a thin line but one corner tilted upward. His green eyes flashed with words unspoken, leaving Vylia to guess at what was going on in that needle-sharp mind of his.

"This way," said Ryon, whose dinner roll had disappeared. He was leaning out of the door and glancing down the hall. "Let me lead."

A jitter of nervousness shot through Vylia's limbs as they followed Ryon past pairs of curious Malaano guards. One of them tipped his head as if in an imperceptible bow, and Vylia hid her face.

But no one made a move to stop them as they reached the map room—an inner chamber where Vylia had met with Brooke before.

Ryon knocked, and a deep voice beyond the door granted entry.

Vylia gathered herself and fixed her posture as Ryon beckoned her inside. The room was just as she remembered, with weapon racks and couches on one end and a large table with maps and figurines on the other. The only difference was that a mountain of a man stood at the head of the table instead of Brooke. Vylia recognized Commander Oda'e from her brief meeting with him in Navarro. The horns and scales of the helmet that sat on the table beside him seemed to change color in the light as she moved closer, gleaming like a water dragon of old.

"Princess." Oda'e bowed low as soon as the doors were closed. He motioned to Tekkyn'ashi, whom Vylia hadn't noticed in the corner. "Fetch her a chair."

"It's all right. I'm happy to stand." Vylia reached the wide table and inspected the various maps drawn on parchment with ink and charcoal. The surface was so high she wouldn't have been able to see anything while sitting, anyway.

Ryon and Tekkyn'ashi stood at each door while Sousuke took his place at Vylia's side. Oda'e seemed to approve of their positions before he spoke. "I can't express how sorry I am for what you have endured recently."

Vylia bit down on rising emotion and released some in a deep breath. "What's done is done. The greatest sin against me was not yours."

Oda'e nodded. "I am at your command, Your Highness, but I fear there are some among my ranks who would do you harm. As we speak, they are being weeded out and reassigned."

Vylia rested her wrists on the table. "Oh? And how do you determine such a thing?"

"By testing whether their allegiance lies with the empire or the land, Your Grace." Oda'e's voice deepened and quieted. "My men and I seek peace with the tribes and independence from the island."

Surprise left Vylia speechless for a moment. Independence? These Malo heritage people—*their* people—wanted to form their own country? For the Malaan-owned tribal lands to be their own?

She stared down at the maps. How badly had the Empire abused the

Navakovrae for them to be willing to risk their lives for this?

Perhaps they deserved to rule their own land. It would be a stunning rejection of her father's expansionism. She couldn't argue with that.

"Then our aims are aligned." Vylia cleared her throat. "It seems you have an unnerving skill for deceit, Commander. You made a fool of me in Navarro. I can see how your rebellion has remained a secret. Though you should know whispers of a revolution have already reached the palace in Maqua."

Oda'e's blue eyes widened before he bowed. "Please forgive me, Princess. We were concerned for your safety but didn't fully unravel the emperor's plot against you until it was too late. I'm so relieved that you survived."

Vylia glanced at Sousuke. "I have my men to thank for that."

"Sir, if I may speak," Sousuke said, but continued before permission was given. "I would like an escort of your most trusted guards to accompany us to Way Maar."

Vylia choked on her breath, rendering her unable to retort before Oda'e did.

"The safest place for her is here," Oda'e said.

"We've heard that before." Sousuke rested his arm on his scabbard. "I have connections with the Lotusfall in Way Maar. We've received word from our comrade that the Lotusfall have a great interest in the princess's safety."

Vylia's mind raced to keep up as Oda'e frowned. Why hadn't Sousuke mentioned this before? Probably because he knew she'd protest. The southern part of Malaan Island was said to be a nest of pagans—especially the swamp near Way Maar. And since when did he have connections with the Lotusfall insurrectionists?

"And you believe these Lotusfall are to be trusted?" Oda'e asked.

Sousuke nodded. "On my life."

Alarm bells clanged in Vylia's head. Sousuke never bet anything on his life. He was all percentages and risks and caution. How could he be so certain of such a ridiculous notion? The Lotusfall had been the most elusive enemy of the imperial monarchy for over a century. They could just want her so they could execute her themselves.

Or perhaps they wanted to use her to strike at her father. To prove that she yet lived would undermine the emperor's reason for declaring war.

Finally Vylia's voice cooperated. "And how do you expect us to remain safe as we travel to Way Maar? The trade route is full of bandits, but it's not half as treacherous as the Sea of Bones. And do you expect me not to be recognized by anyone in My'Eyah?"

"We'll take a smaller port," Sousuke said. "I have heard that the Emberhawk tribe has their navy stationed in Quin'Zamar and the Sekoiako tribe has a port at Rainosek."

Oda'e's expression steeled. "Any Emberhawk city is out of the question. Just because they have the strongest tribal navy does not mean that taking passage from them would be safe in any regard."

Sousuke didn't budge. "And Sekoiako?"

Oda'e didn't speak for a long moment. "They are strong allies of the Katrosi and are certainly hostile to the empire, as their territory borders Navakovrae land to the south. But that does not mean they would be friendly to our cause."

"I have friends among the Sekoiako," Ryon said. "I could arrange for you to take a ship from Rainosek. It's not far from here, and we wouldn't have to take the trade route to Navarro. There's another road that goes southeast that's less travelled."

"Excellent," Sousuke said. "Commander, would you grant us some of your men—"

"Excuse me," Vylia interrupted. She glared at Sousuke, but he didn't look at her.

"Guard Rhu," Vylia said in a flat voice.

Sousuke flinched—the desired effect. Vylia couldn't remember the last time she'd called him by his formal title.

"How long have you been plotting all of this without consulting me?" she demanded.

Sousuke slowly turned to her. "I didn't know if it were a viable option until now, when I had the opportunity to ask."

"I am still the imperial heir," she said, sitting up straight and hopefully appearing as regal as possible. "I will not be shuttled about like a criminal on the run, nor will I be associated with pagans and renegades."

Sousuke frowned. "Did you know that House Rhu would be considered pagan by your priestesses?"

Vylia's lips parted but no response formed. House Rhu worshipped the creator instead of Lillian? But they were a warrior house who had guarded the emperor's family for generations. When had they abandoned the faith?

Wait—did that mean *he* was an unbeliever? How many times had she used the word "pagan" around him, insulting him and his family?

And after her own interaction with the Malo stone, Vylia didn't know who she herself believed in any more. Certainly not Lillian, who had proved herself to be cruel and murderous at the very least.

Did that make *her* a pagan?

"Remember, Hiro said in his letter that the Lotusfall are trustworthy," Sousuke said, and Vylia barely heard him. "My family has been supporting them since before I was born. And there's no way the emperor completely wiped out House Rhu—many of his own guards. We train for situations like that. I guarantee my family is still alive and in hiding. They will help you."

Vylia swallowed, but the knot in her throat didn't budge. This young man had been protecting her for years—he was one of the youngest to ever be assigned as a royal bodyguard, such was his martial prowess and the reputation of House Rhu. He'd risked his life for her and nearly lost it against Aoko. He'd endured elemental fire and smoke at her side.

And apparently she didn't know him at all.

"Trust me," Sousuke whispered. "I won't let anything hurt you."

Vylia met his gaze, tripped into the emerald pools, and drowned in them.

She tore away and looked down at her fingernails with their chipping polish. "Very well," she murmured. "We will do as you say. I—"

Loud banging on the door behind Ryon cut her off. "Urgent news for the commander!" a voice yelled.

Oda'e's brows knitted together. "Not now."

But the door pushed in behind Ryon with enough force to shove him aside.

"Commander!" A man in an officer's helmet barged in.

"Lieutenant Sa'alu, you are in breach of protocol," Oda'e said. "Wait outside and do not interrupt again."

Ryon snarled and rounded on the one called Sa'alu, who stared at Tekkyn'ashi across the room—first with surprise, then with unbridled hatred in his narrowed eyes.

"Sir," Sa'alu said in a low tone. "Are you aware that your son is a traitor?"

Tekkyn'ashi's hand slid to his sword hilt as Oda'e stepped around the table to block Sa'alu from further entering the room.

"What is the meaning of this?" Oda'e growled. Vylia took a step back as Sousuke moved in front of her.

"You know he was on my unit," Sa'alu hissed. "He was to take a message to Navarro and deliver your daughter home safe, but he went missing. Then I heard he was alive in Jadenvive and working for the Jade Witch."

"He was under my command," Oda'e said. "I used him as a spy, running reconnaissance on the Great Hall for the invasion."

Vylia clutched the neck of her tunic, glancing from Tekkyn'ashi to Sa'alu and back again. Which threads were true in the tapestry of lies?

"Corruption at the highest level. You are just covering for him because he's your progen—"

Sa'alu abruptly cut himself off, but no one had interrupted him. Vylia watched his face twist from rage to confusion.

Then he looked directly at her.

Her heart hiccupped as Sousuke moved to block Sa'alu's view of her. Ryon maneuvered between them as well.

"It seems your mind is ill, Lieutenant," Oda'e said smoothly. "I will forgive your insubordination this once. Do not try me again."

Silence stretched thin. Vylia wished she could see what was happening but didn't move from behind Sousuke's back.

Finally, Oda'e spoke again. "For what urgent reason did you burst in here?"

Sa'alu's voice sounded shaken, unsteady. "Queen Illiana of the Emberhawk has arrived, sir. She requests an audience with you immediately."

27

BROOKE

"To the Alliance!"

Brooke raised her glass and smiled as Coriander's men cheered and drank. She hoped she'd made the right decision to commit her best Phoera-skilled soldiers to Coriander's cause. They'd take the throne at Quin'Zamar with stealth, striking and succeeding before Illiana knew what hit her, and removing and replacing the young queen overnight with the rightful royal family. By the time the Emberhawk army awoke the next day, they'd have a new leader, and they'd probably be happier for it.

Minimum loss of life. Minimum Katrosi involvement. Minimum risk.

Heron's stare burned Brooke from across the table. She didn't meet it.

Yes, it could be considered an act of war if any of Brooke's men were discovered. Yes, the cost of failure was high. Yes, it gambled with another conflict from the west at a time when the Malaano could strike from the east at any moment.

But somehow, it felt right. From the elder's prophecy to the sincerity of Coriander's claim to the vigor of his men. It seemed like a danger worth courting, when the reward was so great. Nothing good came to those too afraid to take risks—only entropy. Her father had taught her that.

Brooke stared into her bowl of tuber soup and randomly wondered how she'd have died if she hadn't left Jadenvive that night and the elder's prophecy had come true.

"If only the people back home loved you as much as these guys do."

Nariellyn's voice startled Brooke from her musing. "Hmm?"

"That smile got stuck on your face. Super creepy."

Brooke took a sip of the cocoa-infused brew, then thought better of taking a full drink. She tried not to grimace through the bitter taste as she set the mug down next to her plate of grilled vegetables, chopped spicy meat, and flatbread beside the soup. "Sorry."

From her peripheral vision, Brooke could tell that Nariellyn was examining her. "Something wrong?" the healer whispered. "You know I didn't mean it."

Brooke tried to shake the uneasy feeling, but it clung to her like a faceless shadow. "I, uh . . ." She dared a glance at Heron, who'd returned to his meal, and Lysander, who awkwardly attempted to play with his niece and nephew at Iraleth's side. *I need your help,* she thought-spoke to Nariellyn.

Her friend now looked even more concerned. *Anything.*

Brooke slowly spooned some meat into her flatbread. *I . . . think I like Lysander.*

Nariellyn whooped, but no one seemed to notice amid the noisy celebration.

Stop it! Brooke could feel her face heating and suddenly wished they'd had more time to apply her warpaint in addition to her headdress. Maybe the chalk and charcoal could have helped to hide her embarrassment.

How do I stop it? I'm engaged to another man.

Nariellyn's joy turned to bubbly laughter. *You're asking the wrong person.*

I know, but . . . Brooke slapped a spoonful of peppers on top of her meat. *You're the only other female on my team right now.*

Nariellyn didn't stop giggling. *Sorry, but I don't know how to undo my flawless matchmaking.*

This is serious, Nari! Brooke returned the smile of a drunk soldier across the table, folded her bread, and took a bite. *If you don't want me to be miserable for the rest of my life—that's what you said, right?—then help me. The last time I tried to stop liking him, it didn't work out.*

No kidding!

She was still laughing, curse her. Brooke elbowed her in the side.

Okay, okay! Nariellyn took a long drink. *Really though, I don't think it's possible to stop loving someone. At least, I've never heard of it. Only time can break the spell. Except in your case, apparently.*

Bleed it all. Brooke let the spice sear her tongue and down her throat, but it didn't dull the trepidation in her heart. *I'm a thought-speaker; shouldn't I be able to control my own emotions?*

Did you ever *pay attention to the elder in aether training?* Nariellyn thought. *A thought-speaker isn't the same as a courage-singer. Thoughts and emotions are different, and your gifting is with thoughts.*

Regardless, I'm cheating on my fiancé with these stupid feelings, and I have to stop. Brooke sighed and took another bite. *Why in the green forests are you so happy, anyway? Didn't you admit that Lysander was toxic? Why do you want me to be with him?*

Nariellyn took a huge bite of her pita. *How toxic is he now, would you say, on a scale of one to Heron?*

Nari, please. I just want to do the right thing, and I don't know what to do. Please stop laughing and help me for once.

Oh, I don't think it's funny. I think it's spicy. Nariellyn clanked her dinner knife on a stoneware bowl that held the hottest, brilliant orange peppers. *And I've already helped in more ways than you know.*

Brooke grunted in frustration as she tugged at the pins that fastened her headdress to her hair. The elaborate assortment of horns, fangs, tail-spikes, and feathers was impossible to put on without Nariellyn's help, but Brooke had assumed she could manage to take it off by herself. How wrong she was.

Still, Brooke was glad that her friend was staying late for more drinks after dinner and likely flirting with every other soldier. They hadn't had much to feast about recently. And knowing Nariellyn, she'd probably shrivel up if too much time passed between parties.

Meanwhile, Brooke was looking forward to that coveted rest and time alone. If she had to do that with her headdress on, so be it.

Her mind repeated the fresh memories of the dinner celebration. How good it felt to have something go right for once. And how oddly easy it seemed! She felt grateful to find such like-minded people in a foreign land—people who only wanted righteousness and integrity from their leadership.

Brooke sighed as she gave up on removing her headdress without removing half of her hair with it. Could she ever be happy like Nariellyn again? Could she ever have an adorable young family like Coriander's?

Heron didn't fit in that mental image, no matter how she tried. Maybe he could change with time. Be a good father.

The thought soured her tongue.

Or . . . what if she *could* find a way out of her engagement? And somehow avoid political repercussions . . .

Maybe she could use aether-fabricated emotions and thoughts to make Heron disgusted with her. Make him back out of the marriage.

She hated manipulation.

But could it be worth it? Would the Darkwood join the Alliance if the Emberhawk did, even without the marriage alliance?

The tent flap swished open behind her with a soft sound of leather on fur.

"You're back earl—" Brooke stopped herself as she turned and saw Heron standing there instead of Nariellyn. Staring at her. Up and down.

His head drooped forward until his gaze became a lazy glare. His forehead beaded with sweat. Fists clenched. "Why do you pretend that I'm not here?"

Brooke took a step back, grateful that she hadn't changed into her night clothes yet. "You just barged into a woman's room without—"

"Oh, you're a woman now? I thought you were a leader."

Brooke watched him as if he were a rabid bear. She was used to such insults. Better to respond with something that calmed him rather than start a fight—the fight he apparently wanted.

"Sometimes it is a struggle to be both," she said.

Heron took a step toward her. "That's why I'm trying to help you." His speech slurred. "I was born and raised to be a leader. Why don't you listen to my advice?"

"I listen," Brooke said, holding her ground as the smell of ale on his breath wafted toward her. "I grew up watching my father lead, just as you did."

"You weren't trained from birth like I was. You were just the chief's daughter to be married off to that deaf snake." He took a step toward her and bumped into one of the small tables, wobbling a miniature horse atop it.

Brooke couldn't tell if he'd said "dead snake" or "deaf snake," but she assumed he was referring to Lysander. Her mind grasped for a response, but he continued.

"I can help you avoid stupid decisions like . . ." Heron whirled his arms to encompass the air in general. "*This*. Why won't you listen to me, your life-mate? You treat me like a child."

Brooke steeled herself. He was clearly drunk. She wouldn't stand for this.

"We're not married yet," she said. "I think you should leave. We can talk in the morning."

Heron stared at her with glassy eyes for a long moment as his frown fell into a scowl. "I don't take orders from you. And I've already made plans to fix everything." He smiled wickedly. "You're welcome."

He lunged at her.

Brooke stepped back, but there was little space to dodge. She ducked for Nariellyn's hammock as Heron's hand clamped like a vise around her bicep. He threw her to the floor.

Feathers in her headdress snapped, protecting Brooke's head from slamming onto the wood platform. She wrenched away from Heron as he came down on top of her. Training from ground-sparring leaped into the forefront of her mind, but Heron wasn't sparring. He grabbed one of her wrists and wrenched it hard enough to strain her joint.

Brooke kneed him in the gut, but the only response was a grunt. She kicked at his groin, but he blocked her with his knee.

She reached for her knife sheath with her spare hand. Heron's eyes flicked at the movement, and he jerked her arm up, forcing her hand out of weapon's reach.

Brooke twisted, trying to throw his balance sideways and gain the advantage.

She couldn't. Her training failed her.

He was too heavy. Too strong.

"You are mine." Heron's breath felt hot on her neck. "I'm going to put you in your place, and you'll learn to like it."

28

LYSANDER

Something didn't feel right.

The way Heron had come to Lysander and Dimbae's tipi and pretended to act friendly. How he'd said a lot of words that meant nothing.

Lysander had only heard Heron's drunken thoughts, which were somehow more boisterous yet harder to comprehend at the same time. All Lysander knew was that Heron was up to no good. But what else was new?

He took another long drink of tea, then watched the steam dance upward from his cup. He just couldn't figure it out. What was Heron's aim? Why try to be civil now—after days of making it abundantly clear that they loathed each other?

Heron was probably just a friendly drunk. Nothing else made sense.

Lysander!

He nearly spilled his tea. That was Brooke's voice, louder in his head than he'd ever heard it. But so terrified and desperate that he hardly recognized her.

Help me!

Lysander shot to his feet, and the world spun. Darkness claimed the edges of his vision, creeping inward for more. His knees weakened, threatening to send him back down to the earth.

He gasped as hot tea sloshed over his fingers. *What . . . ?*

He knew this feeling. Sudden, inexplicable exhaustion. The feebleness of his muscles even as adrenaline surged. The dry, tacky sensation on his tongue he hadn't noticed before.

Lysander's pulse drummed through his skull as he looked down at the tea. He didn't need to inspect it to know it had been spiked with dreamthistle.

Heron had poisoned him.

Lysander's hand shot for the vial of antidote on his bandoleer.

Empty. He'd given it all to Brooke.

And the new concoction he'd made for her that afternoon wasn't strong enough. He downed it anyway, coughing as he swallowed the herbs dry. It would have to let him stay alive long enough to help Brooke. Then he'd have to make it to Granny Zelle's pyramid for the missing reagent. Without dying first. Somehow.

He had built up a resistance to dreamthistle as he'd worked with planting and harvesting its toxic roots, but all that would gift him was a little more time. It would have to be enough.

Lysander stumbled through the tent flap and found Brooke and Nariellyn's tipi, squinting at the sunset beyond the jungle trees. Brooke's thought-voice had come from that direction, and her aether presence shone like a beacon of horror.

His breath came in gasps, and his heart spread more poison with every beat. He reached out for the Phoera element to mask the noise he must be making as he ran. It responded like fire in his blood, roaring with his own fear and urgency and rage.

Lysander blinked away the darkness and steadied his swaying as he slipped inside the tipi.

Heron had Brooke pinned on the floor, crushing her with his weight as he yanked at her tunic. She clawed for his eyes but he captured her wrists in a single hand. A tear slipped from Brooke's wide eyes as they flicked to Lysander, pleading for help.

Lysander drew his dagger, took two long strides, and stabbed Heron in the back.

Heron's body clenched, frozen in the pain of death as Lysander's blade struck true. A silent strike for a swift assassination.

Lysander removed his dagger and kicked Heron off of Brooke. Heron rolled under the hammock, his eyes and mouth twitching in his final moments.

Brooke scrambled to her feet and pushed her back into the tipi's wall as if it could protect her. She looked down at herself, seemingly to take account of her body. Her headdress was mangled and a bruise was already appearing on her arm, but otherwise, Lysander couldn't see any injuries.

"Are you okay?" he asked.

Brooke's limbs shook as she stared at Heron's body. Her lips moved, but Lysander couldn't determine what she said through the trembling.

"It's all right." Lysander stepped forward, trying to block the dying prince from her view. "He can't hurt you any more."

She shrank back from him. Her gaze slowly turned from shock to relief to gratitude to realization to anger. She screamed something loud enough for him to hear a faint, distant cry.

Lysander leaned back to give her space as she yelled at him. He couldn't tell what. He cleaned his blade and sheathed it until she remembered that he was deaf.

You killed him!

"Yes."

What have you done?

The darkness returned to Lysander's vision, and dizziness overpowered him. "He . . . I couldn't let him hurt you."

He wasn't even supposed to be here! No one was supposed to know we're here. Tears streamed from Brooke's face. *The Darkwood will declare war over this!*

Lysander tried to control his breathing, but it didn't help the sickeningly sweet feeling that tempted him with sleep. "He poisoned me," he said, but Brooke was screaming something about him being a killer at the same time, so he doubted she heard him.

It didn't matter. He was fading fast. His job here was done, and now there was only one hope for survival.

He turned on his heel and left the tipi, nearly falling as he went.

The wooden platform presented a challenge. He tumbled from it and landed on his knees as his vision retreated.

I'm not going to make it, he thought. There was no way he could make it home to his grandmother's pyramid and take the antidote before sleep claimed him.

With his last remaining strength, Lysander put his fingers to his mouth and whistled for Sorrel, so loud that his ears picked up some of the shrill sound.

Don't fall asleep, he told himself. *Don't fall over. Don't lie down.*

He lost track of time. Brooke appeared beside him, looking dark and desaturated as he battled the shadows.

Did you say he poisoned you? Brooke's voice rang through his mind, breaking through the haze and giving him something to focus on.

"Dreamthistle," he managed.

Can't you drink the tea you gave me earlier?

"Not . . . enough."

He felt Sorrel's warm fur as she nuzzled him. Leaned into her. Collapsed to the earth.

What do I do? Brooke asked.

"Granny Zelle . . . antidote." Lysander didn't have the strength to mount Sorrel, though his vision returned enough to glimpse the gryphon's concerned golden face for a moment.

Brooke lent him her shoulder, and Sorrel lowered her thick neck until Lysander was lying on her back.

You can't ride like this. You'll fall—

"Tie me on." It was impossible not to snuggle into the gryphon's fur. Just like when he was a boy. Napping in the sun . . . So soft . . .

Brooke shoved him hard in the shoulder. *Don't fall asleep!*

Consciousness toyed with Lysander like a cat with yarn. He thought Brooke might be tying his wrists together around Sorrel's neck, but he couldn't tell. Something pulled tight around his back, but he didn't know what it was.

He tried to tell Sorrel to fly home, but he couldn't hear himself speak.

Stay with me! Brooke grabbed his face between her hands. *There's been enough death today. You will make it there and you will live!*

She was beautiful. Such an optimist, even if she took the path of strategy rather than bubbling positivity. Her face was the best last thing he could see, even if she was tear-streaked and bruised. She would survive.

He didn't want to die, but he had to at some point, anyway. He'd been able to avenge himself. To do something good with his final days. And Zamara was dead. What more could he ask for?

Gentle wind through Sorrel's feathers drifted him into the long sleep.

29

RYON

Ryon ducked into an alleyway, leaning against the corner of an abandoned house for support as he released the Phoera energy that shrouded him. He allowed himself a moment to catch his breath. He'd used more of the element for stealth in the past few weeks than ever before. Good practice for his skills, but exhausting. Thankfully Felix had given him plenty of the syn Zamara had released when she'd died.

He shook his head as if trying to jiggle the fatigue loose. If only someone else could make these supply runs, he could focus on escorting groups of people out through the root caves and on to freedom in the forest to the north. The Roanoke received every group with smiles and songs and fish soup, but Ryon wondered how many more refugees the small tribe could handle.

And how many more of these excursions he could make. Eventually, the survivors would have to compromise and allow other elementalists to take the risk of stealthing through the city for necessities. Like that teenage refugee who had an obvious crush on Kira.

Ryon pulled his hood up, lest his silver hair catch the sunlight and draw unwanted attention. No Malaano soldiers in sight, though. Which was probably why Oda'e's quartermaster had chosen this location as the drop-off point.

He found a basket and dug through its contents. Carved bowls, cured hides and quilts, soap that smelled like goat's milk and oats, and torches dipped in fresh sap. Everything Kira had asked for.

Ryon took a deep breath and hefted the basket. Not too heavy this time. "Idryon?"

Ryon startled and turned to find a tall man standing in the shadows behind him. He certainly hadn't been there before.

The man stepped forward into the light. "Do you remember me?" he asked.

He certainly seemed familiar. Emberhawk, to be sure—possibly nobility from the bright glow of his golden eyes and hair the same mercurial color as Ryon's. But he was dressed in leather armor and dark cloth instead of colorful silks.

The man's name emerged suddenly in Ryon's mind. "Xavier."

They'd grown up around the palace together but had never been close friends. Xavier was Lysander's friend. Especially recently. *Too* recently.

Ryon's blood simmered. "You're the one who poisoned Brooke."

Xavier made a face like a child who'd been caught with his cheeks stained by joyberry cobbler. "Normally people are happy when their boss dies." His voice was smooth as honey. "Lysander said he saved her, so why can't anyone find her?"

The basket cracked as Ryon gripped harder. "Do you honestly think I'd tell you where she was even if I knew?"

"Well, you *are* the son of the traitor, so it wouldn't be that far-fetched." Xavier hooked his thumbs on his belt. "But I'm not here to hurt her or you or anyone. I come in peace with an invitation from the queen."

Ryon's muscles remained tense. "Illiana is not the rightful queen."

"She sits on the throne and wears the crown regardless." Xavier shrugged. "And pays well."

"What does she want?" Ryon seethed.

"She wants to speak with you. She's just arrived at the Great Hall. I came to assist you in evading the Malaano." Xavier tilted his head. "Although it seems you don't require help in that regard."

"No thanks." Ryon turned on his heel and headed down the alley.

"A request from your queen is an order," Xavier called behind him.

"She's not my queen," Ryon growled. He summoned the flows of Phoera, which rejected the light around him and cloaked him in darkness.

Just as quickly, the reflection was torn from him like scales from a fish. Ryon lost his grip on the element and felt himself reappear. He cursed and backpedaled to duck into the alley once again.

Two guards chatted at the distant turn of a muddy street, oblivious to Ryon.

He glared over his shoulder at Xavier.

"I'm sorry," Xavier said with an amused look. "But I have orders to escort you to the queen."

Ryon could feel his veins pumping. "I said no."

Xavier watched him for a long moment. Then he disappeared.

Ryon slipped into a crouch, his hand itching for his dagger. Instead he held onto the basket and redoubled his stealth, slipping back into the darkness. Surely Xavier couldn't maintain his own invisibility and sabotage Ryon's at the same time. Escape was just a matter of remaining silent.

He moved from his last known location as quickly as possible. But the earth was soft and sandy—he was leaving tracks.

Ryon heard footsteps a second before something slammed into his back and clamped down on his throat.

He dropped the basket, spilling supplies as he pulled at the arm around his neck. Xavier tightened the chokehold, wrenching Ryon from behind.

Ryon shifted to the side and slammed his elbow backward into Xavier's gut. Xavier grunted but didn't relent.

He gasped for air but none came. He bent his knees, leaned forward, and curled over, hurtling Xavier over his back to slam onto the ground in front of him.

Xavier still didn't let go, bringing Ryon with him in an awkward collapse of limbs.

The edges of Ryon's vision darkened as his lungs burned for air. He released Xavier's arm around his throat, grabbed his knife from its sheath, and drove it toward Xavier's side.

Xavier let go and took Ryon's arm instead, but the blade's tip had already pierced his armor. Ryon gulped in air as Xavier twisted his wrist, wrenching it until Ryon dropped the knife and scrambled up.

Ryon staggered away and reached for his machete.

Xavier disappeared.

Ryon cursed and struggled to summon the element. The syn felt sluggish in his blood. He gave up on the invisibility, grabbed a torch from the ground, and snapped to light it with a roaring flame. He wielded his machete in one hand and the fire in the other, watching the ground for footprints to appear in the sandy soil.

"I don't want to hurt you." Xavier's voice came from the right. "Just come with—"

Ryon directed the torch's flame to lash out like a fireball. It whipped onto the ground, searing the soil with an acrid smell.

The flames bent around a void in their center. Xavier reappeared, the fire extinguishing at his outstretched hand.

Ryon pointed his machete at Xavier's placid face, daring him to approach as he caught his breath.

Xavier drew a shortsword and lunged at him.

Ryon took a step back and parried, his heart slamming into his ribs. He sidestepped and stabbed at Xavier's chest.

Xavier dodged to the side and blocked the strike. His sword screeched along Ryon's blade until it slammed into the hilt and twirled. Ryon's hand erupted in pain and released the machete without his permission.

Ryon shoved the torch into Xavier's face.

Xavier roared. Something connected with Ryon's jaw and his vision exploded. He stumbled back.

Crack. An impact on the side of his head sent him crumpling to the earth.

Time slowed as Ryon's hearing reduced to a high-pitched whine. He squeezed his eyelids open and shut, trying to clear his vision as he struggled to regain his feet.

His body wasn't responding as it should. Terror redoubled and chilled him as realization dawned.

Xavier was a professional assassin. Ryon was just a scout.

He was prey in a tiger's lair.

An arm clamped around his neck from behind, just as before. It cinched tight like a vise.

Ryon embraced his element and screamed with the last breath trapped in his lungs, fire exploding from his skin in a blinding fury. The heat consumed him, alighting his nerves, but the choking grasp released him.

He wheezed and panted as the world tilted. His legs were too weak to lift him, so he crawled. Pulled himself through shards of molten, sandy glass that burned through his clothing and seared his flesh.

His neck constricted again. He couldn't breathe.

His strength was stolen, his element spent.

Kira . . .

Blackness smothered him, and his consciousness flitted away.

30

KIRALAU

Kira's hands shook as she lifted a hand-carved bowl from the earth and brushed sandy soil from it. The supplies she'd requested for the refugees had been spilled, scattered, and forgotten.

Ryon wasn't just late. He was in trouble.

She dropped the bowl and examined the mess of footprints and grooves in the earth, indicating a struggle. One set of tracks looked to be Ryon's. Soft in the way that they pressed into the ground—probably his moccasins, which he wore instead of his boots when he had reason to reduce the sound of his footsteps.

Another set of prints came from further down the alleyway. Bigger, but also soft, hinting that they were shoes made of leather as well.

Kira bit the inside of her lip. Did that mean Ryon's attacker was a user of elemental invisibility as well?

"Here," Tekkyn called.

Kira hurried to her brother's position, careful not to disturb the story the tracks told. Tekkyn pointed to a flickering light in the soil. No—a reflection. Dozens of them. Shards of glass, misshapen and smooth, not sharp as if from a broken vase. Dirty with mud and speckled with sand, as if they'd been melted from the earth itself and left there.

Kira's pulse pounded as she studied the glass droplets. They appeared in a circular pattern, except on one end where it appeared something had been dragged through along the ground. Something heavy.

Tekkyn whistled low. "Must have been some fight to get hot enough to turn sand to glass."

The world blurred as Kira retreated into her thoughts. Who could use Phoera to produce temperatures that hot? Maybe Ryon, with the excess syn Felix had given him from Zamara. But what about the other one—probably a man, since the tracks were larger than Ryon's. If Ryon had won, wouldn't he have returned with the supplies? Had the encounter left him horribly burned?

Please just be alive!

Kira snapped back to reality and hastily searched for blood. Nothing too obvious. After a minute, she found a few dark smears. Maybe just mud.

She dipped her fingers into the thick substance and lifted them to her nose. It smelled of the sharp tang of minerals.

Blood. Congealed and darkened with time. But not fully dried thanks to the moisture of the surrounding earth—perhaps only an hour or two?

"Not enough for him to be seriously injured," Tekkyn murmured as he crouched beside her. "And maybe not even his blood."

Kira stared at the deep red on her fingers. Was this the last of Ryon she'd ever touch?

Where are you?

"Hey." Tekkyn dropped a thick hand on Kira's shoulder. "We didn't find a body or a lot of blood. Which means they might not have been fighting with weapons. Which means whoever did this probably wanted him alive."

Kira shook with the effort to contain a sudden onslaught of horror. Shock. Confusion. Despair.

This was too much. Hadn't they been through enough?

Tekkyn shook her gently, but she didn't meet his gaze. "We'll find him, Frizz. I swear it."

Kira sucked in a breath and her lungs spasmed. "It was probably another light-bender," she said in a constricted voice, trying desperately to restrain her emotions and return to logic and reason. "Or a sound-bender like Lysander. Someone who uses Phoera for stealth." She pointed at the most distinct impression of a footprint. "Aren't they the only ones who wear leather shoes?"

"Sekoiako wear moccasins too," Tekkyn stood, his light armor creaking with the movement. "At least, the ones we encountered on the border last year did."

But that didn't make any sense. "Have you seen any Sekoiako in Jadenvive recently?"

"No. But I heard there were a few who delivered medical aid and food after the Emberhawk attack."

"It must have been a Katrosi," Kira whispered. "Maybe an azure mask."

But what would the azure masks want with Ryon? Had one gone rogue?

"No, most of the Katrosi who wear moccasins have a split for the toe," Tekkyn said.

Kira blinked up at him. "What?"

"They keep the big toe separate. Makes climbin' easier." Tekkyn knelt back down and drew in a clear spot on the sand with his finger. It looked to be a footprint, but with the largest toe distinct from the rest of the imprint. "Their tracks would probably look something like this."

Kira stared at his drawing, understanding his words but not grasping the implications. "That can't be true. If the Katrosi wore moccasins like that, Ryon would too."

"But Ryon doesn't climb as much as he walks. He's a scout—or he was. So this design doesn't really make sense for him," Tekkyn said. "But I've seen it on several orange masks who guard the city. They need to be able to climb all over the tree limbs to stop criminals and such. And a lot of the azures wear this design, too. Trust me; I got a good look when they took me to Brooke 'cause they thought I was involved in the assault."

Kira tried to coax her spinning mind into focusing, but it seemed nearly impossible through the chaos of her emotions. Finally, she got her voice to work again. "So you're saying this man was Sekoiako?"

Tekkyn shrugged. "Maybe, but that seems unlikely."

Kira had seen this style of shoe before. Tribal merchants with whom she'd traded cherry jam. Travellers who'd passed through Navarro—Katrosi and Sekoiako, probably. The Roanoke had been barefoot for the most part. What about the Emberhawk?

Her bones chilled. Lysander wore shoes of this make. And so had Sylendrin, if she remembered correctly.

Emberhawk combatants. Assassins. The arsonists and butchers of Jadenvive.

Surely Lysander wouldn't attack his own cousin. Hadn't he left with Brooke?

But the rest of the Emberhawk who'd attacked the city were dead.

Except the one who'd poisoned Brooke.

Kira's breath caught and a tear escaped. No, the evidence here didn't look like Ryon had been killed by that assassin. But then why would he be taken alive? What did the Emberhawk want with him?

She suddenly recalled their encounter with Zamara in the forest. The one they'd barely survived.

Zamara had tracked Ryon down because she'd wanted him to return home with her. To Quin'Zamar.

To marry her daughter.

Illiana.

"I think Ryon was taken by the Emberhawk."

Kira's father looked up at her with tired eyes. Clearly she wasn't his first meeting of the day.

"What?"

Admitting it out loud made the urge to cry well up inside Kira, so she decided not to repeat herself. Instead she clenched her fists and curled her toes, trying to imprison her emotions while staring hard at the inkwell on the table in front of her. She took a steadying breath, then forced herself to look up at Commander Oda'e.

His eyes cleared of fatigue as he leaned forward and motioned for a guard to close both doors on either side of the map room. "Was he discovered as he led a group out to the Roanoke?"

"No, he was attacked." Kira forcefully cleared her throat. "Here in the city."

Oda'e frowned. "The Emberhawk could not have infiltrated . . ." He trailed off and looked at Tekkyn.

Kira glanced back at Tekkyn to see him nod.

Oda'e let out a curse with a scratchy breath. He mumbled something and ran a hand through his short black hair.

"What?"

He rubbed his eyes. "Queen Illiana was just here for a visit."

Kira's blood ran cold. "Why? What did she want?"

"Her share of the plunder," Oda'e muttered. "Commander Sorrowsong, the one who planned the attack on Jadenvive, struck a deal with Zamara. The Malaano supplied explosives, and the Emberhawk made the initial attack that softened up the city's defenses for the Malaano invasion."

"Did she mention Ryon?" Kira demanded.

"No." Oda'e paused. "But she did make a comment about taking custody of Emberhawk citizens. She wanted the prisoners."

Kira clenched her fists until her nails dug into her palms. Why would Illiana phrase it like that if she only wanted prisoners? She'd been laying claim to Ryon!

She couldn't hold it in any more. She spun on her heel and made for the door. Tekkyn didn't stop her.

"Where are you going?" Oda'e called.

"How long ago did she leave?" Kira's voice shook. "Which route did she take?"

She heard her father rise from his chair and step around the table behind her. "Kira, wait. Do you have any evidence?"

Kira squeezed her eyes shut, allowing a hot tear to fall. She quickly wiped it away. "I have enough."

"You can't just run after her. She has a royal entourage full of—"

"I can and I will." She stepped toward the door.

"Stop," her father said with the voice that commanded armies. "Think about this first or you will meet the same fate or worse."

Kira wanted to scream at him. He'd let Illiana into the city. This was his fault.

But he was right.

She didn't turn around. Her breath came in a halting, quivering gulp.

"There were six guards, several handmaids, and apparently others in hiding if one of them took Ryon." It sounded like Oda'e was talking in Tekkyn's direction instead of hers. "But they rode on tame trace cats—very fast. I doubt it's possible to catch up with them before they reach Quin'Zamar."

Stress lifted from Kira like a sudden flight of doves. The way he was talking—did he mean to allow her to go?

Well, she'd go regardless, but his support would make things a lot easier on her heart.

"We're technically employed by Brooke," Tekkyn said. "I'm supposed to be guardin' Vylia, and Kira's her translator, and somethin' or other about makeup."

Kira swallowed to revive her voice as she turned to face them. "Brooke's gone. And even if she were here, she wouldn't be in charge any more."

Tekkyn gave her a disapproving look. "My word and my loyalty run deeper than that, Frizz, and I thought yours did too."

Kira cringed. "Well, I mean, didn't you give Vylia your best soldiers as guards?" she asked her father. "And Ryon said she was leaving for Sekoiako lands anyway." The mention of Ryon's name cut through her.

It didn't matter what she'd agreed to before. It didn't matter what was right. If she had to choose between her fiancé and her princess—no, the princess of the empire that she loathed and that her people would soon declare war against—there was no contest. She held no ill will toward

Vylia, but she would choose Ryon every time.

Was he technically her fiancé though? Yes, she decided he was. She would find him and marry him as soon as they were able. The fates weren't allowing for any longer of an engagement period.

And if Illiana wanted to marry him for some twisted reason . . . She'd just have to be faster still.

"Let's just go talk to Vylia," Tekkyn said. "She'll understand." He ruffled Kira's hair and smiled softly when she jerked away to ensure the butterfly pin Ryon had given her remained in its place.

"Do not let any harm come to her," Oda'e said to Tekkyn in a low tone. "Take anything you need and go swiftly." He strode to Kira and knelt until he was eye-level with her. His piercing blue gaze shone with concern and determination. And something deeper . . . a father's love.

"I know you're hurting," he whispered. "But don't act out of desperation. Quiet your heart. Use your mind—it's sharp." He kissed her forehead. "You get that from me, you know." He winked.

Kira grabbed him in a tight hug, clanking his armor plates together as a sob tore free. "Thank you, Dad."

"Go get him." He hugged her back, then looked up at Tekkyn. "Vylia is collecting what she can from her ruined embassy. The top platform. Quickly."

31

VYLIA

Vylia turned her coral crown over in her hands, looking for burn marks or other signs of damage. But aside from the smell of smoke, the blue, pink, and purple spires branched outward, unharmed.

A deep sense of loss settled in Vylia's stomach as she ran her fingers over the bumpy sea shells protected by shining lacquer. Her old life was gone. Sousuke would probably say to leave her crown behind, along with her dresses and the rest of her luggage—anything that could reveal her identity.

She sighed and carefully set the crown back on the dresser where she'd left it that fateful day. Best that it stay here, at her embassy that was not meant to be. Where many of the people closest to her had died. Xi. Juli. Uma.

Vylia looked to the stripped bed, where piles of belongings of her lost companions had been neatly piled. A leather-bound journal rested atop Uma's priestess robes.

Tears threatened to rise, causing an odd sensation. Like her eyes were pulling for moisture, but had run dry.

She didn't want to cry any more. She'd been miserable, mourning in the dark caverns beneath the city for days.

I choose joy. Even though I can barely hold my head up, I will force myself to smile and pretend to be happy. The feelings will follow.

Uma had taught her that. It's how she'd dealt with the loss of her mother and her father's coldness. Thrived in spite of it.

Vylia blinked at the uncomfortable feeling in her eyes and moved to the collection of Uma's things. Longing for her mentor tugged hard at her heart as she lifted the small, worn book and examined its binding.

Uma had journaled every day. It felt too soon to open such a private thing. As if her spirit still lingered and would catch Vylia snooping.

But her curiosity got the best of her, as usual.

Vylia unwound the cord that wrapped thrice around the book, holding the folded leather cover tight around the pages. She flipped to the last entry. Held her breath, waiting for the emotions she knew would hit her like high tide.

Uma's handwriting was pristine, reflecting her tutelage under the empire's most renowned scribes.

YEAR 3469. HARVEST SEASON. WANING CRESCENT.

> *I fear I have made a grave mistake.*
>
> *It would be foolish to write about such things, but I must organize my thoughts, and I have no other priestesses to beseech for wisdom.*
>
> *I must remember to remove these pages and put them to the flame when I return to the temple and set things right. Assuming I have not done too much damage already.*
>
> *Vylia is lying to me. I know it. It breaks my heart that she will not confide in me. Perhaps it is because the nature of her situation is confusing. Unthinkable. Forbidden.*
>
> *Heavens, the Emperor will have me killed for this.*
>
> *I think the mirror is speaking to her. Whatever is inside it, no one can say. But it cannot be the goddess. It is deceptive. Desperate. Evil.*
>
> *We all know not to listen to it. Not to speak of it.*
>
> *Simply writing this fills me with dread. And yet admitting it in some form also gives me peace. Recognition of what I*

have done. Acknowledgement of this surreal situation and confidence to do something about it. Though I scarcely understand what's happening or what should be done.

What I do know is this: by removing the Malo Stone from its place in the temple, I've unintentionally removed its restraints. Somehow.

I know that makes no sense. None of this makes sense.

But what if the decorative dais the Stone has sat upon for years has a functional purpose? They say Lillian's mate, Felix Kael Tae, forged it when she ascended to godhood. What if he forged it from glass-gold to prevent a demon from manipulating the stone? Or a spirit from possessing it? Or some dark entity from siphoning the power of the goddess's mirror?

We cannot ignore this any longer. When I return home, I will speak plainly of this to the High Priestess. We must determine what or who the voice truly is. Because of our ignorance, in removing the Stone from its dais, I fear I have placed Vylia in danger.

But the last Empress removed the Stone upon her inheritance, though it was quickly put back to rest for many years. We've heard whispers of Empresses and Priestesses hearing the voice before. Maybe the glass-gold only hinders it. Or something else about the temple, perhaps?

We cannot turn a blind eye for fear of blasphemy any longer. We must determine these things before something terrible happens. Whatever it is must be speaking quickly and clearly to Vylia—I believe she has already tasted its power.

What have I done? Not only have I set something free— or enabled it—I have written of the forbidden. I must destroy these pages. But not until I can read over my scrambled thoughts, pray, and hopefully grasp some shred of truth.

Only one thing is certain: I must return the Stone to the golden dais as soon as possible.

And perhaps, though it is certainly ill-advised, I may have to speak of this to Vylia before she is deceived. Whatever power the voice offers, it surely comes with a price.

Goddess . . . Wind Serpent . . . Creator. Whoever is true, whoever is listening—help me! Let me return the Stone safely to the temple. Let no harm come to Vylia. Let the High Priestess listen to my worries. Reveal to me the truth, and calm my rattled heart.

Vylia stared at the final words in shock. The rest of the pages were blank.

Her beloved mentor had passed into the next life without discovering the truth. But what was the truth? And why had the priestesses not uncovered it?

Vylia realized she was holding the journal too tightly. Asking those kinds of questions would make them sound like pagans to the priestesses. Because the inquiry might prove their precious Lillian to be a false god.

Or nothing but an elemental trapped inside a rock. Imprisoned by the creator for unknown deeds lost to time.

"Your Highness?"

Vylia startled and whipped around. "Oh! Sous—"

It wasn't Sousuke. One of Oda'e's most trusted men watched her with a guilty look, as if she were a porcelain vase he'd just dropped.

He cleared his throat. "Sorry, my lady. I didn't mean to startle you." He took a step back. "Sousuke is guarding the front. Would you like me to retrieve him?"

She almost said no, but in truth, she wanted nothing more than Sousuke at her side. These new guards might be Oda'e's best, but she didn't know them. And she had bad history with guards she didn't know.

"Yes, please."

The guard bowed. "There are two people requesting to see you: a young man named Tekkyn'ashi and a young woman named Kiralau. They say it's urgent."

Vylia nodded. "Send them in."

The guard hurried out and Vylia scanned Uma's last written words again. Glass-gold . . . surely she'd meant the beautiful sculpture that formed a perfect mount for the smooth oval shape of the Malo stone. Vylia remembered seeing it a few years ago in all its splendor—it looked like a lotus flower with a bird resting on top, with petals reaching up and feathers stretching down to meet in gentle crystalline tips.

She hadn't known that the fire-spirit Felix had forged it, and she'd assumed it was made of glass infused with streaks of reflective, glittering color and a golden sheen.

Yet again, everything she'd once thought was wrong. It wasn't glass, it was gold—somehow. Perhaps only an elemental could forge such a thing.

And the pedestal wasn't a piece of artwork for Lillian's mirror to rest upon. With the way the glass-gold petals and feathers touched, it was more like a prison.

Vylia hastily closed the journal and placed it back on top of Uma's belongings. If Uma's assumptions had been correct, there was a chance to set things right.

She would finish her mentor's mission. Or she at least had to try.

Footsteps announced the arrival of Kira, Tekkyn'ashi, and Sousuke. Vylia stood up and instinctively went to straighten her dress before remembering she was wearing nondescript Katrosi garb. It was so comfortable she kept forgetting about it.

"Princess." Kira bowed as she approached, and Vylia waved in an attempt to get her to stop. It would be nice to have a friend who could treat her like a normal human being.

"Call me Vy."

"Vy." Kira came closer with a troubled expression. "My fiancé, Ryon, has been taken by the Emberhawk."

Vylia blinked. "Oh. Oh, no." She gathered from Kira's disheveled appearance and the beaded sweat on her forehead that this had just happened.

"Please release me from service so I can go after him," Kira said.

"Kira," Tekkyn'ashi scolded in a low tone, but his sister ignored him.

Vylia was left stunned. "O-of course," she granted, though selfishly, losing another friend was the last thing she wanted. But what else could she do?

"I'm sorry," Kira said. "It's not that I want to leave you, but I have to find him, and I know it's safer for you—well, you're heading in the other direction. But at least my translations aren't needed as much now that you have a Malaano guard again."

Vylia listened to Kira stumble all over her words. Of course Vylia still needed a translator while she remained in tribal lands, especially to communicate with the Sekoiako. Kira was clearly grasping, but Vylia couldn't blame her.

Sousuke watched from the corner, where an exquisite armoire was marred by what appeared to be a splatter of dried blood that might have been his own from that fateful night. He folded his arms and didn't seem to give Vylia any sign or opinion of his own.

"I release you," Vylia said, although she supposed Kira was more under Brooke's employ than her own. "But please do me one favor first."

Kira was visibly relieved. "Yes?"

Vylia pointed to the bracelet around Kira's wrist. "What is that made of?"

Kira pulled the bangle close to her chest. "It's gold. I know it doesn't look like it, but . . . That's what I was told."

Vylia's jaw went slack. She doubted the golden-streaked, shimmering bracelet was large enough to fit around the Malo stone, but still, it was a start.

"May I have it?"

"No." Kira clutched it tight. "I mean . . ." She looked down at it with moisture cresting in her eyes. "Ryon gave it to me. He said it was his father's." She slowly slid it down and over her hand. "But if it will let me get him back—"

Vylia stopped her by placing a hand over Kira's before she could fully remove the bracelet. "It's all right. I only need something made of gold that's been forged in the same translucent manner. Do you know where else I might find some?"

Kira glanced back at Tekkyn'ashi, who shook his head. "No . . . I've never seen it before this," Kira said.

"Perhaps in the treasury," Sousuke said. "Why do you need it?" His green eyes searched her as if he knew something was amiss.

Vylia took a deep breath. She'd probably sound like a lunatic, but they deserved to know. And at least now she had Uma's diary to support her claims.

She instructed Sousuke to shut the door. Then she told them everything.

Kira listened with a set jaw. Sousuke stood still but his fingers thrummed on his belt as he stared into nothingness. Tekkyn's eyes grew to the size of twin moons and appeared to get stuck like that.

"So, would you please come with me to the treasury?" Vylia asked Kira as her story concluded. "You're the only other person I know who's heard the voice. Help me find a piece of glass-gold, and then you can help determine if it works. Then I can feel safer on the journey back to Maqua, where it can be returned to its proper place in the temple."

Kira looked up from Uma's journal to meet Vylia's gaze with knitted brows and a frown. She could read her own thoughts on Kira's face: Maqua was the most dangerous place on the planet for Vylia. Even more so to be traveling across the Sea of Bones without a wavesinger to protect them from the ocean's wrath, since the Malo stone hampered Vylia's elemental abilities. Finding a piece of glass-gold—if it worked—would increase the odds in their favor.

"I'm sure Dad will let us into the treasury if we explain this to him," Kira said as she handed the journal to Vylia and turned to leave. "Let's go as fast as possible."

32

BROOKE

Brooke stood numbly, watching Sorrel disappear into the distant sky with Lysander's limp form lashed onto her back. If only gryphons could carry more than one person! Since she didn't have a flying mount of her own, all she could do now was hope that Sorrel knew the way and that Lysander's grandmother was a birdwatcher who'd see them coming and get him that antidote as fast as possible.

Everything that had just happened . . . surely it hadn't just happened. It was a dream. No, a nightmare. Several nightmares.

She could scarcely believe Soaring Heron had attacked her and tried to kill Lysander. Sure, he was an entitled prince, but assault and murder were nothing short of criminal. Well, they were criminal in Katrosi lands, at least.

She wouldn't wear the paint of mourning for him.

No, Heron hadn't murdered Lysander. He couldn't have.

Brooke squinted after Sorrel, barely able to see the gryphon on the horizon as she disappeared between jungle leaves. *Aeo, save him!*

She hugged herself and squeezed her eyes shut. She felt hollow, like she'd been robbed. Her strength mocked and her honor violently stolen. Thank the heavens Lysander had been there, otherwise . . . A shudder tore through her.

Lysander couldn't die. It was too much.

How long had she been standing there? It didn't matter. What on beautiful Alani should she do? How could she possibly explain such circumstances to King Raven Eye?

The Tribal Alliance wouldn't survive this. It would only be the Sekoiako, the pacifist Roanoke, and the tattered Katrosi until the Malaano invaded and wiped them out.

Her heart ached. All of her work ruined by a single act. Something out of her control. And yet she'd failed. Failed the dreams of her father and the legacy of her grandfather.

The Katrosi people would not understand. No one would. Except Lysander, but he was as good as dead. Unless he had some sort of resistance to dreamthistle, he could be dead already. How far away was his grandmother's pyramid?

Brooke's mind refused to think any more. Her hands trembled. She knew she had to move. Had to do . . . *something.* Anything but stand there between the tipis in her rumpled clothing and broken headdress.

Dimbae. He'd know what to do.

Brooke headed for his tipi. It was inappropriate to enter uninvited, but she already knew Lysander wasn't in there. And circumstances permitted. Dimbae probably wasn't even in there since she'd given him a break, but it was at least a place to start.

She found Dimbae napping inside on a hammock that looked entirely too small for him. Awkwardness felt dulled in her bruised heart. "Dimbae," she called, keeping her distance. She knew better than to startle him awake.

He woke with a deep breath and looked at her over his shoulder. Watched her sleepily, like he was wondering if she were a dream.

The tears came then. "Heron is dead."

Dimbae threw his quilt aside and was standing before her in an instant. "Are you hurt?" His eyes widened with concern. She must look awful.

"No," Brooke said, but it felt like a lie. "He poisoned Lysander and . . ." Her voice died.

Dimbae's gaze ignited. He cursed. "Where?"

"M-my tipi."

Brooke could barely keep up with him as he left, dashed across the path, and stormed into her tipi with his blade drawn. She ducked under the tent flap behind him and nearly ran into his back.

"Where is the body?"

Brooke moved around Dimbae and stared at the wooden floor in shock. Only a few drops of blood and broken feathers lay scattered.

Horror crested on her like a tide. "He was right . . . here . . ."

Heron's bodyguard. What was his name? Long Root.

Her chance at covering this up had just disappeared with the body.

Sounds muffled and colors dimmed. She couldn't speak, couldn't move, couldn't think. She only existed in this muted, ghastly, hopeless reality.

Dimbae called out to her. Something about the body being dragged.

Nariellyn appeared out of nowhere. She yelled something about the camp being under attack.

But that wasn't possible. Even her luck couldn't be *that* bad.

Orange blur of fire. Dark haze of smoke. Screams. Dashes of running people. Zips of arrows.

Red and gold of Emberhawk armor.

Brooke realized she was in shock. She rejected it. Detested herself for it. Leaders couldn't go into shock.

She grasped for stability and muttered an incoherent prayer. Mental walls rose around her mind, her heart. She shoved emotions outside them. Feelings in this moment would only cloud her reflexes.

Heron must have betrayed them to Illiana—everyone else was loyal, and the timing couldn't be a coincidence. But why?

The Darkwood had always been more closely allied with the Emberhawk than the rest of the tribes . . . Had Heron's father, King Raven Eye, allied with Illiana already? Then . . . could Heron have leaked the location of the encampment for Illiana's benefit?

Lysander had been right.

Curse Heron to the pits of Zoth.

Brooke closed her eyes and recalled her father's lessons. She was a weapon.

Know your enemy. Outsmart him. A fast mind is sharper than a fast blade.

Strike to kill swiftly—this is mercy. Evil will not grant you the same.

I pray you never have to kill a man. But if you do, let the angels guide your spear and the creator sort your dead.

Brooke steadied herself and gathered her surroundings. Dimbae must have moved her. She was near the center lodge, pressed up against the bark of an enormous tree that shielded them from a torrent of arrows.

"Where's my spear?"

Nariellyn handed it to her. "They mustn't see you," she whispered. "You're wearing your headdress. If they recognize you, the queen will know you were here."

"I don't care." Brooke looked around for a target for her spear tip. Emberhawk soldiers were breaching the spike-walls beyond the wigwam barracks. "Where is Coriander?"

"He's fine, but Iraleth is injured."

Coriander's wife? But she was with child!

Wrath consumed Brooke and flickered through her vision. "Go heal her. You stay with them and protect that family at all costs."

Nariellyn nodded but hesitated.

"Go!"

She ran.

Brooke sprinted in the opposite direction. Toward the soldiers. Her spear yearned for blood.

They would pay for this. They would all pay.

Someone grabbed her from behind. Brooke snarled and nearly stabbed Dimbae through.

"You can't fight. We must go."

"I can and I will!"

"They will recognize you. Remember what the elder—"

"Let me go!"

Dimbae hauled her onto a xavi and mounted his own. Pulled the reins so Brooke had to grab the saddle to avoid being thrown off.

Their mounts sprinted through camp at Dimbae's lead. Brooke gritted her teeth and blinked back hot tears. He was right and she hated it. Hated him. Hated the elder. Hated everything.

No. Her mind was a fortress. No emotions could exist within. Her heart would be put in its place.

They broke through a breach in the wall. Sped past a group of soldiers. Into the dark jungle. Over bushes, through bamboo stalks, under vines. Brooke held her spear tight and leaned in close to her xavi, standing in the stirrups and flexing her knees as the saddle bounced beneath. It took every bit of restraint to prevent herself from whirling around and killing as many Emberhawk as fate would allow.

They'd taken her father. Ruined her childhood. Been a perennial enemy her entire life.

Why had she ever hoped for peace with them?

An arrow slammed into Dimbae's back. He flailed, jerking the reins and saddle sideways. His xavi cried out with a loud shriek and stumbled, spilling the both of them to the earth in a wave of dirt.

Brooke's mount reared with a cry, throwing her from the saddle. She hit the earth but didn't register the impact. She ran to Dimbae as their xavi fled, reaching him before she realized how she got there.

"Don't you die on me," Brooke growled as she offered Dimbae a hand. He grunted and staggered to his feet, then drew his blade.

Emberhawk soldiers riding striped trace cats approached from behind. Eight snarling saber-tooths with metal armor curving around their heads, their shoulders, their flanks. No, ten . . . a dozen.

The one with the most extravagant golden armor wore the broadest grin. "What have we here? It can't be . . ." His men crashed through the thicket, surrounding them.

Brooke and Dimbae put their backs to each other, weary of the arrow shaft protruding from his ribcage. She'd let her spear do the talking.

"Take the woman," the Emberhawk said. "Kill the other."

Not on my life!

Soldiers dismounted and advanced with swords drawn.

Brooke screamed a war cry and stabbed her spear at the closest man. He dodged, underestimating her speed. Her weapon slid between his armor plates, catching him in the shoulder. He withdrew as another took his place. She impaled him in the neck. The next was skewered through the thigh.

Another grabbed her spear before she could withdraw it. She yanked at it for only a moment—he was stronger. She shoved it forward, throwing him off balance as she withdrew her knife, leaped forward, and ended him before he could recover.

Dimbae cried out behind her. Soldiers surrounded him. Pierced him as he fell.

One of the men blocked Brooke's line of sight. She dodged around him and stabbed another in the back.

Someone grabbed her headdress. Jerked backward. She stumbled and slashed out with her knife. They released her to catch her balance with one knee to the ground.

The soldiers turned away from Dimbae with bloodied blades. Faced her. Surrounded her.

She screamed at them until her throat went raw.

"Lay down your weapons and you will not be harmed."

Swords pointed at Brooke from every angle, but she ignored them and charged. Dodged the blade in front of her. Drove her knife into the man's gut.

Agony pierced her side from behind. She gasped and whirled, slashing out with her blade. Hitting nothing.

She collapsed to one knee. Pain blurred her vision. Still she held her knife steady, daring another to approach.

The earth shook with an impact behind her. Someone screamed. Something crunched. Brooke looked over her shoulder.

An enormous dragon threw a soldier from its jaws to career into a distant tree. Then it bit another. Arrows deflected from its back and the spikes on its spine as if its scales had been forged from mithril.

Brooke gaped at it, panting through the anguish. It was a wyvern. A lake wyvern with glowing green eyes. Teeth the length of her arm, claws the length of her spear. Wings so broad they couldn't fit into the clearing without crashing into trees, sending cracked limbs down to smash its prey below.

Through the smear of shock and agony, the reality before Brooke's eyes fought against the truth she thought she'd known. Weren't wyverns supposed to be extinct?

The men and their trace cats scattered.

Brooke watched as the dragon ended every last one of them with its jaws or its tail or fire from its gullet that lit up the forest with unbearable heat.

Soon, the only sound was the crackling of dragonfire that fed on the bodies and the environment.

The wyvern turned to look at Brooke with those green eyes. No pupils. Just like the one that had defended Jadenvive from the giant hawk the night of the Emberhawk attack.

Brooke stood so still she didn't even breathe. Only her blood moved, trickling down her leg and dripping to the earth.

The dragon stared at her for a long moment. The fires surrounding them snuffed out in a simultaneous hiss, leaving only smoke to clog the air with foul scents.

Then it spread its wings and disappeared into the night.

33

KIRALAU

Kira regretted agreeing to come along with Vylia the moment she'd done it. Whether or not this was a fool's errand, Ryon felt further away every minute.

Oda'e apparently trusted Kira far more than his soldiers did. The treasury guards looked at her like she was a spoiled teenager poking her nose where it didn't belong.

She couldn't blame them. The Katrosi people had only just begun to recognize her as the one who slayed Zamara. Funny how her own people didn't know her, either.

Kira ignored the guards' stares as they begrudgingly admitted entrance to her, Tekkyn, Vylia, and Sousuke. She let Tekkyn finish up the talking, becoming more annoyed with each passing second it took the soldiers to unlock what sounded like an enormous metal bolt on the other side of thick wrought iron doors.

The faster she found some glass-gold to make Vylia feel safe, the faster she could go after Ryon. The bangle he'd given her hung heavy around her wrist. She wouldn't give it up under any circumstances.

Even if they found translucent gold—and assuming Oda'e let them take it and Brooke wouldn't consider it theft—what assurance did they have that it would contain Lillian any better?

Kira was the first to slip through the opening in the treasury doors as soon as the gap was wide enough.

The room wasn't as large or as well-lit as Kira had expected. Well, she didn't know what she had expected, but it wasn't this—the treasury looked more like a large closet than a dragon's hoard. Gold, silver, and bronze bars were stacked neatly next to boxes full of *rupero*. Copper vases, sculptures, and artwork sat on shelves in various states of patina. A crystalline chalice looked like a bowl balancing on top of a stem, like an oversized wine glass. Boxes that smelled of spices stacked in the corner beside a massive dragon skull.

But some shelves were empty, and the folded d'hakka silk was hardly more than Kira had seen at Monty's shop. How much had Brooke spent and traded already to recover from Zamara's attack?

Kira took a cautious step toward a fist-sized gem displayed on a pedestal in the center of the room. It didn't appear to be a diamond—its facets seemed cloudy. Quartz, perhaps? Why would such an unassuming rock be placed in this position of importance?

There it is!

The watery voice in Kira's head felt so loud that her eardrums might have burst if she'd heard it aloud.

That's the keystone. Get it for me!

Kira covered her ears as if that would stop Lillian's demands. She waited a moment, hoping Tekkyn wouldn't think her mad.

You will be given anything your mortal heart could possibly desire. Take it!

Kira reeled from the intensity of the voice and looked at Vylia, who'd also entered the treasury behind her. The princess looked like Kira felt: confused and scared and bent over in pain.

"I will not," Kira said through gritted teeth, no longer caring what Tekkyn thought. She wasn't alone in this struggle any more.

"Whatever you are, you're evil," Vylia said, her gentle voice growing strong. "I will not obey you, eithe—"

I did not come this close just to be denied by ignorant youth! Lillian's voice slammed through Kira's head like a mallet to her skull. *You doubt me now but you won't as soon as I'm free! You will be my avatar—whichever of you takes it first. Hold it in your hand and reach into it with your aether. You will absorb it, then do the same to my Malo stone. Then I will show you the power of a god, and you will want for nothing ever again!*

Kira gritted her teeth. The stone just sat there on top of its pedestal. She wondered if it would shatter if it hit the floor.

"What's happening?" Tekkyn demanded. "Kira!"

"Find something made of glass-gold!" Sousuke shouted from across the room.

Vylia pawed at her belt. "The creator locked you up for a reason," she growled, taking a step away from the clouded gem on the pedestal. "To Zoth with your empty promises. I'd rather die than let a demon like you free!"

Lillian's voice turned to a shrill shriek, so high-pitched that Kira couldn't fathom anything else. It consumed her in an instantaneous rapture, like a siren who'd lured her prey into an echo chamber. It would scream her apart, piece by infinitesimal piece.

Distantly, Kira felt herself collapse. Something caught her—she couldn't see what. Couldn't think, couldn't speak. Only pain.

Were her ears bleeding? Her brain was bleeding.

She would die. But if she survived, she would not return with her sanity.

Was resisting worth this pain? Worth her life? She didn't know anything about the voice, except that it had the power to rend her sanity. Maybe giving it what it wanted wouldn't be so bad. Didn't the prophecy say that the greater *amos* elementals couldn't be released until the end times? Then surely anything she did would be of no consequence.

I don't want to hurt you. Lillian's voice turned sweet. Soft. Comforting. *Tell me you'll do it, and I'll set you free.*

Kira reeled as the shrieking abated. Just enough to tempt her.

Curse this creature—whatever it was. She would not be manipulated into becoming its avatar, or aiding it in any way. Lillian had asked the wrong girl.

Kira gritted her teeth. "No!"

Agony consumed her. Rocked and tossed and drowned her like a raft in an ocean storm.

She thought she heard Vylia cry out, anchoring her back to reality. But it must not have been reality. Water floated in droplets all around them. Seeping upward through the floorboards. Flowing through cracks in the walls. Streaming through the doorway.

Then I will do it myself.

The droplets joined into a floating current of water, like a river that had been turned upside-down. It swirled into a pouch on Vylia's belt, spinning into a vortex and lifting the Malo stone to whirl and shimmer, flashing with a thousand colors.

The water turned like a snake's head, growing and smoothing into a shape like a cobra. It shot toward the keystone.

Kira cried out, the pain in her head preventing her body from movement. The room darkened and blurred, and she knew they'd lost.

The screaming in her head abruptly stopped, and the silence somehow felt deafening in its absence. Kira gasped as the world righted itself and the pain vanished.

Water crashed onto the floor, splashing her with a chilling burst.

She looked toward the keystone. It was still in its place on the pedestal.

But where was the Malo stone?

Sousuke knelt with both hands on some sort of glass candlestick. No, it was an upside-down chalice he held flat against the floor. No, the cup was too large to be a chalice. The decorative bowl with its long stem?

Kira stared in confusion, then looked to Vylia. She was sprawled on the floor as well, looking just as relieved and bewildered. Tekkyn frantically searched the treasury shelves beyond.

"Where is the Malo stone . . . ?" Vylia's girlish voice cracked.

"Under here." Sousuke didn't move, but his gaze flicked to the both of them, then back down to the glass. "You okay?"

Vylia pushed up to her knees and rubbed her ears. "I . . . think so."

"Is that glass-gold?" Kira asked once her tongue decided to work again. She could just make out the aquamarine opal between Sousuke's fingers and through the crystal.

"I guess so," Sousuke said. "Looks like Uma was right."

Relief flooded Kira, and she saw the same feeling on Vylia's drooping shoulders.

"What now?" Sousuke muttered, both hands still holding the oversized chalice against the floor as if he'd caught a rat inside it.

Kira resisted the urge to badmouth Lillian until she felt better. Her mind was blissfully quiet aside from her own frantic thoughts.

She looked back to Vylia. "Do you hear her . . . ?"

Vylia shook her head. "Either that stopped her, or she decided to stop at the same moment." Her lips pursed and her brow furrowed. "It didn't sound to me like she had any intention of quitting."

"Is there any other glass-gold in here?" Kira shakily pushed to her feet. "Preferably with the weight of an oliphant."

"Don't see any more," Tekkyn called from the back of the treasury. "Plenty of regular gold though, and this gem-like thingy."

"It needs to be transparent gold," Vylia said. "Although it seems this chalice worked, so it must be."

"Thank the creator," Kira murmured as she swept water droplets from her arms. She began to move toward Sousuke, then thought better of it.

Tekkyn jogged over and handed Sousuke a thin crystal serving tray etched with snowflake designs. Kira looked as closely as she could from the distance. Translucent as it was, it didn't have the streak of gold stretching like lightning through its features, nor the faint golden hue that Ryon's bracelet did.

Still, Sousuke carefully slid the tray under the chalice. It clanged against the Malo stone inside as he inched it across the chalice. Had he swiped the opal out of the current of living water and slammed it on the ground? Good thing the chalice hadn't broken.

Sousuke turned the chalice upright and pulled the crystal tray back to reveal the fist-sized water opal. It sat there like any ordinary gemstone, as if it hadn't just spoken to them and nearly shorn their sanity.

Kira wanted to throw it in the nearest volcano.

"Don't touch it," Vylia said. "We should find another piece of glass-gold so it can be fully surrounded until I can return it to the temple in Maqua."

Tekkyn was watching Kira with perceptive eyes. "How about we find the nearest glacier and drop it in an ice crevasse?"

Kira offered a weary smile to let him know she was all right. She looked down at Ryon's bracelet and tugged at it but didn't remove it. "Ryon said the whole palace in Quin'Zamar is made of gold. I don't remember if he said it was translucent, though . . ."

"But we're going in the opposite direction," Vylia said as she moved toward the collection of d'hakka silk. "I have to return this to its place in the temple in Maqua as soon as possible. If this chalice could stop Lillian from achieving her goal just now, hopefully it will be enough to contain her for the journey." She took a piece of purple silk, laid it carefully over the top of the chalice, and tied it tight around the stem.

Kira's hands began to shake as she watched Vylia work—a familiar occurrence after she escaped danger. Something she was becoming more used to every day.

"You didn't give her what she wanted," Kira said quietly to Vylia.

"Neither did you," Vylia said with beaming pride, then looked at Sousuke. "Did you hear her this time?"

Sousuke shook his head. Tekkyn did too.

"Strange," Kira mused.

"She doesn't like men, if the legends are to be believed." Vylia sniffed and glared at the chalice. "It seems our history scrolls need some sorting out."

Kira's heart ached. Vylia seemed as fragile as a lily, but she'd just proven to have remarkable strength. People like that didn't cross Kira's path every day.

"I . . ." She didn't know how to phrase it. She didn't want to leave her new friend. But Ryon . . .

"I know." Vylia put a hand on hers. "I hope this isn't the last time I see you, Kiralau."

Kira returned her hopeful grin. *"Aeo leywa ai shea."*

Vylia tilted her head. "Excuse me?"

"It's a saying in the Ancient language I learned from the Roanoke tribe," Kira explained. "It means, 'the creator be with you and protect you."

Vylia's blue eyes softened. "And with you."

34

RYON

Ryon watched the tails of the trace cats twitch. Striped cats, not like the wild ones. These ones were tame. Shiny saddles.

Maybe he should be scared that they would eat him. But he was happy. They were nice kitties. So pretty.

Pretty.

A blur motioned before him. Soft colors, slow movement.

Oh! A person. Blurry person.

She was pretty. Yellow eyes like the bright sun. Silver hair like his.

The nice lady. The nice cousin. Cousin Illi.

He smiled at her. "Hi."

His voice sounded strange. But that was okay. Everything was okay.

"Idryon?" Illi said.

He heard her voice! Clearer than before. A nice voice. But he didn't like the name she called him. He didn't remember why.

"I'm Ryon," he replied. His tongue felt thick. But that was okay. Everything was happy and good.

Illi turned and said something muffled to another blurry person. Something about salts. He liked salty things. Like cheese.

She gave him something to smell. Strong and sharp! He jerked back.

His head hurt. It was not okay. It was not good.

Ryon blinked through the sudden migraine. What was . . . Where was he?

He focused on Illi. Illiana. Snorted out the smell and breathed deep. "Illi?"

Why had he called her that? He hadn't since they were kids. But then, when was the last time he'd seen her? How many years? His head hurt.

"Yes, it's me." Illiana smiled at him—a beautiful smile. "Do you understand what I'm saying?"

Ryon grimaced at the throbbing in his head and looked around. His vision . . . something was wrong. Many people he didn't know. And yet he felt safe.

"Yes," he said. "Where am I?"

"We're going home," Illiana said. "You've been gone so long."

Home? Ryon frowned. Did she mean the root-cave? Or the palace? He didn't have a real home. He wanted to build one. With a girl. A different girl with bouncy hair. What was her name?

He didn't remember. She was so new. Maybe she'd only been a dream. Yes, she was too perfect. A dream.

Ryon gazed up at towering trees covered with flowering vines. So much green. The jungle . . . ? But the palace was by the beach. Black sand, bright sky. Clear waters. Pretty fish.

Pain skittered from one temple to another, growing worse each time he tried to think. "Emberhawk land?"

"The Emberhawk Sovereignty, yes." Illiana smiled. "How would you like to be king?"

He must not have heard her right, but his hearing was much clearer than it had been . . . however long ago. "Cori is king."

Illiana's face looked like she smelled something bad. Did he smell bad? All he could smell was that yucky salt.

"No, I am the queen," she said. "And if you marry me, you'll be the king."

That was scary. Lysander was supposed to be king. And if he didn't, then Cori. And if he didn't, then Illiana's husband. But that couldn't be *him.* They were cousins. His head hurt.

"No." Ryon shook his head and leaned away from her.

"You don't want to live in the palace? Everyone would listen to whatever you said and love you and do whatever you ask."

Ryon shook his head harder, but it only made his headache worse. He didn't want to marry his cousin. Most royalty did that, but he didn't want to. He wanted Dream Girl and her blue eyes and the way she looked at him. Like she was playing a game she always wanted to win. And she did always win. But he liked that. She was smart and funny and pretty . . .

What was her name?

She liked him too. Definitely a dream.

"Idryon?"

He looked back at Illiana. Her smile wasn't pretty . . . it was fake.

She took his hand in hers, and he realized that his wrists were tied together.

"Please," she whispered. "You will legitimize my claim to the throne. You will have anything you desire. You won't have to give me children—I have a paramour in mind for that. You need only to be my consort, and I will do all the work. Just marry me and live in luxury the rest of your days."

"No."

Illiana frowned. "Don't make this harder than it needs to be."

Ryon pulled against the rope around his wrists. "No!" Pain sliced through the fog in his mind. The world became sharper. Clearer. Darker.

Kira. Her name was Kira.

Ryon shot to his feet, but his legs were rubber. He stumbled into someone. Xavier. He looked sad.

"Muddlewort," Illiana said as she turned away with a swish of her cloak.

Xavier grabbed him. Shoved something liquidy down his throat. It tasted like horseradish. He coughed it out, but more replaced it.

His head didn't hurt so much any more. Xavier helped him lie down.

Everything was okay. The sun came through the leaves so bright. So pretty.

Pretty.

35

BROOKE

Brooke lay on the ground, motionless. Death surrounded her. Nothing moved except the treetops with the occasional humid breeze. Not the piles of golden armor on every side. Not the bodies of trace cats. Not Dimbae.

Brooke squeezed her eyes shut and wondered if death would claim her, too.

She couldn't move without the pain in her back crashing through her. At least the blade hadn't run her through. She couldn't tell how deep the wound was. Deep enough to cripple her. The slightest movement sent a blinding jolt through her nerves.

How much time had passed? How long before infection would set in? How long before she died of thirst?

Was no one coming?

Coriander's camp must have been overrun.

That must be why the vultures hadn't come yet. They were already feasting.

Or they were afraid of a certain lake wyvern. Where had it come from? Why hadn't it killed her, too? Why had it just left instead of consuming its prey?

And if it were really the same one from that awful fiery night, had it followed her all the way from Jadenvive?

It *was* the same one. She'd seen it battling the giant hawk. Same size, same flashing umber scales, same keen intelligence in its strange eyes.

Her people whispered of a guardian fire-spirit. A Phoeran elemental sent by the creator to guard Jadenvive. His name was Felix Kael Tae—the green-eyed fox.

But that wyvern wasn't a fox, and he wasn't guarding Jadenvive.

But elementals could shape-shift.

Brooke lolled her head to the side and admired a paradise flower that blossomed over a dead soldier like a grave tribute. What did the wyvern matter? It was gone.

Perhaps she could get up and walk if her wound closed itself well enough. She didn't know how long that would take, if it were possible. Even if she had the means to stitch it, she wouldn't have been able to sew up her own back.

Better to let it claim her and rid the Katrosi of the biggest failure of a chief they'd ever endured. Heron was already dead, so revenge wouldn't be so straightforward. Long Root could be halfway to Darkwood by now, where she could neither reach nor find him.

She didn't want Dimbae's death to be in vain. But what did she have left to live for? Maybe she could finally be with Lysander—and actually wanted to—but the dreamthistle had surely taken him by now. And her own survival wasn't looking probable, either.

Fate was nothing short of cruel.

A tear slipped through her lashes and dropped into her ear. Somehow she still had tears left.

If only she had been better to Lysander the last time she saw him. Now that she thought back on it, she was glad Heron was dead. He deserved it. But she hadn't known that at the time. If only her last words to Lysander had been understanding or even thankful. She didn't want to think about how things might have turned out if he hadn't shown up.

What would her life have been like if she'd chosen to marry and raise a family instead of chasing after her career? How many children would she have by now? Would she be happy?

She grabbed at her broken headdress. Tore her hair as she wrenched it free. Threw it into the jungle and snarled at the pain.

"Be careful with that!"

Brooke jolted and searched for the source of the voice.

A fox sat behind her, its white-tipped tail curled around itself. Its eyes glowed so brightly that green magic seemed to flit from them and evaporate. Just as the wyvern's had.

Brooke froze. Had that fox just spoken?

"Love-cursed humans have no respect," the fox grumbled, staring after the headdress. It turned back to her. "Are you just going to lie there forever?"

Her mouth opened, but no words formed. Finally she managed, "Are you Felix Kael Tae?"

The fox's tail flicked. "And you're Brooke of House Stillwind. Spearmaiden. Former chieftess. Annoying as a grackle."

Brooke frowned. "I am the current chieftess."

"Wrong," Felix said. "Ulysses is the new chief, since you ran off at the most inopportune time."

Brooke stared at him. She'd only been gone a few days. Ulysses had usurped her?

"That can't be," Brooke said. "The Elder of Aether told me to leave. He said he'd inform the council."

The fox tilted its head. "Yeah, I don't think he had a chance to tell them."

Brooke glared. Clearly she shouldn't trust this strange creature that had randomly popped out of the trees. "What are you, exactly? What are you doing here?"

Felix sighed. "I really don't feel like going over it again." One of his black-tipped ears flicked to the side. "If you don't already know, your spies were the worst."

Brooke narrowed her eyes at him. "Have *you* been spying on me? They say you guard Jadenvive, but I've also heard you're the guardian of chiefs."

The fox laughed—an adorable yipping sound. "Mortals are always so self-centered. No, I'm not your personal babysitter. And if I guarded the city, it wouldn't have been overtaken by the Malaano."

Brooke's insides twisted. "What?"

The strange green eyes pierced her. "Jadenvive now belongs to the children of Malo."

Her pulse stalled. He was lying. He had to be. Jadenvive couldn't have been attacked right as . . . she . . . left . . .

The elder's words shot through her memory. *"You are in grave danger. If you don't leave at nightfall, you will die."*

Had the elder foreseen the attack? No—surely he would have warned her and they could have prepared the defenses. Evacuated the civilians.

But then, why would the creator's vision only include danger to Brooke when the entire city was at risk?

And how could her scouts not have spotted a Malaano invasion large enough to take the city? Only a force with Phoera to cloak them could hope to . . .

The Emberhawk. They'd been working with the Malaano the entire time.

Zamara's attack on Jadenvive had just been the gut punch to soften them up for the killing blow.

Brooke realized she was hyperventilating. This couldn't be true. But somehow, she knew it was. The pieces fit together too well.

She clenched her fists. *Bleed them!*

Felix was still watching her. Like a bear examining a fish caught in a net.

"How do I know this is true?" she whispered.

The fox shrugged his little orange shoulders. "I have no interest in lying."

"Where is Ulysses?"

"He's hiding in the root-tunnels with the survivors who weren't captured. Idryon, Kiralau, and the Malaano princess among them."

Brooke released a breath. That was good news, at least. "And the elders?"

"Most are alive, living trapped in the city like everyone else. The violent one is in prison. The Elder of Aether did not survive the assault."

Brooke closed her eyes. Darkness, oppressive and all-consuming, pressed down on her as if the night sky had slowly fallen to suffocate her.

What could she do? Jadenvive was the speartip of the Katrosi tribe. The other villages didn't have warriors in enough skill or number to retake the city. And even if they did, she was no longer the chief to command them.

Hopelessness stole her strength, her breath. This was the crowning glory of her failure.

Now she could die in shame and be rid of this rotten world.

She looked back at Felix. "What do you want?" she growled.

"I want you to not die and not throw sacred artifacts around."

Brooke scowled at him as her pulse pumped sickly heat through her veins. "Why do you care if I die?"

"Because I can't go near the keystone, and it's not safe here."

The keystone? Brooke found the brilliant cerulean feathers of her headdress wilting in the grass nearby. "That's what you've been after this whole time?"

"Well, no. I protect it from others who are after it."

Brooke frowned. "Who's after it?"

"Anyone with delusions of grandeur. It's the most powerful object on the planet."

Brooke stared at him. She was tired of his clipped answers.

She tried to find a less painful position to lie in. "Take it and go. I don't care."

Felix snorted. "I was a fool to ever trust humans to guard it."

"Do I look like I can guard *anything* right now?" Brooke winced and relaxed into the earth. "Just leave me be."

Felix took a step closer. "Don't Katrosi chiefs make an oath to guard the keystones as they're sworn in?"

"You just informed me that I'm not the chief any longer," Brooke grumbled.

The fur around Felix's snout seemed to droop into a frown. "But you have the keystone now, regardless."

"I just gave it to you," Brooke said. She didn't want to spare the movement to point. "Take it."

"I told you I can't touch it."

Brooke glared at him. She knew better than to ask such an open-ended question like "why." But apparently he wasn't leaving. "Let me guess: it's an elemental thing?"

Felix lowered his head and sniffed at her back. "Turn over."

His eyes struck Brooke as even more unnatural up close. If the brightness of their glow was any indication of magical power, Felix could end her on a whim.

But it sounded like he needed her to carry the keystone or he'd be stuck guarding her headdress on the jungle floor forever. Maybe he intended to help her.

Brooke prepared for the pain as she carefully rolled over onto her stomach, but it didn't help. She hissed breaths through her teeth and gripped the grass hard.

Felix made a pensive sound, almost like a purr as he peered down at her back. "Not as bad as it could be. Still, it needs to be cauterized." He glanced at her face. "Don't move."

Brooke closed her eyes and roared as magma seared into her. Just when she couldn't take it any more, soothing frost extinguished the heat, leaving a dull ache in its place.

It took all of her discipline not to curse the motherless creature and throw his little fluffy body across the clearing.

"That'll do for now, but you'll need some more attention to avoid infection." Felix sighed. "Don't do anything stupid just because you know I'm protecting you now. Humans die all the time, and there's nothing special about you."

Brooke controlled her breathing as pain throbbed through her back. "What a delight you are."

Felix snorted. "Get the keystone. I'll fly you to a place nearby that can tend to your mortal needs."

"Any place nearby would just send me to my grave faster," Brooke said in a constricted voice. "Fly me to a Katrosi village if you want to help."

"Lyzelle won't kill you if she knows Lysander wants you."

Brooke's mouth fell open. "Former queen Lyzelle? Ryon's—er, Idryon's and Lysander's grandmother?"

"Yeah, something like that. I can't keep track of your lineages and generations and whatnot."

Brooke could scarcely believe that there might actually be a friendly haven nearby. "I'm not leaving until my friend is laid to rest." She pointed in the direction she'd seen Dimbae fall.

Felix stared at her. "You're in no condition to dig a grave."

"Please bury him for me. It shouldn't be difficult for a creature of your size."

"He's going to rot regardless. Let's go."

Brooke cringed. "I'm not going to leave him to the wildlife! Do as I ask or you'll find out just how much strength I have left."

Felix seemed to roll his emerald eyes. He scampered over to Dimbae's body. "You want me to bury him alive?"

Brooke choked on her own breath. "He's alive?"

"For now." Felix's voice warped as his form grew suddenly. Wings burst forth and his neck extended. Thousands of scales shot out of his fur and slicked back into a dragon's visage.

He picked up Dimbae's limp form carefully with his clawed feet, spreading his wings for balance. "Pick up the keystone and let's go before you both die of old age."

36

LYSANDER

Sunlight filtered through transparent glass windows and glowed across Selene's perfect skin. Lysander said something clever, and she threw the bed sheets at him. She rolled her eyes and turned away, but he caught her smile.

He couldn't hear her retort, but it was certainly clever. She was always clever. Smarter than him, which he hated about other people, but Selene was an exception. She was to be his queen.

But somehow, he knew it was not to be. Foggy memories invaded to ruin his perfect dream. Zamara threatening him. His refusal. Selene's blood mixing with syn and running silver down the palace steps.

His father never would have let him marry a commoner, anyway.

Suddenly the silver blood was in Lysander's gut. Making him sick. He twisted to try and push it away somehow. It congealed into silver worms, wriggling and biting and spreading to every part of him.

It was his blood. His royal, elemental blood that had killed her.

He should have been born a commoner. Or obeyed Zamara from the outset. Then his love and his mother wouldn't have had to die.

Queen Dierdre's face appeared. Smiling, then melting into the scowl of a silver monster.

The worms began eating him from the inside out.

Lysander screamed himself awake.

The nightmare evaporated, but still his heart raced. Still nausea twisted his gut.

He moaned and opened his eyes. Midday sun beat down on him unhindered. White fur tickled his nose. Sorrel glared at him from the corner of a golden eye.

Lysander cleared his throat and patted her feathery mane. "Sorry."

Sorrel gave a huge sigh and flopped her head back to the ground in dramatic fashion. Her eyes closed and her breathing felt steady beneath him.

Lysander squinted against the light and looked around. Sorrel's slender body curled around him. He lay on the ground and rested his head on the gryphon's belly, but he was covered with a colorful quilt. The soft fabric smelled of jasmine.

Exactly like Granny Zelle—formerly Queen Lyzelle, wife of King Corynath and Queen Mother to King Brynn. Grandmother to Lysander, his siblings, and Ryon and his sister Aegwyn.

Lysander inhaled the sweet floral scent and breathed out. He couldn't believe he was alive, and yet the warmth on his skin, the smells of the jungle, the piercing sun, and the writhing nausea in his gut assured him that he wasn't dead.

He craned his neck to look behind him. The peak of Corynath and Lyzelle's pyramid rose through the green life—he recognized it by the ruby sculpture of a phoenix that graced its zenith.

Lysander patted Sorrel's rump. "You did it, girl."

She raised her head again and blinked sleepy eyes at him, her long feathered tail flicking in annoyance.

Lysander dug into the treat pouch on his belt and emptied the entirety of fish jerky into his hand. He grimaced at the smell, but fish were Sorrel's favorite.

The gryphon leaped up, pranced around him in circles, and crooned loud enough for him to hear faintly as she stretched her wings. Her giant head nuzzled him in the armpit, and he ruffled her feathers as she swallowed chunks of her favorite snack whole.

But the nausea threatened to ruin Lysander's joy. He understood now why he'd dreamed of worms in his stomach—it was overpowering. He couldn't decide whether to throw up or put himself to sleep with fadeleaf.

A figure approached from the direction of the pyramid. It was short with a messy bun of silver hair.

"Granny Zelle!" Lysander called. "Don't come too close—I think I'm going to vomit."

The hunched figure turned back around and disappeared.

Lysander closed his eyes and tried to focus, but it just made it worse. Why didn't he feel the soreness or headache that usually came from dreamthistle poisoning? What on Alani had she given him?

"Here you gooooo!" Granny Zelle hand-signed the last word as if she were singing upon her return. She came close and handed him a thick slice of ginger, her purple dress swishing its silver embroidery as she moved. *"Munch on this. Or, if you can't stand it, I'll make a tea, but it'll take a few minutes."*

Lysander stuffed the ginger in his mouth and reeled from the taste. He pulled it back out and forced himself to chew on a smaller bite. "Thanks, Granny."

She smacked him on the top of the head with her walking stick. He recoiled and nearly choked on the ginger.

"When I said come visit more often, I didn't mean have your gryphon drop off your lifeless body on my doorstep!"

Lysander smiled sheepishly, hoping the innocent look he'd used as a boy would get him out of it. "Sorry. Being poisoned wasn't really a part of the plan."

Granny Zelle harrumphed, and her hand-language flowed fast and sharp. *"So your plan was to stay out for even longer until you were forced to make a pit stop, hmm?"*

"No, I was in jail in Jadenvive, and then I got out and went to see Cori—"

He cut off when Granny Zelle brandished her cane again. He sat up, raised an arm in defense, and forced himself to swallow the ginger.

She leaned her cane on her hip to sign once again. *"How about a 'thank you for saving my life?' Do you have any idea how many years I lost at the stress of seeing my dead grandson flop at my feet?"*

"I did say thank you!"

"Do you have any idea how much those treatments cost? You're lucky I brought you back to life so I could kill you again!" She raised the cane higher.

"Sorry! Thank you! I'm sorry!" Lysander couldn't stop a smile as Sorrel paced nervously behind him.

Granny Zelle's flame-orange eyes narrowed as she examined him. *"Feeling better yet?"*

Lysander took another bite of ginger. "A good distraction. Thank you." The nausea returned as his attention returned to it. "Put that thing down before you hurt someone."

Granny Zelle sank to his level and grabbed him in a hug. Finally she released him and signed, *"Don't you ever do that to me again."*

Lysander pulled her back into another hug, careful of her frail frame. "I'm really sorry," he said. "Thank you for saving me."

"Of course, my dear." Granny Zelle sat back on the soft grass. *"What happened? Thank the stars you have some resistance to dreamthistle. See, I told you all that gardening would pay off one day."*

Lysander waited patiently for her to finish signing and spelling out the long sentence, grateful for something else to focus on. Still, he should probably teach her some more common hand gestures. "And the Darkwood prince is obviously no professional assassin."

The wrinkles around Granny Zelle's brows stretched as her eyes opened wide. *"Soaring Heron?"*

Lysander nodded. "We weren't exactly fast friends. I think he was jealous of my relationship with the Katrosi chieftess."

"His fiancée, yeah?" She stared at him, locked in that wide-eyed position. *"You're referring to him in the past."*

Lysander swallowed hard and munched on the last bite of ginger. "I didn't really have a choi—"

"Sander! What did I tell you about killing people?"

"He was assaulting Brooke! And I didn't have any antidote left so I thought I was going to die. I avenged myself."

Granny Zelle blew out a breath as she shakily pushed to her feet. *"Did you get away with it?"*

"I don't know; I was kind of dying."

She looked at her cane as if she wanted to threaten him with it again, but hand-signing was faster with both hands. *"This could be really bad, you know. You'd better hope the chieftess will sweep it under the rug for you."*

"I'm sure she . . ." Lysander trailed off. He wasn't sure of anything, actually. Brooke had been really upset when he'd killed those border guards to keep their mission a secret. Of course she'd be livid that he'd killed her fiancé. She'd already given him a verbal lashing, even if those memories were dripping with poison.

Hand signs flew in front of his face. *"You like her?"*

Lysander snapped back to the present and found Granny Zelle watching him with an excited expression.

He cleared his throat. "I don't remember saying that."

"You do *like her! Since when?"* She was practically dancing. *"And now she's single again, yeah?"* She stopped abruptly and her jaw dropped open. *"Is that why you killed Heron?"*

"No! She—"

"Good, because that would be very selfish and bad."

Lysander deflated. "It doesn't matter—she hates me now. I've ruined everything politically for her. And maybe doomed the entire Tribal Alliance." He forced himself to swallow the last of the ginger. "If she figures out I'm alive, she'll probably drag me back to her jail and have me tried for murder. Again."

Granny Zelle frowned. *"You weren't involved in the attack on Jadenvive, were you?"*

Nausea unbalanced Lysander even though he was sitting, but he could tell its grip on him was beginning to lessen. "I tried to stop it. But Zamara is dead. That's all that matters."

Granny's signs slowed. *"You said the chieftess hates you now?"* She emphasized the final word with large, exaggerated gestures.

Lysander wondered if everyone's grandmothers were this perceptive. Or if he were just that easy to read.

But he really didn't want to have this conversation with her. It hurt too much. He needed to go somewhere alone to think and process what had happened. Once he could stand up.

"What in Zoth did you give me?"

"Everything I could think of to try and save you. Several of the herbs and minerals were pretty strong." Granny Zelle squatted closer to him. *"I'm so glad to finally see emotion on your face again. I just wish it were something more positive."* She reached out a soft hand and touched his cheek. *"Whatever the situation is, there is always hope. I'm here whenever you're ready to talk."*

"Thank you." Lysander tried to stand, then thought better of it. "How long has it been? Is it almost time for a meal? I'm starving."

"First you can haul your gargantuan body to a bed. I'll bring you your favorite stew, but not as spicy as normal." Granny Zelle eyed him sidelong and tapped her cane on the ground as she straightened. *"Then if you're feeling up to it tomorrow, you can see Sorrel's eggs!"*

Lysander brushed dirt from the quilt and looked proudly at Sorrel. He'd almost forgotten about her nest nearby. "I didn't miss the hatching, did I?"

"Not yet! You might be just in time."

37

VYLIA

"You look like you swallowed a pufferfish."

Vylia turned her glare from the waiting room's tapestry of a snowy mountain to Sousuke as he slouched on the bench across from her. "What does that mean? I look like I'm dying?"

"You look generally unhappy," Sousuke said.

Vylia realized her bottom lip jutted out. She pulled it back in. "I just don't appreciate being ordered about."

"Did Oda'e *order* us here?"

"He might as well have. I have a feeling he would have if I'd refused. As if he has any authority to tell me what to do," Vylia muttered.

Sousuke considered her with a look on his face akin to amusement. "Maybe it's for your safety."

If he said that word one more time, she'd slap him. "What would be *safe* would be us getting on the road, away from the keystone as fast as possible!"

"That's true, but Oda'e let us take a priceless glass-gold artifact and is giving us provisions, men, and a new carriage," Sousuke said. "The least we can do is give him one last meeting before we leave for Sekoiako."

Vylia crossed her arms over her tunic. The fact that it wasn't as soft as her usual silks fueled her annoyance.

The new carriage was a shack on wheels compared to her own, which she'd taken from My'Eyah. Even though it hadn't been damaged in the Emberhawk attack or the Malaano invasion, it was too recognizable.

Taking it was out of the question.

She barely prevented herself from asking if they could just paint her carriage so she could relax on the cushioned seats all the way to the coast. But even then the impeccable woodwork would be obvious. And they didn't have time for a paint job.

Vylia blew out a tight breath. "That's true, but he's kept us waiting for—"

"Princess?" A guard poked his head in through the cracked door. "The Commander is ready to see you now."

"Good." Vylia stood and blew past Sousuke in a flurry of fabric from her skirt. She knew she was acting like a princess, but she *was* a princess, and this was her last opportunity to be treated like one. Being "normal" wasn't so much fun after all.

Inside the map room, she recognized both Ulysses and Oda'e. The Commander looked relieved as she entered and ushered all others out of the room. More guards than usual stood at attention outside.

Unease settled in Vylia's stomach as she observed the guards' behavior. They didn't seem as bored as usual. Hurried, perhaps. Agitated?

She returned a nod from Ulysses as she approached the standing table. "What's going on?" she asked Oda'e.

"Are we ready?" Oda'e quietly asked a decorated soldier.

"Yes, sir."

"Light the purifying fire," Oda'e said.

The soldier bowed and left. The guards moved aside for him, and the door shut with the solid thud of a locking mechanism.

Vylia's unease doubled. She looked at Sousuke. His jaw was clenched tight.

"I apologize for the secrecy." Oda'e removed his helmet and leaned against the table, his shoulders slouching. "We are purifying the city of those who remain loyal to the empire."

Vylia opened her mouth but no sound emerged for two heartbeats. "Already?"

Oda'e nodded. "Many of my men were willing to join the resistance when questioned—even more than we anticipated. Thankfully, we are in the majority. The stars smile upon us.”

"What will you do with those who refuse to join you?" Sousuke asked in a low tone.

"The jail will be quite crowded for a little while," Oda'e said, pointing to a portion of a map that Vylia couldn't see from her perspective. "We may convince a few more to stay after they see our numbers. Those who don't join will be returned to Navarro."

"Are we to stay here for several days, then?" Vylia asked, trying to keep the bite out of her voice. He'd basically imprisoned her in this love-forsaken room.

"Oh, no," Oda'e said. "It shouldn't take long at all. We've planned it quite thoroughly." He offered a weary grin. "I know you're eager to get on the road. But please remain here until the dust settles. We believe the emperor wants all of his people to believe you are dead, but still, any soldier loyal to him could have secretly received orders to do you harm."

Vylia frowned but nodded. She didn't have half a clue what was true regarding her father any more, so she had no grounds to argue.

It didn't matter any more. The only thing she could focus on was returning the Malo stone to the temple as fast as possible.

Oda'e pivoted to Ulysses, who stood like a shadow on the opposite side of the table. "Has there been any sign of Brooke?" Oda'e asked.

"Unfortunately, yes," Ulysses said. "She was in Emberhawk territory. She must have fled just before the invasion." Deep creases accentuated his furrowed brow. "No one took her for an honorless coward who would abandon us in our darkest hour."

"No, that's . . ." Vylia swallowed to clear the pinch in her throat. "That's not right. She told me she had to leave because one of your elders told her to."

Ulysses turned sunken eyes to her. Studied her. "That doesn't make sense. The elder would have told us. Unless . . ." He fell silent for a solemn moment. Then he turned back to Oda'e. "The report also claims that Brooke had the Darkwood prince killed because she wanted to marry another. And that she was plotting against the Emberhawk queen at a rebel camp in the jungle." Ulysses rubbed the back of his neck. "The camp was besieged by the queen's forces, and that's the last anyone saw Brooke. Although I don't believe the Emberhawk captured or killed her, or we'd have heard them boasting of it by now."

Vylia's mind spun with the influx of horrid news. It all sounded so awful she didn't know where to start with a response in defense of Brooke.

But she'd only known the chieftess for a few days. Was it possible that any of those accusations were true?

"Troubling." The chainmail under Oda'e's armor clanked as he shifted. "How likely is it that all of this is accurate?"

"The source was Soaring Heron's bodyguard, Long Root. He carried Soaring Heron's body and broken feathers from Brooke's headdress." Ulysses released a heavy sigh. "Personally, it doesn't ring true to me. But it doesn't matter what I think; the elders have made their decision."

Vylia's gut tangled at his inflection. "Decision?"

"I am to be chief until new trials can be run," Ulysses said.

Vylia glanced at Sousuke, whose face had fallen grim. "But what if Brooke returns?" she asked.

"Then I'd be glad to see her alive, and I'd like to hear her side of the story," Ulysses said, "but she has been removed as chief."

The room fell quiet enough for Vylia to hear footsteps thudding down the hall. Sadness fell over her heart like the last autumn leaf. Somehow, she felt that Brooke was innocent. But then again, so was she, and her life was also in shambles.

Why was life so cruel?

A knock on the door made Vylia jump. The guards exchanged whispers before finally unlocking the door and opening it.

The decorated soldier returned with a bright spark in his eyes. "The purifying fire was successful, sir," he said. "Many more have joined us. The loyalists are being marched to the jail. The city will be fully secure within the hour."

Well, that sounded like a good thing to Vylia. Stress seemed to crack and fall from Oda'e's features like clay casting from a mold. "The stars smile wide." He moved to Ulysses and offered a broad hand. "Jadenvive is yours, Chief."

Ulysses gripped Oda'e's arm in a firm clasp. "The Katrosi will never forget this."

"Then let us be friends once more," Oda'e said as he pried a white lotus pin from his chestplate. "If you'll allow Jadenvive to become the home of the Navakovrae Resistance until we can take Navarro, my men can help guard the city and aid your people in recovery."

Vylia glared at the white lotus as Oda'e dropped it on the table. It had been the symbol of power, protection, and provision for her entire life. Her identity. Her purpose.

Seeing it fall felt like pulling a thorn from her foot.

She noticed Ulysses grin for the first time since she'd met him down in the root tunnels. The charming look of a leader. "I'm in no position to refuse," he said.

Oda'e patted the wolf skin on Ulysses' shoulder, then turned to Vylia. "You're invited to stay for the celebration, Your Majesty."

She bowed her head. "Thank you, but I really must be on my way."

"I understand. Please wait until the loyalists are secured in the jail so they won't see you depart. I will see you personally to your carriage." Oda'e's eyes softened as he looked down on her. "Give my regards to Maqua."

Vylia couldn't return his joy. "I will tell them of your courtesy and civility and purity of heart. But I'm afraid they will only answer you with death."

Oda'e's smile bared white teeth that gleamed in contrast with his dark skin. "Let them try," he said, and Vylia saw where Kira had inherited her fire.

38

KIRALAU

Kira pulled her hood further down around her face. The road twisted ahead of their cart and tired oxen. Which turn would reveal the border crossing into the Emberhawk Sovereignty? Hours ago the air had turned more humid, the vegetation thicker, and the bird calls louder. It had to be soon.

If the road got any bumpier, or her stretched any tighter, she might lose whatever she had for breakfast—she couldn't remember what.

"That's the seventeenth time you've done that."

Kira turned to Tekkyn beside her. "Hmm?"

"Tugged on your hood like that." He leaned back against the wooden bench that sat atop the wagon's front. "If you don't relax, there's no chance they'll buy our story."

"Not all of us are professional spies, okay?" Kira flicked the reins against the backs of the two bulls. "Could you have picked a cover that didn't involve us hauling a load of junk? The oxen are so slow . . ."

"Not sure what other kinda story you could pull, Frizz," Tekkyn said. "Thought this would be most natural for you 'cause of the trade runs you used to make to Navarro from home."

"This is a little different," Kira muttered. "Lee would have taken buffalo for such a heavy load. And I don't even know half of what's in the back, so how am I supposed to sell it?"

She regretted mentioning their little brother as soon as his name escaped her lips. The wound was still raw for both of them. And she knew she was complaining when she shouldn't be. But every passing minute without Ryon stabbed at her anxiety like a cattle prod. Where was he now? Had they reached Quin'Zamar? How long ago?

"Just let me do the talkin', then." Tekkyn's voice lowered and softened. "Try to be calm. Don't look 'em in the eyes if you can't control your face."

Kira's heart seized as a wooden structure came into view. An encampment, a bridge over a wide river, and flags waving in the wind: green with a brown tree for the Katrosi tribe.

Tekkyn reached for the reins, and Kira handed them over. She gripped the edge of the bench she sat on and sent a garbled prayer that was more emotion than it was words.

"We've got this," her brother whispered. "There is nothing illegal about visiting another nation for trade. Relax."

"All right," Kira breathed. She decided to trust him. He'd served under Sa'alu for how long? Two years? And spied for the Resistance the entire time without getting caught. Surely he had the skill to get them safely across the border.

A guard dressed in Katrosi leathers and an amber mask held up a hand as they approached. "What's your business?" he asked in Phoeran.

"Trade," Tekkyn responded.

The guard walked to the back of their cart, lifted the sheet covering their barrels and crates full of wares, and shook his head. "Not a good time to be making deals with Emberhawk filth."

"People still need to eat," Tekkyn said. "I've got buffalo jerky and the best cherry jam you'll ever taste. Want some?"

The man harrumphed and waved them along. "Watch your backs."

Tekkyn nodded and snapped the reins.

Kira finally released a breath as the wagon's wheels creaked against the boards of the bridge. The flags ahead were different colors: blood red with a sunflower yellow phoenix.

"See? Piece of cake," Tekkyn whispered.

"The hard part hasn't started yet," Kira murmured back. She straightened her back to gaze at the current over the guard rails. The River Mossu. Its flow seemed cloudier and more sluggish than it had further north at the Roanoke camp.

A guard in golden armor with a feathered helmet moved to the center of the bridge, and Tekkyn pulled back on the oxen. They stopped once again, chomping at their bits and eyeing the river with wide eyes.

"Hail," the Emberhawk called. His eyes roved over them, and Kira looked down and hunched her shoulders. "What wares do you offer?"

"Many delicious and luxurious things," Tekkyn called. "Buffalo jerky, cherry jam, hides and wax—"

"Do you have any rice?"

Tekkyn hesitated and Kira cringed. Of course real traders from Malaan would have rice to trade—the cheap export from overseas was a delicacy this far west. But Oda'e hadn't been able to spare enough from his troops' rations to sell their disguise.

"Fresh out, I'm afraid. The Katrosi were starvin'."

The guard's expression was flat and dry as the plains. "Then I'm afraid we have no need of you."

Tekkyn balked. "You don't even wanna look through our—"

"No need," the guard said. "We've already plenty of trade for everything except rice. I've orders not to let unnecessary travelers in, and I don't recognize you as one of the regulars."

"I'm not just sellin'. I've got silver to trade for chocolate and spices."

"Do you have any syn to trade?"

"I might," Tekkyn said.

The guard waved for them to back up with a sigh. "Safe journeys."

"I said I might! Give me a second to—"

"Is there a problem?"

Kira looked over her shoulder at the unknown voice. A young woman in a travelling cloak came up swiftly beside them on a xavi. Her long silver braid whipped around her as she pulled her beast to a stop.

The guard glanced from her to Tekkyn and back again. "Are you a member of this party?"

"I am Aegwyn, niece of King Brynn, cousin of Queen Illiana, and sister of the soon-to-be King Idryon."

Kira nearly swallowed her tongue. Her future sister-in-law looked a lot different when she wasn't surrounded by orphans and the hem of her dress wasn't dyed brown from root-tunnel mud. And she'd never heard her use such an authoritative voice before!

The guard squinted at her. "Is that so?"

Aegwyn nodded. "It seems you aren't admitting my people entrance."

Bewilderment crossed the guard's face. *"Your* people?"

Aegwyn's xavi stretched, and she expertly shifted her balance. "They are my slaves."

Kira hoped her hood hid her shock as she ducked further into it in disgust. She curled her lips inward to keep from rejecting the claim outright.

The guard stared at her. "I see no chains."

"Because they are well-behaved and slavery is illegal in Katrosi," Aegwyn said matter-of-factly. "Were you unaware?"

The Emberhawk frowned. "Forgive me, Lady Aegwyn, but I've never had the pleasure of meeting you before and therefore cannot confirm that you speak truth by recognizing you. It's my understanding that you've lived in Katrosi lands for many years."

"That is true. But upon seeing my cousin Illiana in Jadenvive, she convinced me to return." Aegwyn held out her wrist, and a glass-gold bangle slipped down to gleam across the back of her hand.

The guard's eyes bulged as Kira hid her own bracelet further up the sleeve of her cloak. Aegwyn's looked identical to the one Ryon had given her. Their father must have had them both forged from the same elemental jewelsmith.

"My apologies, my lady." The guard bowed low, bouncing the long red feathers in his helmet. He stepped aside to allow the cart room to pass. "Do you require an escort to Quin'Zamar?"

"That's not necessary," Aegwyn said as she urged her xavi forward, which daintily trotted past.

Tekkyn snapped the reins, and the oxen jolted forward, nearly sending Kira tumbling into the crates behind.

They kept quiet and followed the road until Kira was certain she would burst. Finally, Aegwyn looked around and stopped long enough for the cart to catch up with her.

"Sorry about that," Aegwyn said in the gentle voice from Kira's memory.

"What are you doing here?" Kira whispered even though no other soul was in sight.

"Did you think I would just let them take my brother? I'm disappointed you didn't ask me to come along."

Kira sat speechless for a moment. "I'm sorry. I didn't think you were the type."

"What type? The adventurous type? The rescuing type? The fighting type?" Aegwyn flipped her braid over her shoulder. "Well, I might be an orphan tender, but aren't you a farm girl?" she asked with a challenging gleam in her eye that reminded Kira of Ryon.

Kira couldn't help but grin. "I can't argue with that."

"Thanks for savin' our tails back there," Tekkyn said. "Although I would make a terrible slave, so don't expect world-class service."

Aegwyn laughed. "I would never. It was just the best thing I could think of to get you out of that mess." Her xavi sniffed at the fan-shaped leaves on the side of the road, and she gave it some slack in the reins. "If Quin'Zamar is anything like it was when I left, most Malo-heritage people in the city are slaves, so unfortunately it makes for the best cover for you two."

A righteous flame lit in Kira's heart. She'd only seen a few slaves upon her visits to Navarro, but the stories she heard weren't good. "How many slaves are there?"

"Not many. And it's not just Malo people; there are also Emberhawk who couldn't pay their debts, and I heard there used to be a few slaves taken from Valinor before Queen Dierdre married the late king."

Kira felt sick to her stomach. No wonder Ryon hated his own people if this was one of the many evils they stood for. For him to ask her hand in marriage . . . after he'd grown up in a culture where Malo people were normally slaves? This was even more complex than she'd realized.

And her father's approval and support meant that much more. Her mother was a different matter, but that could be addressed later.

She'd dreamed of visiting Ryon's homeland as a romantic getaway to the black-sand beaches he'd described. Luxurious palisades dripping with gold. Exotic fruits. Gentle kisses at a blood-orange sunset.

The mental image was marred by her imaginings of what it must really be like.

"So what's your plan?" Tekkyn asked. "Did you really speak with Illiana in Jadenvive?"

"No," Aegwyn said. "But if I roll the dice right, she'll welcome me back into the palace—I can't imagine that she won't if she's playing nice with Ryon. Then we'd be in a good position to find him and figure out what's going on."

"And let us sneak around the palace if we join the kitchen staff or something," Tekkyn mused.

Aegywn nodded as she fought with her xavi against some enticing smell in the jungle. "I can't lie—I have no idea if any of this will work, and I'm so nervous I think my hair will start falling out."

"Well, you got us through the border like an expert." Kira's heart warmed with affection. Aegwyn was shaping up to be the sister she'd always wanted, including some of Ryon's own unexpected traits. She wondered how much of that was inherited.

"Thank you," Kira said. "I don't know what we'd do without you."

"You'd find Ryon regardless, I'm sure." Aegwyn won the battle of wills against her xavi and charged down the road. "But I'm glad I can help. Let's go!"

39

BROOKE

If Brooke could have told her past self that within days, she'd no longer be chieftess, that she'd have affection for a killer, and that she'd be flown through the Emberhawk jungles clutched in a dragon's claws, she'd have checked herself into a home for the unwell of mind.

She hoped the various types of pain she was experiencing while hanging on for her life would be worth the flight. Felix seemed like he really didn't care if she slipped from his grasp and plummeted to her death in the green canopy below. And yet he'd finally revealed himself to her, after he'd been nothing but a rumor for years.

Her mind couldn't spare the space for the questions. All she could do was focus on maintaining her grip on the bumpy flesh between Felix's umber scales and massive claws. And pray the next jolt from the wind didn't tear her wound anew.

Brooke sensed their descent and twisted her neck to confirm it. To the northwest, the mountains of Valinor beyond the Darkwood territory. The east, behind them. Vast ocean stretching on the southern horizon. And below, a giant glass pyramid fast approaching as branches cracked and leaves bowed to Felix's wings.

She hoped Lysander was here. He'd mentioned that this was the only place with the antidote to dreamthistle, since he'd given her all of his. But Sorrel would have to fly at the speed of lightning for him to be alive at all.

At least if he's dead, we don't have to have a horribly awkward reunion . . .

Her chest constricted so hard she couldn't finish that thought. He had to be alive. She *needed* him to be alive. After all the chaos of the last several hours, Lysander was one of the only shreds of sanity she had left to hold onto. Until she could find Nariellyn and Ryon and the elder—

Brooke grimaced as Felix shifted his legs, preparing for a windy landing. *Creator, please let them be okay. Let it all be a lie.*

But even if Felix had lied, and the Malaano hadn't taken Jadenvive and she was still the chieftess, Soaring Heron would ruin her from his grave regardless.

Please at least let Dimbae survive.

Brooke closed her eyes, tears filtering through her lashes as she braced for impact.

Her braids whipped around, smacking her in the face as the claws of Felix's other foot stabbed the earth. She cried out as his grip tightened to prevent her from slamming into a cobblestone pathway.

"You didn't drop it, did you?" the wyvern rumbled.

Brooke gritted her teeth. "You didn't drop Dimbae, did you?"

Felix craned his long scaly neck to look at his back. "He's still breathing."

Brooke relaxed as Felix gently laid her down on the stone, further destroying the feathers of her headdress. She didn't care. All that mattered was being still. Lying down and not moving until the torture stopped, one way or another.

"Brooke!"

That was his voice. He was alive.

But how? It didn't make sense.

She couldn't look at him or she'd cry.

She squeezed her eyes shut. Maybe she'd cry regardless.

"What happened?" Lysander's voice sounded rushed, frantic.

"Illiana," Brooke managed, then remembered he couldn't hear. She opened her eyes and caught his maroon gaze.

She'd never realized how handsome he was. No—he'd always been attractive, and she'd definitely noticed before. But there was something more now; something beyond. A depth to his eyes, like a deeper understanding or wisdom she hadn't seen before.

Was this the same man who'd sat slumped and broken in Jadenvive's prison just days ago?

Brooke sent a thought into Lysander's mind. It morphed into memories of the attack, only moments after he'd flown away. Of sending Nariellyn away to help Iraleth and Coriander. Of fighting for her life beside Dimbae.

Dimbae needs help, she thought to him.

"Granny!" Lysander yelled, then bent closer to her. "Don't worry. You're both safe now."

She choked on a sob and let the resulting pain carry her tears into a steady flow.

Strong arms lifted her from the earth. Cradled her to his chest.

She felt Lysander move toward the blurry pyramid. Shoulder through the door, then stride through tall flowers and sit on a flat boulder before a trickling waterfall adorned with ferns.

He didn't say a word. Didn't let her go.

Brooke clutched his tunic and let her sorrow run free. Embarrassment gnawed at her. What was she doing? This man wasn't safe. Opening up wasn't safe.

But he was the only one she had left. Who else could she turn to now?

He smelled like leather and spices, and she hesitantly allowed herself to breathe it in. To take some minor comfort in the security he offered. To enjoy the sudden peace and stability.

Still he didn't say anything, and yet somehow, it didn't feel awkward. Even her embarrassment slowly slipped away as she stared into the ripples below the falls. The quiet was enveloping. Healing. Somehow, he understood that. Understood her.

Despite the chaos Lysander had caused, despite his past, and despite what he was capable of, she acknowledged in that moment that he was a good man. Or at least, he wanted to be.

There were the *balembas* again.

"I'm sorry," he murmured. He made a slight movement as if offering her a way out of his arms.

I know. She didn't let him go.

Instead, she let go of all of her stress and fear and anger. They melted away in his arms.

She couldn't carry the weight of the war on her heart. Or the Alliance. Or even her own tribe. She was just one human.

But for the first time since she'd lost her father, she didn't feel alone any more.

They returned to silence until finally Lysander spoke again. "Let me treat that wound."

Brooke relished the lingering moment until she realized she probably smelled like sweat and looked like a half-dead bird. *Okay.*

Lysander stood once again, and Brooke was surprised his arms weren't shaking by now. He'd barely let her rest on his legs as they sat to avoid agitating her wound.

Wait, she thought to him, not wanting the moment to pass.

He paused and looked down at her with a raised eyebrow.

Did you kill him just so he couldn't have me?

"No. I had many reasons." Lysander glanced at a door on the other side of the indoor garden. "The only thing that got him killed was attempted murder, and . . ." He frowned, then replaced it with a smirk. "But if I'd known I could kill for you earlier . . ."

Brooke huffed. *You say that like we're an item.*

He paused and looked down at her with that smoldering gaze until she squirmed and broke eye contact.

He grinned and continued walking. "Mm-hmm."

"Excuse—" Brooke began to escape his grip until the wound changed her mind. She grimaced and relented.

Well, if she really wasn't the Katrosi chief any more, and her life and reputation were already ruined . . . why not dig the pit a little deeper?

You just want me so you can learn thought-speak.

"If that were true, I'd prefer Nariellyn, since she's been the one teaching me."

Brooke recoiled from the sting of truth. Had she promised to be the one teaching him, specifically? Perhaps she should make that right.

Lysander gently adjusted his grip as he took a flight of steps downward one at a time. "You just want me because I'm a royal, and it would be politically advantageous."

Brooke was taken aback. *That's not true,* she thought to him. *Although it's convenient. But politics don't matter since I'm not the chieftess any more.*

"You're not?" Questions flickered in Lysander's gaze, then he seemed to suddenly dismiss them. "Hmm," he mused. "Somehow I think politics will always be important to you."

She didn't want that to be true, although she didn't know why. *Okay, well, I'll have you know that killing people is your least attractive quality.*

"Is it, now?"

Yes, and you refraining entirely from violence is my first condition.

"No can do," Lysander said. "You attract trouble at an alarming rate. I'll take out the trash when needed."

Brooke pursed her lips to control her expression. *I will be the one determining when it's needed.*

"Okay," Lysander said. "Can I kill Heron?"

She slapped him. His black beared seemed to absorb the impact.

He looked down at her with a disapproving look. Questioning . . . playful. The fire in his eyes wasn't an angry one.

She grabbed his tunic and pulled him into a kiss before she realized what she was doing.

Something in the back of her mind warned that her darkest moment was the worst time to begin a relationship.

She ignored it.

40

RYON

Ryon walked through the gardens with Illi. It was so pretty. Pretty.

Blurry white flowers everywhere, and lots of green. Light pink, too, and gold stuff. Statues and treasures sitting on big white things beside the path. The path was hard to walk on, but he tried to do a good job. Illi had asked him to. And she gave him good food.

Illi was so nice.

He remembered another nice girl. Her skin was darker. Pretty blue eyes, like clean ocean water. Curly black hair held back with a bandana thingy. She always wore a bandana thingy. But now she wore it around her neck sometimes. He couldn't remember why.

Why did he remember her at all? He couldn't really remember anything. But why not?

Something about the other girl just seemed . . . right. He grasped for the mental image of her.

He couldn't remember her name. Dream girl.

Illi said something, but he couldn't understand her. Oh, she was probably talking to that other person. There were lots of people now.

He smiled. Smiled for the people. Illi had asked him to.

They all looked so happy. He was happy, too. Everything was good.

Illi took his arm and led him further down the path. It wasn't as difficult now, and the colors of the flowers looked dimmer. The edges of their petals seemed more crisp. The roses had thorns.

He remembered what the white things were called. Pedestals. It sounded like petals, but different. There were lots of pedestals and white petals in the arboretum.

Yes! That's what this place was called. This was Granny Zelle's arboretum. His grandfather, the old king, had planted it for her because she missed the jungle.

But it didn't look like it should. It used to have bright silver syn-sculptures on the pedestals. Now the art was marble or granite, or they weren't art at all.

This one looked like a crown of feathers and dragon horns. Like Brooke's, but bigger and with more horns.

Brooke. Who was Brooke?

His head hurt. Brooke was a friend. Yes . . . but not Emberhawk. She was from a different people. A people who had no gold or silk like whatever he was wearing. Wood and trees and leather.

Katrosi. They were Katrosi.

He was Katrosi.

His head hurt. He grimaced and rubbed his temple. How could he be Katrosi and Emberhawk at the same time?

"Idryon?" Illiana smiled up at him, her eyes laced with concern. "Are you all right?"

He tried to remember how to work his tongue. It was thick and lazy. So he just nodded.

But he wasn't all right. Everything was pretty, but it felt like a lie.

Illiana handed him a cup. "Drink this, dear. You must be overheating." She turned to the crowd. "Zamara's mercy, it's so hot today!"

Ryon took the cup and looked down into its waters. Something told him not to drink it. Something was wrong.

"Where is she?" he mumbled.

Illiana leaned closer. "What was that, dear?"

Pain lanced through Ryon's head. His fingers twitched and he dropped the cup. Cool liquid splashed his pants. Why was he wearing dress pants?

His blood felt like pond scum, sludging through his aching muscles. And someone must have driven a spear through his temple for it to hurt like that.

Why was he here?

He backed away from Illiana.

"Xavier!" Illiana called. "Will you help him, please? He's in distress."

A huge man appeared from the concerned crowd on his left. The man who'd kidnapped him.

Ryon ran.

Thick hedges tore through his clothing and clawed into his skin. The sensation jolted his senses awake.

Kira. Her name was Kira.

Illiana screamed for guards behind him.

There was a wall beyond the hedge in front of him. It ran all along the edge of the arboretum and joined the palace behind.

He was walled in.

Ryon tried to focus and summon the Phoera element to make himself invisible. It eluded him.

Footsteps pounded behind him. He rushed for the arches of flowered vines and ducked into the purple-tipped grasses.

His body felt sluggish. Miserable. He must have been drugged.

Muddlewort. He'd heard Illiana say it before. Lysander had said it was an herb that clouded the mind.

Shaking overtook Ryon's limbs as the footsteps grew closer. He burst onto the pathway, crashed into a screeching woman, and ducked into the hedge on the other side.

The wall was made of cobblestone. Too smooth to climb.

Phoera still wouldn't answer him.

Nowhere to hide. No way to escape.

Ryon cried out in prayer. *Aeo, help me!*

Someone grabbed him from behind. Forced him to the ground. He struggled as they shoved something bitter down his throat.

His pain faded. The haze returned, brighter this time.

Everything was okay.

A lion formed in the mist, its eyes flickering like embers. Its mane waved like tongues of flame. Ensorcelled with fire but not consumed.

Fear branched through Ryon. He knew the lion wasn't real, but somehow, it was. It was not a tame lion. But somehow, he knew it was good.

The nice man helped him to his feet. The garden was peaceful and pretty and dull.

And all was well.

41

LYSANDER

Lysander's heart swelled with gratitude as he watched Brooke sleep on her side in Granny Zelle's guest room. Despite the warped cauterization on her back he'd smeared with green salve, her face was tranquil. Such a rare sight.

Just days ago, he'd thought there was nothing to live for. How glad he was now that he'd held on despite the pain of emptiness and loss.

Was this your doing, creator? He thought in a silent prayer. He closed his eyes and took a deep breath. Maybe he should at least listen to Ryon next time he got preachy.

You look at her like you love her, but you left her to die.

Lysander's soul nearly fled his body. Then he realized the creator's voice didn't sound like Felix. Hopefully.

He spun and found a glow-eyed kitten watching him from the doorway, its tail flicking with annoyance.

Lysander remembered to breathe, quietly stood, and snuck to the door. "You scared the life out of me," he whispered as he shut the door behind him.

That would be an improvement upon the world, Oathbreaker.

Lysander wanted to punt the kitten down the hallway, but the power it would call upon was far greater than an angry trace cat mother.

"I didn't leave her to die," Lysander said quietly. "I didn't know the camp would be attacked, and I left because I was poisoned."

You don't look poisoned, said Felix.

"Granny Zelle saved me. And I built up a resistance to dreamthistle."

Ah yes, because you cultivated it to assassinate innocents in Zamara's name.

Lysander bit down on his irritation. "Look, I'm sorry you see my working for Zamara as breaking your oath. And I'm grateful you helped me in Jadenv—"

I don't "see it as breaking my oath." You started following Zamara and gave her all of the syn I'd given you. That was literally you breaking the terms of the oath you took when you became my vessel in the clearest possible way.

Lysander raised his hands. "Take all my syn, then. And I have a stash you can have, too. But if you think I followed her willingly, you're not so bright."

Felix's vibrant eyes flashed. *You must not know what "willingly" means. She threatened you, and you caved to her. That was your choice.*

Lysander huffed and strode past, highly aware that his next step might be his last. It was a bit scarier now that he actually had something to lose. "What was I supposed to do? Just say no and let her kill me? She'd have gone after Coriander and my defiance would have accomplished nothing."

At least your honor would have been intact for your trip to the afterlife.

Lysander clenched his fists and continued down the hall without looking back. "Well if you'd have shown up, I would have stood with you to bring her down. But you didn't show, did you? You let her take Selene and my hearing and everything."

There was a slight pause. Then Felix's voice sounded in his mind once again: *You know I don't make public appearances. That was a trap Zamara laid for me, and I refused to step into it.*

Lysander stopped. Glanced over his shoulder. "And yet you showed up as a wyvern to save Jadenvive in full view of everyone."

That was to protect the keystone, Felix said, his green eyes flashing. *And I didn't reveal my identity. That wyvern was just a beast from the lake as far as any humans know.*

Lysander gave him a deadpan look. "Lake wyverns went extinct a couple generations ago. And they don't have elemental eyes."

No, they're just endangered . . . right?

Lysander sighed. "You're just bored, aren't you?"

Extremely. The kitten trotted forward and pounced up the stairs to the indoor garden. *Listen, I didn't kill you the first time because I saw you try to kill Zamara. And I won't kill you this time if you'll convince your woman to stop running around and putting the keystone in the maximum possible danger.*

Lysander followed him up into the greenhouse area of the pyramid and relished the air heavily laden with the scents of plant life. "Well, if Jadenvive has been overtaken by the Malaano, we can't exactly return there and lock it in the treasury."

That's the problem. First I taught you Emberhawk and gave you glass-gold, and it only took five generations to completely forget everything and lose the keystone to the Katrosi. Then the Katrosi seemed promising only to have them frolic off into enemy territory, practically begging to have it stolen by kai'lani knows who.

Lysander inspected a patch of slender-leaf hyssop, then flowering feverfew, impressed with how well Granny Zelle had kept up with everything in his absence despite their differing water needs. "Do you expect me to ask Brooke to stay here until a safer place arises?"

No can do, Brooke's thought-voice called.

Lysander turned to find her climbing the stairs behind him. He grinned and brought her under his arm as she tousled her braids and yawned.

The kitten's fur stood on end and its mouth moved, but Lysander couldn't read kitten lips. "Hey, either take human form or whine in some way we can both understand."

Felix glared at him, then coughed up what looked like a silver hairball. The syn unraveled and lifted into the air to form floating Phoeran script: SHE ISN'T WEARING HER HEADDRESS. WHERE IS IT?

"It's back in the guest room," Brooke said, or at least, that's what Lysander thought she said—it was difficult to see her lips when she was cuddled into his side. "Skies, you're paranoid. Can't you sense it or something?"

ONLY THE GREATER ELEMENTALS CAN SENSE IT, the letters

read before shifting to: BECAUSE IT BINDS THEM TO THEIR STONE PRISONS.

"Oh yeah, I forgot you're a *lesser* elemental," Brooke said.

Lysander determined her emphasis by the way she slowed the word "lesser." He grinned.

The kitten's eyes thinned into slits. The silver dust changed into new letters: DO NOT LEAVE THIS PYRAMID UNTIL I CAN FIND A SAFER LOCATION.

"What are you so afraid of?" Lysander asked. "I thought there was a prophecy about the greater elementals not being released until the end times."

I HAVE BEEN TASKED BY THE CREATOR WITH PROTECTING IT REGARDLESS, said the letters that floated over Felix's tuft-tipped ears. Then, EVIL ALWAYS FINDS A WAY.

Brooke glanced up at Lysander, and he joyfully met her gaze. She felt so small under his arm. She might not need his protection, but he would protect her anyway. He would learn how to treat a woman right this time, no matter how much work it took. He couldn't lose another love.

"Well, I have to find Nari," Brooke said. "I told her to stay with Coriander's family and heal them, and I've no idea what happened to any of them."

"Illiana would have jailed them," Lysander mused. "She would lose her reputation with the people completely if she had them killed. And Nari would have been kept alive because . . ." he chose his words carefully as he considered Brooke's expression, "she is living proof of Katrosi involvement."

Faint lines creased between Brooke's brown eyes. "Then I have to break her out."

NOPE. SORRY.

Brooke slipped from Lysander's side to flick her hand across Felix's letters. The syn powder floated outward like a silver cloud. "It's my fault she's in this situation, so I'm going to make it right," Brooke said. "We can just leave the keystone here."

Felix's letters re-forged themselves in midair: I'M NOT GOING TO LEAVE IT HERE TO BE GUARDED BY A GERIATRIC HUMAN.

Lysander caught movement from the corner of his eye. Granny Zelle approached, swiped her cane through the floating script, then nearly whacked Felix on the head. The cat dodged, whirled, and bared its little fangs.

"Careful, Granny!" Lysander laughed. "He's wild."

"I know full well what he is," Granny Zelle said. "He's a no-good liar who never comes to visit."

Felix dipped his head. His fur rippled and his body swelled in size as it took the shape of an orange fox. His letters rearranged. I HAVE BEEN WATCHING OVER YOU, LYZELLE.

"And never coming in for tea?" Granny Zelle demanded. She raised her cane again. "And you come in here like a feline thinkin' I won't recognize you?"

Felix shrank. SURELY YOU ARE AWARE OF WHAT A HANDFUL YOUR GRANDSONS ARE.

Granny Zelle's cane fell slowly, landing on the ground to support herself. "Well, I can't argue with that," she said with a grin. She winked at Brooke. "Let that be a warning to you, young lady."

"Oh, I'm well aware," Brooke said, shooting Lysander a mischievous look. Before he could protest, she bowed to Granny Zelle. "Thank you so much for your hospitality."

"My pleasure. Haven't had this much company since last year's harvest festival!" Granny Zelle squinted at Brooke's tattered clothing. "I can get you some fresh clothes if you like, though I don't have any armor for women like that. How are you feeling, dear?"

"Much better," Brooke said. "Thank you all."

"You can't be feeling well enough to storm the palace prison," Lysander said in a low tone. "Why don't you—"

"You're one to talk," Brooke interrupted. "I still don't understand how you're not dead."

"You're leaving already?" Granny Zelle's mannerisms told Lysander she was yelling.

"We think Cori's imprisoned in Quin'Zamar," Lysander said. "I have to get them out and talk some sense into Illiana."

"Cori's what?" Granny Zelle exclaimed. "I'll pack your favorite dinner!" She whirled and hobbled toward the kitchen.

Lysander stepped close to Brooke, taking her hand. "Please stay here with Felix. You're hurt and the consequences of you being captured are too great."

"I'm fine. Felix cauterized the wound."

"That doesn't mean it's healed," Lysander said.

Felix formed some letters beside them, which they ignored.

"Your salve really helped," Brooke said.

Lysander gave her a knowing look. "I'm deaf, not blind. I can see every time you wince."

The letters floated closer, but no one looked at them.

"My healer is the one in prison," Brooke said. "But you don't want me to go after her?"

Lysander tilted his head. "You're too crafty for your own good."

The letters flew in between them. They faced Brooke, so Lysander read them backwards: IF YOU DON'T STAY HERE, I WILL TURN INTO A WHALE AND SWALLOW YOU.

"I thought you couldn't touch the keystone, but suddenly you can swallow it?" Brooke said. "And how would a beached whale protect it?"

Somehow, the fox appeared to be vexed.

Lysander folded his arms. "Felix, I know you're bored. You can't tell me honestly that you don't want to go with us and overthrow Zamara's legacy."

The fox's tail twitched. The letters disintegrated, then after a moment, the silver cloud formed: IT'S TRUE THAT I CANNOT SAY THAT HONESTLY.

Lysander smirked. "My one condition is that Illiana not be harmed.

She's young and was brainwashed by Zamara, but she's still my sister. Got it?"

Felix laid his ears flat. NO PROMISES.

"Promise," Lysander demanded.

I WILL ACCOMPANY BROOKE. THIS IS THE BEST DEAL YOU'RE GOING TO GET, OATHBREAKER.

Lysander sighed and turned to Brooke. "Let's go together and split up once we reach the palace walls. Felix can easily sneak you into the prison to release everyone, while I'll go through the front gate and speak with Illiana. We have a good relationship—I can speak peacefully with her."

Brooke frowned in concentration. "I don't like the idea of splitting up."

"Me either, but you can't go directly into the palace. Illiana is the paranoid type so she keeps a ridiculous amount of guards. We can't risk you being recognized."

"Why doesn't Felix just sneak me into the palace, then?"

"I thought you were rescuing your healer."

Brooke pursed her lips. "Of course, but we also need to put Coriander on the throne."

"Then you'll have to break him out of prison first, right?"

She sighed, but her eyes flickered with allure. "Touché."

Granny Zelle reappeared, waving a bulging sack. As she hobbled closer, Lysander kissed Brooke on the forehead. "Felix is all talk. He won't let anything happen to you."

I MIGHT IF YOU DO SOMETHING STUPID. I HAVE OTHER VESSELS.

Brooke ignored Felix. "I've already experienced his protection first-hand." She pushed up on her toes to kiss Lysander on the cheek, lighting him aflame. "You won't have the same luxury, though. Be safe."

"Here you go!" Granny Zelle shoved the bag into Lysander's hands. Then she used sign language uncomfortably close to Lysander's face. *"Don't hurt Illi. Don't get hurt. Bring Cori and Iraleth and my babies back here, okay?"*

Lysander leaned back. "Yes, ma'am."

"Bring her back here, too." Granny Zelle looked at Brooke with a roguish sidelong glance. *"I have questions."*

42

KIRALAU

Vines and branches gave way to sunlight cresting on an idyllic coastline and distant mountains. Black sand accentuated deep blue waters and vibrant green palms along the shore. The beach was interrupted by magnificent docks that housed ships larger than Kira had ever seen—some with sails taller than a house.

And as their cart continued along the hilly path, which sloped down into Quin'Zamar, foliage retreated to afford them a view of the gleaming city at least four times larger than Navarro. Straw-topped huts surrounded a colorful marketplace and pyramids made of glass. A sprawling castle crowned the city from a cliffside where the river met the sea. The blinding palace appeared to be made entirely of glass-gold.

Kira gaped. She'd never seen a more breathtaking sight made by the hands of man.

Perhaps Vylia could have just brought the Malo stone here.

"Don't fall off the cart." Tekkyn was watching her with a teasing grin.

Kira had trouble retrieving her jaw. "How can you not be impressed? Have you been here before?"

Tekkyn shrugged. "Been lots of places."

Kira glanced back at Aegwyn, who rode her xavi behind their cart. Her eyes were wide, and her olive skin paled. She looked like she was going to be sick.

"Hey," Kira called to her.

Aegwyn startled and found Kira's face as if she'd been lost. "Yes?"

"You okay?"

"Uh, yes." Aegwyn sat up straighter and made a clicking noise to guide her xavi beside the cart. "Let me lead. There's a guard tower around this turn."

Kira watched her for a long moment, concerned about whatever had her spooked. "You sure you're all right?" she asked as quietly as the space between them would afford.

"As good as I can be." Aegwyn flashed a smile. It was unconvincing.

Kira turned her gaze downward to Quin'Zamar. "What makes the beach black like that?"

"The volcano, Sleeping Panther," Aegwyn said, pointing to the closest mountain to the west. "The lava it belches cools into black stone. It slides into the sea and becomes sand."

"Amazing," Kira breathed. Ryon and Aegwyn had grown up in this paradise? Why would they ever want to leave?

"Beauty can be deceptive," Aegwyn said under her breath. "Stay close. Illiana no doubt brought Ryon to the palace. I can get you inside by giving you as gifts to the palace staff, assuming they have a couple of open positions."

Kira found the idea of "giving" a human being revolting, but it did seem like a quick way to get behind whatever guards surely watched the palace. So she swallowed her opinion.

"And they'll just let us run around over there?" Tekkyn asked.

"I really can't say," Aegwyn said as she led her mount around a curve in the road. "My bangle should allow me some leeway up front, but honestly I don't know how Illiana will react when she sees me. If she's done something awful to Ryon . . . I . . ."

"Have we thought about how we're getting *out* of this place after all the fun's over?" Tekkyn said. "If we go in as slaves, they'll come after us when we escape with Ryon."

The girls looked at each other. "I've been trying not to think that far ahead, honestly," Aegwyn said.

Even entering the city seems like a monumental task for her, Kira thought to herself. "Do you have a better idea?" Kira asked.

"Not without lookin' at the grounds and guard posts and whatnot," Tekkyn said.

"We don't have time for that," Kira said. "And you know what? Ryon can use his invisibility to sneak us out, no problem."

Tekkyn didn't appear convinced, but he tipped his head as if to concede that point.

A roar from a thousand throats suddenly split the air. Kira craned her neck and found a crowd—no, a multitude—gathered in the market square below a balcony overhang that gracefully dove from the palace above.

Two figures strode out from the palace and stopped, but the cheering continued.

Kira's guts knotted. They were so far away, but her heart dared to guess who they were.

"Wait," Kira said to Tekkyn, and he pulled the reins until the cart slowed to a halt and stopped creaking.

"My good people!" A young woman's voice warbled as its volume was amplified by Phoera sound manipulation.

"Illiana," Aegwyn whispered.

Kira's heart pounded as she squinted at the figures. One appeared female in a flowing white dress, the other male.

Ryon?

"I present to you your new king!"

43

BROOKE

"All right, get off." Felix transformed from a dragon to a trace cat the moment he landed, sending Brooke and Lysander tumbling from his shape-shifting back in a heap.

"Hey!" Lysander yelled.

Felix shuddered, tossing his thick beige mane. "Romance nauseates me." He hacked up a chunk of silver that dissolved into mist, then formed Phoeran script in the air between them.

"We didn't do anything on your back!" Lysander protested at the same time Brooke said, "Didn't you have a mate once?"

Felix's hind quarters plopped on the forest floor. "Say your goodbyes and let's go." His letters followed suit.

Brooke straightened her split riding skirt and went to fix her headdress, then remembered it wasn't there. She'd left it at Granny Zelle's pyramid after extracting the keystone, which rested hidden in a large leather pouch on her belt. She wasn't wearing face paint either, but her clothing and the style of her braids would give her away as a Katrosi if anyone gave her a second glance.

She pulled up her hood and looked up at Lysander. His enormous frown looked as reluctant as she felt.

"It'll just be an hour or so." Lysander took her hands in his. "We can use thought-speak to find each other in the palace. This will be over before a d'hakka strike, and then we can finally have some peace."

Brooke found his optimism foolhardy yet adorable. How had they become so inseparable so quickly? It was like they were two mag-stones, pushing away from each other by some unseen force for so long. And now that their situations had flipped, that same force brought them together with startling speed.

Her feelings felt childish. And yet they made her so inexplicably happy that even her rational nature couldn't stop her from enjoying Lysander's presence. The warmth of his embrace and the strength she felt in his arms. How small her hands felt in his.

Still, she gave herself a healthy warning: love wasn't a feeling. True love was a commitment.

A commitment she didn't want to think about yet.

Brooke moved her head to eye him sidelong as she sent a thought to his mind. *A d'hakka strike? Could you at least use a different analogy for your deceptive assurances?*

"Not deceptive." Lysander looked up at the sky. "As fast as a . . . xavi." His grin put boyish glee on his masculine face. "I hope you know the only reason I'm leaving you is because one of the most powerful creatures on the planet is keeping you safe."

"Your hair is a powerful creature," Felix called, and his syn-script changed in mid-air to match his words.

Brooke giggled as Lysander ran hands through his windswept black hair. His efforts did little to fix the problem.

I will probably accompany Felix to guide the prisoners to safety, Brooke thought to Lysander as she reached up on her tiptoes to help tame a stubborn lock. *We'll see how the timing works out. But I'll find you regardless.*

Lysander took advantage of her closeness to kiss her forehead. "Promise you won't take any chan—"

"Ryon is here," Felix said, drowning out the rest of Lysander's words.

Brooke's smile turned downward. "What?"

"I can sense him." The trace cat's enormous head drooped low in the direction where Brooke assumed Quin'Zamar lie ahead. "But he has a lot less syn than I left him with."

Brooke hurried to Felix, but couldn't see anything but vine-wrapped trees in the direction his pupilless eyes gazed. "It can't be Ryon. I left him in charge of . . ." She trailed off. If Jadenvive had been overtaken by the Malaano, any number of awful things could have happened to Ryon. But how could he have ended up *here?*

"It's him. But he's not with other silverbloods—he's alone. So I don't think he's in the prison." Felix's eyes swirled like galaxies, as if he were peering through the veils of time and space and magic itself. "He's higher up. Must be the palace, but in the upper rooms or a tower or something."

Brooke watched Felix's ears lie back on his head. A low growl rumbled in his throat.

"Something else is wrong," Brooke said as more of a statement than a question.

"That half-blood who calls herself the queen," Felix muttered as the silvery script flowed and wove itself into new words. "She has more syn than what's safe for a *trai'yeth*. If she's not already lost her mind, she'll be mad or dead or both before long."

"That can't be right." Lysander came alongside, his boots cracking fallen leaves beneath.

Felix's letters shifted into new ones: THERE IS NO MISTAKING THAT LEVEL OF POWER. THAT MUCH SYN WOULD KILL ANY HUMAN. THEREFORE IT MUST BE THE HALF-BLOOD.

Lysander looked crestfallen until Brooke took his hand. He gave her a quick glance of appreciation before turning back to Felix. "Okay, so we tell her it's dangerous and remove some of her syn?"

SHE WAS RAISED BY ZAMARA; SHE KNOWS. BETTER TO WAIT AND LET HER DIE THAN RISK CONFRONTING A MADDENED YOUTH WIELDING THAT MUCH POWER.

"She's my sister." Lysander clenched his fists. "I'm not going to just—"

SHE IS A NARCISSIST WHO HAS ABSORBED A CONTINENT WORTH OF SYN. Felix's letters grew larger and thicker. He turned his head to focus on Lysander. HAVE AN IOTA OF PATIENCE, AND THE

SITUATION WILL SORT ITSELF OUT.

"Maybe it's dangerous for you, but not for me," Lysander said. "I have to at least try to save her."

Brooke sent a gentle thought toward him. *Remember what you are risking. It's not just your life any more; it's also my heart and our future.*

Lysander's eyebrows raised, and Brooke realized too late how he might have interpreted that.

A moment of silence passed. Lysander's brows knit together before he spoke again. "I'll get Ryon out first. If the syn has driven Illiana mad already, there's no telling what kind of situation he might be in. Once he and the others are safe, I'll confront her."

Brooke squeezed his hand. *Can you do both safely?*

He smirked. "It's me and Ryon we're talking about here. Unseen and unheard are the best ways to get around, wouldn't you say?"

All Brooke knew was darkness, the coarse coat of Felix's trace cat form, and the softer patch of fur on his throat that she clung to as she leaned down on his back. She could discern his pace by the way enormous shoulder blades moved beneath her and guess at their location from echoes and voices.

The sounds were faint now: soft murmuring, dripping water, distant footsteps. She couldn't hear the insects of the rainforest or the commotion of the streets any more. And the air now felt stuffy and smelled of mildew.

Were they inside the palace prison already?

Going in with Felix felt like cheating. Everything was less terrifying and more exhilarating than it should have been.

His tail tapped on Brooke's back twice. She squeezed her arms around his neck to signal her readiness. Then she sat up straight on his back and held her hands up, palms out into the darkness.

Light returned in a blinding instant. The sound of crumpling armor alerted Brooke to two guards crashing to the ground on either side of her before her eyes could clear. She moved her hands to aim at each of them, pretending like she'd downed them herself.

It must have looked awesome to anyone who watched. She should take credit for Felix's powers more often.

A long hallway stretched out before her with prison cells on either side, metal bars stretched from floor to ceiling. Dozens of pairs of wide eyes peered out at her.

Brooke slipped from Felix's back and patted his head as if he were no more than her mount. She moved to one of the fallen guards, looking for keys and trying to avoid the horrified expression frozen on his face. She didn't want to think about how Felix had dropped them so suddenly.

She found the keys on the wall inside a small guard post instead. She glanced over her shoulder before hurrying into the prison, toward the desperate whispers and pleas for her attention. She didn't see anyone in the hallway behind where Felix sat and groomed himself like any other tame trace cat.

Brooke raised a finger to her lips as she approached the first cell, but the noise from the prisoners only grew more excited. She scanned face after face of people stuffed into the large cells, not recognizing anyone. She couldn't just release Quin'Zamar's most dangerous criminals.

"Brooke!" Nariellyn waved from a cell in the back.

Relief surged Brooke forward. She dodged reaching hands as she found the lock on Nariellyn's cell and fumbled with the keys.

"Thank the skies you're okay," Nariellyn breathed. Her clothes were smeared with mud and her hair unkempt. "Where's Dimbae? What's with the cat?"

A pang of worry for Dimbae knifed into Brooke's chest. Hopefully Granny Zelle was right to be optimistic about his recovery. "I'll explain later. Is Coriander here?"

"He's in the back." Nariellyn pointed down the hall.

Brooke tried a thick metal key and glanced at the faces of the people crammed into Nariellyn's cell. She dropped her voice to a whisper. "Are these people . . . ?"

"Yes, they're Coriander's." The bolt clanged, and Nariellyn grabbed Brooke in a hug as the door swung open. Men poured out but didn't leave the prison. Instead they watched her, waited, and pointed out other cells for her to open.

Brooke went straight for Coriander's cell as soon as she saw him. His children clung to his legs. Her heart melted at the sight.

"Good to see you." Coriander patted the heads of his children and instructed them to stay near him as other prisoners slipped out.

Brooke handed him the keys, but Coriander gave them to another man beside him as he turned back to walk further into the cell.

"Are you all right?" Brooke asked. He seemed healthy, but her breath caught as she saw Iraleth lying on the floor, cradling her belly. Iraleth gave Brooke a weak smile, but her face was pale and sweat plastered her silver hair to her forehead.

Coriander carefully helped his wife to her feet. "Bless you," Iraleth said.

Brooke bowed, trying not to let her concern show on her face. "I have a way to sneak you out."

"All we needed was the keys." Coriander addressed another man who waited by his side. "Get the women, children, and injured to safety." The man nodded and offered Iraleth his arm.

"Be safe." Iraleth leaned toward Coriander to kiss him on the cheek, and he hugged her gently while whispering in her ear.

"You're not going with them?" Brooke asked.

Coriander studied her as he embraced his children and told his son to look after his mother. "I get the sense that you're not, either."

Brooke knew she should accompany Felix and continue pretending that his powers were hers, but she would much rather continue sneaking around the palace until they found Lysander and Ryon. Maybe Felix would continue to follow her if she just started off in a dangerous direction.

"What's your plan, then?" Brooke asked.

Coriander waited until his family was out of earshot. "I'm going to kill my sister," he murmured.

Brooke had a small intake of breath. She hadn't taken him as someone capable of such . . . darkness.

"You don't understand, or you wouldn't look at me that way," Coriander whispered. "She drained Iraleth's syn. While she was injured and pregnant. In front of my children."

Brooke grimaced and glanced back at Nariellyn, who nodded and said, "She's weak but she will recover."

"Thank you for healing her," Brooke said. "Well done."

Nariellyn gave a thumbs-up.

"Illiana is beyond saving," Coriander said. "She has lost her sanity to the syn. Absorbed too much of it. If not by her actions and words, you can tell by her eyes." He took a blade that one of the men handed him and stuffed it into his belt. "She will die from it sooner rather than later. Ending her before then will be a mercy killing."

Brooke frowned. She'd been an only child and had always wanted siblings. But in this situation . . .

"You're certain we can't save her?" Brooke whispered. But she remembered Felix's words—she knew the answer.

"If there was a way, I would take it." Coriander's stature went rigid, as if tensing his muscles could protect him against the tragedy of what had to be done. "She has done this to herself."

44

KIRALAU

The dishes on the serving tray chattered together as Kira's hands shook. She took a deep breath and willed her nerves to calm.

Anyone who looked at her for half a second would know she wasn't a slave. Her posture was too straight. Her gaze not downcast. Her clothes completely wrong.

She'd only gotten this far because of Aegwyn and Tekkyn covering for her, but now she was alone. Lost in the heavenly palace with a tray of food that would by no means serve as an excuse for her to see the king.

Ryon. The king.

Kira's eyes misted again before she desperately blinked the tears down and focused on her stride down the long, empty hallway. The pounding of her heart was almost as loud as the clacking of her shoes on the polished floor. Silk curtains flowed toward her from the open windows and brushed her leg, sending a chill up her spine.

She would never find Ryon in this maze. But even if she did, how would he react? He'd married Illiana. His cousin. Instead of her.

Ryon's glass-gold bangle weighed heavily on her wrist. *I'll end up in prison for sure. Aeo, help me!*

Kira slowed her pace as she neared two columns at the end of the hall. She peeked around the corner, looking for guards and hopefully some extravagant doorway beyond which a king might reside.

"Go right," said someone behind her.

Kira was so startled that a glass tipped and fell off her tray. It shattered on the floor, sending hundreds of shards skittering down the hall.

It's me!

The voice in her head sounded like Lysander. But when Kira looked behind her, she only saw the curtains billowing on the breeze.

Footsteps sounded beyond the hall and to the left. Fast approaching.

A strong grip took Kira's arm and pulled her to the side, behind one of the pillars. Her vision went black.

Quiet. Lysander's thought pressed upon her mind.

It took all of Kira's strength not to resist or drop the rest of the tray's assortment. She wanted to greet Lysander and curse him at the same time. But he wouldn't hear the curse so she'd hit him instead.

You can hit me after this guard passes.

Kira wondered if he could hear her thoughts.

The footsteps came frighteningly close, then stopped. "Hello?" a man called.

Yeah, your thoughts are louder than most.

Kira stayed as still as her nerves would let her. She couldn't decide whether Lysander's invasion of privacy into her mind was worth not having to write to communicate with him as she'd done the last time, since she didn't know the Phoeran hand-language.

Did you have to scare the light out of me? Kira thought. *What are you doing here?*

I thought you'd recognize my voice, Lysander returned.

I've only met you like once! Kira snapped.

You still hate me, huh?

You gave me enough reasons to. Kira wondered if he could sense her frustration, too. But she reminded herself that it was Lysander's suggestion that led to her finding the herbal cure for her mother's cloud sickness. So he couldn't be entirely evil.

Was he trying to rescue Ryon? But hadn't Lysander disappeared with Brooke? Did that mean Brooke was nearby as well?

A sigh emanated from where the guard must have stood, not three foot-lengths from them. He grumbled something about people leaving things on pillars in the windy hall.

We both want Ryon back, Lysander thought. *Isn't that why you're here in that cringey travelling merchant costume? I'm shocked you got this far.*

Kira clenched her jaw. *Let go of me.*

Lysander's grip on her arm eased. *Stay close. I think I know where Ryon is.*

Kira took a deep breath and let it out as silently as possible. *Thank you. I . . . I'm sorry.*

His deep laughter rumbled through her head. *No you're not, but it's fine. This way.*

Kira followed Lysander's lead as he gently pulled her along. Walking blind was difficult enough, but the tray made everything more tedious. She wished she could set it down, but she didn't want to spare the time or risk the suspicion of leaving it somewhere.

The stairs were the most difficult. Halfway up the spiraling staircase, Lysander took the tray from her. For some reason, she didn't hear him set it down, either.

Here.

Kira continued on and gasped when her vision abruptly returned. She stood in a different hallway, this one circular with the sun and orbiting stars bejeweled into the tile floor. A door just ahead.

Lysander knocked.

No answer.

He knocked again. "Ryon?"

Kira wondered if Lysander could hear Ryon's thoughts. And if these were the king's chambers, where were the guards?

"His thoughts are . . . off," Lysander muttered. "These aren't the king's chambers; they are the heirs'." He turned the doorknob. It clicked, and the door slowly swung open.

Ryon sat on a lonely chair in the center of the curved room. He didn't respond to their presence. He stared at the wall.

Kira rushed to him. "Ryon!" She crouched in front of him, interrupting his vapid gaze. "Ryon, it's me." She took his hands in hers.

He met her gaze with unfocused eyes. Slowly smiled. Said nothing.

"What's wrong?" Kira yearned to hug him, but something wasn't right. Everything wasn't right. Her heart ripped in two different directions at once.

And where were his lenses?

The tray clattered as Lysander set it down and drew his dagger.

Kira followed Lysander's gaze to the window that overlooked the beach and distant mountains. She didn't see anything.

"Reveal yourself," Lysander said.

A figure melted into existence not an arm's length from Kira. She gasped and staggered back, then lurched forward to place her body between the man and Ryon.

"Who's this?" the man asked. He raised his hands and took a step back.

"His fiancé," Lysander muttered.

"Oh. Not any more, eh? Unfortunate." The man's face grew solemn. He took another step back and addressed Kira. "I am Xavier."

"What did you do to him?" Kira demanded. She pulled a throwing knife from the sheath she'd hidden inside her tunic. Pointed it at Xavier's throat.

"Muddlewort," Xavier said, as if that was supposed to mean something to Kira. Lysander rummaged around the vials of herbs that were strung across his chest.

"You were the one who took him," Kira accused, having no idea if it were really true.

Xavier dipped his head. "Queen's orders."

Lysander growled as he took a cup from the serving tray and poured a vial of dried herbs into it. The liquid began to steam. "How do her orders compare to Zamara's?"

"I am ever loyal to the throne," Xavier said. He lowered his hands, ignoring Kira's knife. "And we have new blood on the throne now, eh?"

Kira narrowed her eyes at him. What was he implying?

It didn't matter. She would kill him.

Except Xavier hadn't drawn a weapon, and his body language didn't imply any kind of threat.

She stepped to the side as Lysander approached Ryon, but still stayed between him and Xavier. Lysander handed the cup to Ryon and guided him into drinking.

Lysander must have heard the confusion in her thoughts, because he explained, "They drugged him. This is the antidote. There, no—careful. Good." He tossed the empty cup aside—at least, that's what Kira assumed from the clattering sound since she didn't take her eyes off of Xavier. "He'll be responsive soon."

Xavier prevented hope from flooding Kira like a stalwart dam. He glanced at the door behind him. "You have me to thank for that. At the amount she wanted me to administer, he might already have sustained permanent damage."

Kira's blade didn't waver as she tried to puzzle it out. "Then you don't always follow orders?"

Xavier fixed her in a lionlike stare. "I am ever loyal to the throne," he repeated.

"You just didn't want *her* on the throne," Lysander said.

Xavier said nothing, but Kira sensed words unsaid hanging in the air: *no one* wanted Illiana on the throne.

"She wanted a king. I gave her a king." A thin smile stretched across Xavier's lips.

Kira contained a shudder. She couldn't figure this man out. Whatever he was, he gave her goosebumps.

How long would Lysander's antidote take to work? She wanted nothing more than to tend to Ryon but refused to remove her blade from Xavier's direction.

"Are you going to try and drag him back to Jadenvive?" Xavier asked. "Kira?"

Her stomach leapt into her throat at Ryon's voice. She whirled.

Ryon grinned weakly at her. "You're not a dream."

Kira collapsed on him and hugged tight. Wept. Didn't let go.

Ryon squeezed her back with a grunt of discomfort. He glared at Xavier. "You."

Xavier dropped to one knee and bowed his head. "My lord."

"You really married her?" Kira managed, her voice unsteady.

"No! I didn't . . ." Ryon swallowed and squinted at his reflection in an ornate mirror that hung from the wall. He rubbed his eyes with the back of his hand. "At least . . . I have no memory of that. And I'm pretty sure you have to be aware of . . . anything . . . to actually make a vow." Ryon grimaced and looked up at Lysander. "Thanks. You got anything for a beast of a headache?"

Lysander nodded and disappeared.

"The vow was . . . accepted," Xavier said. "Legally."

Ryon looked sick in more ways than one—mirroring Kira's own feelings. "I didn't marry her," he said. "I'm not married."

Kira buried her face in his shoulder. He hadn't truly betrayed her.

"But I want to marry you. Only you, ever." Ryon gently brought her face up to meet the fire that reignited in his orange gaze. "I've proposed to you like three times now, and they've all been lame. I wanted to take you to the waterfall or do something with chocolate or paradise flowers, but with the attack and . . . and then the other attack, and . . ." He gritted his teeth and squeezed his eyes shut and rubbed his temples.

"Hey, it's okay." Kira placed his hand over his. "I don't need all that fancy stuff. I love you."

"I love you, too!" Ryon grinned wide despite his obvious discomfort. "Your dad gave his blessing, you know."

Kira felt heat rush to her cheeks. "He did?"

Ryon made an obstinate noise and rolled his eyes. "Of course he did." He lifted an eyebrow and gave his signature lopsided smile, then paused to gauge Kira's reaction. She couldn't stop an awkward grin.

"I mean, we're in a castle, right? So that's kind of romantic, yeah?" Ryon slid out of the chair to get down on one knee, nearly fell over, and caught himself before taking Kira's hand. "Will you marry me?"

"At the first opportunity." Kira swiped at moisture from the corner of her eye. "I just have one question."

Ryon looked like he was strung so tight that if she flicked him, he might. "What . . . What is it?"

"How old are you?"

He blinked. "I'm twenty-three. Is that okay? How old are you? Am I too old?"

"I'm eighteen." Didn't he already know that? Kira resisted the urge to toy with him when he was so vulnerable. "Works for me. Let's get married, old man."

45

LYSANDER

Lysander slunk down the opulent halls, trying to keep himself from panting. He'd be nearly exhausted by the time he reached Illiana after stealthing Kiralau around the palace, having to use Phoera to manipulate both light and sound energy. It pushed his skills to the limit, and his limit was much lower thanks to the dreamthistle he was still recovering from.

It was a good thing he wasn't planning on fighting Illiana, because by the time he reached the Grand Balcony, he'd be barely able to fight a branch runner.

But if Ryon changed his mind and decided to leave his room and follow Lysander after all, things could get ugly. And Lysander didn't really expect Ryon to remain in his beautiful prison for long. The fact that it kept Kiralau safe was Lysander's only winning dice roll.

Still, he retained his invisibility to prevent Ryon from following him to Illiana and complicated everything.

Until he remembered that Ryon grew up in the palace, too, so he'd know his way around whenever he regained clarity of mind.

Lysander had to knock some sense into Illiana—fast—or else there would be blood. Whose blood, he didn't want to guess.

The service stairway that led from the kitchens to the Grand Balcony was packed with servers like ants in one of their tunnels. It further confirmed a fact that Lysander didn't want to be true: Illiana was hosting some kind of large banquet there. Which meant the private conversation he wanted with her would instead be in front of a large number of nobles and in view of the entire city, as the balcony stretched out elegantly over the marketplace.

But Lysander had to confront her immediately, or Coriander might find her first. Felix and Brooke might have released his brother by now, and as soon as the guards became aware of a jailbreak, chaos would descend on the palace like a tornado.

Somehow Lysander doubted a confrontation between Coriander and Illiana could have a peaceful ending.

He reached the open double doors to the Grand Balcony. The guards on either side saluted sharply, causing the upright red feathers on their helmets to wave. Lysander nodded to them as he entered.

He imagined the expansive room was loud because of the laughter and clapping and drinking he saw the nobles doing. Dozens of them sat at a long table that ran beside the railing that was open to sea-salted air. A throne of sorts sat in the middle, upon which perched his little sister.

Golden spikes crowned her head, and her necklace flashed and glittered in the midday sun. A scarlet red dress covered her like blood. Glowing orange eyes watched fire-dancers twirl on the opposite side of the table, spinning with ribbons and sparks and tongues of flame.

Her eyes—they were actually glowing. He'd never seen a human's eyes glow like that. Illiana was half elemental, but still, it seemed . . . wrong.

Foreboding pumped through Lysander's veins as he entered. Rounded the table. Approached Illiana's royal seat.

She saw him and her face lit with joy. She stood and called out to him— words he couldn't quite make out on her lips. As he approached, Illiana leaned in and embraced him.

He hugged her back, wary of her crown and the fragility of her frame. Anxiety drained from him as they embraced. Perhaps Xavier hadn't reported him as a traitor after all.

"Brother," Illiana greeted as she pulled away. She made an attempt to hand-sign, but she'd never been good at it. Her movements were clumsy, and she wore strange golden claws on her forefingers that made her movements even more difficult to decipher. She made an obvious gesture at a chair beside her, and a noble stumbled out of it. "Sit and eat! Tell me: where have you been?"

Lysander didn't sit. "May I speak with you in private?" he asked quietly, hopefully being heard over the obvious noise of the room. "I realize it's a bad time, but it's urgent."

Illiana sat back down with effort—her gown didn't appear to be made for comfort—and took a drink of wine. He couldn't see her lips to discern her dismissal.

Lysander leaned over the table, close to her ear. "I wouldn't interrupt you unless it was extremely important. It involves your safety."

Illiana shot him an annoyed look. She waved at the now-empty chair beside her. "Then sit and speak."

He really didn't want to have his movement restricted by the table, so he pulled the chair out and sat on its edge. "Did you attack Cori's camp?"

Her face soured. She sat her glass back down, hard. "He was plotting against the throne."

"Do the people think it's *his* throne?" Lysander asked.

Illiana snapped her eerie gaze on him. "Does it matter?"

Lysander couldn't determine what she said next through lip-reading, but he could safely assume her message.

"Yes," Lysander whispered. "Isn't that why you married Idryon? To win the people's favor?"

Illiana's lip curled, and she looked back at the fire-dancers. Lysander couldn't tell what she said.

He grew annoyed and looked into her mind.

Thoughts swirled around his presence like a maelstrom, jolting abruptly in different directions. It was *loud,* but not loud like Kiralau's clear and distinct thoughts. It was a cacophony with each chaotic thought screaming for attention. He'd never encountered a mind like that before. But he was new to thought-speak. Maybe it was normal.

Even so, he backed out of Illiana's mind and tried to guess where their conversation left off.

"Marrying Ryon won't change people's opinions enough," Lysander said. "Coriander is next in line, and everyone knows it."

"Treason!" Illiana looked back at him with ethereal fire in her eyes, her jeweled earrings catching in her hair with the sudden movement. "It was mother's wish that I be her heir, and you know it. It was her plan to claim Idryon for me. Are you jealous, brother?"

"No, I'm concerned about you," Lysander said, his hand itching for his dagger in case her twitching hand snatched that steak knife. "I fear a coup."

"The coup is locked in the dungeons and will soon be dealt with." Illiana turned back to the entertainment and took another drink.

Lysander stared in silence for a long moment. Did she mean to execute Coriander? What about his family and his men? And all of his sympathizers in the city?

He didn't have to return to her mind to confirm it. Her thoughts vomited gore.

"Illi, please, consider peace," Lysander said. "You will always have a home in the palace. We have larger threats to—"

"The only threat is the Katrosi, and I've ruined them. Not even father's war caused as much devastation as I've inflicted on them." Illiana's face stuttered in soundless laughter. "Did you know your mission to set fire to Jadenvive was my idea? I'm a genius. That's why mother appointed me as her heir." Her expression abruptly fell into a twist of sadness and anger. "But you let her die. I didn't know she could die."

Lysander leaned away from her. "How much syn have you absorbed?"

"As much as I want," she said. He didn't catch what else she said as she turned away, but it involved her being a half-blood.

"Illi, even *trai'yeth* elementals have a limit to how much syn they can hold before—"

"No! Mother didn't have vessels like—" She stopped herself. "She held as much as she could."

"And it drove her mad, too," Lysander murmured.

Illiana shot to her feet, knocking her elaborate chair back. Her nose wrinkled like a wolf's as she screamed something unintelligible at him. "Mother was a goddess! And I am a demigod!"

All movement in the room suddenly stopped. Lysander followed the direction that the nobles had turned their stunned faces.

Coriander stood in the doorway. Instead of the guards, he was flanked by Brooke and Felix in trace cat form.

A gleaming blade pointed at Illiana. "Step down," Coriander said, his thoughts ringing with cool-forged anger, "and you will be treated with mercy."

Illiana crouched like a cornered cat and bared her teeth. She whirled on Lysander and thrust her hand at him.

It felt as if she'd taken control of his bones and thrown him across the room with them. He flew backward and slammed into the elegant metal struts of the balcony railing. Pain arched up his back as he caught sight of the marketplace a lethal drop below.

Silver mist appeared in Illiana's hand and coalesced into a long spike. She reared back and the spike followed her movement in mid-air. She pointed it at Coriander as if to hurl it at him, and it shot forward at a sudden and terrifying speed.

Coriander dodged and sprinted for a fire-dancer's pedestal. The dancer jumped down and cowered beside the prince for cover.

The nobles scattered like bees from a jostled hive.

Lysander noted the pillars lining the sides of the room that displayed busts of his forefathers and previous monarchs. They weren't thick enough for someone to safely hide behind. He glanced at the double-doors that nobles and servers ran screaming from. That was the only escape route, unless someone had a way to fly or climb from the balcony.

Brooke hurled her spear at Illiana. The silver mist that surrounded the queen ballooned outward, then solidified into a shield before Illiana. The spear slammed into it and dropped to the table, sending cakes and wine splattering over the decadent display.

Illiana reached a hand out toward Brooke, whose eyes went wide as she lifted into the air.

Lysander tackled Illiana, hitting her hard enough to send them both crashing across the table. Her metal claws dug into his shoulder, but he didn't let go until he caught a glimpse of Brooke falling back to the floor and gasping for breath.

A whirl of movement spun over him. Lysander glanced up into the enormous face of a green-eyed ember hawk. Blue-white flames danced inside its beak as it inhaled.

Lysander scrambled to his feet and ran as searing heat exploded behind him. He covered his face and didn't stop until he was at the edge of the room. Yet still the inferno raged hot enough to sear his clothes.

Through the flames, he saw his sister shielding herself with an outstretched hand to Felix. Fire consumed her dress and hair, and the spikes of her crown drooped like wilting leaves.

Felix reached the end of his breath and the flames ceased. He reared back with massive wings glistening like cinders, then down again to snap Illiana in his curved beak.

Instead he got a mouthful of syn spikes that formed in themselves faster than a blink. Silver lances protruded from his red-feathered face, and he roared loud enough for Lysander to hear.

"How dare you take her form?" Illiana said as Lysander rushed to stand between them, arms outstretched with a plea for them to stop. He noticed a drip of silver blood falling from Illiana's nose, then the world tumbled end over end. He hit something hard.

Silver blades shot from Felix's open mouth like ice shards. They crashed into Illiana's syn shield and absorbed into it. She laughed as the mist surged into her skin, her dress still alight with flame.

"Illi, stop this!" Lysander yelled.

She dodged a strike from Felix and sent a silver spike into his chest.

Felix stumbled back, his wings flailing as he collapsed onto the floor.

Lysander stared in horror as Illiana strode to Felix's still form and reached a hand out to him. The silver blood that poured from his wound flowed to her palm and skittered along her skin.

"Illi!" Her name tore from his lungs.

This time she turned to him with a crazed smile. "Now you will all face my justice."

Illi, listen to me. Lysander sent the desperate thought to her mind, doing his best to strip it of his panic and reinforce it with command. *You are hurting yourself. The syn is killing you!*

His body froze. Miniscule spikes of pain sparked to life by the thousands. They pushed from his veins and out his skin like needles.

Illiana said something about his half-Valinorian heritage, but Lysander couldn't lip-read exactly what it was through her expression of disgust and his haze of pain.

He was being ripped apart from the inside out. The feeling was familiar from when Zamara had nearly killed him.

Lysander heard himself scream, distantly, like his broken ears only picked up the echo through the resonance of his skull.

He couldn't survive this a second time.

And Illiana couldn't be saved, he realized with a sadness that dulled his agony. The little sister from his memories would never have done this to him. To anyone.

She was already gone. And Lysander wanted someone to avenge him.

The pain stopped abruptly, changing from a horrible ripping to a sort of aching relief. Lysander gulped in air and looked around, trying to orient himself. His gaze landed on Ryon and Kira in the doorway.

"Illiana!" Lysander read from Ryon's lips. His cousin's eyes were sharp with clarity and ablaze with rage. "Put him down!"

46

BROOKE

Brooke rushed to the table to grab her fallen spear and run Illiana through, but someone grabbed her arm and yanked her back.

She snarled over her shoulder at Nariellyn. "Let go!"

"You'll tear yourself apart," Nariellyn said. "Did you forget about your wound?"

"She's killing him!" Brooke roared, and the injury in her back sent a skewer of agony through her. Her vision swam and she nearly lost her balance.

"Give me a minute!" Nariellyn sent healing energy lancing through Brooke's back like ethereal stitches. The sensation was even more debilitating than the cut in her back that had re-opened when she'd thrown her spear.

Brooke went down on one knee and steadied herself, cursing her friend but knowing she was right at the same time. Warm blood poured down her back and slicked her riding-skirt.

"The two of you are friendly now?" Illiana glanced between Ryon and Lysander, then considered Ryon as if trying to determine how much of a threat he was. "You still haven't figured out that we killed your father?"

Brooke's pulse stalled as Ryon's face paled. They looked at Lysander, who had collapsed to the floor in a heap. It was apparent that he hadn't heard what Illiana had said.

Lysander, Brooke called to him with thought-speak. *Did you assassinate Ryon's father?*

What? No, came Lysander's exhausted reply. He met Ryon's disbelieving gaze. "I . . . I trained her but I didn't know who the target was."

"Liar," Illiana spat. "You knew full well." She smiled as silver blood from her nose spilled onto her lips, and she licked it up. "I was the perfect choice because the traitor never suspected me—I was so young. But my success guaranteed my place as mother's heir. Alunette was too weak to target family."

"I didn't know!" Lysander insisted. "Otherwise, I never would have . . ." He begged Ryon from his collapsed position on the floor with wide, desperate eyes. "Ryon, I'm sorry. Forgive me!"

Ryon looked like he'd been struck by lightning, but Kira's hand on his arm revived him as guards approached them from behind.

"Stand down!" Ryon yelled at them. "Am I your king or not?"

The soldiers slowed as they neared him, then turned their backs to Ryon, forming a wall between him and anything that might approach from the hall.

Brooke released a breath as the red-feathered guards complied. Kira took a bow and quiver from one of them, nocked an arrow, and aimed it at Illiana.

"Illiana, you're outnumbered," Ryon called in a firm voice. "You can't win. Stand down."

"Surrounding and threatening an unarmed girl. How pathetic you all are," the queen sneered. Silver mist hovered around her like a shining cloud on a summer day. "But I'm not alone. Xavier!"

Movement caught Brooke's eye. Ceiling-length curtains waved to reveal a side door. An Emberhawk man stepped out—one who matched the description her azure masks had given of the assassin who'd poisoned her tea with dreamthistle.

He hauled a young woman out by her arms, which were tied behind her back. Her wide eyes fixed on Ryon. She screamed his name.

Aegwyn? Brooke grabbed the dagger on her belt.

"Stay still," Nariellyn commanded as her ethereal stitching continued, and Brooke gritted her teeth.

"Let's see what color her blood is after I drained her," Illiana said. "Slit her throat. The rest of the traitors will die this day."

Xavier didn't move. He looked at Ryon.

"Release her," Ryon said.

Xavier withdrew a blade. His face was blank as he cut Aegwyn's bonds. The girl fell forward and staggered to her brother.

"You are *all* traitors!" Illiana screamed. A silver lance coalesced from the mist and shot toward Xavier. It skewered him through the middle, and he fell.

Brooke ripped free of Nariellyn and dashed for her spear.

Illiana saw her and swiped her hand sideways as if backhanding Brooke from afar. Brooke felt her body seize up as she careened into the chairs the nobles had fled from. Her vision darkened and returned slowly with floating spots.

Realization dawned on Brooke. Even though she wasn't a Phoeran elementalist, or a royal silverblood, she was still of Phoeran descent. Syn still swam through her blood. Syn that Illiana controlled.

They were all Phoeran.

Except Kira.

Brooke breathed through the pain and rolled onto her side to catch a glimpse of the Malo girl who exuded more ferocity than her small body should be able to hold. Illiana must not know that Kira had been the one to end Zamara.

Kira fired her arrow. Illiana's mist became a shield again in the next instant, and Kira's arrow clattered across the marble floor.

Illiana bore a demon's grin. Her shield dissipated and formed hundreds of silver spikes. With a wave of her hand, they shot like knives at every human in the room.

Brooke squeezed her eyes shut and braced for the pain. But it never came.

She dared to open her eyes and saw a misshapen blade hovering a hand's length from her face. It shuddered, then exploded into silver dust.

Brooke held her breath as she looked at Felix's still form. The giant ember hawk had one eye open. Each spike the green eye focused on fell into a pile of silver dust like sand from an hourglass.

"Bleed you," Illiana swore as she turned on Felix. The pool of silver blood that poured from his wound flowed into Illiana's hand and absorbed into her skin.

Brooke reached out for her aether. It resonated from her spirit, quiet and timid, yet strong. She gathered her energy and hurled her presence into Illiana's mind.

Inside was a typhoon of incomplete thoughts. Insecurity. Defiance. Rage. It was so dizzying that Brooke nearly lost her own identity. Never before had she felt a mind so . . . wild. Detached from reality. Self-absorbed.

Get out of my head, witch.

I am no witch, Brooke replied as she gathered herself. *My abilities come from the creator. He offers forgiveness. Abandon your syn before it ends you.*

I am the only god I need!

Hatred swirled around Brooke's presence like the cutting winds of a desert storm. But this desert had a black sun and a blood-red sky.

Brooke concentrated and created a visage of Zamara from memory. A tall, beautiful stature. Ruby lips and judging eyes.

Stop this madness, Brooke made the image say. *Reach out for peace.*

You only say that because you're losing, Illiana thought. *That's not my mother.*

Illiana's memories of Zamara emerged through the haze of stinging sand. The voice of the dead elemental spoke all at once from a dozen images in a cacophony.

Never compromise. Never surrender. If you even consider it, I'll kill you myself before you can disgrace me any further.

My last half-blood daughter in the Kioan desert wasn't half as weak as you.

If she is truly your friend, then kill her as a sacrifice to me.

You cannot be my heir until you show true strength by spilling the blood of family. You will kill your uncle, the traitor, and if you fail, you will take your own life instead.

You're only a half-blood. You will never truly gain the adoration of our people until you transform into an ember hawk and fly from this palace balcony.

Brooke reeled from the onslaught of horrifying scenes. How had this creature ever called itself a mother?

Illiana focused on the last memory. Repeated it. Again and again.

Your mother was evil! Brooke called through the haze. *Reject her and let us help you!*

Felix cried out like a dying eagle as Illiana ripped more syn from him. "I am a godkiller," she yelled, "and the power of a god is mine!"

Illiana ran and leaped from the balcony. She spread her arms and disappeared below the edge.

Brooke rushed to the edge and looked down.

Illiana hadn't flown. She hadn't transformed into anything except a broken body on the marketplace pavement far below. Screams echoed as a pool of silver blood grew around the queen's burned dress.

Brooke looked at Lysander, who remained frozen with a terrified expression. She'd have to console him later.

She rushed to Felix. His massive chest of blazing yellow feathers still rose and fell with breath.

"She's gone," Brooke said as she leaned close. "Are you okay?"

"No," Felix said with effort. "I can't survive this."

Brooke's heart sank. "What do you mean?"

"I mean I'm dying." Felix closed his giant emerald eye. "But not yet, apparently. I think she nicked my core. I'm bleeding out."

"What can I do?" Brooke placed her hands over the wound, but it was too large to hold closed. "Illiana . . . doesn't need her syn any more. Would that help?"

"It might keep me alive a little longer. But I can't slip out of this one." Felix's beak twitched as others approached and Ryon tried to help Brooke stop the bleeding.

Felix's form slowly shrank, the fiery feathers slimming and tightening into fur until he became a fox once again. Brooke cradled him in her lap and gently turned him to examine his chest. A puncture wound still oozed silver blood.

"When I die, keep my stone," Felix said with effort. "You can resurrect me in seven years with aether and a willing vessel. When I wake up, the world had better not be overrun with evil. Understand?"

"I'm not gonna let you die," Ryon said as a tear slipped down his determined face. "There's tons of syn here. We can get you as much as you need to heal."

"That's not . . . how it works when my core is damaged," Felix said. His eyes fluttered open, dimmer than before. "Don't pretend like you'll actually miss me."

"Shut up!" Ryon yelled. "How much time do you have?"

"Not enough. So get me that syn and stop crying. It's not befitting of a king."

47

VYLIA

"**T**his carriage is so bumpy. I might rather walk."

Sousuke rolled his eyes. "You are *such* a princess."

Vylia squeaked as the carriage jolted again, harder this time. She wasn't entirely sure the thing wouldn't splinter to pieces at the next pothole.

She folded her arms and raised an eyebrow at Sousuke. "Is this the first time you've ridden in a carriage?"

Sousuke glanced out the small window in the door as if he'd rather be walking alongside Oda'e's troop of guards. "You know the answer to that."

Vylia frowned. "I've been considering renouncing my crown, but you'd never speak politely to me again."

Sousuke turned his green gaze on her. He looked so different without his bulky plate armor on. Smaller, and yet he wasn't small compared to other men. Just younger.

"I don't think you can just renounce your heritage," he said in a low tone.

"Of course I can," Vylia said. "Although I'm sure my father would still want me dead."

Stern lines drew across Sousuke's face. "Why consider it, then?"

"Freedom." Vylia heard a shout outside but couldn't tell what was said. Probably the rear guard complaining about their pace again. "If I weren't a royal, I could do whatever I want without worrying about impropriety all the time. I could live where I want. Marry who I want."

Sousuke huffed a laugh. "You will always be a royal."

"See? You are so mean all of a sudden!" Vylia pulled out her fan, flicked it open, and waved humid air toward her face. "You never used to talk to me like that before Jadenvive."

The jostling increased as the carriage appeared to increase in speed. Sousuke leaned toward the window and peered out. "Would you prefer I treat you like an imperial again?"

Vylia pulled at a strand of hair that stuck to her forehead. "What? You're an imperial too."

"Not any more." Sousuke's hand drifted to his sword hilt.

Vylia shrank. "What's wrong?" she whispered.

"We're going too fast," he murmured. "I can't see . . ."

Dread flooded Vylia as she struggled to recall the shouting from earlier. The carriage's cloth padding made it difficult to hear any outside noise, which had been lovely for taking a nap earlier.

"Can't see what?" Vylia nudged Sousuke until he moved out of the way, and she stuck her face in the cloudy glass.

The trees rushed by much more quickly than before. She realized then what he couldn't see: the guards. They would have to run to keep up. And yet she saw no men in their former positions alongside the thick wheels.

"Oh no," she breathed.

She looked at the chest tucked under her seat that contained the glass-gold chalice and the Malo stone. Was this a robbery by common road bandits, or were they after something more?

"What do we do?" Vylia whispered.

"Can't do anything until we stop." Sousuke had drawn his sword, awkwardly keeping it against the wall in the tight space. "When I leave, you lock this door behind me and don't—"

"Don't leave me!"

"I won't. I'll never leave you." Sousuke put his free hand on her arm and caught her up in that familiar stare. "Princess or not."

Vylia swallowed and nodded. She sat back down, then regretted the movement when Sousuke removed his hand.

She could almost feel the Malo stone beneath her like an ill omen, drawing chaos and malady toward itself.

"Who would you marry?"

Her head snapped back up. "What?"

"You said you wanted to marry whoever you want," Sousuke said from the door, crouching in a ready stance and bracing against the walls. He didn't look at her, instead glaring out the window with sharp eyes. "Who do you want?"

"I . . ." Vylia gripped the seat as they hit another bump. Were they slowing down? "You're just trying to distract me so I won't panic."

"I wouldn't ask if I didn't want to know," Sousuke said.

The carriage *was* slowing down.

"I don't know," Vylia blurted as her pulse thrummed pulses of heat through her. She blinked sweat from her eye. The fan wouldn't help her now. "Anyone *not* from a royal house."

"Is House Rhu a royal house?" Sousuke gripped the door handle.

"Y-yes, but I didn't mean—"

He ripped the door open.

No sooner had Sousuke leapt from the carriage than a sword ran him through, piercing through his armor and out his back.

"No!" Vylia screamed as Sousuke fell to reveal a Malaano man on the other side of the blade. One she recognized with horror as others pulled Sousuke to the side.

Lieutenant Sa'alu.

"Don't hurt him, and I'll do whatever you want!"

Sa'alu glanced at Sousuke as he crumpled to the road. "A bit late for that," the lieutenant said in his agonizingly calm, slow voice. He looked back up at Vylia. "But we might not hurt him *again* if you tell me where—"

He cut himself off. Stared at nothing in particular for a long moment. Then looked directly at the chest under Vylia's seat.

"Never mind." Sa'alu pointed his bloodied sword at the chest. "Be a dear and hand it over."

"She speaks to you?" Vylia didn't move. "You can't listen to her. She's evil. She's not a god."

"But she *was* a god. And she will be again." Sa'alu waved his blade in the direction of the chest. "The longer you delay, the more blood he loses."

Tears blurred Vylia's vision. "Will you save him if I do?"

Sa'alu shrugged. "He might be dead already. And let's be honest, Princess—I can take it whenever I want." He took a step forward.

"I'll cooperate! I'll do whatever you want," Vylia cried. "Please!"

Sa'alu's eyes thinned in apparent annoyance. He raised his sword at Vylia but stumbled before she could scream. Sousuke's dagger stuck in his ankle.

The lieutenant roared and thrust his blade into Sousuke's shoulder, pinning him to the ground. Sousuke gasped in pain and coughed blood.

"Stop!" Vylia screamed, but Sa'alu wasn't listening. His gaze had once again gone distant.

Then he refocused on her with a dark anger.

She shrank back into the carriage as a sob wracked her.

"You'll cooperate, you say?" His voice was like that of a python.

"Y-yes, just please don't kill him," Vylia stuttered. "Please don't let him die."

Sa'alu ripped his sword free from Sousuke's shoulder, eliciting an agonized cry.

"Give me the stone," Sa'alu said with excruciating slowness.

Vylia's hands shook as she clutched the chest beneath her seat. Opened the lock. Removed the chalice. Pulled back the silk holding the Malo stone in place. Offered him the artifact.

Sa'alu's eyes widened as he took the opal in one hand. He turned it over in fascination as the sun caught its aquamarine facets and refracted the light into dozens of colors beneath its smooth surface.

"Very well," he murmured as if speaking to the stone. "But my price will be higher."

He paused for another long moment. Then smiled.

It seems you require a new escort, little minnow. The familiar voice floated through Vylia's head like perfume on the breeze. *Let's go home.*

48

KIRALAU

Kira fidgeted in her borrowed dress. It was so heavy-laden with black pearls she might as well be carrying a backpack full of rice.

Ryon had immediately stepped down to pass the crown to Coriander, so why was her wedding as extravagant as a queen's? And how had the palace staff prepared everything on such short notice?

She wondered how much was left over from Ryon's last wedding.

Kira scolded herself and redoubled her effort to focus on the here and now. The white flowers were fresh—so many that they clustered over the archway and spilled onto the moss-covered cobblestones they stood on. Jars of fireflies hung from jomoco trees that waved in the evening breeze. And the sky blazed with multicolored clouds as the sun retreated, as if the creator himself had painted a masterpiece on tonight's canvas.

Even in her dreams, her wedding was never this breathtakingly beautiful.

" . . . cornerstone: the creator," the priest said, distracting Kira from her fidgeting. He placed a square tile on the pedestal between her and Ryon.

Ryon. He looked at her like she was the only thing with any importance in all of history. He exuded a sense of gratefulness as his eyes drank her in, despite what he'd endured only days ago. She knew he was still suffering from withdrawal from the muddlewort, and yet she'd never seen him so happy.

Concern that his mind might be permanently damaged wriggled in the back of her mind, but the clarity of his gaze muted that fear. But even if that was a struggle they were destined for, they would face it together.

"I commit to love," Ryon said loud enough for the small crowd in the arboretum to hear. He placed an ivory tile beside the one the priest had laid down.

Kira tried to ignore everyone except for Ryon as she placed a cool tile next to his. It fit perfectly. "I commit to joy," she said.

"I commit to peace," Ryon said as he placed another tile without looking away from Kira.

She felt her cheeks flush. "I commit to patience." She decided against joking that she would need a *lot* of patience to stay married to this jokester.

"I commit to kindness," Ryon said. A lifted eyebrow might have meant he was impressed or asking if she was doing all right.

Kira smiled awkwardly and tried to remember the next line of her vow. Oh, right! "I commit to goodness," she said a little too quickly to make up for her delay. Her tile clacked into place.

"I commit to faithfulness," Ryon said. "Always."

Kira knew her smile must look terribly goofy. She couldn't help it—they'd found his lenses in the palace and she'd fallen in love with how they looked on him. "I commit to gentleness."

"I commit to self-control." Ryon slid the last tile into place, completing a mosaic on the dais.

The priest nodded. "With these vows, may your home be filled with holiness."

Kira tuned him out as Ryon took her hand. Was he supposed to take her hand? What was she supposed to—

Relax, Ryon mouthed. He winked.

She swallowed hard. Why was she so nervous? She knew that he was the man for her without a doubt. Still, something about swearing her life away in a foreign city without her whole family in attendance made her nervous.

Her mother would kill her.

But she'd exercise forgiveness as soon as Kira and Ryon conceived the first grandchild.

"I will protect," Ryon said, placing a miniature pillar on top of the tile foundation.

Kira fumbled for her own piece of marble. "I will orchestrate."

"I will provide," Ryon said.

"I will support." Kira set her second pillar in the last corner.

"And the creator will cover you with his blessing," the priest said, balancing a small ceiling on the little house.

The crowd burst into applause, startling Kira. Ryon laughed, pulled her close, and kissed her.

That whoop sounded like Tekkyn.

Kira melted half from embarrassment and half from joy. If all the Phoeran marriage rites were finally over, maybe she and Ryon could finally have some quiet time alone.

"I love you, *balemba,*" Ryon said, resting his cheek on her forehead. "Forever."

"I love you, too," Kira said, and her heart soared.

"So, where do you want to live?" Ryon asked as he pulled away with a smirk. He led her down the steps and along the path that led to the palace, raising his voice over the crowd's roar of approval. "I kinda have this castle . . ."

Kira felt her cheeks flush at the whistles, struggling not to trip on her dress. "Can we have a chicken coop in a castle, though?"

Ryon chuckled. "Touché. Were you thinking of your family land, then? It might be nice to have some land that's not, you know, underground."

Kira's mind flipped through possible responses her mother might give and the future implications. "Our land is on the border, though. The worst possible place to be in the middle of a war."

"Well," Ryon said, "since Jadenvive has been attacked like fifty-eight times now, I'm thinking of getting the orphans out of there, yeah?"

She couldn't argue with that. She skipped a step to catch up with Ryon as he squeezed her hand. "We could fix up my grandfather's old house and live there," she said. "I just have one condition."

Ryon ducked under a shower of cocoa beans as audience members tossed them. "Anything."

"Never tell Mom that you were stealing her cherry jam from the root cellar."

Ryon's mischievous orange eyes and fiendish smirk sent Kira's heart thudding against her ribs. He reached out and touched the butterfly clip he'd given her, which had allowed one of her curls to escape and tickle her forehead. "You underestimate my legendary charm."

Then he turned his head back to the audience as they retreated. "Hey, Brooke!" he called. "I quit!"

49

BROOKE

Brooke nodded at Ryon and clapped as he swooped Kira up in her wedding dress and carried her behind the arboretum's gazebo, then down the path that led to the palace. Aegwyn chased after them, tossing cocoa beans over their heads in an Emberhawk fertility tradition.

As chieftess, Brooke had promised to pay for their wedding. Oops.

Her headdress poked her ankle from under her chair as she shifted. She'd have to get it repaired or hunt another alpha xavi to replace the stiff turquoise feathers. But what was the point if it would just be put on a mannequin in the Great Hall, marking the end of her severed term as chief with shame?

At least Ryon had found her grandfather's missing headdress in the arboretum. Brooke wondered how and when Zamara had stolen it, and how long it had been sitting there like a trophy with wyvern horns as long and heavy as the High Chief's legacy. It would feel so right to put it in its place in the Great Hall.

She decided to just pay a courier to deliver both headdresses to Ulysses. She wasn't ready to show her face again in Jadenvive. They'd heard news that the Navakovrae Resistance had taken the city and returned it to the Katrosi tribe—such a fortunate circumstance that Brooke found it impossible to believe until she met with Commander Oda'e personally and searched his mind for motives. But she'd let the people rejoice without a reminder of the first female chief whom they thought abandoned them.

Maybe one day they'd learn the truth. But until then, where would she live?

She loved the wilderness. Perhaps she could live near the Roanoke in secret. Yes, they'd help her, especially if she foraged truffles from the Gnarled Wood where they dared not tread.

"I love you."

Brooke jerked out of her thoughts and realized she was still clapping as the crowd began to disperse. Lysander towered before her, looking down at her with an unreadable expression.

"Oh . . ." She put her hands down, feeling like an idiot.

What had he said? That he loved her? How was she supposed to respond to that?

"Thank you," she signed, proud of herself for knowing that single hand-language gesture. Maybe her hand-signing for the first time would distract him. She retrieved her headdress from the soft grass and ducked around him.

A moment passed before Lysander called after her. "I know you love me too. I can sense it."

That's cheating, she thought to him without turning around. Where was she going? The buffet table, yes. There was jomoco gelatin with joyberries and cream.

I learned from the best, Lysander thought.

Brooke noted that there weren't as many servers as she thought might attend a reception in the palace gardens. They were probably preparing for Coriander's coronation tomorrow, when he would officially revert Quin'Zamar's name back to Quin'Alor—its original name meaning "Pyramid of the Guardian." Felix had suggested that Brooke consider giving the keystone to Coriander for safekeeping—apparently the glass-gold walls of the palace would protect it somehow.

This is true, Brooke thought back to Lysander. *And as the best, I sense that you have an objective of some sort . . .* She snatched a cheesy cracker and popped it in her mouth. This might be the last time in her life to eat the delicacies only afforded to royalty and chiefs. *If I say I love you back, you'll ask me to marry you. Is that it?*

She could feel Lysander's presence close to her back. Very close.

"Is there any reason to wait?" he asked.

Brooke scoffed and grabbed a plate. *We've only been seeing each other for like a week!*

"Technically we've been engaged for a dozen years or so."

Brooke looked over her shoulder at him with narrowed eyes. *That's not true and you know it.*

"Will you marry me?"

Probably. Later. Brooke turned back to the table and grabbed a handful of crackers. They seemed dry enough—maybe she could save some for the road.

Lysander rounded the table to face her. "What kind of answer is that?"

Brooke didn't look at him as she waited for a kid to take a scoop of the joyberries and cream. *By the skies, you're emotional for a man.*

And you're not for a woman. Doesn't that make us a good pair?

Brooke sighed as the kid dropped some of the delicacy on the grass. *I love you too, okay? Are you happy now?*

His grin stretched wide. "Yes. Will you marry me?"

Well, she wasn't getting any younger. *Fine.*

Brooke awoke to sunlight streaming through white curtains and a sweet-smelling jungle breeze tickling her skin. She slowly opened her eyes and stared out the open window of Granny Zelle's pyramid. She admired the distant mountain range and wondered which one was Sleeping Panther.

Maybe they should go somewhere *away* from everything for their honeymoon. Away from an ominous dormant volcano. Away from

Lysander's creepy toxic plant garden downstairs. Away from his adorable grandmother with her happy squeals and opinions and questions about great-grandchildren. Away from the Darkwood, which now surely wanted one or both of them dead. Away from the Emberhawk people, who rejoiced over their restored Slain Prince and new princess.

Ugh. The worst thing about marrying Lysander was becoming a princess.

At least if Ryon teased her about it, she could point out that he'd been kidnapped and held captive in a foreign castle for a forced marriage like a princess in a children's tale.

Brooke rolled over, but her husband's place on the bed was empty and his sheets pulled up neatly. Where had he gone so early? Or had she slept in?

At least not being chieftess any more meant she didn't have to wake up at the crack of dawn to work every day. Although the lack of work was beginning to gnaw at her soul.

She stretched, preparing to do her morning exercises, prayer, and schedule. She should check on Dimbae, whom Nariellyn said was recovering so well that he might be able to get out of bed today. And of course Brooke should go to Sorrel's huge nest and see the three baby gryphons again, because their little fluffy bodies, soft downy feathers that stuck out in every direction, and huge heads and eyes were cute enough to cure depression worldwide. Maybe Brooke could arrange for Dimbae to pet one to liven his spirits.

She remembered Felix with a gasp. Was Lysander gone because . . . ?

Brooke pulled her robe tight and dashed through Lysander's suite, up the stairs at their strange angle thanks to the pyramid's shape—she'd have to get used to that—and into the upper room where they'd piled as much syn as they could collect into gleaming silver heaps. A fox lay on the large ottoman near the balcony, surrounded by pillows and covered with a blanket.

Felix's eyes were closed as Brooke knelt by his side. She gently lifted the blanket and observed the wound that still slowly oozed silver.

Brooke had no idea how to help him aside from feeding him the syn. He'd sounded like his death was inevitable, but he wasn't dead yet or he'd have reverted to some sort of stone or gem as Zamara had. The least she could do now was let him sleep. Assuming that elementals slept.

She felt guilty for confronting Illiana after Felix had warned about how powerful she was. She should have known he'd fight to protect her—rather, the keystone. Lysander also felt guilty for not being able to save his sister. But he couldn't have known how she would react, and their guilt couldn't change anything now.

The door opened slowly to reveal Lysander carrying a tray with a heaping breakfast. He brightened when he saw her, but she put her finger to her lips and indicated that Felix was asleep. She motioned to the table, where Lysander set the tray.

He leaned in to kiss her forehead, and she relished his scent. Being with him felt so *right*, especially after so many failed engagements. Did this mean her curse was finally broken? Maybe it would be worth a return trip to Jadenvive to flaunt her happy marriage in front of Ulysses's mother. She wondered if people would keep calling her a witch.

"Good morning, Princess," Lysander whispered.

Brooke wrinkled her nose at him and snatched a muffin. She took a bite, then waved it in his face. *You'd better watch it.*

He grinned and handed her a letter. "From Jadenvive."

Uh oh. Did they want her back to stand trial for leaving?

Brooke snapped the wax seal with a tree symbol—the Katrosi emblem. She stopped eating as she unfolded the parchment and read:

> *Brooke,*
>
> *You either have the best timing or the absolute worst.*
> *The Elder of Aether told his granddaughter about his prophecy and the instruction he gave you before he had a chance to tell the council. We saw her memories, and your*

name has been cleared.

But unfortunately the council already removed you as chief. As much as I didn't want to, I stepped into your position as vice and led the tribe during the incursion, when our people needed a leader more than ever. The elders have decided I am to serve as chief for the remainder of your term, at which point we will return to the trials as normal.

I wish this could have happened in a more respectful, traditional manner. I am sorry. I hope to have your understanding and approval.

Now that I am chief, I can see how completely overwhelmed you must have been. I do not have the same tolerance for stress that you do. Because our people and our city require my full attention as we rebuild, I do not have the time to also worry about leading the Tribal Alliance.

As such, I have decided to form a Tribal Alliance council. The leaders of the other tribes have recommended representatives from among their own peoples to serve on this council, which will oversee diplomatic foreign affairs and promote peace and goodwill among the tribes.

I would be honored if you would consider representing the Katrosi tribe in leading this new council. King Coriander mentioned he would offer the position for Emberhawk representation to Lysander. Congratulations, by the way.

Regardless of your decision, please return to Jadenvive as soon as you are able. I have many questions about the day-to-day as chief, could use your advice on pleasing the patriarchs and matriarchs, and would like to know of any promises you made which I might uphold.

Your headdress will be placed in a position of honor. I will also need the keystone, as its double has been stolen from the treasury, and I look rather silly trying to lead with a large empty hole in my new headdress.

Strength and humility,
Ulysses

"What does it say?" Lysander asked, clearly studying her reaction.

He wants me to lead a new Tribal Alliance council, she thought to him, re-reading that portion and taking another bite of muffin, chewing slowly.

"Will you do it?"

I don't know . . . she mused as the desire to say yes swelled within her. This would be an opportunity to carry on her grandfather's legacy, even not as chief.

She hadn't failed him, then. Hadn't dishonored House Stillwind. Hadn't truly left a dark smear on the history scrolls as the first female chief.

"What's wrong?" Lysander asked.

Brooke's face must have shown her confusion as she read over the last paragraph again. "Apparently someone stole the keystone's double from the treasury."

"The keystone has a double?" Felix's voice sounded from behind her.

Brooke put the letter down and went to his side. "How are you feeling?"

"Terrible," Felix growled. "Why would the keystone have a double?"

"To protect it," Brooke said. "My grandfather had a quartz gem crafted to look exactly like it. When he would go into battle or another dangerous situation, he would have it removed from his headdress and stored in the treasury, while taking the double out with him." She petted his soft fur, avoiding the wound, and offered him a silver chunk. "Here's some syn. Is there anything else we can do for you? Maybe an aether healer like Nari—"

"Bring me your headdress."

Brooke glanced at Lysander and tried to hand-sign: *"Could you get my headdress, please?"* She was certain she butchered the word "headdress."

He rolled his eyes. "You really don't have to learn hand-language. I told you I prefer to hear your thought-voice." But must have understood her signs, because he retrieved her headdress from across the room and brought it to her.

Felix stared at the gem, closer than he'd dare approach it before. "So this one is the fake?"

"No, this is the real keystone," Brooke said. "I left Jadenvive in such a rush that I didn't have it swapped out."

Felix inched his nose toward the cloudy facets, and Brooke pulled it back. "Hey! Didn't you say something bad would happen if you touched it?"

"I'm going to die anyway." Felix struggled onto all fours, hopped off the ottoman, and touched his nose to the stone.

Nothing happened.

A deep, guttural growl rumbled from Felix's throat. "You mixed it up at some point, you fools!"

Brooke sat there, stunned. "So the real one . . . was stolen?"

Felix sprinted to the balcony, jumped onto the railing, leaped off, and transformed into a wyvern in mid-air. He gripped the railing hard enough to bend the metal railing and roared in pain.

"What are you doing?" Brooke cried.

"Get on my back," Felix snarled. "There's no time!"

Brooke held onto her robe against the gust from his wings. "But aren't you about to . . . ?"

"I'll try not to die in mid-air." Felix's eyes flashed. "This is bigger than me and you and your tribes and the empire now. All of Alani is at stake, and it may already be too late."

THE STORY CONTINUES
IN THE KATROSI REVOLUTION BOOK 3: LOTUSFALL

ACKNOWLEDGMENTS

Thanks so much to everyone who exercised patience and understanding as this book was written and produced slower than usual. To the amazing fans who sent me messages of encouragement. To those who saw the delay and pre-ordered anyway. I couldn't have done it without knowing that y'all were excitedly waiting for this sequel. I hope it was worth the wait!

I could not have done this without the guidance of my incredibly talented editor, Sarah Grimm. She drove halfway across the country not once, but twice to help me iron out these crazy plot threads. Sarah, you are one of the very few who truly get me and my writing style. Your friendship is priceless to me, and I can't thank you enough.

To my incredible alpha and beta team members: Amanda, Becky, Chantal, Danae, Desirae, Hann, Keanan, Kimberly, Laurel, Mackenzie, and Rob. Thank you so much for dealing with this manuscript in such a raw form and offering fantastic insight and suggestions. Y'all are the best!

To the ARC team, promoters, and my friends who supported me even when times were tough for all of us.

To my husband, my daughter, and the rest of my beloved family for their everlasting patience and loving support (even the Muggles).

And last but never least, I'm grateful to the one true Creator who gave me this calling and guided me along this rugged path. Take joy, my king, in what you hear. May it be a sweet, sweet sound in your ear.

AUTHOR BIOGRAPHY

Jamie Foley loves strategy games, dewberries, and Texas winters. She kills vipers with her great-grandfather's rifle but she's terrified of red wasps and mimics in *Dungeons & Dragons*.

When she's not writing clean sci-fi/fantasy, Jamie specializes in digital typesetting. With over a dozen years of experience in graphic art and online marketing, she is currently the Director of Marketing at Enclave Publishing and the typesetter for The Christian Writers Institute and Fayette Press.

Jamie's husband is her cowboy astronaut muse. They live between Austin and the cattle ranch, where their hyperactive spawnling and wolfpack roam.

Get a free short story when you sign up for Jamie's email newsletter at www.jamiefoley.com/newsletter. You'll get behind-the-scenes goodies, giveaways, and exclusive opportunities like first dibs at joining Jamie's beta team, ARC review crew, and cover reveal ninja squad.

@jamiesfoley
www.jamiefoley.com

FAYETTE
— PRESS —

If you enjoy *The Katrosi Revolution*,
you'll probably love these other clean fantasy series:

A DRAGON BY ANY OTHER NAME

THE STONES OF TERRENE

CAPTIVE & CROWNED

This time, beauty is the beast. And she wants prince charming dead.

Welcome to Terrene— where dragons exist, the past haunts, and magic is no myth. Welcome aboard the Sapphire.

The half-dragon King of Torva needs a queen, but the human bride he has captured may prove to be more trouble than she's worth.